DREAMS AND
NIGHTMARES

DREAMS AND NIGHTMARES

STRANGER MAGICS,
BOOK SIX

ASH FITZSIMMONS

Print Edition ISBN: 978-1-949861-12-9

Cover design by BespokeBookCovers.com

www.ashfitzsimmons.com

CHAPTER 1

To be fair, I passed the patrol car doing at least a solid ninety.

There was no reason not to, aside from the nagging signage at the Arizona line—it was a lazy Saturday afternoon in mid-June, and the road through the reddish scrubland was wide open under a smattering of puffy clouds. I had places to be that day, miles to cover, and rubber to burn, and I've always had something of a lead foot. So yes, the patrol car was well within its rights to shoot onto I-40 in a spray of gravel and throw on its lights, but I still accompanied its acceleration toward me with an internal soundtrack of profanity. Had I not had a four-year-old passenger in the back of the well-worn Suburban, I'd have been far more vocal about my displeasure.

As a longtime—albeit former—police detective, I rankled at the notion of getting ticketed. Back in England, I'd have got a wave, maybe a finger wag of mock reprimand, had I been stopped at all. But in the States, driving with a forged license, I couldn't very well pull out my old credentials and appeal to transatlantic fraternity.

I saw my passengers' worried expressions in the rearview mirror as the siren wailed behind us. "Nothing to fret about," I told them with forced cheer. "Might have been going a touch on the speedy side. Just remember our story, and we'll be fine."

By the looks on their faces, they didn't buy my reassurance, but I couldn't blame them. We were a decidedly odd lot in the SUV: a middle-aged

Englishwoman behind the wheel, two black teenage boys in the seats behind me, and a young white family of three on the rear bench. The Ford brothers had made their way west from Detroit by a combination of hitchhiking and Greyhound, while the Delacroixes had, after much persuasion, driven themselves out of the Louisiana bayou to join our camp in New Mexico. Little Gracie was sleeping, but her mother slunk down in fear, and her father, who wore the scruffy, haunted look of an escaped convict, kept the tip of his wand poised in the gap between the Fords' chairs. Ethan Ford, only sixteen, had no wand to ready—the boys were lesser bloods, one-eighth fae and barely skilled at magic—but he held a pistol out of sight under one thigh. His little brother, Elias, who hadn't spoken since he shot the Arcanum assassins who'd murdered their parents and three sisters, looked straight ahead, silently gritting his teeth.

I tried to project serenity, though my guts roiled as I pulled onto the shoulder and cut the engine. My New Mexico license might have been a magical forgery, but a forgery it was nonetheless—as was the insurance card in the glove box. My cousin Arnold, who was a more technically skilled wizard, had assured me that the paperwork would withstand scrutiny, and our American hosts, Zeb and Carey Jones, had confirmed that the fakes were good, but still I feared that something would go wrong, that my license wouldn't show up in the computer and I'd be hauled in for questioning. And since I'd survived the last year by staying off anyone's official radar, ending up on the wrong end of an interrogation seemed like a very bad idea indeed.

Any officer worth his badge would take a good, long look at us. The cover story we'd worked out was that the Delacroixes had adopted the Ford boys, and I, a local guide, was driving them to Sedona for a family hiking holiday. If questioned, I'd learned enough about the area by then to make my role convincing, and it didn't hurt that

I'd stashed ropes, a tent, and a couple of pairs of dirty hiking boots in the rear to give credence to my lies. But the rest of our cover was flimsy at best. Wes and Jemma Delacroix, who were still in their mid-twenties, didn't fit the "adoptive parents" mold for a couple of teenagers from the other end of the country. Moreover, the Delacroixes were from two old shrimping families—kind and resourceful people, but neither wealthy nor particularly educated. By contrast, the elder Fords had been professionals—he a mundane cardiologist, she a quarter-blooded defense attorney—and their sons were the well-traveled products of private schools. The boys' trainers were probably worth more than the Delacroix family spent on a month of groceries, and Ethan's gun, as our firearms aficionada Amy had declared, was a high-quality piece of German construction—"That ain't a Saturday night special," she'd said wistfully as he packed it back into its case. But under the circumstances, we were doing the best we could, and my passengers were more than willing to play their parts if it meant getting them out of the mortal realm.

I waited with the window down and my hands on the steering wheel, watching in the side mirror as the state trooper ambled toward us. Khaki shirt and trousers—definitely Arizona. Though he was perhaps a tad shorter than average, his shoulders were broad, and his shirtfront was flat above his black gun belt. As he neared, I picked out details: a tanned face, dark stubble along his jaw, and large, mirrored sunglasses several decades out of style.

He tapped the back of the SUV as he passed, then peered in my window and touched the brim of his hat. "Afternoon, folks. How're we doing, Badger?"

I exhaled, fighting the shaking in my suddenly limp arms. "Lou. Bloody *hell*, you scared me."

He grinned, exposing gapped front teeth and dimples, and suddenly looked much younger than thirty. "And are we engaging in a spot of human trafficking today?" he asked in a mincing faux-British accent that would have embarrassed even Dick Van Dyke.

"No more than usual." I turned to my passengers and tried not to show my relief. "Everyone, this is Lou Martinez. He's with the Minor Arcanum."

The others released their weapons and waved weakly, and Lou shook his head. "I won't keep you, then. Got that ammo Amy needed—Zeb said you were heading this way today, so I thought I'd catch you and save the trip. Do you have room in there for a few boxes?"

"Front floorboards, the boot's full," I told him, and waited while Lou returned to his car to retrieve the goods. "That kid's going to give me a heart attack, I swear," I muttered once he was out of earshot.

"He's a *wizard*?" Ethan asked.

"Barely more than a witch, to hear Carey tell it, but yeah, he's got a wand. The Minor Arcanum tend to look on wizardry as more of a hobby than a career path," I explained. "He's an officer who happens to be a wizard, like Carey's a vet who happens to be one."

He frowned in thought. "Kind of like Fringers, then?"

"Precisely. Anyway, he's on our side," I assured them, and Wes and Jemma nodded from the safety of the rear.

A few moments later, Lou returned with a reusable grocery bag slung onto one shoulder, which he deposited in the passenger seat beside me and took pains to hide on the floor. "That's a lot of assorted ammo, now, so try not to get stopped again," he told me. "Let's slow it down a little, huh? Speed limit's seventy-five, Ms. Parsons." He slammed the door before I could protest, then came around to my window again. "What's your rush? You've got hours until it'll be dark enough to hit the canyon. Take your time, enjoy our lovely state. Buy some souvenirs. You're not going to find much Diamondbacks merch in Faerie."

"Eat 'em up, Tigers," Ethan muttered in reply.

Lou's grin widened. I seldom had much to say about

baseball, and Ethan had issued a challenge. But knowing what was ahead, I nipped their banter short. "I want time to rest before we hike," I told Lou. "If I'm to keep to the speed limit, we need to press on."

"Uh-huh. This rush of yours wouldn't have anything to do with your boyfriend, would it?" Catching the sudden shift in my expression, Lou chuckled and patted the door. "Zeb said you'd be in a hurry today."

"Zeb needs to learn when to keep his mouth shut."

Laughing in earnest, he stepped back to wave us on. "Drive safely!" he called, then lifted a hand in farewell as I merged into the light traffic.

When we'd left him behind, Jemma cleared her throat from the back seat. "You didn't tell us you had a boyfriend," she said in her—at least to my ear—nearly unintelligible drawl.

I looked at her in the mirror and felt myself smile. "He's been away. Coming home tonight." Around a bend, I spotted a sign for a truck stop and flipped on my indicator. "Who needs a snack? Maybe a drink after that little traffic incident?"

"Maybe a new pair of pants," Wes grumbled, and I looked back just in time to see Elias grin.

Lou was right, of course—I had hours to kill before I could safely lead the Fringe evacuees into Boynton Canyon, but that didn't make me any less anxious to reach Sedona. When we crossed the city limits, the sun was still too high for hiking, and Gracie was getting restless after a long day on the road. Turning off the main street, I spotted an inoffensive Tex-Mex restaurant and pulled over to wait for sunset.

Our server, a chipper blonde with a tanning bed glow and multiple hemp bracelets, seemed unfazed by our assorted party. She took our drink orders, brought the little one a plastic lidded cup without being asked, and was only too happy to keep the warm tortilla chips and salsa coming. The elder Delacroixes soon found their appetites, but the Ford boys were ravenous from the start, ordering massive combination platters and bowls of queso. When our server departed again, I leaned across the table to them and whispered, "There are tacos where you're heading. Good ones. *Proper* ones. This isn't a last-meal situation."

Elias's eyebrows rose, and Ethan, dubious, asked, "How do you fake good tacos?"

"You don't. When you get settled in, go downtown and find La Hacienda. They've got two chefs: Amos Dunwoody runs the Tex-Mex side, and Rosa Flores runs the Mexican side. She does roasted corn to die for."

"And it's…*free?*"

"Absolutely free. Now, let me let you in on a little secret," I continued, waiting while the others leaned closer to our huddle. "You'll both be in school—oh, don't give me that pout," I told Elias. "There's no point in twiddling your thumbs while you wait out the Arcanum, and from what I hear, the classes are pretty laid-back. But if, say, you went by the restaurant every now and then and washed dishes or what have you…well, I understand that Rosa saves some of her best meals for the staff. Just a suggestion, mind, but if you were to get bored…"

Ethan crunched into a fresh chip and nodded. "I could be bored."

"*After* school, now." I helped myself to the queso and turned to Wes and Jemma. "If there's something you'd like to do, feel free, but it's not required. Get adjusted, meet your neighbors, play with Gracie, and then, if you're restless, do as you like." I chewed for a moment as I considered their situation. "You both know your way around a fishing boat, yes?"

"Born and raised on the Gulf," Jemma confirmed.

"The settlement's not too far from the sea. If you wanted to run charters, I'm fairly sure that someone would set you up. But again, the important thing is to rest first." I glanced around to be certain that the neighboring diners were engrossed with their own conversations, then asked, "How long *were* you down there, anyway?"

Wes shook his head and sighed. "Nine months. Nine very long months."

"Nine months, two weeks, and three days," Jemma murmured. "Not that I was counting or nothing."

Her husband gave her a half-smile and wrapped his arm around her tense shoulders. "Nice to get A/C again. Or a roof that don't leak."

I could only imagine how the Delacroixes had lived. Even in the shadow-on-shadow color scheme of the dream space, the shack in which I'd found them was beyond salvaging, little better than a rotting lean-to on stilts above the swamp. They'd hidden it among a cypress grove and camouflaged it with Spanish moss, far from the main waterways and miles from a real road. Fortunately, their preventive measures did nothing to hide the pale golden glow of their bodies as I sleepwalked, searching the distant terrain for hiding Fringers while I tranced back in New Mexico. It took me three visits in as many months and several long conversations with them before I was able to convince them that I meant them no harm, and as the miserable Louisiana summer neared, they decided that the possibility of a real bed was worth the risk that I was an Arcanum plant. Of the two, Wes had been the stronger holdout—finding his extended family murdered had, naturally, made him skittish, especially of strange, glowing foreigners who only visited in his sleep—but when Gracie had contracted pertussis, he'd packed their few belongings into their motorboat and headed for civilization.

Carey, the veterinarian who'd spent much of the last year patching up every Fringe refugee to land at the ranch, finally had to cry uncle and call in Penny Morris, the Minor Arcanum's lone doctor, from Vermont. Having done a few volunteer tours in third-world countries, Penny was no stranger to making the best of her circumstances, and she'd flown out that afternoon with several bags of equipment and medication. We knew there was no chance of doing the sensible thing—taking Gracie to the nearest hospital—because of the questions that would raise, and so Penny moved the child into a private bedroom, made her comfortable, and put her on heavy antibiotics while Carey handled the healing spell that would speed her recovery. Still, Gracie was kept in near-quarantine for a month until Penny deemed her safe to travel. As far as anyone could tell, there were no infectious diseases in Faerie to worry about, but there was also a corresponding lack of medical facilities. I'd coordinated with Vivi Stowe, my young counterpart in the other realm, to let Penny speak with the few Fringe doctors and caution them of what was heading their way. The Fringe refugee community came from all corners of the world, after all, and there was no account of who'd been fully vaccinated before making the escape.

If the Delacroixes had it bad, hiding had been no more a picnic for the Ford boys. All five Ford children had been home from their Episcopal school on the morning that the Arcanum attacked, beneficiaries of the religious holiday. The girls had been waiting at the table with their father, and their mother had just gone to the staircase to call the boys to breakfast when assassins broke down the door and began shooting. As Ethan recounted it, their mother had been the first to fall, and then the attacking wizards had taken out their defenseless father and sisters. He'd panicked at the sound of the chaos below, but by the time the wizards came upstairs, Elias had taken the gun from their father's nightstand and was waiting. He'd shot each wizard in the chest as they came around the bend in the staircase, then followed with shots to the head, emptying the pistol's magazine into the wizards and the wooden floor. When Elias's ammunition had been spent, Ethan had seen there was nothing to be done for their family, realized that nothing good could come of two dead wizards in the foyer, then packed what he and Elias could carry and hurried his blank-faced little brother out of the house.

They'd left the family cars, opting instead to take a series of busses into Detroit, where Ethan had found a Starbucks with Wi-Fi. While Elias had picked at a muffin, Ethan had logged on to the Fringe network on his tablet to put out a call for help. Instead, all he'd found were similar reports of death and people on the run—and then, suddenly, a beacon of hope: an evacuation meet-up just a few blocks away. Ethan had begun to gather his things, but seeing Elias's drawn face had made him hesitate. They'd been taken by surprise once that morning—who was to say that this promised assistance wasn't another trap?

In the end, the Fords had stayed low and made their way out of town. Assuming the police and the Arcanum would be looking for them, Ethan had put as many miles between them and home as he could as quickly as possible. He'd withdrawn every penny from his and his brother's savings accounts, then jumped on the Amtrak to Chicago. From there, they'd taken busses into Wisconsin and onto Michigan's upper peninsula, eventually working their way south toward home as the months passed. By the time they'd returned to Detroit in September, their money had been nearly spent, and they'd made do with church handouts and occasional nights in shelters, arriving late and leaving before anyone could call the authorities.

Sleepwalking, I'd found them in one such shelter, huddled together on adjoining cots, their bodies glowing with the pale white light of the slightly fae. Elias had said nothing when I'd pulled the two of them from true sleep into the shared dream space, but Ethan had been willing to trust me—not enough to give me an address to which I could wire train fare, but he'd been willing to come closer. I'd tracked their westward movement and sent Carey's younger brother, Jim, to fetch them from a truck stop east of Albuquerque. Jim, who made a much better morning

DJ than wizard, had come unarmed and struck up a quick rapport with the boys through cheeseburgers and milkshakes, and then he'd driven them to the ranch, where Zeb had plied them with enchiladas until they were nearly sick. Finding other Fringers on the property had finally put their minds at ease, and the boys had crashed onto clean sheets until noon the next day.

Both parties had spent a year in hiding, and I knew that what they needed was time—time to breathe, to rest, to properly mourn, and to rebuild their lives. School would give the boys structure and routine, and being around other children who had lost parents and siblings in the so-called unravelling—the Arcanum's devastating surprise attack on the Fringe—would at least give them a community. Many of the orphaned children lived together. Although couples and families had opened their homes to fosters, the sad reality was that a great number of the evacuees we found were children who'd been overlooked when the Arcanum came after their witch and lesser-blooded parents. Primary-school kids couldn't live alone, of course, and so Vivi, as coordinator of the Fringe in exile, had commissioned a dormitory for them, keeping siblings together and giving the occupants a makeshift family for meals and socialization. To her surprise, her brother Rufus, a former university professor who had spearheaded the settlement's school, and his partner, Poppy, moved in as dorm parents. The arrangement seemed to work—Rufus wound up teaching the refugee children, found that he actually enjoyed it, and was happy to help with homework at night, while Poppy kept the rowdy ones in line. Being a lupine shifter, she did command a certain respect, and she seldom had to bare her teeth.

As for the Delacroix family, I knew there was a suite waiting for them in the settlement's "guesthouse," the bungalow near the center of town where newcomers stayed until they had a sense of the terrain and a place of their own. Building a house meant perhaps an hour of enchantment for the settlement's de facto architect (and one of Vivi and Rufus's many older brothers), Robbie, but he took pride in his work and insisted on perfection, which meant that putting up a house was often preceded by a week or more of planning it with the new homeowners. No one knew how long the exile would last, after all, and Robbie, who was finally unburdened of the restrictions of construction crews and physics, enjoyed flexing his creative muscles. "Besides," he told me on one of my infrequent trips across the border, "why paint every wall eggshell when they really want a Provençal scheme and a coordinating mosaic backsplash? It's no trouble to personalize."

One nighttime hike more, and my charges would be safe—well, as safe as anyone of minimal magical talent could be in Faerie. But there would be counselors on the other side to help them cope with the trauma, neighbors to help them get acquainted, and a community to help them recover a sense of normalcy, even if the new normal was exile. The only thing I couldn't give them was any timetable as to when they might return to our native realm. *That* question hinged on how quickly we could rescue the Fringe hostages the self-appointed grand magus had taken and drive him out of power—and if I had my way, into an active volcano. But our information about the Arcanum's inner goings-on was virtually nonexistent. The organization had closed its ranks in the last year, resettling its member wizards in or near the seven installations. Aside from the few assassins who were still spotted from time to time, there was little visible activity outside the Arcanum's strongholds, and to our dismay, they'd completely neglected their responsibility to mend the gates that spontaneously opened into the Gray Lands, the only one of the three realms without useable magic and the source of many of the mortal realm's monster stories. Cleanup duty had instead fallen into the lap of the Minor Arcanum, a confederation of wizards and witches far smaller and less disciplined than the Arcanum—but on the plus side, the Minor Arcanum had become an ally to the exiled Fringe, and seeing as the Arcanum wanted us dead, any ally was a welcome ally.

I looked across the table at Gracie, who had abandoned her crunched-up chips to concentrate on the purple squiggle she was drawing on her placemat, and smiled to myself. No matter what they'd managed in this realm, the Arcanum didn't have a prayer of invading Faerie. Gracie would grow up in relative safety instead of hiding in the darkest corners of the bayou. The Ford boys would continue their education without having to worry about feeding themselves, and someday—whenever that might be—they would be prepared to come home and start over.

And someday, perhaps, I would be able to join them. Not yet, not with so many still missing, but someday, maybe I'd be able to ride out the storm.

That was a nice thought, though impractical, and I pushed it aside while I dug for the bottom of the queso bowl.

There were three primary downsides to using the Sedona gate as our entry point to Faerie. First, the gate was near the heart of a supposed "vortex," and any trip into Boynton Canyon meant there was a strong possibility of encountering hippies. Vortex hunters tended to be friendly, but I'd had to learn enough about the area to fib my way around the question of what I was doing on the trail after dark, especially if I was leading a party past the alleged epicenter. Plus, running into people on the way out meant that I had to be certain they'd gone before I headed back, as I'd have had a devil of a time explaining why I'd left half my party in the canyon. Second, the trail wound through the backyard of a luxury resort, and I'd learned through trial and error to time my visits around their planned nighttime hikes. But the third reason the gate gave me such a headache was its location—it was invisible from the trail and accessible only by a difficult leap off a particular rock formation (or, as was usually the case, via levitation out over the canyon and through the nearly hidden hole in the fabric of the realm), and I had to lead my groups out well after nightfall.

We'd floated the idea of opening a gate from the ranch, but no one, least of all Carey and Zeb, wanted to take the risk of drawing the Arcanum's attention to our base camp. And so Sedona it was, a long drive, a dark hike, and a leap of faith.

Fortune was with us that night, and we made the trek undiscovered and uninjured, the boys behind me toting their packs and the Delacroixes bringing up the rear with Gracie in a carrier. When we reached the meeting spot, I called a halt and pointed up at the cloudless night. "Take a look at the stars," I told them. "They're different on the other side."

Ethan looked around, then squinted at the underside of the gate. "Is that it?"

"You see the spillover?" I traced the edge of the gate with my finger, watching the inactive magic surge and ebb as it pulsed out of Faerie.

"Yeah." He gazed at it for a moment until a passing bat broke his concentration. "Hey, Badger?"

"Mm?"

"Think we'll find any family over there?" he asked in a quiet rush. "I mean, Mom never knew her dad, so maybe…"

"I wouldn't get your hopes up too high," I said as gently as I could. "There are people over there who can check for you—ask Vivi if you can meet with Toula Pavli. But if you were anticipating a big family reunion—"

"I'm not, just…maybe."

I squeezed his shoulder, knowing all too well the impulse to reach for any family, no matter how questionable. I'd been lucky to find a cousin who didn't hate me and to reconnect with my long-absent fiancé in the aftermath of the Fringe's unravelling, but many, particularly the lesser bloods, had lost everyone. The Ford boys' long-lost grandfather was half fae—who knew if he was still alive, let alone interested in the well-being of grandsons he may never have known existed? That was, after all, why our Amy had never gone in search of her fae kin. "My parents were the product of one-night stands or worse," she'd confided to me one evening over our third cups of tea. "They never told me the details. But whoever my grandfathers were, they were fae. You think they'd want anything to do with *me*?"

"Don't worry," I told Ethan, "they're going to take good care of—*ah*. On time."

A white orb shot out of the top of the gate, illuminating our section of the trail and the lip of the canyon beside us as it hung in space. Right behind it was a familiar profile, and I waved as I recognized Rufus. "Hello! All set, then?" I called.

I'd yet to grow accustomed to the odd placement of the gate, which made anyone emerging from the far side seem as if his head and torso were being pulled from thin air at an odd angle. Rufus looked about for his bearings, then spotted me and waved back. "Hi, Badger! Five, was it?"

I'd also not yet fully internalized that the former professor, who appeared more like a graduate student, was in his mid-nineties. Dark-haired and somewhat boyish in his expressions, Rufus was equally happy to talk about the state of the NHL, the problems of electronica as a musical genre, and the reputation one could cultivate as a black-market don during World War II when one was fae and willing to make rations available on the cheap. He was also deeply enamored of his partner, who, though perhaps a third his age, gave him his marching orders. Pickup duty was an inconvenience most of the time, as our clock seldom aligned with Faerie's, but if I sent word that I was bringing unaccompanied minors along, Poppy insisted that Rufus be there to look out for them. And as I'd learned over my year-long acquaintance with them, what Poppy wanted, Poppy got.

"Five," I confirmed. "The little one's being carried." Wes pivoted to reveal Gracie sitting behind him, her eyes wide and her thumb firmly lodged in her mouth.

"Perfect." He shaded his eyes from the orb's glare and grinned. "You two must be the Fords. Ethan, yes? Want to show your brother how easy this is?"

I could tell the boy was nervous, but he nodded and tensed his legs. "What do I need to do?" he called up.

"Not a thing." Rufus beckoned with two fingers, and Ethan stifled a cry as he rose into the air. "I've got you, kid, you're not going to fall," Rufus soothed, waving him closer, and Ethan sailed out over the canyon and up toward the lip of the gate. When he was within arm's reach, Rufus grabbed him and guided him in, and I watched below as the boy's feet and legs disappeared through the hole. "That's Liza down there, she's going to take you the rest of the way," Rufus told him, and Ethan barely had time to wave goodbye before he vanished.

Elias followed his brother without hesitation, and Wes sent Jemma ahead of him. "Thank y'all for everything," he told me, pumping my hand as his wife started her decent into Faerie. "If we can ever repay—"

"We're Fringe, we're family," I said, cutting him short. "Take care, dear. And you," I added, giving Gracie's pigtail a tug. She smiled and swatted me away, and I watched as the two of them sailed to safety.

Finally, I was alone on the trail, and Rufus looked over his shoulder toward the forest floor below him. "Ready? Hang on, I'll give you a lift."

Five seconds later, another young face appeared at the edge of the gate—a face I knew nearly as well as my own. "Hello, love!" I called, waving as Seamus steadied himself. "Miss me?"

"Terribly," he called back, then turned to Rufus. "I think I can take it from here."

Seamus sounded confident enough, but Rufus still seemed doubtful. "Sure about that? At least let me spot. The canyon floor looks unforgiving."

Moving as deliberately as if he were navigating an unmarked minefield, Seamus maneuvered himself through the gate, then floated beside it, buoyed by an enchantment of his own making. Ever so carefully, he steered himself over the abyss and onto the trail, then dropped the last couple of meters and made a running stumble into my arms. "Missed you so much," he murmured into my hair as we held each other. "Let's not do that again, all right?"

I glanced up when the orb's light winked out and saw that we were alone. "Looks like you learned something, at least."

"Oh, loads. Did you know that it's possible to break the same bone three days in a row? Hurts like hell every time."

"Poor boy," I said, and kissed him. "About magic, I mean. Surely Val did more than beat you up for the last month."

"Yes, but there *was* a fair bit of beating."

We kissed again, and I leaned my head against his chest, feeling the soft cotton of his T-shirt beneath my cheek. "Kip's been practicing. Think you can still take him?"

"Once the latest crop of bruises heals." His arms tightened around me, and I felt his quiet sigh of contentment. "The long-distance thing is shite. If I go over for more punishment, you're going with me."

"That's what phones are for, Seamie."

"Poor substitute for this. I *need* this."

"So do I."

We stood together under the stars, each of us drinking in the other like water after a drought. After a long moment, Seamus mumbled, "Are we driving back tonight?"

"You know, it's late. I thought we'd get a room in town, make the drive in the morning." Cutting my eyes to his, I caught their hungry gleam and chuckled. "Easy, boy. Hike first, cuddle later."

"Mm. Just cuddling?"

"Maybe more if you behave." I released him and cocked my head toward the distant car park, and he took my hand to walk with me through the darkness. "Oh, and Seamie?"

"Yes?"

"You're looking rather young tonight."

He groaned and closed his eyes, and in my torch's light, I watched him age twenty years as he replaced his glamour. "Forgot," he muttered. "Sorry, Badge."

I squeezed his hand and kissed his now stubbly cheek. "Perfect. Come on, then," I said, shining the light on the trail ahead. "You and I have some serious catching up to do."

CHAPTER 2

The air conditioner was too loud and rattled each time it started up, but I didn't mind. With the room almost unpleasantly chilled, I had every excuse to burrow beneath the piled-on spare blankets and enjoy the feeling of Seamus's body spooned against mine. Spent and still healing, he slept curled beside me in the middle of the bed, his slow breaths barely stirring my hair, one arm thrown over me as if he feared I'd run out in the middle of the night. I relaxed in the comfortable routine—despite my teasing, Seamus was seldom able to stay awake more than a few minutes after sex, leaving me to gradually drift off while he warmed my back. Then again, seeing as I had a tendency to snore—he'd recorded it one night to put a stop to my denials—perhaps his talent for dropping off to sleep was a self-preservation measure.

Having made my warm nest in the starchy sheets, I closed my eyes and started to clear my thoughts, the better to focus on the task ahead. Part of me cried out for sleep—it'd been a long day on the road, after all, and I was rather relaxed—but if I was going to do any snooping on the East Coast that night, I needed to sleepwalk *now*. Fighting the urge to surrender to restful unconsciousness, I chided myself for my sloth. I was comfortable and fed and, if not safe, at least armed and capable of defending myself—how many other Fringers could say that? How many were hiding in the wilderness and the darker corners of cities, cut off from support and fearful of being killed in their sleep? How many were unprotected children?

Too many. I'd seen far too many disturbing sights in the last year, and I say that having spent a good portion of my previous career working homicides.

Turning my attention to the task at hand, I blanked my mind, ignored my physical sensations, and let my body go limp as the dream space expanded before me, the motel room now rendered in a palette of shadows as I entered a plane beyond the purely physical. I climbed out of bed, unfazed by my sleepwalking form's glow, and looked back to find Seamus unbothered beside my darkened body, bright white and stripped of his glamour of age. There were no illusions in the dream space, no way to disguise who and what one was and what sort of power one wielded, which suited my purposes well. My quarry were the dimly glowing sleepers, the ones too weakly talented to be called wizards or too human to be considered proper faeries. Finding them took a fair bit of work, but at least I always knew what I was seeing. Wizards like me were bright and obvious, and aside from a select few, were best avoided.

Satisfied that my room was secure, I rose through the ceiling and high over dreaming Sedona, keeping my eyes peeled for unexpected flashes in the dark. As I banked east, I was surprised to see another wizard approaching me—Carey, the only other wizard in the area who could sleepwalk, still refused to hunt Fringers for fear of drawing the Arcanum's attention. But as the nearing glow resolved into features, my momentary panic turned to concern. "Hua?" I called, hailing her with a wave. "What are you doing here?"

I held my position until she closed the gap between us, and I reassured myself that yes, the sleepwalker floating somewhere over the Arizona–New Mexico border with me was Liu Hua, one of the Minor Arcanum's rising stars in China. Though barely twenty-five, she shone with a radiance nearly as strong as my own—and unlike me, she always made it a point to sleepwalk fully clothed. I had a nasty habit of forgetting my shoes, or worse.

"Badger," she said, nodding. "I had hoped to catch you tonight. I have news of the gate."

Language was meaningless in the dream space—to my relief, I'd yet to find another dreamer who couldn't understand me. Though I knew from a phone conversation that Hua was fluent in English, she had no perceptible accent in our nighttime communications, and I trusted that whatever version of Mandarin she was hearing from me wasn't terribly mangled. "What's your time?" I asked. "What are you doing asleep right now?"

She smiled. "Early afternoon. And put your mind at ease—I only wanted to relay that the gate has been closed."

My tension drained like a deflating balloon. "Wonderful. That's fantastic news, dear. You're certain that the patch is strong?"

"Very strong. We would have fixed it sooner, but bringing enough people to *Tibet*…" Her nose wrinkled as she shook her head. "We have a wizard in Lhasa, but she's very old, and she's been ill of late. I had to convince the Chen twins to come from Shanghai, and both of them had to make arrangements with work…you see the trouble, right?"

The middle-aged Chen sisters, a relative rarity among their generation, were excellent wizards, but they were also busy wives and mothers with stressful jobs in the Party bureaucracy and could be prickly if called out on short notice. And like the majority of the Minor Arcanum, they couldn't sleepwalk. As such, I had yet to speak to them, but from the stories I'd heard, I didn't envy Hua.

I'd been fortunate to land on the doorstep of one of the few wizards who could teach me sleepwalking, but as I was introduced to other members of the organization, I realized how rare the skill actually was. Perhaps only a dozen could sleepwalk reliably, but once they understood the Fringe retrieval mission, most were happy to pitch in and at least point me toward likely targets. More importantly, the sleepwalkers were the Minor Arcanum's first source of news when sensitive information needed to be spread—the larger branches of the phone tree, as it were. Given how little we knew about who and what the Arcanum might be monitoring, people were careful to keep their contacts limited and personal. Whereas the Fringe had been able to rely on our secure computerized network to broadcast information, the Minor Arcanum spread news between individuals and often by telephone. Sleepwalker-to-sleepwalker conversations simply saved on phone costs.

Gates, especially, were never discussed by e-mail. In the last year, the Arcanum, long the guardians of our realm, had ceased to concern themselves with encroachments from the Gray Lands. Had the Minor Arcanum not stepped in, anything that chose to wander over would have had free rein to do as it liked to the unsuspecting mundane populace. Since our primary strategy for survival over the centuries—wizard, witch, and lesser-blooded fae alike—has been avoiding detection by mundanes who see the magically gifted as a threat to be eradicated, letting things from the Gray Lands run about unchecked would have been a *bad* idea.

That's not to say that letting things from Faerie run about in the mortal realm is necessarily better, mind. The fae are best treated with caution, as even the most decent-seeming half faerie can be deadly if provoked. And they're not the only race in that realm to worry about—thanks to natural gates, there's been a fair bit of cross-pollination over time, and races like the merrow cross back and forth regularly. (I had to explain once to a young witch why the merrow are so troubling. Think less mermaid, I told him, and more shark. There aren't many reports of merrow hunting humans, but it's happened, and it seldom ends well for the prey.)

But if Faerie is worrying, the Gray Lands is terrifying.

Aside from Kip, our resident centaur in hiding, I'd never heard of anything good coming across that border—and most creatures that made the trip were at least peckish when they arrived. Worse, the natural gates that formed into the Gray Lands were devilishly tricky to close, requiring at least a couple of experienced wizards to complete the job. Why the Arcanum had abandoned its responsibility was a mystery to us, but we had too much to lose to leave the gates alone and hope the other wizards eventually got the hint. And in recent months, it seemed to me that gates were opening more and more frequently. True, I didn't have much on which to base my hunch—for all I knew, the number of gates naturally waxed and waned—but at any rate, they had kept us occupied.

The latest gate, Hua's project, had formed not twenty miles from Lhasa—tucked into the surrounding Himalayas, at least, but still far too close to civilization to be left alone. "Any signs of movement?" I asked her.

"It would be easier to tell if the gate had opened over snow, but our initial evaluation was good," said Hua. "Just one yeti, a young male. We think he headed for higher ground—the local females are in heat, so perhaps he got a whiff and investigated."

"Good to hear. Let us know if the situation changes and you need back—"

We both stiffened and fell silent as a third wizard rushed toward us, and then I saw Hua relax and smile. "Jean-Claude, hello," she called. "I was telling Badger that the Tibet gate has been sealed."

By then, I'd recognized the elderly man in the cardigan as the Minor Arcanum's lone Canadian sleepwalker, a Québécois pharmacist who'd been among the first to join our cause. "Ah, Badger, there you are," he said, then nodded to Hua. "Ms. Liu, good evening. Napping, are you?"

"It's been a long week," she replied. "Good night to you both."

With that, Hua vanished, and Jean-Claude smiled fondly at the place she had been—according to Carey, Hua had been sleepwalking since she was five, and the older ones looked at her like a favorite granddaughter. "That's good to hear about the gate," he said. "And I also have news for you. My cousin located a witch in Paris this afternoon."

"Fantastic. Is she receptive to talking with us?"

His smile widened, exposing yellowed teeth and the silvery glint of a crown. "More than receptive. She's on a plane to New York as we speak, and I've been told that she's booked through to Albuquerque. Can you collect her? The ticket options weren't great, so she's not landing until about five-thirty tomorrow afternoon."

"We'll make it happen," I assured him. "Thanks for passing that along. Let me get back to the ranch, and I'll wire your cousin the money—"

He snorted and waved the offer aside. "Henri has no need, but thank you. He did tell the girl that you would be contacting her. Would you—"

"I'm on my way. Her name?"

"Nina Lesage. Fourteen years old. Henri said she's in poor shape, but at least she has a passport."

"I'll have Carey on standby. Let's hope this Nina can sleep on a plane," I told him, then took my leave and sped east.

I hadn't given much thought to how many planes cross the Atlantic on a daily basis until I was hovering miles above the ocean, trying to spot a glowing needle in a haystack. It took me the better part of an hour to register a flash inside a westbound plane, and then came the problem of *catching* the damned thing. I'd never tried to "land" inside a 777 before, but I could sleepwalk at great speed, and my spectral form slid through the thin skin and into the aisle without a hitch. With a moment's concentration, I was able to stay on the plane instead of shooting myself out through the tail, and then I began my search of the cabin for the young witch.

Transoceanic flights were hell on the system, and I wasn't surprised to find at least half the passengers still awake, staring at the screens in their seatbacks or in their laps. A baby fussed as his mother rocked him near the galley, shadows moving against shadows. And then, at the front of the coach section, I spotted the telltale light of a witch in one of the aisle seats.

I hurried closer for a look and found the likely target. The passenger was young and female, wearing a jacket over a black T-shirt that billowed from her thin frame. Black leggings with a hole in one knee and worn trainers completed the ensemble. Her hair was dark and stringy—she'd gone far too long without a trim—and her fingernails were ragged, gnawed-down stubs. She slept with a canvas tote clutched to her chest, and I suspected her wand was hidden in there, close at hand. But it was her face that gave me pause: her cheeks were too angular to be healthy, and her eyes, even with her makeup, appeared sunken and bruised. She didn't look fourteen, but rather seemed to vacillate between girlish ten and hard-ridden twenty as I moved around her.

The poor thing looked like she hadn't slept well in some time, and I mulled over whether I should leave her to her rest and try to find her again later. As I stood by the first-class curtain, waffling between waking her and moving on, her eyes popped open, and she gasped when she saw me. "Oh! Oh, good evening," I rushed before she could panic, "I'm Badger. I'll be picking you up in Albuquerque."

She clutched at her chest, then stared around her in surprise. "Where…where am—"

"You're asleep, Nina, still on the plane. And I'm out in Arizona right now. I just wanted to introduce myself so you'd know who'll be meeting you."

As I talked, she seemed to calm, then managed to nod. "You…Henri mentioned your name, he said you would take me to Faerie…"

"Exactly. We'll take you out to a lovely little ranch for a few days, put some good meals down you"—Nina's eyes lit up at the mention of food—"and then we'll be on our way. Ehm…" I looked about for a seat, then settled for the armrest of the sleeping mundane across the aisle from Nina's chair. "If I might ask, what are you seeing right now?"

"You, ma'am," she replied. "And…oh. I'm glowing, too, aren't I?" she said, twisting her hand back and forth in front of her face. "This is odd."

"I'll explain it all tomorrow. But…you can't see the plane?"

Nina shook her head. "No, just us and a lot of black. Should I see it?"

"No, I was only curious," I said, smiling to reassure her. "Well, I'll let you get back to sleep, dear. We'll meet you at the airport, yeah?"

"Okay." Her smile was still shy, but she seemed far less likely to bolt. "How do I sleep from—"

"Close your eyes and relax. Your mind will sever the connection on its own." I stood and smoothed her mussed hair, and she snuggled back against the seat she couldn't see. "Rest, now. Everything's going to be fine."

Within a minute, she was deeply asleep again, and I stepped away so as not to accidentally wake her a second time. Concentrating, I took a deep breath, focused on the feel of my abandoned body…

…and I was back, awake, panting softly, and horizontal, curled against Seamus, who slept undisturbed by my nocturnal wanderings. Dislodging his arm, I slid out of bed and padded to the bath, then ran cold water in the basin and splashed my face while I readjusted to physicality.

With the water running, I didn't hear Seamus until he

was standing behind me, and I almost jumped when he rubbed my shoulders. "Badger?" he said in a voice thick with interrupted slumber. "What's wrong? Are you feeling sick? Do I need to—"

"I'm fine," I told him, and blotted my face dry against the thin hand towel. "Been walking."

"Ah. Any luck?"

"We're picking up a French girl in Albuquerque tomorrow—well, tonight," I amended, spotting the bedside clock in the mirror. "She's on a plane right now. I said hello."

He held me in the dark and stroked my back. "You've been busy, love. Come to bed. You can't find them all tonight."

I let him lead me back to our abandoned bed and crawled in beside him. As his arm pulled me close, I murmured, "Seamie?"

"Mm?"

"I did it again."

"Did what?"

"Woke her. I didn't touch her, and she woke anyway."

"Maybe she can sleepwalk," he said through a yawn.

"No, she couldn't see anything. I…I was just thinking about whether I should wake her, and she woke…"

"Don't worry about it now," he mumbled. "Sleep, Badge."

I could feel it when he passed out again, but I stared at the wall for another silent ten minutes before sleep finally came for me.

Exhausted as I was, I still slept fitfully until first light, when I woke to the rustling of a paper sack. Cracking one eye open, I saw Seamus standing over the room's faux-wooden table for two, unpacking boxes and cutlery from the brown bag. He looked up when I shifted in bed, smiled guiltily, and swept a hand over the matching cardboard containers. "Huevos rancheros? I had a craving around four. Val's not bad at food, but he doesn't understand proper salsa."

I'd yet to find huevos rancheros anywhere as good as Zeb's take on the dish, but my empty stomach wasn't feeling particularly critical that morning. Grunting in the affirmative, I untangled myself from the sheets and shambled to the table, where an open box and a takeaway cup of black tea awaited me.

The caffeine proved ineffective against the oversized portion of eggs and tortillas, however, and Seamus insisted on driving us back to New Mexico. "I'm jetlagged," he said as he dug the keys to the Suburban from my purse. "Wide awake. Go on, go back to sleep."

Too weary to argue, I climbed into the passenger seat and closed my eyes as we turned toward the Interstate. When I opened them again, Sedona had vanished, and I blinked in blurry confusion at the familiar fences and stubby trees until the two-lane road to the Joneses' ranch came into focus.

"Better?" Seamus asked as I stretched and scowled at an abandoned shack.

"Maybe. How long did I—"

"You've barely stirred since we left the hotel. You snore less when you sleep upright, did you know that?"

I rubbed the grit from my eyes, wishing I'd showered that morning before checkout. "Sorry. You should have awakened me."

"Not feeling suicidal today." He grinned, then slowed at the faded wooden sign for Second Chance Ranch and turned off the main road. "Seriously, are you all right? Rough night?"

"Not my best, but yeah, I'm…here." I smoothed my tangled bob, felt a crust at the corner of my mouth, and wiped off the dried saliva as discreetly as I could. "Better. Tell you what, I'll drive to Albuquerque, eh?"

"Assuming you can stay awake for more than an hour

at a time, deal."

Seamus crawled as we approached the circular terminus of the long driveway. To the right lay the Joneses' house, a modest red-brick homestead with navy shutters and an overgrown flowerbed border—with everyone's schedules, something had to give. To the left were a pair of barns, one occupied by the last of the pregnant mares and the other housing Carey's veterinary equipment. The Joneses' vehicles, a tidy SUV and a pair of battered farm trucks, sat in a neat row in the grass, and Seamus parked in an empty space on the end. As he climbed out, one of the resident barn tabbies hissed in terror and fled up a tree—par for the course with a faerie on the property, though I did pity my partner, who'd never had as much as a friendly lick from an animal. Ignoring the rude welcome, he locked up, tossed me the keys, and sloughed off his thin leather gloves, his second skin for any situation involving proximity to iron. "Shower?"

"God, yes," I sighed, and led the way down the dirt path to the third "barn," the slightly disguised bunkhouse we'd installed for passing Fringers and for ourselves, the Joneses' long-term unexpected guests. As I neared, I heard the dull thump of amplified bass coming from inside the building and braced myself for whatever sonic horror waited on the other side of the door. Exchanging a knowing look with Seamus, I shouldered my way inside and cringed.

Amy, our teenage crafter, had appropriated a room near the far end of the bunkhouse as her personal workshop. Her bedroom was simply too small for her growing collection of curing woods and glass jars, and she needed a place to sprawl and a door on which to post her black-and-red *STAY OUT* sign. Crafting was delicate work, after all, and the last thing she needed while building a wand core was Seamus or me popping by to show off some new trick we'd mastered—or Kip poking his head in to break her concentration.

And the girl stayed busy. Crafters were a rare breed, found only among witch-bloods, those few with both wizard and fae heritage. They seldom had any real talent for magic, but some could manipulate it in the ways necessary for the construction of wands and less common magical devices, a skill that no wizard could match. Amy's late mother had been one of the best, and her daughter, young as she was, showed great promise. Every wizard of the Minor Arcanum who needed a new wand had received one from Amy's workshop in the last year, and she kept a stash of stronger wands around for the Fringers who came through so that no one went to Faerie emptyhanded. That day, however, the door was wide open, and we found her shaping wand shafts with the thick shades drawn, sanding and polishing as she attempted to spit along with Eminem in her soprano South Carolina drawl.

"Afternoon!" Seamus yelled over the racket. "Are you deaf now?"

She jumped on her stool, then muted her sound system—a cheap tablet connected to Zeb's old speakers and subwoofer—and beamed as she swiveled around. "Hey! Welcome back! Sorry, didn't hear y'all come in," she said, unfazed to find herself with an audience. "You still in one piece, Seamus?"

He lifted his T-shirt, revealing a fading patchwork of green and yellow bruises. "More or less. Have we been copying Zeb's music library again?"

Amy nodded. "Needed something to get me in the zone. Sanding's tedious, you know?"

Seamus glanced at the tablet's screen. "Bought that one on CD back in the day. Were you even *alive* when this was popular?"

"Eh, barely. I was born in 2000."

His shoulders slumped, and I laughed at his sudden despondence. "She's a baby, Seamie," I said, patting his arm. "It's only going to get worse from here. By the way," I asked Amy, "where's everyone hiding? We have a pickup at the airport later tonight."

Her pale eyebrows rose. "Yeah? That was fast. Uh…Carey's on a house call—sick bull or something—and the boys are out back." Leaning over her workbench on tiptoe, she was just able to raise the shade, giving us a view of the training ring behind one of the real barns. The shapes of the people out there were indistinct, but I could name them by their relative size and movement. Zeb, tall, tanned, and sporting a dark ponytail, leaned against the rail fence with his strong arms folded while he watched the younger two circle each other. Kip, tallest and lankiest of the three, moved in a half-crouch, his bronze chest bare and his red hair blowing loose. And then there was Arnold, prematurely gray, a head shorter than his opponent, and still recovering from a bad sunburn, who clumsily mirrored Kip's movements. As I watched, Kip suddenly shifted and charged, and Arnold struggled in his grip. The two danced around the ring for a moment, locked together and jostling for holds, until Kip twisted and pinned Arnold in the dirt.

"Well, that looks like fun," Seamus muttered beside me.

"Zeb thought they could use a bit of instruction in the fine art of street fighting," I explained as Kip pulled Arnold to his feet. "Kip's fast, but he still kicks too much, and Arnie…"

"Is Arnie?"

"Is a well-trained magus who could do with a gym membership. One does not engage in manual farm labor when one has a perfectly good wand at hand."

He snorted. "Meanwhile, Secretariat keeps forgetting about those missing back legs."

"Be *nice*," Amy chided as she packed her tools into her tackle box. "He can outrun you."

"Of course he can, he's still a damn centaur under that spell."

She glowered up at Seamus, and I looked away before she could see my smile. Kip and Amy, both recently orphaned, had decided almost immediately upon meeting that they were friends—and anyone with a drop of intuition could tell they were heading for something more than friendship. But in light of the circumstances, the adults on the ranch weren't about to prod them any closer to each other than they'd naturally become. Amy was only seventeen, and Kip was decidedly inhuman, so our consensus was to let those chips fall without our meddling.

We watched for another few rounds, all of which ended with Arnold meeting the ground, and Amy finally huffed her impatience. "He's making the same mistakes," she said, then abruptly left the room and headed outside. Seamus and I followed, only to see Amy slinking close to the wall and staying low—an ambush, I realized, and held Seamus back. "Watch," I whispered, and started for the ring by another trail. "Hello, everyone!" I called. "Look who I found!"

They turned at my voice and waved, and we hurried up the path to greet them. With the guys distracted, Amy slipped around the far side of the ring, then squeezed through the fence rails and sprinted across the dusty circle toward Kip. He grunted in surprise when she grabbed him around the waist and threw her slight weight to the right, but he held his balance and pivoted, then pried her loose and tossed her, kicking and laughing, over his sweaty shoulder. "That's hardly fair," he said as she tried to wriggle loose. "Oh, did you want me to put you down?"

As she shrieked, he jogged across the ring toward the half-full water trough, then dumped her in. She splashed him back, and while the two started a water fight, I shook my head and turned to the other nominally responsible adults. "How's it coming?"

"Slowly," Arnold muttered. "I don't suppose the police have any tips?"

"If you want to take him down," said Seamus, "there's one *highly* effective way."

"And I've already forbidden groin strikes, so no," Zeb

interrupted. "Welcome back, man. How was it?"

Seamus eyed Arnold, who was dirt-streaked and already beginning to discolor. "You think he has it bad? His limbs are still intact."

Zeb winched. "Ouch. Your uncle won't cut you a break?"

"He'd consider it an insult, I think. Lucky me."

"And while Seamus whinges," I interjected, "we're meeting a Fringer in Albuquerque tonight. She's flying in from Paris. Fourteen, scrawny. Needs a good feed if nothing else."

"I'll get a bed set up," Zeb offered. "Carey should be back any…" He paused, cocking his head, then nodded as the sound of an engine crescendoed. "Speak of the devil. Come on to the house, I've got burgers ready to grill. Hey, kids!" he yelled toward the splashing twosome. "Lunch! Call a truce!"

They rejoined us, both dripping, and Arnold shook his head. With a mutter and a wave of his hand, Amy and Kip were clean and dry again, and my cousin rolled his eyes as he gave himself the same treatment. "If you'd be so kind as to not tell Carey exactly how badly I performed," he mumbled, "I'd be much obliged."

"French, you say?" Carey mumbled around a bite of her second ketchup-dripping cheeseburger. Ravenous after spending the morning with a cantankerous bull, she'd inhaled her first burger as soon as it came off the grill. "Do any of you *parlez*? Because that's about the extent of my ability."

I looked around the long table at the shaking heads— all but Amy, who lifted a finger. "I had French freshman year, but I haven't exactly been keeping up with it."

"No worries," I told her. "Seamie, you'll need to come along to zap English into her. And since I told her I'd be there, guess you two are off the hook," I added, pointing to the Joneses.

"We'll make the next Sedona run," Zeb offered. "Once we've got enough passengers. You think this kid's sick or just hungry?"

"Hard to tell, but—"

"I'll be up tonight," Carey interrupted, "and I'll shoot Penny a message just in case. I don't think she keeps weekend office hours," she said as she chewed, then grabbed a napkin to save her shirt from escaping condiments. "This is *really* good, babe."

He smiled and passed her the napkin stack. "Considering your patient, I thought a burger was appropriate."

"Ugh, that boy's a brat," she muttered, and saluted her husband with the remains of her bun.

I offered to clean up after lunch, and Carey stayed close while I rinsed the plates, picking cold chips from the baking pan. "Good trip?" she asked when I shut the tap off.

"Successful. Thought I was in trouble when Lou pulled me over, but other than that…"

She snorted and moved the pan out of my soapy reach. "I'll have a word with him. When did you hear about this girl?"

"Last night. Jean-Claude was waiting for me, and I found her plane."

"Nicely done," she replied as she pulled the ketchup from the fridge. "And these are too good to waste."

"You're just hungry."

"Famished," she agreed.

I dropped the plates into the basin while Carey continued her lunch behind me. "Something *did* happen," I said after a quiet moment. "Sleepwalking."

"Oh?"

"Yeah. I…" I paused, trying to recall as many details as I could, then said, "I was on the plane, trying to find the kid. When I did, I wasn't sure whether I should wake her—she looks like she's been sleeping rough," I explained over my shoulder—"but then she woke on her own. I didn't even touch her."

Carey picked a burnt chip off the pan with her fingernail. "It happens," she said, sounding unconcerned. "Just proof that you're getting better at sleepwalking. I didn't have to touch you to wake you into the dream space that first time."

"You didn't?"

"Nope. What's happening is the dream space is responding to your unspoken desires. Part of you wanted to wake her, and it did the work for you. Now, you're going to have to work on controlling this," she cautioned. "Like everything else, it'll come with practice. I mean, you don't want to accidentally wake every wizard you run across out there, right?"

I thought of the brilliant glow of the Arcanum silo in the dream space and shuddered at the implication. "How do I control it, then?"

"Keep your intentions clear. Be mindful of yourself. You got out there in that shared space—now, you have to remember to be aware of your own power. Don't worry, we all went through this phase," she said, waving a chip for emphasis. "Nothing new."

"Though I suppose I'd better stay away from the silo for now, eh?"

Carey grimaced. "*Far* away. Hell, I wouldn't get too close, and I've been sleepwalking for twenty years. Better to not risk it." She scraped the last of the chips into her palm, then passed me the pan for soaking. "It's going to be fine, Hannah. I'm here to help you, okay?"

"Okay," I replied, but my stomach continued to knot long after Carey had left the kitchen.

CHAPTER 3

Around three, after he caught a quick burger-induced nap, Seamus and I loaded into the Suburban and struck out for Albuquerque. I hadn't bothered to ask Nina for her flight information, but everything coming in that evening appeared to be on time, and I didn't want to leave her waiting by herself in the terminal.

As we made our way south on I-25 with the air conditioning cranked against the warm afternoon, Seamus flipped through the radio presets until he found his preferred rock station and settled back with a satisfied sigh. "Missed this," he said as he unscrewed the cap of his Pepsi.

"Even the terrible local adverts?"

"Even those. No one's tried to sell me a Chevy in weeks. It's bizarre."

I chuckled and overtook an old woman in an oversized Cadillac. "So, how *did* you spend the last month?"

Seamus closed his eyes. "Sore, mostly."

"Care to elaborate?"

"Sore and tired."

"*Seamie.*"

He grinned at my exasperation. "I was going to stay with Toula, since she has an actual guestroom in her suite, but Val wanted me close at hand—"

"And Toula would have yelled at him for beating you up."

"That, too. He stuck me in one of the empty guard rooms, and whenever he wasn't working, we were training.

Mina subbed in a few times for extra practice. Once he thought I'd made enough progress, he called in Harry Stowe to spar with me—Vivi's youngest older brother, yeah?"

"Yeah, I've met him. That doesn't seem fair…"

"Of course it wasn't. Harry wiped the floor with me for a week. I mean, we're close in age, but he's been at this a lot longer."

"Did you ever beat him?" I asked.

"Once," Seamus muttered. "He felt guilty about everything, and he *had* broken my leg the day before…"

"Bloody hell."

"*Bloody* is right." He drank and stared out the window for a long moment. "But Val did teach me gates. Intra-realm gates aren't that difficult, really. He said I'm not at all ready to close a Gray Lands gate by myself, but hey, progress."

"Sure," I replied, fumbling for my own drink between the seats.

We drove in silence for a time, listening to the radio and the numbing rumble of the road under the tires. After a while, I thought that Seamus might have fallen asleep, but when I glanced over, I found him staring into space. "Seamie? You okay?"

"Hmm?" he said, startled from his reverie. "Oh, ehm…yeah. Yeah, I'm fine."

"Are you sure?"

He said nothing, but I bit my tongue, letting the uncomfortable quiet linger until he gave in. "Val…talked about you."

"Oh. Is he opposed to—"

"No, no, he has nothing against you. Ehm…" Seamus squeezed the half-empty plastic bottle between his palms while he sought the right words. "He asked me about our plans for the long term."

"What did you tell him?"

"That we're focusing on the time being for now."

I nodded. "Sounds good to me. What, he wanted our ten-year plan?" I joked.

But Seamus didn't smile. "He…well, he tried to impress upon me certain facts that I already knew."

"Such as?"

"Such as the fact that you're not getting any younger, Badge," he mumbled.

I hardly needed a reminder of *that*—I saw it in the mirror every morning, especially since I'd stopped dying my roots. The silver threads in my once-dark hair didn't exactly coordinate with my lifelong white forelock, but there was nothing I could do to halt their proliferation. "Well," I said stiffly, "seeing as mortality is generally an incurable condition, I don't know what he wants me to do about it."

Seamus hesitated before speaking again. "You know that you have an open invitation to Faerie, don't you? Vivi's not territorial."

"And leave you here? The realm still hates you, doesn't she? Honestly, I don't see how you got through a month without—"

"Faerie's got over me. She's not giving Coileán and Eleanor headaches anymore. Took a week, but I guess I passed whatever test she's worked up." He put his drink aside and turned to me. "We could move over there together. Get a place in the settlement, yeah? You'd be with the rest of the Fringe, and whenever you needed to come back here, you could go through Sedona."

I cut my eyes to his hopeful face, then quickly looked back at the road. "That wouldn't do any good."

"Sure it would, you wouldn't age—"

"Every time I left, I'd age all at once. For that plan to work, I could never come back here. And aside from that, I can't sleepwalk from there. I tried back in January when I spent that long weekend with Toula. I'd be useless."

"You wouldn't be *useless*—"

"Seamie, I'm the only coordinator left here. Who's

supposed to pick up the slack? Amy can't do it, and Arnold—"

"What about Vivi? You've done more than your fair share—why can't Vivi take a turn on this side?"

"Vivi is where she needs to be," I murmured. "With her family. She has the same little mortality problem that I do, remember."

"So why does she get to be safe? Why not you? And what about *us*?" he insisted, squeezing my shoulder. "How long until the Arcanum comes to its senses, Badger?"

"I don't know," I muttered, staring at the cement mixer ahead of me.

"Another year? Ten years? Twenty? Thirty?"

"I don't *know*, Seamie. But while we've got missing people—"

"No offense, but sod them. What if something happens to *you*?"

"I—"

"What if this goes on, love? What if we're still here thirty years from now and you have a stroke? Or develop Alzheimer's? Cancer? Or…hell, what if you drop dead of an aneurysm?"

I could hear the fear in his voice, but I tried to keep calm while I drove. "That's the risk of living, I suppose. Happens to us all eventually."

"But it doesn't have to! Not to you!" He struggled, then quietly said, "I'm just fucking terrified that something's going to happen to you that Carey and Val can't fix. Badge, I…I walked away once. I don't want to lose you again, not like that. Think about it, okay? Please? I'm not saying you have to decide tonight, but…think about it. The settlement's lovely, it really is."

I nodded, and he released his grip on my shoulder. As Seamus turned away, I tried to suppress the nagging fears that he'd stirred up all too well. I'd been flirting with death for most of my life—one assumed the risk when one joined the police service. But in the last year, with every close encounter with the Arcanum, I'd practically been poking death in the eye. We'd had several near misses in our pickups, Fringers who were still well on the Arcanum's radar, and once, I'd pressed myself against the back of a wall and clutched my wand, praying that the wizard on the other side wouldn't hear me breathe and come around to investigate. No, I didn't especially want to die, but someone had to hold the line.

And what if our standoff continued for another couple of decades? What if I woke up one morning and couldn't move half my body? Or what if the Arcanum came around, released their hostages, and I was, oh, eighty? Perhaps a spry eighty, but still well past my prime? Sure, I could go to Faerie then with a clear conscience, but would Seamus still want me? What if, a hundred years hence, he decided that he wanted a family—something I could never give him? What if he fancied screwing a girl of twenty instead of coming home to me?

There were certain difficulties inherent in any relationship with an immortal, but I couldn't dwell on them that afternoon.

I reached across the center console and took his hand. "Love you, Seamie."

He clasped my fingers so hard that I almost winced. "Love you, too, Badger. Always will."

The plane from JFK landed only five minutes late, and Seamus and I paced around the baggage claim until the passengers began to trickle in. I had no idea of whether Nina even had a bag to check, but there was no better location from which to scout.

The alarm for incoming luggage sounded, and as the passengers jostled for position around the belt, Seamus tapped my arm. "Is that her?" he asked, pointing across the room. I squinted at the scrawny child, then nodded and started her way.

Nina's ripped black ensemble might have suggested toughness, but she clutched her tote too tightly and worked her bottom lip with her teeth as she looked around the room. She didn't even have a backpack, I realized as we neared—all of the girl's possessions were being carried in a glorified grocery sack. Waifish and lost, she hunched near a rubbish bin and tucked her dirty hair behind her ear as she scanned the crowd.

"Mademoiselle Lesage?" I asked, and she jumped and spun to find me, eyes wide and frightened. "Oh…oh, dear, it's all right, you're all right," I hurried, showing her my empty hands. "It's Badger, remember me? So glad you're here."

Her brow knit as I spoke, and she paused before replying. "You…you go me…euh…l'avion? Oui? Quand je dormais?" Receiving no immediate response, she raked her chapped lip again. "Comprenez-vous?"

"I, ehm…I'm sorry," I said slowly, "but I don't speak French. Don't worry, we'll fix this…" I noticed Seamus typing furiously on his mobile and asked, "What are you doing?"

"This is probably going to be glitchy, but it might help," he said, and showed me the screen. "Translation app. Maybe this'll be enough to get her to the car."

Nina waited, puzzled and nervous, until Seamus finished tapping and handed her the phone. Her dark eyes lit up in comprehension, and she nodded. "Okay," she said, flashing a thumbs up. "Okay. Allons-y."

We hustled Nina out of the airport as quickly as we could and led her to the Suburban. She climbed into the back without hesitation, and as I started the engine, Seamus began to write another message for her. He passed her the mobile as I backed out, and I watched her scan the text in the rearview mirror. When she finished, she looked at him doubtfully. "It, euh, thing, hurt I…euh…"

"Write," he interrupted, miming a keyboard, and she tapped out a reply and passed it forward. Seamus read it quickly, then turned back to her and shook his head. "No. It does not hurt. Pull off, Badge, will you?"

I found a deserted corner of the car park and stopped the vehicle, and Seamus got out and joined Nina in the second row. Nodding reassurance, he stripped off his gloves, then rested his fingertips on her temples and closed his eyes. She gasped and jerked, but he held on for a few seconds until the enchantment took full effect. "Do you understand me?" he asked as she rubbed her head.

Nina scowled. "You said this would not hurt."

"It didn't, did it?"

"Felt strange."

"But not *painful*. And it worked, right?" She paused, then nodded, and he slipped his gloves back on. "All right, then. I'm Seamus, that's Badger up front, and we've got about two hours on the road. Dinner will be waiting, but are you hungry now? Have you eaten?"

"Pretzels," she replied, speaking slowly as she experimented with the foreign words. "On the plane."

"That's hardly a meal," I told her. "There are some fast food places on the other side of the city—we'll pull off and find something quick." I started the engine again, then glanced over my shoulder. "You're not a vegetarian, are you?"

"Madame," she replied, "if it is food, I will eat it. I am not particular."

Given her thin frame, I could only imagine.

Nina's welcome to the States was a bag of chicken nuggets and chips, but she wolfed down every crumb and licked the grease from her fingers. The three of us kept up light conversation for a time, until I saw that she was no longer looking out the window, but rather dozing against it.

We didn't hear another peep from the back seat until we were within ten minutes of the ranch, and by then, the sun was already down. "It's nicer by daylight," Seamus told her, "but the stars are pretty, too. Light pollution's not bad at all out this way. Ever seen a true dark sky?"

"Not like this," she replied, leaning against the glass to look up. "It is never so dark in Paris."

"Same goes for most of Europe, actually. You're Parisian, then?"

"I was. When they killed my parents, I left the city. I have been moving around—Tours, Bordeaux, Lyon…I was in Nice for a month, but everything is more expensive by the sea."

Our rule was not to ask about the deceased unless our passengers wanted to open up, and Nina was making it clear that this wasn't the time. "Well, if you'd like to stargaze, you're more than welcome to do so after dinner," I said. "Feeling hungry again yet?"

"A little."

That, as it turned out, was a gross underestimation of Nina's appetite. I had no idea where she managed to hide her third helping, but she seemed slightly green when Amy led her out to the bunkhouse. When their footsteps retreated, Carey shook her head and sighed. "Kid hasn't eaten well in weeks, at least."

"Maybe she's just hungry," said Arnold.

"Did you see her hair? Her eyes? You don't look like that unless you're starving." She picked up her plate and Zeb's and went to the sink. "Jean-Claude called while you two were out. Turns out cousin Henri didn't give him the full scoop before he shipped Nina off."

"Oh?" I asked.

She flipped the water on and scrubbed the plates clean, then returned to the table. "He caught her dumpster diving and took her home for a meal. She saw his wand and freaked, he told her he wasn't Arcanum, and that was that."

"Nice of him to feed her," said Seamus.

Carey smirked and sipped her water. "Henri's seventy-some years old, and Nina went with him without a fuss.

While they were eating lunch, before she spotted the wand, she asked him…what she could do to *repay* him, to be polite about it."

"Jesus," I muttered.

"Yeah. Henri said the kid's been living in hostels when she can, living on the street when she can't, and rendering certain services to feed herself."

Seamus looked sick. "She's *fourteen*."

"And resourceful," said Carey. "Penny's going to catch a flight out tomorrow. I want a full exam on that kid, and I can't do the bloodwork she needs to have done. There's no telling what she's picked up in the last year."

"I've, ehm, got better at gates," Seamus offered. "If Penny wants to save the trip—"

"Not an emergency, so we're not going to risk Arcanum attention," Zeb interrupted. "But thanks."

"And there's no need to poke and prod her tonight," Carey continued. "Let her get settled in with Amy and Kip—that's bound to do her good."

Zeb and Arnold took Seamus down to our usual watering hole for welcome-back beers, but Carey, who'd been going strong all day, begged off in favor of spending some quality time with her neglected bed. Finding a television to myself, I opted to loaf about in the Joneses' basement while the boys were away, giving me a chance to relax without bothering the kids.

Around ten, catching myself dozing through more than the commercial breaks, I forced myself back to the surface and out toward my bedroom. There would be no sleepwalking that night, I decided. I deserved at least one decent span of uninterrupted slumber, and as long as nothing was burning, I didn't need an update until morning.

But as I passed the training ring at the spare barn, I picked Amy's silhouette out of the shadows. She sat alone on the fence with her face trained toward the clear heavens, her feet tucked under the lower rail to steady herself. Everything seemed harmless enough, but my intuition told me to check on her all the same.

"Gorgeous night, isn't it?" I said, announcing myself well before I was upon her. "Have you got your star app handy? I'm rubbish at constellations." I heard her sniffle then, and my heart sank. "What's wrong, love?" I asked, hurrying closer. "What happened? Are you hurt?"

"No," she mumbled, and wiped her bare arm across her face. "Sorry, I'm fine."

"Nonsense. What's going on?"

Amy said nothing, and I leaned on the fence beside her, letting the silence stretch, until she sighed. "Nina saw my workshop."

"Yeah? And?"

"And she realized what I am, and she…she stepped *back*. Like I was contagious or something."

"Amy, dear, you know you're not—"

"At least most everybody can pretend and be polite. She didn't even try. Didn't really want to talk to me after that. *Kip*, now, Kip's all right with her, but God forbid she sit too close to a mongrel. It might be catching," she said bitterly.

I straightened and wrapped my arm around her waist, and Amy leaned against my shoulder. "Don't let her get to you," I murmured. "You're an incredible young woman, Amy, and we're very proud of you."

"I think you're the exception." Amy looked at me, and I could see the sheen of her eyes in the security lamp's glow. "I really do. No one seems to mind me as long as I'm making something they need, but when I'm not being useful…"

"Have Carey and Zeb said anything like that?"

"No," she admitted, "but…I saw how it was with Mama and Daddy. Fringers came around when they needed wands and stuff, but no one got *friendly*."

As much as I wanted to deny it and reassure Amy that Nina's reaction was a fluke, I couldn't lie to her. Nominally, the Fringe welcomed everyone on the weak end of the magical spectrum. Witches? Sure. Lesser bloods? Not a problem. But throw a witch-blood into the mix, and no one was sure what to do with him. Even though witch-bloods made the finest magical tools available, both witches and lesser bloods tended to view genetic comingling as distasteful, and wizards and full faeries even more so. I knew of only one Arcanum-born witch-blood—Slim, our captured coordinator—whose wizard parent hadn't kicked him out as soon as it was convenient. Witch-bloods happened in the Fringe from time to time, but that didn't mean that the Fringers of purer stock were always thrilled to be associated with them.

"You know what?" I said. "There are many Fringers hiding out in Faerie right now, and only a few of us here. You're doing something most of them are too scared to do. Hold your head up, girl."

Just then, we heard Kip call her name, and he jogged over when I hailed him. "*There* you are," he said, climbing the fence to sit beside Amy. "I lost you. Going to bed any time soon? Nina's asleep."

"Good," she mumbled. "That's…good."

Kip frowned at her response. "Is something wrong?"

"No. Not at all," she said, a bit too brightly. "And yeah, bed sounds like a good idea. Shall we?"

He slid off the fence, then held her hands while she made the short jump to the dirt. Bidding me good night, they linked arms and walked off together, and I stared up at the sky, looking for answers in the unfathomable stars.

Penny arrived the next afternoon, mussed from the long trip but ready to go. "And where's the patient?" she asked almost as soon as she'd cleared the car door, glancing about her as if Nina might be hiding in the scrub. "We've got work to do."

Nina, who'd spent most of that day catching up on lost sleep, groggily followed the doctor into the basement, which Penny had appropriated as a makeshift surgery. Arnold carried down a heavy suitcase full of equipment and vials surrounded by padding and cold packs, then was unceremoniously ordered out of the room.

They didn't emerge for an hour, and both looked rather drained by the experience. As Nina slunk back to the bunkhouse, Carey and I cornered Penny for the scoop. "Not nearly as bad as it could be, all things considered," she declared as she repacked her kit on the scuffed basement coffee table. "At least she's not pregnant."

"But…" Carey coaxed.

"*HIPAA*," Penny retorted. "You can make what you will of my spell—I told her not to let anyone touch it for at least three days. Give the antibiotics a fighting chance." With a cocked eyebrow for Carey, she returned to her work. "And that's all I'm telling you. Your patients may not have confidentiality issues, Dr. Jones, but mine do."

"Can you tell us how soon she'll be cleared for travel?" I asked before Carey could argue.

"Honestly? She's safe to go now, but leave her here for a few days, why don't you? Maybe a week, if you're feeling generous. Put a few meals down her, eh? Kid's rocking the 'heroin chic' look without the heroin."

"You're sure of that?" asked Carey.

Penny gave her another disapproving look, but she replied, "She's clean. I ran a full panel." Latching her case, she asked, "How're the rest of you holding up? Anything you need me to check on while I'm out here? Scrips? Allergies?"

"Well, Kip had a cold or something last week," I told her, "but that seems to have cleared up on its own."

"Good," she muttered. "I mean, guessing at dosage is always a delightful adventure, but if I can avoid it, so much the better."

"I've been doctoring him," Carey added. "And yeah, nothing makes you feel quite as confident in your skills as making quasi-educated guesses."

"Hey, at least you know horses."

"That's only the back end of him," she replied with a snort. "You should see the X-rays. That kid's skeletal structure is unbelievable, and he's got redundant organs all over the place, to boot."

That piqued Penny's interest. "Yeah?" she asked, leaning over her case. "Redundant?"

"Dupes everywhere—he's got a heart and lungs in the human-ish bit, but he's got a second set in the equine chest. I mean, with a body like that, he needs the second heart just to keep his circulation going, I suppose, but the bigger lungs don't seem to get much use unless he's running. Only one stomach, I think, but *damn*, he's complicated."

"Let's hope he never gets more than a bad sniffle, then." Penny carried her case to her open luggage and continued her packing. "My return flight isn't until tomorrow morning—any chance that I could crash here tonight?"

"Of course," said Carey. "Hope you like lasagna."

"Zeb's?" She grinned. "Oh, yeah. I keep telling you, lady, you found a good one."

The drugs in her system did nothing to dull Nina's raging appetite, and she spoke little during dinner as she tucked into helping after helping of pasta and garlic bread. Penny was more vocally appreciative of the cuisine, but I noticed that Amy ate little and was oddly quiet during the meal. Glancing about the table, I saw a flicker of unease cross Kip's face from time to time, especially when his comments to Amy garnered only brief responses. Though I felt for the poor, confused boy, it wasn't my place to explain Amy's reticence, nor would it have been wise to tell him why Nina had put as much of the table as she could between herself and Amy. I'd seen how protective he could be when he thought Amy was in trouble—nothing good would come of cluing him in to the fact that the newcomer, who apparently had picked up the worst of the Fringe's internal prejudices, thought his friend was subhuman.

Arnold scraped his chair away from the table, shaking me from my uncomfortable thoughts. "Who's ready for pudding?" he asked as he rose. "Penny? Take your plate?"

She passed it over Nina's bent head and smiled her thanks. "I could be convinced. What kind of pudding?"

"Well, I tried my hand at Zeb's chocolate cake with cinnamon cream, if you're willing to risk it."

Her brow wrinkled. "That…isn't pudding."

"It is on our side of the pond," I explained, stretching to give Arnold my dishes. "And I'll chance it. If it's half as good as the one he made last month—"

Before I could finish, the antique house phone began to trill, and Carey rolled her eyes as she stood. "Sorry, I *did* sign up for the Do Not Call list," she said as she crossed the kitchen, then pulled the sun-faded yellow handset off the wall and twirled the spiral cord around her finger. "Hello?" she barked, tensed for a quick exit to the unwanted conversation, but her face softened in the next instant. "Oh, hi, Joyce, long time no… Oh. Oh, dear, that…" She listened for a moment, then whistled low. "Shit. Are you home?… Good. Stay there, we'll be down shortly. Bye."

She rang off and turned to face the suddenly silent table. "That was Joyce Killian," she said, looking at Zeb and Penny. "They've got bodies. We need to get down there ASAP."

"Down where?" Seamus asked, pushing his plate aside. "And *bodies?*"

"South Florida, they live in the Everglades. And three

dead skunk apes, she says. The troop actually sought Boone out tonight, so it's probably serious."

My partner's confusion only deepened. "The hell's a skunk ape?"

"Floridian bigfoot," Zeb offered. "Bigfeet. Bigfoots? Whatever, they're simian."

"And intelligent," said Carey. "The Killians have been interacting with a troop of them for decades. They're kind of like the cracker version of Jane Goodall."

Penny coughed into her fist. "That's…*generous*. Did Joyce say what killed them?"

"Boone wasn't sure. They're worried that a gate's opened somewhere in there," she added, leaning against the kitchen counter.

"*Another* one?" Arnold sighed. "How many does this make this month, three?"

"Four," Carey replied. "And if there's a new one out there, then God knows what's come through. Heck, they've already got alligators and giant snakes to worry about."

"That's a lot of wetland to cover," Zeb muttered. "And unless you were planning on rearranging our schedule tonight, we aren't going anywhere."

Her eyes narrowed. "What are you—*oh*. Damn it," she spat. "Colorado. *Shit*."

"They're picking up a pair of rescue mares tomorrow," Arnold explained to Penny. "It's going to be a long week around here."

At that, Kip lifted a finger. "Maybe it would be best if Seamus and I aren't here when you bring them in. We could go in your place."

Zeb rubbed his chin as he mulled that over. "Seamus, yeah," he said after a pause. "With Hannah and Arnold. The three of you should at least make up for the two of us. But Kip—"

"If there's a gate, then y'all will need a dark magic detector," Amy interrupted. "I've been working up a better one for a few weeks, but the controls are a little wonky. I'll go along to run it, and Kip can keep me from getting eaten by a gator. There, problem solved."

The Joneses and Penny looked at each other in uncertain silence, but Arnold jumped in before they could realize all the ways this scenario could go wrong. "Sure, we'll take the kids. A change of scenery's nice every now and then, isn't it?"

"Dude," said Penny, "it's a *swamp*. It's June. Why are you trying to punish them?" she asked, sweeping one manicured hand toward Kip and Amy.

"You haven't spent much time in South Carolina, have you, Dr. Morris?" Amy retorted. "I'll be fine. *They'll* be miserable," she added, cocking her head toward my end of the table, "but I'm well acquainted with humidity and mosquitoes."

"Yes, that sounds delightful," I grumbled. "We'll go, Carey. Have you got a picture for the gate?"

Ten minutes later, equipped with our overnight backpacks and half of Arnold's cake in plastic bags, we waited as Carey returned to the kitchen with a printout of the front of the Killians' house. Taking the paper in hand, Arnold squinted at the image, then looked back at Carey. "Why stilts?"

"It floods," she said with a shrug. "I generally aim for the ground—less chance of accidentally walking off the porch that way."

Seamus glanced over Arnold's shoulder to see the target. "I could—"

"We're not risking it tonight," Arnold interrupted. "Practice gates during daylight hours—that's just good sense. Always better to see where you've landed, eh?"

He couldn't argue with that, and we stepped back to give the magus room to work. Gates were one of the great magics, a high-level skill that many never mastered, and they weren't Arnold's strong suit, though he was certainly faster at them than I was. On the other hand, having watched a few faeries casually rip open gates like they were flicking away an obnoxious fly, I found it painful to wait the few minutes while Arnold carefully created and assembled the necessary channels of active magic. From the look on his face, Seamus concurred, but before we reached the limit of our patience, the gate blazed to life, a hole in the fabric of space between the Joneses' kitchen and the dirt path leading to the Killians' front staircase. "That should do it," said Arnold, shouldering his pack and tucking his wand away in his waistband. "Shall we?"

"Be careful, guys," said Zeb as we filed through, and I looked back in time to catch Carey's wave before she sealed the rift, leaving us in the cacophonous darkness of the summer swamp.

I was reaching for my torch, moths be damned, when a door above us squealed open, spilling warm yellow light through the porch floorboards onto the frog-infested weeds below. "Carey? That you?" came an older woman's voice.

"Friends of Carey's," I called back, waving my torch to get her attention. "Hello! May we come up?"

The woman on the porch, an indistinct silhouette against the open door, cocked her head, then asked, "You that Badger girl?"

"That's me."

"Thought so. Figured you'd talk funny." She stepped back from the railing and motioned us closer. "Come on up, y'all, get out of the muck. Skeeters have been having a field day of late." As we clomped up the sagging staircase, she folded her arms and studied our company. "Didn't expect so many. Boone!" she called into the house. "Get out the guest hammocks, we're gonna need 'em."

The Killian abode had character in spades but not much in the way of insulation or modern amenities. It was, Boone explained with pride, largely his mundane father's handiwork, and he'd inherited the old homestead years ago when his ailing mother had been forced into a nursing home in the nearest town. I had no reason to doubt Boone's father's carpentry skills, but the years since the house's erection had been cruel, and the structure was still standing only thanks to the spells reinforcing its joints. The entire structure listed about ten degrees, the result of one hurricane or another, and the old floral wallpaper in the guest bath was peeling from its glue, victim of the constant humidity.

There was, to my dismay, no air conditioning, not even a boxy window unit. A pair of ceiling fans spun lazily overhead, offering slight assistance to the breeze that barely stirred through the screened windows. But while I could feel a trickle of sweat already dripping down my spine and wicking into awkward patterns on my shirt, our hosts seemed unbothered by the warm night. Joyce and Boone passed around cold glasses of sugar water masquerading as tea, then settled into matching rockers with sagging rattan seats and gave us the details of the situation.

"Y'all know much about skunk apes?" Boone began as I choked down a sip of iced tea. "Don't really have any in your neck of the woods, do you?"

Arnold, who had made the rookie mistake of taking a proper gulp of tea, forced himself to swallow even as his eyes bulged. "No," he said through a sick smile, "we haven't got any in England, and I've yet to hear of such around the ranch."

"That was rhetorical," Boone replied. "They're unlike any other yeti population in the world. Darker than the ones in the Himalayas, bit smaller, and *fragrant.*"

"He means they stink to high heaven when they're scared," said Joyce.

"And mating, but that's a ways off. No way to know for sure how long there's been a population in the 'Glades, but I'd betcha they've been here longer than we have."

"They *know* this turf," Joyce cut in. "Really well adapted. You hardly ever hear reports of 'em that are more than drunk stories."

I nodded along, catching every other word as I acclimated to their drawl, but Amy seemed untroubled. "We get plenty of bigfoot sightings in the Carolinas," she said, already halfway through her vile drink. "And there's the Lizard Man story, too."

"Your bigfoot's a different animal," said Boone as he wagged his finger. "Related, maybe another subspecies, but the ones north of here ain't the same critter. And I don't know nothing about no lizard men." He peered at her and sipped from his sweating glass. "Carolina, huh? Who're your people, hon?"

Amy began to flush and drank, stalling for time. "Well, uh…my daddy's mama was a Levey out of Louisville, and my mama's mama was a Waterston out of Macon, and my folks settled in Charleston."

Joyce put her glass onto a coaster on the wooden floor and rocked forward to examine Amy more closely. "You're the crafter everybody's been talking about, ain't you?"

"Yes, ma'am," she mumbled.

"Well, now, it's lovely to make your acquaintance," she replied, and Amy jerked in surprise. "We saw a couple of your wands not too long ago…who was that, Boone?"

"Cole and Toby Graves," he said. "Remember, they were heading to the beach for their honeymoon, and they stopped by for a tour?"

She smacked her forehead. "Of course. They're such sweet gentlemen. But yes," she said, turning back to Amy, "they said they'd gotten new wands from you, and those were *gorgeous*. You been crafting long, sugar?"

Her flush deepened, but Amy's smile was genuine. "A few years. My mama was teaching me before everything went to he—*heck*," she said, catching herself before she could curse. While we'd expanded Amy's vocabulary in less than ladylike directions, she remained cautious around strangers, afraid of giving offense.

If Joyce had noticed the hiccup, she gave no indication. "I guess something stuck, didn't it? Say, you don't do repairs by any chance, do you?"

"Sure, I do," she chirped. "Brought my travel kit. Got something that needs patching?"

Five minutes later, once Amy was busily prying open the Killians' antique wands, Joyce topped up everyone's tea, and Boone resumed the debriefing. "Joyce and I have made a study of the skunk apes, if you will. We're out here, they're out here—might as well get to know the neighbors, right? And we're out there so often that we found their camp."

"We run tours," Joyce added. "Airboats, you know? Y'all ever been on an airboat?" We shook our heads, and she shrugged. "Don't matter. We'll fix that tomorrow morning."

"Anyway," said Boone, "I was out late this afternoon, going after a gator—"

"Before y'all turn your noses up, they're good eating," Joyce insisted.

"They are that," he nodded. "So I'm out there, minding my own business, and I see three of the skunkies bearing down on me in a canoe. They build their own boats, you know. Huts, too. Whatever they are, they're sharp. They know us—we're friendly, we bring gifts, do a bit of magic for them—but they don't come out to find us unless something's really wrong."

"They keep to themselves," said Joyce. "Kind of like us, I guess."

"Little bit," Boone allowed. "So they had their translator with them—Mimi, we call her."

"It's not *real* sign language, but it works," Joyce explained. "They grunt and howl and stuff, but we can't make heads or tails of it."

"*Anyway*," said Boone, giving Joyce a pointed look,

"Mimi told us they had three dead. She didn't say what killed them, but we went through the usual suspects, and it wasn't any of those. So I told them to wait, went back to the house, got Joyce, and we followed them out to camp." He shook his head and drank his tea. "Two kids and the oldest male—the troop's in chaos. They just lost their leader, see, and there's three likely contenders, and that's just going to mean fighting, no way around it—"

"They looked like they'd been strangled," Joyce interjected. "Dark marks around their necks, bulging eyes, y'all know. Wasn't pretty. My first thought was a python, but a python would've eaten them. It wouldn't have left good meat lying around, and it wouldn't have killed *three*."

"And the skunkies know what to do with snakes," said Boone. "They got trophies back at camp. The fact that something was able to take down Big Boy is…well, pardon my French, but it scares the piss out of me."

"Where are the bodies now?" Seamus asked.

Joyce sighed. "The light was getting real low out there. We wanted to bring them back here overnight so we could figure out what killed them, but the troop wouldn't let us take them."

"They, uh…they got some interesting funeral practices, you might say," Boone offered. "Little ritual cannibalism. It ain't pretty, but it's their way."

"But seeing as there might be something nasty out there, we told them we'd bring some friends out to help," said Joyce. "I know Carey and Zeb have a dark magic detector…"

"Brought a better one," Amy murmured, not looking up from her work.

"Well, that'll do nicely, then," she replied. "So why don't y'all get some sleep, and we'll head out there at first light? We've only got the one guest bed," she said apologetically, gesturing to the fold-out sofa upon which Kip and Amy had landed, "but we've got enough hammocks to fit everybody."

Arnold, Seamus, and I shared a look, and I cleared my throat. "Ehm…we could make extra beds for the night, if you don't object."

She brightened at the offer. "Really? Me and Boone…well…"

"You're witches," said Amy as she tamped down filler material into a wand core. "This one's a dragonscale. I'd know it anywhere."

The old woman smiled sheepishly. "Guilty. We can't do a lot of the fancy things, but folks in the Minor Arcanum are nice enough to help us out. Y'all, um…y'all are all wizards, I guess? 'Cept you, hon," she added, gesturing at Amy.

We stood in awkward silence for a beat, none of us sure how to proceed, but from the weight of the boys' eyes on me, I understood that I'd become the designated spokesperson. "Arnold and I are wizards," I told her, pointing to my cousin. "Kip and Seamus are…ehm…"

"Other," said Kip.

"*Other* other," Seamus chimed in.

"Mm." She studied us carefully, then shrugged and headed for her bedroom. "Guess it's really not nice to pry. Just don't burn the house down, now."

CHAPTER 4

Morning only added heat to the oppressive humidity, and I stewed in my own juices at the kitchen table while Boone passed around a plate of sausage patties. The flavor was slightly different to the sausage I'd had in the past, but something warned me not to ask about the ingredients. Beside me, Amy shifted in her chair, peeling her bare legs from the vinyl-covered seat, while the boys finished rinsing off and dressing on the wrap-around porch. There were no neighbors, and with only one bathroom, it was easier for them to each take a stretch of decking.

I'd packed my well-worn trainers and jeans, but as I watched Joyce and Boone tidy up the breakfast pans, I reconsidered my wardrobe choices. Both had opted for T-shirts and khaki shorts with hiking boots, and whereas Boone had pulled on a baseball cap over his bald spot, Joyce had chosen a floppy straw hat, which had perhaps been white several decades ago. Before I could truly reevaluate my clothing, however, they gave me something else to worry about: Boone slung a rifle over his shoulder by a nylon strap, and Joyce completed her ensemble with a black shoulder holster and what appeared to be a .45.

"Ehm…are you anticipating trouble with the apes?" I asked, pushing my plate aside.

Joyce secured her pistol and shrugged. "Them? Nah. It's everything else out there that concerns me. We get aggressive crocs every now and then. Not a real big concern," she added as my eyebrows rose, "but I'd rather be safe than sorry."

Amy pushed back from the table and headed for her bag. "Y'all don't mind a third person with a gun?"

"More the merrier," said Boone as he picked up the coffee pot. "Refill, Hannah?"

I took him up on the offer, if only to keep my itchy hands away from my wand. The swamp hadn't grown any quieter with daylight—the calls had changed, but the place still set my nerves on edge. The rest of our party seemed no more at ease than I was, but our elderly guides were calm as they checked their ammunition and encouraged us to eat up.

All too soon, we trooped down the creaking staircase to the clearing that served as the Killians' driveway, and Boone directed us along a narrow dirt trail to the water, where the airboat awaited.

Having passed the night in a sweat on the lumpy pull-out bed, I was unsure of what to expect from the Killians' boat, and I'd begun to fret about its seaworthiness once I saw the leaning house in the morning light. But while the dock appeared to be worse for wear, the boat was tidy and well-kept, a flat, fiberglass craft with chrome accents and a jaunty red stripe down the hull. Behind a low windscreen, four rows of benches occupied most of the boat, while a lone chair rose at the back, directly in front of a massive, caged propeller, the sort of equipment that would look far more at home on an airplane than attached to an overgrown fishing boat.

Boone turned back to us and smiled proudly. "I'll be piloting. Y'all get comfortable and hold on."

As Joyce helped us into the boat, Arnold took a seat at the far end of his bench and preemptively gripped the handrail beside him. "Just, ehm, curious," he said, looking back as Boone climbed to his perch, "but how fast does this thing go?"

"Well," Boone drawled, "in deep, open water, I've taken her close to sixty, but we won't go nearly that fast today."

His eyes bulged. "*Sixty*?"

"It's a fun ride. I'd show you," he added apologetically, "but it's not safe here. No brakes on these things, see?" He paused and peered at my cousin's face. "You get carsick, don't you?"

"On occasion," Arnold mumbled.

"Uh-huh. Sit in the middle of the boat. Trust me on this, son."

Magus or not, Arnold knew when to follow directions. As soon as he was situated, Joyce stepped aboard, and with a buzzing roar, we were off.

I had to assume that Joyce's hat came with a chin strap, as the rush of wind was enough to whip my hair into my face. We picked up speed and turned down a narrow channel of blue-gray water between islands of thick mangroves that spread their branches over us in a nearly complete tunnel. Between the wind and the propeller, I couldn't hear the sounds of the swamp around me, and I relished the first truly moving air I'd felt since arriving. Just then, I saw the end of our channel approach at a T-intersection, and I braced myself before Boone could kill us all. But the old witch was a master pilot, and he banked to port in time to keep us smoothly traversing the waterways. Of course, in so doing, he'd caused the other side of the boat to briefly rise above the water, and I looked back at the sound of a high-pitched yelp to find that poor Arnold was green and clinging to his seat.

Fortunately, Monday morning seemed to be a slow time for tour boats in the Killians' part of the Everglades, and we passed no one as we headed deeper into the swamp. Boone slowed as the channels narrowed and grew more choked with vegetation, and eventually, he took us down to a crawl, barely more than drifting as he navigated a tricky passage. I heard a splash to starboard and turned in time to see something log-like fall into the water, and Joyce tapped my shoulder. "Gator," she said over the sputtering engine, and I smiled weakly as my hand went for my wand.

But if the alligator was hungry, it chose to pursue easier prey. After nearly an hour's trip through the labyrinthine swamp, Boone drifted against an unremarkable mangrove island, and Joyce jumped out to tie off the boat. "We're here," he announced. "Take your gear, just in case."

We disembarked, some more gratefully than others, and Arnold clutched the nearest tree until he recovered his land legs again. "Don't worry, hon, it's a short hike," Joyce assured him. "Just look out for snakes."

As we picked our way through the trees, Joyce joined Boone at the head of the pack, called a halt, and let out a whooping cry. We waited while the echoes died, and she frowned. A second whoop also received no response, to her visible consternation, and Boone scratched his stubble. "Maybe they're hunting," he offered.

"Not with Big Boy dead, they ain't," she murmured.

"Feast would have been last night. They might be sleeping it off."

"No. Morning after is the memorial. They should all be at camp…"

Just then, a faint call sounded in the distance, and the Killians' heads jerked toward it. "Betty," said Joyce. "That ain't good."

They hurried toward the noise, and we struggled to keep pace behind them. "Who's Betty?" I asked as I climbed over a rotting log.

"Junior female," said Boone. "*Low* down the totem pole. She shouldn't be giving the okay."

"We call ahead to let them know we're close," Joyce explained. "If they want us or not, they let us know, but it's always Big Boy or Mama who tells us."

"Head male and female," Boone added. "He was her mate, so why isn't she at his memorial? Why've they got a kid doing the honors? She's, what, two? Three?"

"At most."

Familiar with the uneven terrain, they raced onward,

putting the rest of us to shame as we stumbled along behind them. But after another few minutes' slog, the light ahead brightened, and we pressed through into a clearing at the center of the island.

Looking back, I don't know whether the sight or the smell hit me first. I remember seeing the huts, neat shelters constructed of branches and built into the surrounding mangrove trees, and at their center, a large fire pit made of hard-packed earth and ringed with stones. There were blackened bones in the pit, resting atop the ashes, and other bones of various sizes sprinkled in the dirt around it. Between the pit and the huts were several dozen furry hillocks, some brown, some black, that I quickly recognized as the skunk apes we'd come to find. On first glance, they looked like overgrown, hirsute teenagers who'd gone camping and passed out after one too many beers around the bonfire.

But the smell…

Dear God, the *smell*.

The Killians had prepared us for the apes' natural funk, and yes, the camp seemed to be permeated by an odor not unlike rotten eggs, a sour note over the green smells of the island. Mixed with that was the sharp scent of burnt wood and a hint of roasted flesh—almost like roast pork, I thought, and silenced my thoughts before I could correct myself. Above that, however, rising from the camp like a noxious miasma, was a stench I knew all too well from my previous work, albeit never so concentrated. I looked to Seamus, who had covered his mouth, and caught a flash of movement as Albert retreated to the trees to be sick.

The apes weren't asleep. They were dead, and the muggy swamp was doing everything in its power to speed along the decomposition.

"Hody *shid*," Amy mumbled through her pinched nose. "Whad—"

"Back," I ordered, pushing her and Kip toward the path before they could get too close. "Keep Arnold out of the way."

"Bu—"

"*Stay*," I insisted, then joined Seamus and the gobsmacked Killians, both of whom were silently crying at the scene. On closer inspection, the carnage was striking: apes of all sizes lay scattered in the dirt, many of them with their dinner still in their hands.

Seamus squatted beside one of the smaller apes and checked its back for injuries, then flipped the body over and looked at the face and neck. "No visible wounds," he reported. "What do you suppose—"

A faint whoop cut him off, and we spotted a small, brown ape staggering out of one of the huts. "Oh, *Betty*," Joyce cried, and ran across the camp to catch her. Though a juvenile, Betty was nearly Joyce's height and perhaps half again her weight, and Boone jogged after his wife to help her.

After a moment's struggle, they helped Betty to sit, and Joyce knelt to look at her half-closed eyes while Boone pulled his water bottle from his pack. Once she'd had a drink, Betty pointed to the hut from which she'd come and grunted, and, expecting the worst, I peeked inside.

A larger black ape lay curled on a bed of leaves, shaking in spite of the heat. I could smell her vomit and covered my nose before I gagged. Her eyes rolled toward me, and she raised one hand, then gestured as if she were waving me closer.

"Mimi," said Joyce behind me, and I stepped aside to admit her. "Poor old girl," she murmured, dropping beside the ape with the water bottle. "Drink, now." The ape took the nozzle in her lips and sucked weakly as Joyce smoothed her matted hair from her eyes. "This is our translator," she told me. "If she's strong enough, maybe she can tell us what happened."

But Mimi proved barely well enough to lift her arm and grunt in pain, and after a few attempts to sign with no response, Joyce stood and shook her head. "I don't know.

She was fine last night…you think they were poisoned?"

By then, Boone and Seamus had joined us in the hut, and Seamus cleared his throat. "I…may be able to help," he said softly. "No guarantees, but I might be able to learn something."

"How?" Joyce asked.

"Explain later. Wish me luck," he added, then sat beside Mimi and closed his eyes.

I saw his face work as he sat in silence, now grimacing, now flickering with pain, and the Killians watched worriedly until he drew a deep breath and looked at us again. "Okay, Val did *not* prepare me for that," he muttered as he stood. "Her thoughts are jumbled, but—"

"Her *thoughts*?" Boone echoed.

Seamus nodded. "Difficult to put them in any firm order, but it seems like the sickness started after dinner." He couldn't hide his disgust. "They roasted the bodies, split them up, and passed out the pieces. Then there was a signal, and everyone ate. The ones who ate the fastest and the most got sick first, and a few of the others had sense enough to stop. By then, it was too late for many of them." He pointed to the nearest of the corpses outside the hut. "Mimi's been in pain all night, but she's feeling somewhat better now. Betty only had a bite or two, and she's been tending to Mimi as well as she can. Mimi doesn't know about any other survivors. She crawled in here when everyone started dropping."

Boone goggled. "How did you—"

"Fae," he murmured. "Not entirely proficient at it, but—" He paused as the Killians backed off in alarm, then spread his empty hands. "Zeb and Carey sent us to help, that's all."

"They didn't say anything about—"

"Yeah, because Carey thought she would be coming herself. Seriously, I'm not going to hurt you. Don't shoot."

I eyed the Killians—particularly Joyce, whose hand rested on the butt of her pistol—but neither drew, and I let out the breath I'd been holding. "Right, then. Joyce, I think you almost had it. It sounds like whatever they ate was toxic. Seamie, did you see anything—"

"Just meat. I didn't see them add any spices or such," he replied. "Which means—"

"The bodies themselves were toxic," I finished, "and whatever was in them was strong enough to survive roasting. Some sort of venom?"

"One hell of a venom," he muttered, then turned to the Killians. "These pythons you mentioned, are they venomous?"

"Burmese pythons," said Boone, shaking his head. "Constrictors. They'll squeeze the life outa you, but they ain't like water mocs. I've never seen nothing like this," he said, glancing out the door at the bodies.

"That makes two of us." Seamus sighed. "Badger, are you thinking what I'm thinking?"

"If you're thinking we need to find that gate, then yes. Boone, we're going to need the boat."

He and Joyce looked stricken. "We can't just leave them!" he protested. "They're sick, they're dying, they need help…"

"And whatever killed them is probably still out there, maybe with friends," I retorted. "Right, here's the plan. Boone, you're piloting. Joyce, stay here and take care of the apes. We'll be back as soon as we can."

They followed Seamus and me out of the hut and toward the trail. "What about the young'uns?" Joyce asked. "They could stay here and help."

"True, except Amy has the detector," said Seamus, "and she has an oversized shadow who answers to 'Kip.' They're with us."

He jogged ahead to rally the others, but Joyce grabbed my elbow before I could escape, then pulled me close and whispered, "Is Kip also…"

"No," I told her when her voice trailed off. "He's not fae."

"Good," she muttered. "I'm sorry, I don't mean to be ugly, but I know what they can do." She paused, struck by a thought, then added, "If he ain't fae and he ain't a wizard, then what—"

"Gray Lander. Maybe we should leave it at that," I replied, and freed myself before Joyce had time to digest the latest revelation of the morning.

Even as small as Amy was, the pilot's seat on the airboat was barely large enough for Boone, and there was no way the two of them could safely share it. Still, she couldn't very well give him directions from the middle of the boat over the noise of the propeller, so Amy clung to the scaffolding around his seat with one arm and held the detector outstretched in her other hand. By shouting at the top of her lungs, she was able to direct him through the mangroves.

After ten minutes, I hurt for Amy. The detector was the size of a paperback but much heavier, and the weight had to make her arm ache. I'd seen palm-sized detectors in the past, but those were crude by comparison—they pointed to the greatest source of dark magic, but they could do nothing else. Amy's detector was a digital device of her own design, and its continually updating readout provided a direction, approximate distance, and degree of deviation from the background magical spectrum. Judging by the data she'd shown us before we left the apes' island, the gate wasn't far—but then again, any distance grew longer when one had to hold one's arm out for the entire journey.

I was watching the banks for signs of alligator activity when Amy's detector trilled a warning chime. "Two o'clock, slow it down!" she yelled, and Boone maneuvered until we were drifting. "There," she said, pointing down an open channel.

I stared down the waterway until I spotted the gate in

the distance, the source of the strengthening dark magic around us. Though it hung perhaps a meter above the surface of the channel, it had apparently opened underwater in the Gray Lands, as water poured from the hole in a short cascade even as dark magic flowed out into our realm.

"Is that it?" asked Kip, squinting at the sourceless waterfall.

"Presumably," said Seamus.

"And have you given any thought as to how you're going to close it?"

At that, Arnold, who had been queasily staring straight ahead for the duration of the ride, finally looked at Seamus and me. "Hannah, you and I can do it. Just keep your focus, and you'll be fine. Seamus, ehm…"

"I'm on reptile patrol," he replied. "Get the hole patched, and then we'll worry about whatever's slipped through."

Boone pulled alongside the gate and dropped anchor, and Arnold and I carefully moved to the side of the boat to start casting. In truth, the exercise unnerved me. Though I'd grown substantially as a wizard after nearly a year of tutelage, I still had to think about the techniques that were second nature to my younger cousin—to put it another way, while he raced a Lambo, I settled for steady progress around the track, occasionally forgetting to punch the clutch before I shifted gears. Someday, Carey insisted, I'd be his equal—a promise that never failed to make me laugh—but for the time being, and especially for a technical job like gate closure, I was happy to let him take the lead. I just didn't want to leave him hanging.

To my relief, however, the construction began smoothly enough, and soon Arnold and I found our rhythm. While I crafted the channels that would funnel magic into an impermeable barrier, he did the more delicate work of piecing them together, then began filling the pockets he'd made with raw magic, a battery upon which the gate could draw while it fought against the outflow of dark magic that would batter it down. So engrossed had I become with the task at hand that I almost missed Seamus's cry.

"*Snake!*" he bellowed, pointing to the nearest mesh of mangroves, and Arnold and I wheeled around to see the cause of his alarm.

Nestled in the pale roots was a flash of brilliant orange at least as thick as I was—and I've never been a waif. Its head rose above the water to study us, weaving back and forth as if hypnotized by an invisible charmer, and its fire-colored hood flared in warning.

Kip, who'd been sitting behind me, began to hyperventilate as the snake reared higher and higher from the channel. "Get out! *Go!*" he screamed at Boone, who was steadying his rifle for the shot. "No, no, don't fight it, just go. Forget the gate, we have to go!"

"It's okay, Kip, it's not going to get us," said Amy, gripping his shoulder briefly before she pulled out her own pistol. "Don't worry, he's about to be dead. Now, if the boat would just stop *rocking*…"

"Allow me," I said, and climbed onto the bench beside them. "Save your ammo, kid, I can take him out."

"No, *don't!*" Kip shouted as I released the killing bolt from my wand. I focused my thoughts and will until the magic flowing through the stick sharpened and hardened, and it struck the snake's neck like a scimitar. The snake barely knew what had hit him before his head fell into the swamp, and the bleeding stump of his neck quickly slid beneath the surface.

"Nice work," said Arnold, clapping me on the back. "That was a clean kill if I've ever seen one. What sort of snake was that, do you suppose?"

"That ain't a python, that's for sure," said Boone as he lowered his rifle. "Damn thing's way too fat, and you don't see 'em that color. Not around here, at least."

"Or hooded, I'd think," said Amy. "Isn't that more of a

viper thing?"

But Kip was still in a panic. "Leave, please," he begged Boone. "You don't understand, it's not dead, it's going to be angry. We have to leave *now*."

Boone chuckled indulgently and gave Kip's ponytail a yank. "Boy, that thing's deader than dead. You'd think a big feller like you wouldn't be afraid of a—"

"Hydra."

We turned to Seamus, who stared wide-eyed at the undulating orange coils in the mangrove roots. "*Hydra*," he repeated. "I saw two heads, watch for it to surface…"

"The hell're you—" was as far as Boone got before the snake reared again, now with a pair of heads forking from its neck. I was no great judge of snakes, but to my layman's eye, neither head appeared to be particularly happy to see us.

"*Go*, damn it! I told you!" Kip yelled, shoving Boone toward his chair. "Get us out of here!"

"Bloody *hell*," Arnold muttered as he leveled his wand. "Seamus, I cut, you—"

"Cauterize, got it." A blue fireball was already burning in his hand. "Hit him."

Arnold lashed out with a spell much like mine, severing both heads below their juncture. Before the neck could slip away, Seamus threw his fireball, which clung to the snake even as it writhed. By the time the snake fell, the stump was blackened and smoking, and it sizzled as it went under, leaving nothing but rippling water and a smell like spoilt, burnt chicken.

Seamus and Arnold waited until it vanished, then laughed weakly and high-fived each other. "I knew four years of Greek would come in handy someday," said Arnold, tucking his wand away.

"That's Roman mythology," Seamus protested. "Labors of Hercules."

"Who would be *Heracles* in the Greek. Don't fight me, I read Classics at Oxford."

"Well, *excuse* me. At Durham, most of us were clever enough to take courses that actually mattered—"

"*It's not dead*!" Kip shouted. "You can't kill it that way, idiots! Let's go, before it…"

Whatever he intended to say was replaced by unintelligible cursing as the hydra, now with four heads that rose around the cauterized wound, surfaced again.

"Oh, fuck me, that's not even fair," Arnold muttered as Boone and Amy drew on the beast. "You cut it, you cauterize it, it's dead. That's the way hydras work. Unless…oh, *shit*, the venomous blood variation. If we cauterize the stumps with the thing's own blood…"

Before he could hazard a proper plan, Amy screamed Kip's name as he ran down the bench and took a flying leap off the boat and onto the hydra's back. I saw a glint from the boot knife in his hand, a gift from Zeb, just before he plunged it into the snake and twisted. The monster bucked in pain, and the heads turned, hoods flaring and mouths open, before they lunged for him as one.

Kip yanked out the knife as they started their strike, and at the last moment, he held his breath and flung himself into the canal. Too late to abort, one of the heads managed to graze its own back…and then the hydra began to writhe, churning the water in a roiling frenzy. Within seconds, it sank again, and Kip popped up beside us, panting and glowering from the swamp. "The next time we encounter something out of the Gray Lands, *listen to me*, yes?" he snapped, heaving himself aboard. "There is only one way to kill those," he said as he wrung out his shirt over the side of the boat. "Its weakness is its own venom, and you've seen what that venom can do. *I* have seen what that venom can do on more than one occasion. Grown men die in *agony*." Angry but exhausted, he stretched out on the bench and stared up at the mangrove branches. "Hurry up with the gate."

Arnold, Seamus, and I looked at each other

uncertainly—and, if we were being honest, with more than a little embarrassment. "Is there something else we should know?" I asked softly.

He glanced at me and sighed. "They mate for life. Hunt in pairs. There's a second one around here somewhere, and there's a lot of rotting meat not too far away."

If competitive gate closure were a sport, Arnold and I might have set a new speed record that morning. As soon as the last links were in place, he activated the array, deemed it passable, and held on while Boone gunned the engine. Spurred on by fear, our pilot took the curves sharply enough to throw us into each other, and Arnold, gripping his seat as if his life depended on it, stared into the distance with a look of nauseated determination.

We had barely reached the apes' island before Boone had leapt from his chair—a feat, given his age—tied off the boat, and was running for the camp, calling for Joyce. The rest of us followed as quickly as we could, and before long, we crashed into the clearing. "Joyce!" I yelled. "Where are—"

"*Shh!*" Boone hissed, then pointed to the other side of the fire pit. Following his finger, I spotted Joyce standing outside one of the huts…and mere meters away, a fat, reddish snake.

"The mate," Kip whispered. "Seamus, if you can grab her—"

The hydra's head darted forward, and we held our breath as its tongue flicked at the air. When it paused in its progression, Seamus muttered, "Wish me luck," then vanished. A blink later, he reappeared beside Joyce, wrapped his arms around her before she had time to scream, then disappeared again and returned to our end of the clearing. "Stay here," he told her as she whipped around with wide eyes, then beckoned to Arnold and pointed to the snake. "Let's get her."

"Could be a him," said Arnold.

"Just kill it," he said with a sigh, and created a fresh fireball.

They hadn't taken two steps before Betty emerged from the hut on shaky legs. Seeing the hydra, she froze, and her barrel chest began to rise and fall more rapidly as the creature locked on to her.

"No!" Joyce yelled, and slipped from my grasp to dash to her aid. "Betty, run!" She whooped an alarm, but the petrified ape could only stand there and watch as death took its sweet time.

Seeing his wife break free, Boone ran after her, calling for her to stop. As they neared, the hydra finally noticed them and turned its attention from the ape, who weakly scrambled up a mangrove to momentary safety. Before Joyce and Boone could backtrack, the hydra was advancing, and I watched in horror as it lunged.

But Seamus was faster. He flickered beside me, and then a blur slammed into the snake's neck, knocking it away before it could inflict the fatal bite. His aim was imperfect, however, and one of the hydra's fangs, already beading with venom, scraped along Joyce's bare leg as it passed. She screamed and collapsed, and Boone rushed to her side to stare helplessly at the dark discoloration spreading toward her thigh.

"Distract it!" I yelled to the others, then pulled out my wand and shouted an incantation. The force that flew from the tip of the wand that time was gentler, but it whisked the Killians off the ground and shot them back to me. While Arnold and Seamus kept the snake occupied, I beckoned Amy and Kip closer. "I'm going to try to stop the progress," I told them, pointing to Joyce's leg as she cried in pain. "Watch my back."

Amy nodded and pulled out her gun, and I began to cast over Joyce, willing into being a healing construction that would counteract the venom in her system. At the very least, I tried to numb her leg. Forming the spell took all my concentration—I wasn't half the healer that Carey and Arnold were—and so I didn't hear it when the hydra tired of playing keep-away with the boys, changed course, and headed straight for us.

My first inkling that something was amiss was when I heard Amy fire three rounds. Before I had time to turn and look, Seamus yelled at us to get out of the way, and Amy and Kip paid heed. As for me, when I finally glanced back, the hydra was almost on top of us. I tried to get my wand in front of me, but I felt like I was moving through wet cement until suddenly, a blow threw me off my feet and sent me sailing into a mangrove. I slammed into the tree with a crack that I distantly thought might have been a branch until I landed and my brain registered the pain in my left arm and the back of my head.

Dazed and fighting my sudden need to be sick, I watched as Seamus peppered the hydra with fireballs, and the confused beast turned around, sparing the Killians. While Kip and Amy ran back to pull them into the trees, the snake sped for Seamus, giving Arnold the opportunity to aim and behead it. As soon as the hissing head hit the dirt, he grabbed it, pulled its jaws apart, then stabbed the hydra with its own fangs, holding on until the body ceased to twitch.

Aching, I struggled to stand, but Seamus was at my side before I could find my feet. "I'm so sorry, love," he murmured, helping me upright, then called to Arnold, "I'm taking them over! Joyce needs help!"

Arnold shook his head. "It's already morning in Sedona—"

"Don't care. Can you clean up here?"

He looked around at the corpses, furry and scaly alike, then nodded. "I'll see to the living, too."

"Good. Boone, Amy, get Joyce up if you can. Badge, can you walk?"

"Think so," I mumbled, though the world spun around me.

"Okay, I've got you. Kip…help Arnold," Seamus ordered, then opened a gate onto the Boynton Canyon trail before anyone could stop him. "Go, hurry," he said to Amy and Boone. "Amy, show him the way. We're behind you."

"Wait," Kip protested, "I—"

"Watch for Arnold," Seamus insisted. "Buddy system. I'll bring her back soon," he added, then half-carried me through the gate and closed it behind us. As he hurried us down the trail, he pulled his mobile from his pocket and dialed. "Hello, Val?" I heard as the trail began to go gray in my vision. "Please, I need help…"

CHAPTER 5

I woke several hours later in one of Coileán's guestrooms, stiff but no longer dizzy. My arm was both splinted and surrounded by a haze of enchantment…which extended to my head, I realized, seeing active magic pulsing across my field of vision. Experimenting, I looked to my left and spotted Seamus standing at the window, gazing out at the eternally blooming garden. He'd lost his glamour of age again, but at that moment, I was too confused to even consider giving him a hard time about it. Blacking out was bad enough without waking to find oneself in the home of a faerie king.

Hearing me shift against the sheets, Seamus hurried across the room and brushed my hair from my face. "How're you feeling, love?" he murmured, smiling tightly.

"Not sure. What happened?"

He winced. "My bad aim. Broke your arm, cracked your skull, and concussed you. Other than that, you should be all right. I'm sorry, Badge, it was coming at you…"

Slowly, I sat up in bed, then wiggled my fingers on my injured side. "Feels fine now."

"Val said to keep the splint on until it's hardened, just to be safe. And lie down," he urged. "Give it time to work."

"I—"

"You have a head injury. Let it heal."

Though frustrated, I knew he was right, and I eased myself horizontal again. "Joyce?"

"We got her here in time. Barely. She was convulsing

when we went through the gate." Conjuring a chair from the ether, Seamus sat beside me and squeezed my hand. "If she'd had a larger dose of the venom, she'd have died in Florida. As it is, Val's not sure how much damage she's sustained—he knocked her out and got the enchantment going, but at her age, if her heart's affected…"

"She seems tough," I replied, entwining my fingers with his.

"That only goes so far. Boone's resting with her now, but…" His eyes searched my face as if looking for bruises his uncle had missed, and then, almost inaudibly, he said, "I could have lost you."

"But I'm still here," I said, flashing a half-smile.

"That thing would have killed you if—"

Before he could finish his thought, he turned at a sharp rapping on the door, and Amy let herself into the room. "Hey, there!" she said, jogging across the oversized suite. "You're up! Glad I caught y'all both—Aiden is taking me out to the settlement for a bit."

"What's going on?" I asked, starting to sit up again before Seamus, my overly cautious nurse, nudged me flat.

She grinned. "He heard I was here, and he's been pestering me to come out to Vivi's office and run checks on the Fringe net for the last hour."

"Amy's been keeping Boone company," Seamus explained.

"He seems stable." She shrugged. "Anyway, Aiden says the network's due to go live in another week or two, so the sooner we get through the last tests, the sooner we get connected." Her smile widened. "He's, like, *really* excited to do this. I may be out there for a few hours—come get me if I'm not back by morning, okay?"

We promised to rescue her if called upon to do so, and as Amy took her leave, Seamus gave me a look and chuckled to himself. "All right, Seamie," I said, "what do you know?"

My partner shook his head. "He stopped by not too

long ago. You'd think Christmas had come early, listening to him tell it."

I couldn't help but grimace. "Still fancies her, does he?"

"Seems like it, poor kid."

Having shared more than a few girl talks with Amy over the last months, I had to pity Aiden. Ever since she'd left Faerie, Amy had consulted with him on the Fringe network project, offering suggestions and helping him troubleshoot on occasion when he ran up against a wall. She was friendly in her texts and almost always willing to chat when he needed a sounding board, but never had she suggested that their friendship evolve into anything more intimate. Amy had her crafting, our team, and the unflappable mare that Zeb was teaching her to ride—and whether she was aware of it or not, she had Kip. She didn't need a boyfriend in another realm.

"Aiden keeps bugging me about when I'm coming back to stay," she'd griped to me one night after ending a two-hour phone call. "I'm running out of ways to say, 'I don't know, please drop it.'"

"Well," I told Seamus as I settled into the mattress, "Amy did say she's going out there to work. Maybe Aiden will be too busy to pester her." Seamus looked at me doubtfully, and I made a face. "It's a *thought*."

"Mm," he grunted. "Hit your head pretty hard, I see."

By nightfall, Seamus was sufficiently convinced that I wasn't about to drop dead to let me shower in peace. When I emerged, still bruised but smelling far more presentable, I found that an aide had brought us dinner, and Seamus was on the phone to Carey, giving her an update. "Joyce is stable," he told her while I sat and tucked in. "Weak, but stable. She woke about an hour ago. Val thinks another day here would be good for her—give the enchantment the best chance of working, you know?" He paused, listening, then grimaced. "No, she's *not* pleased, but all things considered, I think that's better than the alternative."

As I ate, ravenous after a day in bed, Seamus brought me up to speed. Arnold had returned to New Mexico only a couple hours before, having spent the time since our quick departure tending to the few surviving apes. Though he couldn't understand them, he apparently made his intentions clear enough for the sick to emerge from hiding, and no one tried to stop him when he burnt the corpses. Kip had assisted him as well as he could, mostly by half-carrying the apes too weak to walk from their huts to the shelter Arnold had magically erected in the middle of the camp—complete with oversized fans. As for the Killians' boat, neither man wanted to risk driving it into a tree, but Kip remembered the way back to the house, and Arnold was able to steer it on a slow-moving cushion of air, saving both of them from his motion sickness and from a fiery wreck.

"And now that they're sure everyone's alive, Kip wants to know when Amy's coming back," Seamus reported, turning to his pie.

"I hope you gave them a vague answer."

"Naturally." He scooped a bite onto his fork. "If the network hits a snag—"

The door slammed open, and we dropped our utensils in surprise as Amy stormed in, red-faced and scowling. "Sorry," she muttered, closing the door behind her. "Door's lighter than I thought."

Seamus was already out of his chair. "What's the matter? Are you all right?"

"Fine," she snapped, and stomped to an empty seat at our little table. "Got any leftovers? I haven't had dinner yet."

He slid her his pie, and we watched as she shoveled it down, glowering into space. "Do you want to talk about it?" I finally asked once she'd cleaned the whipped cream from her plate. "If it's a problem with the coding, I'm afraid we're no help, but other than that…"

I let the thought hang, and after an uncomfortable silence, she pushed the plate away, folded her arms on the tabletop, and faced me. "He won't take no for an answer, and he's driving me up a wall."

"Who, Aiden?"

She grunted her displeasure as she nodded. "All that talk of final testing was…*bullshit*. He didn't need me out there—he just wanted me cornered," she spat, and glared at the table. "You gonna eat that last roll?"

I surrendered it to her appetite. "Why?" I asked, worried that I knew the answer already.

But Amy allayed my immediate fear. "He wants me to stay," she mumbled around the bread, her cheeks puffed like a squirrel's. "And I said *no*, I've got things to do in New Mexico, and I've got people over there I've been helping, and that's that." She stole my water glass, drained half, and resumed. "He won't listen. All afternoon, he kept bringing it up again—*it's not safe, look at what happened to Hannah, things are so much better here*," she said in a scornful sing-song. "I mean, I know the risks better than he does, but does that matter? No, of course not, *I'm* the unreasonable one…"

"Don't hit me for saying this," Seamus replied, "but he's got a point. You'd be safer here—not that I'm trying to get rid of you," he hastened when she shot him a death glare. "All I'm saying is that technically, he's not wrong."

"Fine. Whatever. But he's not going to change my mind by whining about it every ten minutes." She looked around the table at our meager leavings, then settled for Seamus's leftover green beans. "I'd have gotten *so* much more work done out there today if he'd have let me concentrate."

Seamus and I locked eyes over her head as she bent to the task of hoovering up every last crumb of food. Before either of us could speak, someone knocked at the door, and Amy paused with my spoon in her mouth, preemptively peeved. "Come in," I called.

The door cracked open, and Aiden stuck his head inside the suite. "Sorry to bother—"

"*Go away,*" Amy interrupted, half-rising from the table. "We're busy."

He paused, momentarily unsure, then opened the door a little wider. "Did you, uh…we could get some dinner at—"

"I've eaten, thanks."

"Oh." Aiden rubbed the back of his neck, which had begun to flush. "I, um…I didn't see you leave."

"You'd gone down the street to find Vivi. I thought I'd start back."

His eyes widened in alarm. "You walked back here *alone?*"

She spread her hands in mock confusion. "Well, since Faerie's *so* much safer than New Mexico, I don't see why you're concerned."

"That's…that's not…I didn't say—"

"That's *exactly* what you said."

"I meant the settlement!" he protested, finally working through his flabbergasted stutter. "You can't just walk around here by yourself! Are you insane? No one knows you, no one knew you were out there—"

Amy sighed and waved him away. "You're not my mother," she said, resuming her seat, "and I don't need a babysitter. Why don't you get back to work, Aiden?" she added with a contemptuous smirk. "You know, so the next time I'm over here, you'll actually have something for me to test?"

Aiden's embarrassment blossomed into a full-face flush. "I'm sorry, I wanted to get you out to the office for a little while—"

"The truth would have worked. I'm happy to help with the net."

He fished for a response, growing more discombobulated by the second as Seamus and I watched, then blurted, "I like you, okay? And I'm really worried that something's going to happen to you if you go back."

Amy's voice was cold as ice. "There is no *if*. I'm going back with everyone else. You're supposed to be a smart guy—how is this so difficult for you to understand?"

"But—"

"This isn't your decision. I need to be over there."

He struggled to find a loose brick in her wall. "Look," he finally said, "I...I know you miss your parents, okay? I know you want to do something about it. But you might have family here, too. Family you're ignoring," he rushed as her mouth opened. "I can't know for sure, but—"

"My parents were murdered by those monsters," she interrupted, her tone dangerously low. "If you think for one second that I—"

"*Lots* of people's parents were murdered, Amy. They're making new families now. They're getting by. They're *safe*. If you'd just stick around for a while, you might—"

"Might *what*?" she snapped, going to her feet. "I've lived here, I've tried therapy. Maybe that works for some folks, but I guess it didn't take with me."

"They'd want you to be safe."

"They'd want me to do the right thing," she retorted. "And the right thing for me isn't sitting here, waiting to be rescued. That's not who I am. If that's confusing to you, then maybe you haven't been listening."

I sat there, holding my breath. It takes a brave person or an extremely foolish one to tell off a high lord, and Amy wasn't pulling her punches. Fortunately, she was winning, and I could almost see Aiden's tail tucking as she chided him.

Once she broke for air, Aiden held up his empty hands in pacification and took a step backward toward the door. "I hear you, all right? But will you do one little thing for me, please?"

She folded her arms and arched an eyebrow.

"Let Toula check your aura," he said. "It'll take, like,

five minutes, and you'll at least know if you're not alone."

"Amy's not alone," I interjected. "She's part of a team that's better for having her."

Aiden began to stammer again. "I just meant that she might have blood—"

"Oh, you think it takes blood to make family?" Seamus cut in. "I'll be sure to tell my birth parents if I ever meet them. That'll be nice."

Sensing that he'd managed to annoy all three of us, Aiden mumbled an apology and headed for the door. Before he could slip away, however, Amy said, "I'll do it." He paused and looked back at her, and she held up a finger to silence him. "To satisfy my own curiosity. Not for you, and I'm not staying. If you want to be my friend, Aiden, you'll respect my wishes."

He gently latched the door behind him, and she sighed as she sank back into her chair. "Thanks, y'all," she mumbled, reaching for the now-cold beans.

Seamus caught her wrist before her fork could stab them. "Cheese quesadilla?"

"Thought you'd never ask," she replied with a grin.

One problem with recuperating in bed all day is that one is then awake all night. Late that evening, when it became evident that I wasn't going to be sleeping any time soon, I put Seamus to bed, then walked the halls, making sure that Amy was in and that Joyce and Boone were all right. The Killians had seen better days—Boone was still a nervous wreck from nearly losing his wife, and Joyce was weak— but for a couple of old witches finding themselves in Faerie, they were holding together remarkably well. I left them playing canasta and wandered through the quiet castle, eventually finding myself a window nook with a stone bench and an open window onto the garden. Though there wasn't much to see by starlight, the night breeze was pleasantly cool and carried with it the smell of

Coileán's roses, a welcome respite from the warming ranch.

I leaned against the wall and closed my eyes, enjoying the breeze as much as the silence, and suppressed the voice that nagged at me for not sleepwalking. I *couldn't* sleepwalk between realms, so I had no reason to feel guilty that night. I could sleep as much as I liked—real, deep sleep, the kind that actually refreshed me—although, I mused, I'd wake with an awful cramp in my neck if I fell asleep in the window nook.

I was deciding whether dragging myself back to bed was worth the trouble when I heard soft footsteps on the hallway runner and opened my eyes to find Joey Bolin approaching. Despite the late hour, he was fully dressed in jeans, a long-sleeved shirt, boots, and a black duster that looked slightly worse for wear, and he lit his way toward me with a keychain torch. "Evening," I said, lifting my good hand. "Just getting in?"

"Been out with Georgie all day," he replied. "If I seem a little bow-legged right now, you'll know why."

Given Georgie's size, I had no idea how he stayed atop the dragon for more than a couple of hours. As he neared, I sat up and made room on the bench, and he sank down beside me in a swish of leather. "Seamus has gone to sleep," I told him, "as has Amy. She and Aiden had a disagreement today."

He fished his mobile from an inside pocket, showed me a screen of text messages, and flashed a lopsided smile. "Yeah, I heard all about it." After putting the phone away, he turned off his light and sighed. "You understand why he's acting like this, yeah?"

"His sister, I assume."

"That's my theory." Joey hesitated, then quietly asked, "Any sign of her?"

The hope in the boy's voice was heart-wrenching, but I couldn't lie to him. "I haven't seen her or met anyone who has, but then I also haven't looked in the silo. Arnold's convinced that she's in there, but he doesn't have firm proof."

Another pause. "I don't mean to tell you how to do your job, but could you tell me why you haven't looked there yet?"

I could hear the pain through his politeness, and I felt for him. Jocy had been nothing but supportive of the Fringe recovery effort, but I knew it had to hurt every time another refugee arrived who wasn't his wife. In truth, I'd hoped to locate Helen months before, but the problem was stickier than I'd first imagined.

"It's not that I don't want to poke around the silo," I told him. "Believe me, if I could, I'd be all over it tonight. But it would be very dangerous, and for everyone else's sake, I've stayed away. All the sleepwalkers have."

"Dangerous? How so? If everyone's asleep…"

"The problem is that sometimes, people wake into the dream space. Carey's asked me to stay away from large wizard concentrations just in case, and lately…"

"Lately what?" he pressed.

"I've, ehm…I'm not fully in control of my talent," I admitted.

Joey snorted in the dark beside me, and suddenly, a flame ignited in his hand, bathing his face in its flickering blue glow. "Join the club, Hannah."

"I don't know, Seamus seems to think you have it together."

"Yeah, well, we've both got a long way to go." The fire died, and Joey settled back against the cool stone wall. "So what, if you get too close to too many wizards, you wake them up?"

"Not necessarily, but I've accidentally done it a few times. And since the goal is to keep the Arcanum from knowing what we're about, going there now would be a terrible idea. All it would take would be one of them figuring out how to sleepwalk, and we'd be compromised worldwide."

He said nothing, and I thought he was mulling over potential work-arounds until I heard a wet sniffle beside me. "Oh, Joey, dear, I'm sorry," I murmured, groping in the darkness for his shoulder. "I want to find her—we're *going* to find her—but I can't risk everyone's safety right now. Once I learn how to control this, I promise you, I'll go to the silo."

When I touched him, I felt the telltale shaking as he tried to cry in silence. Sitting up, I wrapped my arm around his back and pulled him against me, and Joey did his best to stifle his tears. "We have no reason to believe she's not alive," I said. "She's out there. We'll find her."

Soon enough, he'd pulled himself together, and I heard him wipe his eyes dry when I released him. "Sorry," he muttered, "I just…sometimes…"

"There's nothing to apologize for."

Joey continued as if he'd not heard me. "I've been worried sick about Helen for more than a year now, and…" He let out a shuddering breath. "The baby was due last fall."

"We'll find the both of them."

"*If* the baby's alive. Did they even let her have it? They hate me—do you think they let our baby live?" he mumbled, resting his head in his hands. "I can't do a damn thing to save my wife or our child, Hannah. Right now, you're my only hope."

With a weary sigh, he rose and took his leave by the gate he casually opened in the middle of the corridor, and I curled up on the bench, listening to the night and wishing I knew what I was doing.

"I don't care what it says. I'm not staying here."

Amy perched uneasily on the edge of one of Coileán's smaller dining room tables, which could have seated twelve. Her legs, too short to reach the floor from even a modest height, swung back and forth into the creamy linen tablecloth until she caught herself, stilled the pendulum, then forgot all about it ten seconds later and renewed her twitching. She clutched the edge of the table and tensed as if preparing to launch herself onto Toula, who stood by with empty hands and a reassuring half-smile.

Never particularly formal in her dress, Toula had chosen a thin pink sweater over black leggings for the occasion that morning, complete with coordinating fleece boots—at first glance, the uniform of a slouchy young thing just arisen from a weekend lie-in, whose spiked black and blue hair hinted at wild revelry the night before. The truth was rather different: Toula was closing on forty, the most powerful witch-blood on record, and persona non grata to the Arcanum that had raised her. Daughter to an executed wizard terrorist and an exiled faerie queen, Toula was frightening enough for her mere bona fides—and that didn't include the damage she'd done the last time the Arcanum had her on its kill list.

But she had more than a soft spot for the rest of her kind, witch-bloods who hadn't won the genetic lottery. She nodded at Amy's defiant scowl, then knowingly cut her eyes to Aiden, who stood against the wall with his arms folded, awaiting the results. "Understood, babe. What you do with this information is up to you—I'm just the messenger. Besides, I may not find anything," she said, shrugging. "There are no guarantees in this business. All I have to go on are the faeries I've tested."

That seemed to mollify Amy to a degree, judging by the slight loosening of the tautness in her shoulders, but she still appeared displeased with the situation. "Just as long as we're clear."

"Crystal. Sit still, now. This won't hurt a bit—right, folks?"

Aiden nodded, and Seamus and I followed suit when Amy's eyes found us across the room. We'd stuck around after breakfast on the off-chance that Amy would need moral support once she received Toula's findings, but as I watched her lick her lips, I sensed that our presence was welcome regardless of the results. Amy had proven herself to be tough enough, but at the end of it all, she was still seventeen.

As Toula approached with her hands outstretched, muttering a nonsensical mantra, Amy closed her eyes and grimaced in anticipation. After a brief moment, a white mist appeared in front of the girl's face, which condensed and solidified into a spherical crystalline lattice. The sphere then began to take on color, quickly resolving into a chaotic swirl of red and green.

"Open your eyes," Toula urged, and Amy, still trying to hide her trepidation, reluctantly obliged. "See? Painless," said Toula, then gestured toward the sphere. "And definitely a witch-blood signature. Let's see what we get from your parents, huh?"

With a flick of her fingers, the sphere dissolved and reformed as two spheres, each still a combination of colors. "Here's Mom and Dad, but I can't tell you which is which, sorry. Anyway, you're certifiably a double witch-bl—uh…"

She fell silent as Amy reached for the orbs, and Seamus and I shared a look.

"They're not actually solid," said Toula as Amy's fingers passed through the orbs. "I'm, uh…I'm sorry, sweetie."

We waited while Amy studied her parents' auras. The girl had escaped with only a handful of photograph of the family she'd found murdered—this was as close as she'd come to her parents since the Fringe's unravelling, and Toula seemed to sense that this wasn't the time to rush her.

While Amy probed, I studied the orbs for a different reason. Whereas mine had been the green of a wizard and Seamus's the red-blue of the half fae, Amy's parents' glowed with the markers of both magical lines—brilliant but virtually useless in terms of power. What struck me was their vibrant color. Whoever they were, all of Amy's grandparents were strongly talented. She'd been robbed by the blending of their gifts, and though her own talent as a crafter was considerable, the orbs hinted at the wizard—or faerie—she could have been.

After a time, Amy withdrew her searching fingers, and Toula cleared her throat. "Okay. Ready for your grandparents?" she asked. Amy nodded, and Toula split the orbs again.

And there they were—two red, two green, all pulsing with potential. "What do you know about your grandmothers?" Toula enquired.

Amy bit her lip. "Names. Neither wanted anything to do with me."

"I feel you, kid," she muttered, then pushed the green orbs aside. "Now, as for your grandfathers…" With another gesture, the red orbs flattened into sheets, and Toula raised her left hand, on which she wore a large ring made of solid quartz. "Give me a sec to look for matches," she said as the ring began to glow from within.

Seamus and I watched the stored lattices in Toula's ring database appear and flicker in front of her as the spell powering the ring compared them to Amy's grandfathers' signatures. Suddenly, one image froze, and Toula frowned, surprised.

"Oh, God," Seamus muttered, "not another of Mab's—"

"Not this time, and you *know* you love Val and me," she retorted. "No, this isn't quite right…" She waved at Amy's lattices until they split a third time, then pointed to the one on the far left and snapped her fingers. "Great-grand. There it is."

"Match?" Amy mumbled.

"Yup. Just on one, now—I don't have anything on your other grandfather," she explained, pushing the unmatched pair away to join the green orbs, "but *this* one…well, I've got one great-grandparent, at least."

Amy tensed anew. "Yeah?"

"Yeah. Oberon."

"*Oberon*?" Aiden yelped.

Shocked, Amy gripped the table as her eyes darted among Toula, Seamus, and me. "Um…well, uh," she mumbled, "that's…interesting…"

I caught a flash of light from the corner of my eye and looked up in time to see Aiden disappear through a gate of his own making. "This doesn't change anything, Amy," I reassured her. "And no one has to know any of this but you. Seamus and I won't tell the others anything you don't want discussed—right, Seamie?"

He nodded emphatically. "Not a word, love. Nothing to worry about."

Amy still seemed dazed, but I couldn't blame her. It was one thing to go through life as a witch-blood, knowing that she had fae kin out there somewhere whom she would likely never meet. But to learn she was descended from one of the Three, the original faerie king, who'd held the Arcanum silo itself under siege before Aiden had beheaded him…that had to be disconcerting, at least.

"So," said Toula after a moment, "on the plus side, you do have family around here. Whether you actually want to make contact with any of them is up to you, but—"

She fell silent as another gate opened, then sighed as Aiden emerged, half-dragging Eleanor through the rift. The queen, as always, presentable in spite of the hour, and briefly, I envied her dark blue twinset and smart herringbone trousers. Like Toula, she barely seemed twenty-five, an attractive redhead in her prime. Only if I studied her green eyes for too long did I begin to see that Eleanor was better than seven hundred years old.

She shook Aiden off and frowned at the room. "Sorry to interrupt. Aiden said I was needed?"

He gestured across the room at Amy, who hunched away from the gate. "She's Oberon's great-granddaughter."

"Oh. Is that so?" Eleanor took two steps toward Amy,

considered the girl's posture, then paused and clasped her hands. "Bit of a surprise, dear?"

Amy nodded mutely.

"He was a right bastard," she said in a confidential murmur. "Which, ehm, child—"

"Don't know," Toula interrupted. "Not in my database yet, so there's no telling."

"Ah," said the queen. "And with everything in recent years, there's a decent chance that person is no longer living."

"Would have been a son," Amy muttered. "My grandmothers are wizards."

"That's little help, unfortunately. Oberon had hundreds of children. He was barely a father to any of us, mind, but he did sire an impressive number of offspring." Seeing that Amy had yet to bolt, Eleanor slowly crossed the room and hoisted herself onto the table beside her. "It doesn't matter who your grandfather is or was. If he was one of my brothers, then you're my…grandniece? Is that correct?"

"I think so."

"Well, that's all right, then." She slumped to better see Amy's worried face. "Glad to know."

Amy's brow creased. "You…*are*?"

"Don't sound so surprised. You've made an impression, Amy." The corner of her mouth twitched. "*Lady* Amy, I should say."

"I—"

"Your grandfather is or was a high lord. The title passes with the blood."

"You, uh…you do realize I'm half wizard, right?"

Eleanor snorted as she pointed to Toula and Aiden. "You're in good company. Anyway," she said, patting Amy's knee, "you've nothing to worry about. I've never been close to my siblings, but I certainly won't hold that against you. Call on me if you need assistance," she added, sliding off the table, "and the next time you've over, do stop by—you and I should at least have a nice chat."

Before she could take her leave, Aiden stepped between her and the gate and held up his hands to stop her progress. "Make her stay."

The queen cocked her head. "I beg your pardon?"

"Make her stay. Please," he added. "She's planning to go back, you know how dangerous it is—"

"I'm aware, yes."

"She has to listen to you. Make her stay here."

Eleanor considered him for a long moment, then turned around and looked back at Amy. From my vantage point, I couldn't see the queen's expression, but I saw the slight smile creep across Amy's face.

"Dear boy," Eleanor said, turning to Aiden, "that is absolutely not my decision." He began to stammer, and she lifted a finger to silence him. "First, she's Fringe. I have no right to order her about. Second, assuming I did have that right, I wouldn't force her to stay here. Amy's doing good work in the States, and as long as she's willing to assume the risk, it's not my call."

As Aiden searched for a rebuttal, Eleanor turned again to Amy. "You are, naturally, welcome here, and should you change your mind, I'd be very pleased to have you. But if you feel that you need to be elsewhere, then I'll wish you all success and see you on your return. And *certain* children who don't know as much as they think they do should mind their own business."

Knocked down a few rungs, Aiden stood aside and let Eleanor leave, and then, with a last look at Amy, he closed the gate and reluctantly headed for the door. When the latch clicked behind him, I told the others I'd be back and followed him into the hallway.

"Wait," I said, and he turned, surprised to find himself with company. "Come here." Beckoning, I led him into an empty salon and drew him away from the door. "You're concerned about her safety. I appreciate that, I do. And I know that a lot of your worry has to do with your sister."

Aiden hesitated, then sighed and slowly nodded. "If I

knew she was okay…"

"I understand, and I'm sorry. I spoke with Joey last night. Believe me, Aiden, if I could safely sleepwalk into the silo, I'd do it right now. As it is, though, this is going to take more time. We haven't forgot Helen—we've just got to be clever about this. As do you." He frowned in confusion, and I jutted my thumb toward the dining room. "While I appreciate the impulse that led to that little ambush, you're going to push Amy away if you keep this nonsense up."

"I only want her to be safe," he protested. "She's out there, she's not talented, you guys can't always protect her—"

"You've got to stand back and let her find her own way. If you're truly her friend—and I think you want to be," I said, looking into his eyes—"then you need to let her make her own decisions. *Yes*?"

"Yes," he muttered, then glanced away. "I…I should go apologize, shouldn't I?"

"I wouldn't," I replied, to his surprise. "She's *peeved*. Honestly, you're probably one of the last people she wants to see right now. I'd give her space, were I you."

"But—"

"Apologize in a few days. Let her cool down and digest everything, then assure her that you've learned your lesson and this will *never* happen again." When Aiden seemed poised to protest, I shook my head to cut him off. "You can't strong-arm her into liking you, love. That's not how this works. Go on, have a think, then text her late this week."

Resigned, he started to leave, but he paused a few steps from the door. "You're, uh…not going to tell Coileán about this, are you?"

"No, but something tells me your brother's going to find out anyway. You *did* just drag Eleanor over here."

Looking slightly queasy, Aiden took his leave.

CHAPTER 6

By our best calculations and Coileán's reliable office clock, the local time in Faerie—variable though the days could be—was then roughly an hour ahead of Arizona. As such, we were stuck in the realm until late that evening, which gave Amy time to sit in her room alone and the Boones a chance to tour the Fringe settlement. Sure, there were more beautiful sights in Faerie than the settlement, but the old witches were uneasy being in the realm, and the prevalence of benches in the little town allowed Joyce ample opportunity to rest. Though the worst of her venom scare was past, she remained weak and somewhat unsteady on her feet, and so I found a park bench, a cup of tea, and a youth pick-up football game for her when she began to flag.

"They're really safe here, you think?" Boone asked me, watching the screaming players run back and forth across the neat park lawn.

"Safer than back home," I replied. "You've heard the stories?"

"Bits and pieces. Whole thing's messed up, ain't it?"

"That it is." I sighed, then turned at the sound of footsteps. A false alarm, I quickly saw—a pair of joggers out for a few laps in the warming morning—and I tried to compose my face into a disinterested expression before they were upon us. I'd hoped that Seamus would be along, but having spotted his uncle lurking before I took the Killians out, I suspected that my poor partner was in for another day of pummeling.

My supposition proved true, and the going was slow that night as we traversed the Boynton gate. Seamus limped through at the head of the pack, and by the time the rest of us were safe on the canyon trail, he'd opened a gate back to the Killians' home. "You'll let us know if you need anything?" I said, taking Joyce's hand.

They promised to be in touch with an update on the ape situation, and Seamus sealed the gate behind them, shutting our door into the night-dark swamp. With another moment's concentration, he opened a fresh gate to the ranch, and the three of us remaining hurried through before any late hikers could spot us.

While Seamus and Amy headed for the bunkhouse, I made a quick stop at the house to let Carey and Zeb know we'd returned. After a moment's search, I found them in the basement, snuggled together on the couch with the true crime channel on. "Evening," I said from the top of the stairs, then grimaced as the program went to the evidence photographs. "Ooh, *that's* unfortunate."

They turned to find me, and Zeb raised his hand. "Two head shots at close range with a .45. My money's on the boyfriend, but Carey's going with the creepy neighbor. Want to watch and find out with us?"

"Eh, that scene looked like Jackson Pollock had a red period. I'll pass, thanks. Seamus and Amy have gone to bed, and I'm on my way out."

"Sounds like a solid plan. Hey, don't forget to make Arnold put your blocking spell back in place tomorrow morning, yeah? And welcome back," said Carey. "Glad to see you in one piece, Hannah. Joyce and Boone got home okay?"

"They're *home*. Whether they're okay remains to be seen, but…"

The Joneses nodded in understanding, then returned to their gristly entertainment.

Seeing myself out, I pulled the kitchen door closed, then picked my way through the darkness toward my waiting pillow. Nearing the proper barns, however, I caught a glimpse of two figures sitting on the training ring fence beneath the security light, and I paused, smiling to myself to find Amy and Kip catching up. I knew I shouldn't snoop, but Amy had been withdrawn all day. Rationalizing my spying as being responsible and checking in on her, I crept around the side of the barn, taking care to avoid the light and keep my steps quiet, and shamelessly eavesdropped.

"And then he runs out of the room," I heard her tell him. "A few seconds later, he's back with *Eleanor*, and he's trying to get her to make me stay over there."

"What's *wrong* with him?" said Kip, sounding more than merely agitated. "He has no right—"

"I know, and Eleanor set him straight, but…" She groaned and leaned against Kip's shoulder. "Long day, man. Long day."

He reached around her and pulled her closer, rubbing her arm as she nestled in beside him. "Don't talk to him again."

"Not an option. I want the new network up before I'm ninety, and he comes knocking whenever he has a problem. I think he'll back off," she continued as Kip shifted his grip on her. "He slunk away after Eleanor got onto him, and obviously I'm here now, so—"

"Do not talk to him."

She twisted to look at his face. "*Excuse* me?"

"I don't want you to talk to him," said Kip. His tone had a new edge, and he slowly shook his head as he regarded Amy. "His actions are inappropriate, and I want you to ignore him from now on."

Amy pulled away and slid down the rail. "Okay, first, I just said we're still working together. Second, that isn't your call. You don't get to tell me who I can and can't talk to."

"I can tell you—"

"No, you *can't*," she snapped, then jumped off the

fence and stormed away.

"I only—"

"Leave me alone!" she yelled over her shoulder.

"Amy, wait!" Kip called after her, but she melted into the darkness, and his shoulders slumped.

Though I debated the wisdom of revealing myself, I couldn't just leave him out there, and I cleared my throat to announce myself as the bunkhouse door slammed. "Evening."

When Kip turned, I saw the distress in his eyes. "Hannah—"

"Let her go. She'll speak to you again when she's ready. May I?" He nodded, and I climbed the fence to take Amy's vacated spot. "What's the trouble, Kip?"

He sighed and stared out at the pasture, from whence came the occasional nicker or snort as the horses made themselves comfortable in the dark. "He was going to keep her there," he mumbled. "That…*arsehole* was trying to steal her."

Kip's accent had migrated toward the American end of the spectrum, but he'd picked up much of his profanity from Seamus and me. "He fancies her, yes," I replied, "but I do think he's learned his lesson. If Amy reciprocated, she wouldn't have come back with us." He said nothing, and I squeezed his arm. "When are you going to tell her, love?"

Kip straightened as suddenly as if he'd been caught reading comics under his maths book. "Tell her what?" he asked too quickly.

"That you also fancy her," I murmured. He began to stammer, and I cut him off with a pat. "It's obvious. If she hasn't realized it yet…well…Amy's clever enough, but in some areas, she's oblivious. So if you want something to happen, you'll need to make the overtures."

I watched his face as several emotions flashed across it in rapid succession, all of them muddled by the unnatural shadows of the security light. Finally, he muttered, "She's not of my people."

"Granted. Nor you hers, for that matter."

He looked back at me with impatience. "Then why do I want her?"

"*That*, I can't tell you. But everyone else on this ranch knows that the two of you are more than friends."

Even with the odd light, I could see he was blushing. "Everyone?" he mumbled.

"It's nothing to be ashamed of, dear."

"You don't understand—"

"Well, seeing as I sleep with a *faerie*, I beg to differ. Now, listen to me," I said, reaching up to turn his chin back toward me. "I'm not going to tell you how to manage your affairs, especially in matters of the heart. But I've interviewed loads of people over the years, Kip. I've learned to read them fairly well. And I know for a fact that you two have feelings for each other. How you handle that is your business."

But he shook his head. "You're wrong about Amy."

"Oh? Has she said something?"

"No," he admitted, "but…she would never feel this way about me."

"What makes you think that? I *have* been watching you two for some time, you know, and I've got a decent track record."

Kip's jaw clenched, and he flung one hand toward the dark pasture and the drowsing horses. "Because *that* is what she must think of me."

He looked miserable, and I slid closer to him. "Don't be ridiculous. There's no way she puts you and *Dan* in the same category."

"Dan is easier to harness, I suppose," he muttered. "But she knows what I—"

"Hear me, Kip: Amy does *not* think of you as…as a beast. Put that out of your mind."

He shrugged, unconvinced. "If not a beast, then a monster."

"Why on earth would you—"

"What else comes out of the Gray Lands?" He looked away as he wrestled with his thoughts, then said, "We're not of the same people. Better to tell her nothing."

"And always wonder?" I prodded.

"I don't need to wonder. Good night, Hannah," he said, then slid off the fence and turned toward the quiet bunkhouse alone.

I rose from my body almost as soon as I closed my eyes that night. A four-day break from sleepwalking was far too long—irresponsible, I chided myself as I floated through the ceiling and up over the slumbering countryside—and I had catch-up work to do.

As I drifted east, looking for flashes in the dark, I tried not to ruminate on my accidental awakening the last time I went out. If I stayed calm and kept my wits about me— and didn't give the dream space any reason to wake sleeping Fringers before I decided the time was right— then I'd get past this little blip in my training. Maybe a few more trips, I mused, a bit more practice at staying focused while out in the dream, and I'd have this thing perfected. And *then*, if I could talk Carey into a nighttime excursion to Montana and the silo…

I looked down as I passed over the gently rolling farmland of eastern Texas and spotted a familiar pair of bright lights below. Whose lights they were, I couldn't say; I'd avoided them for months on the suspicion that they were Arcanum wizards who'd managed to avoid going underground. But I was rested that night and determined to work past my dangerous little hiccup, and so, throwing caution aside, I descended toward the brighter of the pair.

They weren't in the same house, as I'd originally suspected, but they were neighbors. The brighter glow came from a modest cottage at the end of what appeared to be a short gravel driveway, while the dimmer one was perhaps a kilometer away in what appeared to be a ranch house much like the Joneses'. Taking aim, I dropped from the starless heavens toward the shadowy form of the cottage's roof, then plunged through and landed in a tidy bedroom beside a wooden four-poster.

The glowing form was female, a youthful and pretty brunette, I quickly ascertained—and on closer inspection, her light was white, not gold like mine.

Fae.

Before I could backpedal my way out of there, she opened one eye, then sat up in alarm. "What the hell—"

"I'm sorry, I'm sorry," I said in a rush as I backed toward the wall. "Wrong, ehm, address, I didn't mean—"

She held out her hand to stay me. "No, wait, don't go anywhere. Uh…" Glancing down at her nightclothes, a long gown that surely had a quilted robe to match, she frowned in consternation, then shrugged off her appearance and climbed out of bed. "Sorry, I guess we're having a pajama party. I'm dreaming, yes?"

"Yes…"

"Which explains why the glamour's not working. Oh, well." She folded her arms over her old woman's nightie and gave me a quick inspection. "Hi. Who're you?"

I wasn't sure what was more disconcerting, the fact that I'd accidentally awakened a faerie with a distinctly Texan drawl or the fact that she seemed utterly unbothered by the situation. "Ehm…Badger," I managed.

"Badger? Your mama named you *Badger*?"

"Nickname. I…I, ehm…" Finally recovering, I stuck out my hand. "Hannah Parsons, with the Fringe. My apologies for the interruption, Miss…"

She met my handshake and grinned. "That's more like it. Call me Bonnie. And Fringe, did you say? I haven't seen any signs of the Fringe around here in months."

"You know about us?"

Bonnie chuckled and leaned against her bedpost, though how she'd located it without being a sleepwalker herself, I couldn't say. "Knowledge keeps one alive, don't you agree?"

"Certainly. But you didn't hear about the Arcanum coup, then?"

Her thin eyebrows drew together. "No, what coup? When? What have those idiots done this time? And, uh…mind telling me *how*, exactly, we're dreaming together?"

She listened without interrupting while I told her of the Fringe's unravelling more than a year before—the kidnapping of the Arcanum's young grand magus, who had not only refused to cut ties with her fae half brother but had also married a man who'd turned out to have blood in two courts; the former grand magus's coercion into letting the new regime access the Fringe's extensive database of witches and lesser bloods; the swift attacks on Fringers around the world, paused only for a frantic hour in which a fraction of our people were evacuated out of the mortal realm; the Arcanum's continuing attempts to eliminate the Fringe stragglers in the wild and their use of the ones they'd kidnapped as hostages to keep Faerie out of the picture; and our efforts as survivors to find the Fringers left behind and the ones stolen away. "I didn't think you were Fringe, but I wanted to be certain," I explained.

"Good of you." Bonnie shifted against the post, shaking her head. "Well, that would explain why I can't find a Fringer to save my life."

"Can I ask why you need one?"

"Nothing nefarious," she replied, and felt her way back on the bed. "There's a baby down the road."

"Yeah, I saw the light—"

"He's half fae, and he's not quite two. Already beginning to find his talent. You see the problem, yeah?"

"Ehm…I don't mean to be rude, but…*yours*?"

"Oh, *no*. His mama's a dear little thing, but I was at the fair with her the night she went home with a handsome stranger, and I'm old enough to know that he wasn't human."

"You didn't stop her?"

A flicker of guilt crossed her face. "None of my business who she shacks up with. I mean, things could be worse for the baby—I'm half-blooded, and I've gotten by all right. But as I was saying, he's already started showing talent. I was going to make the Fringe aware of him, but…well, I guess I have, haven't I?" she added, gesturing to me. "So, any thoughts?"

"To be honest, you'd both be safer in Faerie," I replied.

At that, Bonnie broke into a long fit of trilling laughter. "You're joking, right?" she finally asked, wiping one eye. "There's no way I'm taking him over there."

"The king and queen have recalled the courts," I pointed out. "There's no reason why—"

"Ah," she interrupted. "You said the king and queen. The new ones, I presume?"

"Yes, exactly."

Bonnie smirked. "The only queen to whom I've ever held the slightest loyalty was killed a few years ago, I hear. Correct me if I'm wrong, now. I haven't seen since she tried to order us all into the Gray Lands, and that was some time ago."

My stomach began to knot. "Wait…*you're*…"

"One of Mab's. Nominally, I guess. Now, how would you like me to take the baby over there?"

I didn't know half of what an Arcanum education would have taught me about the courts, but I knew that if Bonnie remembered Mab's expulsion from Faerie, then she was well over a thousand years old and correspondingly powerful, and I chose my words carefully. "Mab's two surviving children are there already, and her grandson is helping the Fringe. Under the circumstances, if you sought shelter, they might—"

"Or they might not. Anyway, I'm not leaving Texas. Been here too long," she explained with a smile. "Came out on a wagon and liked what I saw."

"Understood," I replied. "What if I took the baby over, then?"

"Unh-uh. No chance you're getting him away from his mama without force, and I'd take exception if you tried," she added with a hint of warning.

"She could come, too."

"The Rockwells have been out here almost as long as I have. Fat chance." Bonnie squinted into the distance, thinking, then looked back at me. "Then again, I don't think she'd have much of a prayer if the Arcanum came to call. So here's my thought: I'm going to try to guide him along, keep him out of trouble, but if the situation changes…"

"Think you can remember my number between now and the time you wake?"

"I've always been a light sleeper," she replied, and stretched out again. "Let's try."

I woke the next morning to a blinking indicator on my mobile: a text message from an unfamiliar number that read only, *Testing—B*. Sitting up, I sent back a confirmation text, then shuffled to the bath.

When I was presentable, I headed for the house in search of food. Given the quiet of the bunkhouse, I assumed the others were already at breakfast, and I hoped someone had at least left me a few pieces of toast. To my surprise, however, I found breakfast spread but still untouched when I entered the kitchen, and I followed the sound of voices into the den. Poking my head around the corner, I saw a familiar man standing in the middle of the huddle: Jim, Carey's little brother, wearing a thick black braid and a paint-splattered T-shirt from the country music station where he worked. Catching Jim on the radio always threw me for a loop: "Jim Dandy" sounded like a middle-aged good old boy from the Deep South, whereas Jim Wheeler was twenty-six and plainly Navajo.

Spotting me, he waved and beamed. "Hey, there! Got another one for you."

Jim patted the shoulder of the man beside him, who, though apparently Caucasian, had tanned darker than Jim's natural complexion. His long hair had bleached nearly to white, and what I could see of his arms beneath his rolled-up sleeves was mainly sinews. The man squinted at me, then asked, "You Badger?"

"I am," I told him. "You're…"

"Jerry Thorne."

"*Gila!*" I pushed through the crowd to take a closer look. While I hadn't known many American Fringers before the unravelling, nearly everyone had heard of Gila, the crazy witch who posted gorgeous photos from his treks through the wilderness. "My God! We thought the Arcanum got you!"

"Bastards got close, but they weren't fast enough. Not when I'm living on the edge of a decent-sized cave system."

"You've been underground all this time?"

He chuckled at my shock. "Nah, just sleeping down there. Got pretty good at living off the land, but I busted my leg and tried to hitchhike to the ER. Lucky for me, this one here picked me up," he said, slapping Jim on the back. "Had some magic crap in the car, we got to talking, and here I am."

He wore a black brace around his knee, and from the look of the spell around it, I suspected that Carey or Arnold had already been at work. "I'm so glad you're all right," I said, and pointed to Nina, who skulked uneasily on the edge of the huddle. "That's two. We'll put a call in and see if we can't get you across in the next few days."

"And in the meantime, breakfast," said Zeb.

Jim didn't have to be told twice, and Zeb hung back to help the newcomer to the table. Before I could follow the pack, Arnold caught my shoulder and pulled me aside. "Blocking spell," he reminded me. "I already took care of

Amy."

I stood still while he cast the spell again, making me invisible in case the Arcanum thought to run a blood trace from my grandparents. "How are things?"

"Eh, fine," he muttered as he finished up. "More or less. Are you going to tell me what's going on with Kip and Amy?"

"Why do you think something's going on?"

"Oh, I don't know." He stepped back, considered his handiwork, and nodded to himself. "It seemed odd when she called Aiden this morning."

"In front of Kip?"

"Well, at first, then he went outside to sulk."

Arnold's eyebrows inched upward, but I only shrugged and headed for the table. "I know nothing, Arnie."

"Bollocks," he muttered, but followed me toward the smell of Zeb's breakfast casserole.

To say that the atmosphere in the bunkhouse that day was tense would be a gross understatement. As Jerry settled into one of the unclaimed private rooms to sleep and let the healing spell work, Amy took up residence in her workshop, but not to work on new wands. She spent much of the morning and early afternoon on the phone with Aiden, troubleshooting the network's final bugs and laughing too loudly at his jokes. I couldn't help but notice that she did so with the door wide open.

After an hour or so of listening to Amy's one-sided conversation, Kip gave up on the book he'd been reading and stalked out to the training ring, where he restlessly paced until Zeb and Seamus dragged Arnold outside to spar with him. Nina, who avoided Amy like a cat confronted with a spray bottle, sat on the fence and watched the men go at each other, and after a time, I joined her. I quickly pitied my cousin; Kip wasn't playing around, and when Arnold did occasionally get a blow in,

Kip's resulting glare was enough to give anyone pause.

Dinner was unusually subdued—Amy still wasn't speaking to Kip, Nina kept to herself, Jerry was groggy after a long day's rest, and poor Arnold's jaw was black and blue—but the rest of us did our best to keep the mood light and the dishes circulating until the meal drew to its end and the kids scattered. Carey offered us a movie night in the basement, and I gratefully accepted, even when her film of choice turned out to be *Scarface*.

I sleepwalked again that night, finding no one new but at least catching up with a few of my Minor Arcanum contacts. All were eager for news of Joyce and Boone, and I passed on what I knew. "I would send flowers," Jean-Claude told me, "but I do not know if anyone delivers to the swamp. Boone told me once that they receive their mail by boat."

Dawn found me on the phone with Vivi, who had made the arrangements for a pickup that night on the other side of the Boynton gate. Agitated by the continued tension in the bunkhouse, I went for a run with Seamus before breakfast—anything to avoid the loaded silences. As we rounded the far pasture and the terrified horses fled from my partner, he panted, "Are you sure about the drop-off? I don't mind…"

"You've barely stopped since you got back," I replied. "Take a breather. I'll get Amy out of the house, and that should help things along."

He wiped his dripping brow on his T-shirt—the morning was clear and beautiful, and the mercury was already on the ascent. "You really think it's a good idea to put Nina and Amy in a small space together for several hours?"

"No, but I think it's even worse to leave her here."

"You could take Kip instead."

"Kip can't drive."

"Right," he puffed, and jumped over a low rock in our path. "You don't actually plan to let Amy take the wheel, do you?"

"I'm not *mental*, Seamie."

After lunch, I packed the evacuees into the Suburban, kissed Seamus goodbye, and hurried Amy into the shotgun seat for the long drive west. The girls had little to say to each other, giving Jerry and me a chance to chat. He regaled us with a litany of the inconveniences of cave living as we crossed the Arizona border—a bat colony and an abundance of cockroaches topped the list—and by the time we stopped in Sedona for dinner, I knew more about backcountry survival than I'd ever cared to learn. Spending months on the run in England had been unpleasant, but at least I'd never resorted to drinking a snake's blood.

Once the sun was down, I led our little pack out through the canyon and found Rufus waiting to take them the rest of the way. "Want to spend the night over here?" he asked once Nina and Jerry had vanished. "Plenty of beds in the settlement."

"Thanks, but we're going to push on tonight," I told him, and then Amy and I began to pick our way through the starry darkness to our waiting vehicle.

"Jerry seems nice," she said after a few minutes of hiking, "but *ew*. He's got no filter."

"I'm surprised you and Nina were able to eat at all," I replied. "The look on your face when he started talking about the rats…"

"Why would you worry about Nina? She never met food she didn't like."

"Retract the claws, please."

Amy muttered but dropped the matter, and we spoke little until we'd refueled and purchased caffeine for the drive home. "All right," I said once I'd reached cruising speed on the Interstate, "you and I need to have a little talk."

"I'm sorry," she said with a sigh. "Nina's just been so annoying—"

"This has nothing to do with Nina. I see you and Aiden

made up."

"Oh, uh…yeah." She opened her crisps packet and tucked in. "He said he was sorry, and with the net this close to being finished, I thought we could put it behind us and get the work done."

"Mm. And this would have nothing to do with Kip, would it?"

I glanced her way in time to see a flash of guilty surprise. "Don't know what you're talking about," Amy mumbled.

"I might have overheard your fight. Want to tell me what's going on?"

Guilt shifted toward annoyance. "If you heard it, then you know why I'm not talking to him."

"Enlighten me anyway?"

"Because he's being a *jerk*!" She jammed a handful of crisps into her mouth and glowered out the window. "He's trying to boss me around like I'm some dumb kid. Excuse me, I'm not stupid, and I'm not helpless. He can't just tell me what to do."

I sat quietly for a moment, choosing my words. Like it or not, Amy was still young enough that she could do with guidance, but she had seen far more than most girls her age, and I couldn't ignore that fact. I also wasn't her mother, but that night, I was the closest thing she was going to find.

"Kip was wrong," I told her. "He shouldn't have said what he did. If you want to talk to Aiden, that's your right."

"*Thank* you," she muttered.

"But you're also being a brat. *Listen*," I insisted as she began to protest. "Nothing Kip did was any worse than what Aiden did, so why are you punishing one and not the other?"

That flummoxed her, and Amy wrestled with the question while she ate. When the packet was nearly empty, I said, "Let me tell you a little secret, Amy. It's always worse when the ones we care about hurt us."

She startled, then turned to the task of recovering every barbeque-flavored crumb. "What do you mean?"

"I mean that it was obnoxious when Aiden tried to mess with you, but when Kip did, it stung. Am I wrong?"

"He's supposed to be my friend," she mumbled.

I hesitated, wondering how much I should say. "Amy…why do you suppose Kip told you not to talk to Aiden anymore?"

"Because he's trying to boss me around like I don't know how to handle—"

"He was *angry*, love. I mean, I'm no mind reader, but from what I could see—and I spoke with him after you stomped off," I added, gauging her reaction from the corner of my eye, "he was furious that Aiden was trying to steal you. That wasn't bossiness talking—that was *jealousy*." I paused, but Amy wouldn't look at me. "Now, that's not to excuse what he said. He owes you an apology. You owe him one as well for those lovely, *loud* conversations you've had with Aiden of late—and don't think we didn't notice, dear. We're old, but we're not deaf."

Amy nibbled her lip. "But he said—"

"I know what he said. That doesn't give you any excuse to act like a spoilt child."

She went quiet again, and in the darkness, I couldn't tell if she was thinking or merely sulking until she murmured, "Why would he be jealous?"

I sighed. "Amy, open your eyes."

"You don't think…" She nervously laughed to herself, then crushed her empty bag in her fist. "Kip doesn't *like* me like me. We're just friends."

"Sure."

"*Hannah!*"

"I'm not saying anything else," I told her, flipping on the radio. "All I'm suggesting is that Kip got possessive because he thought he could have lost you forever. That's it."

"What do you know about—"

"That's *it*, Amy."

She huffed and slouched lower in her seat. "You are *so* wrong about him."

"Mm," I said, and turned the volume louder.

Before Amy could protest again, her mobile began to trill, and she tapped the line open. "Aiden? What's up?" she began, then paused. "Wait, seriously? Hang on, I'm putting you on speaker."

"Aiden?" I asked once Amy held the phone toward me. "It's Hannah. What's going on?"

His voice was fuzzy with the distance, but I could hear his triumph all the same. "We're going live tomorrow, that's what's going on. Amy, can you stay with me while I run the last checks?"

"Heck yeah, I can," she replied, and cut off the radio. "Whenever you're ready."

It was convenient, I mused, that our faerie-tweaked phones never needed to be recharged…but on the other hand, I feared I was in for a long, lonely drive home while the network geeks babbled in their incomprehensible dialect.

CHAPTER 7

Though it was well before dawn when we drove back onto the ranch, Amy went straight to her computer and booted, talking to Aiden over the speaker the entire time. I dropped my bag inside my dark bedroom—at least Seamus was getting some shut-eye—and looked back as Kip's door creaked open. "Net's going live," I whispered to him while he blinked in bleary confusion. "They've been at this for hours." Satisfied, Kip retreated, and I left Amy with a cup of tea before crashing until daylight.

When Seamus nudged me awake and coaxed me into the main room, I found the others crowded around Amy's workshop door, watching as she continued to type and talk in a voice grown raspy with continual use. At first glance, I wasn't certain how the girl was still awake, but the litter of tiny bottles of energy shots around her desk seemed to solve that riddle. After listening to her phone conversation for a moment, I imagined that the situation was much the same on Aiden's end of the line.

"Come on," said Carey, ushering us out of the bunkhouse, "we can't help them right now." When Kip dawdled, she caught his arm and gently tugged. "Waffles, eh? Go on inside, Zeb'll get started."

Though it was only Friday, neither Carey nor Zeb had any appointments scheduled until the afternoon, and we took advantage of the situation to eat a leisurely breakfast. Finally, as the hour neared nine, when the last of the batter was spent and we were slouching at the table, almost comatose with syrup and bacon, Amy stumbled in, carrying her laptop over her head like a prizefighter's belt. "We are *on*!" she shouted, and slammed the computer onto the table with a clatter of rattling dishes. "*Whooo!*"

I glanced at Carey, who casually pulled her wand from beneath her T-shirt and aimed it at Amy's head. "Catch, dear," she murmured, then breathed an incantation. The sleeping spell took immediate effect, and Zeb saved Amy from tumbling to the tile.

"Heavier than she looks," he grunted as he carefully lowered her to the floor. "Who's carrying her outside?"

"How about the couch?" said Carey, then floated her into the next room. As she left us, she called over her shoulder, "See how it is, will you? I'm curious."

But there, we encountered a slight problem: Amy had locked the system, and my credentials wouldn't work. "They changed the entire login scheme," I told the rest of the table after my fifth error screen. "Makes sense—this should keep Harrison and the Arcanum out—but I can't poke around on here until I get a working passcode or two."

Though I was eager to get a glimpse of what the kids had assembled, Amy was already snoring—and having seen her mania, I didn't want to try my luck with Aiden. Temporarily defeated, I put her computer on the sideboard for safety while we cleaned up the kitchen, then made a fresh pot of tea and settled down with my own laptop to catch up on the news I'd missed over the last days. I still made it a point to visit the local Durham sites, which left me homesick every time I clicked away. As gracious as the Joneses had been, I missed my cozy house on its quiet street and the delicious freedom of coming home, throwing on sweats, and marathoning terrible television without suffering anyone's disapproval. True, my tiny garden had been mainly weeds—"wildflowers," if I were being generous with myself—and all the fixtures could have used an upgrade, but the place was home, convenient to work and the shops, and even my parents, who'd insisted for years that I come to Sunday dinner. Seldom did my mother ever produce a proper Sunday roast, but she'd made up for it with the recipes she'd learned back in Texas, and I'd gladly taken the leftovers home with me, grateful to be spared the time in the kitchen after a long day at work. Maybe Durham wasn't the most exciting city on Earth, or even in northern England, but it was familiar and comfortable—*home*.

I still owned the house, though the only people who'd been inside for more than a year were the Malones, Seamus's parents, who'd found my murdered parents just before I went on the run. Having lived next door to a witch for five decades—and having seen a hint of what their long-absent adopted son could do—they'd asked few questions of me beyond what they could do to help. Once I'd begun to breathe in the States, I'd transferred my bills to a new account and sent them money to keep my creditors at bay. Surely they had to wonder when my funds would dry up, as I'd formally tendered my resignation to the Constabulary months ago, but if they worried about my financial state, the Malones kept their concerns to themselves.

I was lucky to have them. Dad's kin in the Arcanum either ignored me or, like Arnold, were unaware of my existence, and Mama's surviving family had never been more than the occasional call or Christmas card. But the Malones, my childhood neighbors who had nearly become my in-laws, still treated me like a daughter. I couldn't tell them much about my hiding place or about what had happened to the Fringe, for their own safety as well as mine, but with Seamus's permission, I'd finally been able to give them a word about their son: *Seamie's with me. He's safe.* It wasn't much, but they were grateful for any news of him. Whereas I'd resigned, Seamus had simply disappeared after he'd hopped a plane back to England, having accidentally set a suspect on fire in Belfast. He'd stopped responding to e-mail and taking phone calls, and his parents had eventually received word from his landlord that his lease had been terminated. They'd retrieved his belongings, not knowing if their son were dead or alive, and when I'd relayed the news to Seamus, he had allowed me to give them at least that sliver of hope. Having avoided them for years for fear that he'd lose control and kill them, Seamus wasn't ready to face his parents yet, and I respected his wishes. Though my dad had told them years ago of his suspicion that Seamus was fae, I had no idea how they would take confirmation of that hypothesis.

I was reading the latest batch of Durham obituaries, hoping to see no one I knew, when Amy's computer screen flashed to life and an alarm began to blat. Jumping from my chair, I ran to the sideboard to see what the matter was, but the lock screen refused to relent, and I could see no way of silencing the machine short of shutting it down. As I tried to think of what Amy's passcode might be, Carey hurried into the kitchen with her hair in a towel turban, and Zeb followed a moment later, shirtless and tying his bathrobe sash. "I didn't do it," I told them. "It started on its own."

They peered at the screen, a red background with pulsing black text requesting the passcode, and Zeb shrugged. "How deeply is she sleeping, Carey?"

"Shouldn't take much to nudge her back," she replied, then helped herself to my teapot while her husband went to the other room to wake Amy. By the time he shepherded her into the kitchen, Carey had fixed a mug, which she passed into Amy's hands. "Sorry to cut your nap short, but what's it doing?" she asked.

Amy, groggy from her magical sleep, sipped her tea and stared blankly at the screen for a few seconds until the last of the fog burnt away. "*Crap*," she muttered, putting the tea aside, then rapidly tapped her passwords until she gained access. What appeared then was far more advanced than the basic lock screen had suggested: a detailed world map, pocked with white diamonds and framed by a flashing red border. One of the diamonds, located over eastern China, flipped between white and red in time with the alarm.

"What's going on?" I asked as Amy navigated through the map screen.

"Dark magic."

"Come again?"

She spared me only a brief look before resuming her work. "When Aiden and I designed this, we built connectivity into it for my dark magic detectors. Net went live, detectors automatically engaged, and now one of them is going off."

I pointed to the map just as it vanished. "That one—"

"Hua's. I shipped it out a few weeks ago."

"Shit," I whispered, and looked at Zeb and Carey. "We've got a gate in Beijing."

"Damn it," Zeb muttered, "fifth this month—"

"Not necessarily," Amy interrupted through a yawn. "I mean, yeah, it's another gate, but it might not be in Beijing. I made the range on those things pretty wide. If we had more, we could triangulate, but right now…"

"How far from the city could it be?" he asked.

She looked up again. "About a thousand miles."

"A *thousand*—"

"I don't have all the onboard information connected with the network yet, but Hua should get more accurate readings. How far ahead is she?"

I pulled up my computer's clock and did the quick calculation. "About fourteen hours. Carey—"

"On it," she said. "Let's try to sleepwalk and touch base…"

Before we could leave the kitchen, the wall phone began to ring, and Carey answered with a barked, "*Hello?*" She softened almost immediately. "Oh, Hua, hello, I'm sorry, we were about to… Yes. Yes, we saw. Do you know… Okay… Okay, got it. We'll be waiting."

She hung up and folded her arms. "Hua has an idea of

where the gate's opened, but it's going to take her a few hours to verify."

"Where?" Zeb asked. "Not the city, I hope."

"No, Beijing's safe. She thinks the signal's coming from somewhere in the Huangshan range."

Amy's face screwed up in thought. "If it's somewhere in the mountains, the situation can't be all that bad."

But Carey shook her head. "It's a major tourist destination. If a gate's opened somewhere in those mountains…well," she muttered, "let's just hope nothing on the other side comes exploring."

As Hua reported over a series of e-mails to Carey that day, her fastest route to the mountains was via a flight into the closest notable city—also called Huangshan—particularly seeing as Hua didn't own a car. The earliest flight wasn't until half-seven in the morning her time, however, which meant she didn't reach her destination until ten that night to us. While Carey and Zeb went about their scheduled appointments that day, the rest of us packed the essentials and waited for word about our travel plans. Around dinnertime, we were surprised to see Jim wander into the bunkhouse with a backpack slung over one shoulder. "Carey called me," he said. "Something about China?"

Before we retired late that evening, Carey received another message from Hua: *It is here, somewhere. Signal strong. Taking bus to Tangkou.* I moved the pin in the map we'd printed out, and Carey promised to wake us if she had news overnight.

But Hua stayed busy, and her next call didn't come until six Saturday morning. Carey, who had given Hua her mobile number the day before, carried her phone into the bunkhouse and woke us so that we could hear her report firsthand. "All right," she said, holding the phone out on her palm like a platter, "how bad is it?"

Hua sounded weary, and she kept her voice low. "Bad.

I am sorry about noise around me, I am camping, and there are many people here. Difficult to find privacy. Wait…" After a moment of shuffling, the ambient noise subsided, and Hua resumed. "Rental sleeping bags are not recommended. At least I could clean mine."

I grimaced in sympathy. "Have you been hiking all day?"

"Or queuing for a cable car. Many tourists. But I think I found the gate."

"You saw it?" Zeb asked.

"No, but I circled it. I left the trails…probably not allowed, surely not encouraged," she muttered, "but I think I have narrowed the search to the area around one peak."

"That's helpful," he replied.

"Well…yes and no. I think it is somewhere in Xihai."

I hurried to the map we'd tacked to the wall and scoured the named peaks for the reference point. "Ehm…which was it, again?" I called toward the phone.

"Xihai," she repeated. "Uh…Xihai Grand Canyon?"

"Got it," I said, moving the pin. "That sounds nice enough."

"It is beautiful," Hua agreed, "but a problem. The trail is long and uneven—"

"Good thing we're in decent shape, then," Zeb interrupted.

"And part of the route is *closed*," she finished. "Maintenance issues. The paths and rails must be repaired, you see, and the routes into the bottom of the canyon are not available this month."

Zeb frowned at the phone. "Then how did you—"

"Light bending spell. Not difficult to hold together, and with the crowd, no one noticed me slip away."

Seeing Seamus's confusion, I whispered, "Invisibility-lite. You blend into the shadows. Unless you're standing in the middle of the desert at noon, it's not a bad tactic."

"*Ah*," he said, and nodded.

Invisibility, like all such glamours, was child's play when one had enchantment at one's disposal, but it was difficult to establish true invisibility with a spell, and even more challenging to maintain it when one's attention was diverted elsewhere—say, toward not falling down a mountain staircase. With Seamus set to rights, I turned my attention back to Hua, who had been discussing mountain espionage tactics with Zeb.

"If I was noticed," she told him, "then no one stopped me. Believe me, you do not want to attempt invisibility and hike Huangshan at the same time. Do you have any idea how many thousands of stairs I walked today? My legs are aching tonight."

Carey's eyebrows knit. "Can you not cast—"

"Oh, I cast, and it is duller now, but I don't have half your skill." She grunted as she shifted position. "And there is something else I noticed today. It might be nothing, but…"

"Yeah?" said Carey.

"Smoke. I saw smoke in the canyon three times. Not much, but enough to tell me something is down there."

At that, Arnold drew closer to the phone and cleared his throat. "Not to be a skeptic, but this is Huangshan we're talking about, yes? Isn't it rather known for its clouds?"

"I know what clouds look like," Hua replied testily. "And clouds generally are not localized, thin, and black. From what I could see, it was as if someone was trying to make a little fire."

Kip, who had been standing close to Zeb, took a step away from the outstretched phone and muttered, "Raiders."

"Sorry," said Hua, "what was that? I didn't hear."

"Raiders," Zeb echoed, wrapping his arm around Kip's tense shoulders. "They're humanoid, more or less…black cloaks, ride scaly horse-ish things, carnivorous…"

"They move in packs," Kip added. "Never fewer than

three."

"I cannot say what I saw," Hua replied, "but it is possible. There is sufficient tree cover in the canyon…but moving horses around would be difficult if they didn't use the paths, and I saw nothing on the paths today." She sighed deeply, then said, "I am tired, but I doubt I will sleep. Not with the gate open. Will you come now?"

"If you can show us the way," said Carey, nodding as the rest of us headed for our clothing and our packs.

"Photos in a moment," said Hua, and the conversation ended.

By the time we'd scrambled into our clothes and grabbed our gear and granola bars, Carey's mobile was beeping with the notifications of arriving pictures. Hua had taken a three-hundred-sixty-degree shot of her surroundings, and a final text message confirmed that the coast was clear. Staring at Carey's phone, Arnold concentrated for a moment, then motioned open a gate onto a chilly mountaintop clearing beneath a sprinkling of stars made bright by elevation. We hurried through toward Hua, who leaned against a boulder while she waited for us, and he closed the rift before any curious campers could stumble across the flash of sudden daylight.

Hua straightened and regarded the eight of us as our eyes adjusted to the night. "More than I had anticipated," she murmured. Her gaze lingered on Amy, who had slung a gun case over one shoulder and was barely concealing her holster with her jacket. "Perhaps it would be wisest if the crafter remained here," she said as we clustered around her. "A lookout. If she sees anything while we are away, she could contact us."

Amy's hand went to her unburdened hip. "I'm a good shot."

"I never said you weren't," Hua countered, "but surely six wizards and…*him*"—her head jerked toward Seamus, though she otherwise kept her distance—"can manage this. Stay here, you and you," she said, indicating Kip as well. "Watch for us."

Amy began to protest again, but Kip beat her to it. "If there are raiders in the canyon, then they're *mine*," he quietly insisted. "Do what you want, but I'm going that way."

"And I didn't come here to hang out at a campsite," Amy added. "So what's the plan?"

Though Hua seemed unconvinced, she surrendered. "I have pictures of the bottom of Xihai, but in the dark…"

Arnold nodded emphatically. "If it's all the same to you, I'd rather not open a gate onto the Gray Lands gate by accident, especially not when I can't see what's lurking. Shall we wait for morning, then?"

She consulted her mobile. "Dawn is still seven hours away, and the campsite is packed. I say we do it on foot. Less chance of being noticed if we head down in the dark."

"Not to be a wet blanket," said Carey, "but didn't you say the trails are closed for maintenance?"

Hua shrugged. "We will go slowly."

For a forty-eight-year-old woman, I was relatively fit. No, I wasn't running marathons every weekend, I couldn't bench press twice my weight, and I had yet to scale the Seven Summits, but I'd always kept pace with my younger colleagues at the Constabulary and put in my time at the gym. With my background, I thought I was prepared for Huangshan.

I was not.

Huangshan is beautiful, a landscape of jutting granite peaks, sheer cliffs, and deep ravines partly covered with variable green forests of hardwoods and bamboo and twisting pine, plus frequent seas of rolling clouds—an alien beauty to one who grew up on the gentle hills of Durham, to be sure, but striking for the scars of the geological violence visible in the jagged range. This I knew largely from photographs, however, as I could see little of the famed beauty as we felt our way down the mountain on which Hua had paused to camp. True, the paths were well-maintained and wide enough for us to comfortably walk two abreast, but the route was dark, lit only by the small circles of our torches, and the way was steep.

I lost count of the stairs we descended after the first two hundred, but given their pitch, I was grateful that I couldn't see the view. A quick mumble and flick of the wand gave me a much-needed walking stick, and the others quickly did likewise while I conjured up sticks for Amy and Kip. As we passed our first half hour, I knew my knees were going to be cross with me by morning, and Carey had already begun shoring up the numbing spell Hua had built for herself. Our guide limped, but she didn't complain.

After an hour, the path began to flatten, and I luxuriated in the feeling of level ground—a feeling that was snatched away almost immediately as Hua led us toward a barricaded fork in the trail. She paused to consult her map, held up her dark magic detector to be certain, then nodded and stepped over the chain. "This way," she whispered. "Stay close and watch your step."

Within a few minutes, the only sounds around us were the wind through the trees, the slap of our shoes on the stone path, and our labored breathing as the trail undulated. Focusing on our footing and struggling to climb the endless stairs that clung to the mountainside, we had little energy to spare for conversation. Every few minutes, Hua called a halt to check her detector again, but the signal remained strong. "I fear," she confessed during one of our too-brief breaks, "that the clouds will be strong tonight. When the bottom of the canyon is visible, the view is spectacular…"

"It's okay," said Carey, patting her shoulder, "you don't have to sell us on the scenery."

Hua sighed as she adjusted her pack. "I seldom have

foreign visitors. You come to my country, to one of my favorite places, and it is too dark to show you anything."

"And there's a new gate," Seamus added.

"Yes, and that," she muttered. "Come on. Maybe we will have a nice sunrise."

We fell in behind her, narrowing our group to a single-file line as we walked to better take advantage of the handrails. Certain passages lacked even that reassuring aid—the steps seemed to drop off into the abyss—and I slunk close to the mountain and sent up a grateful prayer that I couldn't see the drop. I stumbled twice on the four-hour trek, Seamus and Carey fell at one point, and by the time we called a halt at a trail fork just above the cloud level, Arnold was limping as badly as Hua was from a twisted knee. "This had better be one hell of a sunrise," he grumbled to me as we took a break. "And what happens if the tourists look over and see us here? I'm not going to be able to bend light if I'm focused on a shield."

"One step at a time," I told him, then drank deeply from my depleted water bottle. "Hua, is there potable water at the bottom?"

She held up her nearly empty canteen and shook it. "Maybe. I am willing to take that risk."

Overhearing us, Seamus took my bottle and concentrated for a few seconds until it refilled. "Maybe it's best not to play with untested water, eh?" he said, passing it back to me.

I sipped with caution, but the water tasted normal. "That'll do. Hua, top-up?"

If she was hesitant around Seamus on principle, she threw caution aside at the promise of water, and she wasn't the only one thrusting a bottle toward him in the dark. "Honestly," he said after refilling the last of them, "you people should have *said* something. This is easy."

"Casting water is mostly done by drawing it from the atmosphere," Arnold explained once he'd slaked his thirst, "and that takes time. Didn't realize you had that in your arsenal."

"Val doesn't just beat me," he replied. "Mostly beatings, but sometimes he throws in something useful like that." He considered the rocks rising above us, shadows against the starry heavens, then said, "You want to descend in the dark?"

"That was the plan," said Hua. "My readings suggest the gate is down there…"

"I'm just thinking that if the gate *is* down there, and something's come through that's capable of starting a fire, do you really want to surprise it under these conditions?" asked Seamus.

Kip passed his torch from hand to hand. "If it's raiders, we can surprise them. They can't see in the dark any better than we can."

"That's a big *if*. What if it's not raiders? What else could it be?"

He paused as the group turned to him, then began counting off on his hand. "Any of Nath's people. What they call themselves, I don't know…we always called them the strangers. And there used to be faeries among her people, or so I heard—"

"There were," I interrupted. "If I'm not mistaken, they've ended up over here."

"Maybe some are just now coming through, then," said Kip. "There are another people among the strangers who pay homage to Nath, but keep to themselves. They seem somewhat human, but they are slighter, with purplish skin and black hair, and they live in the great caves north of Nath's citadel."

"They use magic?" Arnold interrupted. "Well, dark magic?"

Kip nodded. "So I heard, though I've never seen them up close. Too dangerous. We called them deep dwellers."

"Svartálfar to the Arcanum," he replied, turning to me. "If one or two of them is camping around here, we would do best to draw them away from the gate. No sense in fighting them near a firehose of dark magic."

"Anything else come to mind?" I asked Kip.

He thought for a moment. "There is a chance that some of my people have found their way over, but…unlikely. This terrain is not ideal."

"I—I'm sorry," said Hua, flicking her torch on him, "but did you say *your* people?"

Kip shielded his eyes from the beam in his face. "Uh…yes. Would you mind—"

Before he could finish, Amy pushed Hua's torch down and stepped between them. "He's with us. Whatever else he is doesn't matter. Yeah?"

Hua seemed troubled at this news, but she let it go. "What else could be down there?"

He sighed as he mulled over the possibilities. "Troll? They can build fires. Or"—he lowered his voice to a near-whisper—"the Little People."

"Come again?" said Seamus.

"They're small, no more than this high," he said, holding his hands about half a meter apart. "They live underground, like the deep dwellers, but they can't use magic. Don't need it," he added, shuddering. "They hunt in swarms, men and women, old and young, all together. My father said he saw what they did to another village when he was a boy—there was nothing left but ashes and bones. When they bite, they don't let go."

I looked at Arnold, who could only shrug.

"Yeah, I've got nothing. Going to go with 'evil gnomes' for now," I said. "But really, I'm liking none of this. I'm with Seamie—let's wait for daylight."

"If we wait, we lose the advantage of surprise," Jim countered. "If they can't see us coming—"

"Only an idiot breaks down a door without having some inkling of what's behind it," Seamus cut in. "Or at least the proper weapons. We don't know if we're dealing with bloodthirsty midgets or just a wayward hiker, so why don't we sit still for a few hours, take a load off, and wait to strike until we can at least see what we're striking?"

The others sat silently for a moment, and then Carey said, "You know, we should probably listen to the cops. Head on just a bit—I think the path widens up ahead. And Badger?"

"Yes?" I replied.

"Up for a sleepwalk?"

The night was incredible, clear and moonless, and I leaned against Seamus's chest and watched the clouds roll in below us, thick mist barely visible by starlight. We turned the torches off and lowered our voices to whispers, and Seamus and I kept tabs on the others as they catnapped. Poor Hua, weary and sore, had tucked herself against the mountain and propped her head on her backpack, and Jim and Arnold had curled up beside her, pressed close for warmth. Kip and Amy kept to themselves, I noticed, but the Joneses were drowsing together. Carey's spellwork had taken care of the worst of my aches from the hike, but I was alert—it was barely lunchtime in New Mexico, and my brain refused to shut off. For once, Seamus appeared to be in the same boat, as his breathing never slowed to the telltale tempo of sleep.

But even with insomnia, I could put myself into the trance necessary for sleepwalking, and I soon found myself standing beside my unconscious body.

"Took you long enough," said Carey, who'd been leaning against the mountain while she waited. "Shall we?"

I nodded and leapt, letting myself hover over the canyon for a few seconds until Carey joined me. We sank beneath the obscuring clouds, looking for glowing bodies, but none of the telltale pinpricks of light appeared. Soon, I could make out the gate, a wide hole in space hanging just above a little lake. I saw nothing else—no trolls, no centaurs, not even a sleeping bird...

And then I look a closer look at the shadows and

realized that the massive mound I'd taken for a rock formation was very much alive and sleeping.

"Oh, *shit*," I muttered, pointing it out to Carey. "You see that?"

She peered at the gray around us until it resolved for her as it had for me, and she floated back in alarm. "Is that, uh…"

"Dragon," I confirmed. "*Great.*"

Carey and I decided to let the others sleep until morning—all but Seamus, who was waiting for an update when I returned from my sleepwalk. He urged me to nap and promised to keep watch, but there was no way I was getting real rest, especially in light of what was waiting at dawn. Still, my vigil wasn't entirely terrible. I had my partner's arm around me, a thousand stars to contemplate, and a peaceful night. Aside from the fact that we were perched on a walkway stuck onto the steep side of an off-limits mountain with a gate and a giant lizard somewhere below us, the scene would have been perfect. Well, that, plus the annoyance of my sweat-damp clothing, which had turned clammy in the cool wind. I scrunched closer to Seamus, taking advantage of his body heat, and felt his arm tighten around me.

Slowly, ever so slowly, the hours crept past. I dozed and jolted myself awake half a dozen times before the sun began its creep toward the eastern horizon. The soft glow lit up the world below us, brightening the sky and turning the clouds into a sea of pink-topped waves, and I coaxed my stiff limbs to move enough to let me free my mobile and snap a few pictures. By then, the others had begun to stir as well, and Carey called everyone close for the bad news. "At least it's not evil gnomes," she said as the others' faces fell. "But this is going to be tough. Be on guard, have your weapons close, and let's not take stupid chances down there."

Wincing after the night, we rose and began our final descent, moving as quietly as possible. I hiked behind Hua, feeling my ready wand shift against my spine as I navigated the trail. The steps ahead were steep, and I resolved not to look down at the presumably lovely scenery—that was hardly the time for vertigo. But soon enough, the trail descended into the clouds, and we bunched together in the fog, all of us moist and partly blinded, feeling our way with our sticks and torches once more.

The sun was well and truly up by the time the trail began to level off, and my sore legs rejoiced at the thought of reaching the bottom of the ravine, even if the rest of me dreaded what I'd seen lurking down there. "The path should drop us just past that boulder," Hua whispered, pointing to a rock made indistinct by mist. "I will go first and see if anything is awake."

She had nearly disappeared in the fog when I saw her come to an abrupt stop, and I hurried after her and almost bumped into her back. "See it?" I whispered.

Hua nodded.

"Sleeping?"

"I will check."

Just as I'd seen in the dream space, there was a lovely pool near the end of the trail, surrounded by a forest of bamboo and pine, green fingers rising through the thick air. The gate we'd come to close hovered a hand's breadth over the water near the middle of the lake, a hole far too bright for its surroundings. By its pale light, I could see the ripples on the pond as the gentle wind stirred the water—and there, across the pond, tucked with its back to a convenient stone, lay a massive dragon the color of dried blood.

Hua inched her way around the water toward the behemoth. Looking more closely, I could see where a pine tree near the dragon had been blackened on one side, and it wasn't hard to deduce that we'd found the source of Hua's mysterious fires.

While she crept closer, the rest of our pack joined me and stared in silence at the sleeping lizard. After a moment, Seamus ventured, "Maybe it's friendly."

"*Friendly?*" Arnold whispered.

"I've ridden one that size, and she's friendly enough."

"That's not Georgie," I replied. "Georgie's bonded to Joey, and she understands a couple of languages. What do you want to bet this one's wild and can't understand a word we say?"

"Must you be so negative, Badge?"

I shot him a look and eased my pack to the ground, the better to maneuver. "Right. We deal with the dragon first, then worry about the gate."

"Agreed," said Arnold, who dropped his damp bag by mine. "Maybe we can scare it through the gate, what do you think?"

Before I could respond, Hua hurried back to us, wide-eyed and pale. "She has a clutch," she whispered. "At least five eggs. See how her body is curled around them?"

I squinted through the fog and could barely make out whitish oblongs at the center of the dragon's coiled mass. Though the mist and distance made the dragon's exact size difficult to pin down, she was probably the size of a jumbo jet, and the eggs had to be almost as tall as Amy and several times wider.

"And there goes that idea," Jim muttered. "Mama's not going to leave her babies behind. So now what?"

We looked at each other, no one wanting to be the first to give voice to the unpleasant task ahead of us, until Kip pulled one of Amy's pistols out of her bag. "If she sees us, she'll roast us alive," he said quietly as he checked the magazine. "Strike first, strike hard. Go for the eyes and the underbelly—the rest of the hide is tough."

"I still think we could possibly coax it back the way it came," Arnold began, but before he could elaborate on his scheme, Amy raised her trusty rifle, took aim, and fired.

The girl might have been useless from a magical

standpoint, but Amy had a sharpshooter's hands, and her shot hit its mark. Now most definitely awake, the dragon roared as she swung her head from side to side, giving us a clear view of her ruined left eye. She rose to her feet, baring far too many teeth for my comfort, and belched a jet of fire at the mist above her as she sought her assailant in the fog. More terrifying to me was the voice I heard bellowing in my head, which alternated between wordless rage and a thought my mind translated as *WHERE?* That dragons were telepaths I already knew, but I had no idea whether this one could track us by our thoughts alone.

"You had to go and piss off Smaug, didn't you?" Jim muttered as Amy lined up her next shot.

"Are you going to criticize or be useful?" she snapped, then let fire another round. The dragon took the second bullet in the side of the neck, where it buried itself between the tough scales, and Amy swore softly as she aimed again. "She's moving too erratically. I need to get closer—"

"Hold back," I ordered, and stepped out from behind our semi-protective boulder with my wand raised. "Let's see how she likes lightning."

With a quick mutter to steady myself, I shot a long, arcing blast of energy toward the dragon. She saw the flash, however, and she screeched in pain as she intercepted the bolt with her wing. I could tell that I'd charred a hole through the thick membrane, but I seemed to have only incensed my quarry, who by then knew exactly where we were hiding.

My shield barely held against the flames that she shot our way, and Arnold quickly strengthened what I had thrown together. When the fire dissipated, I saw through the haze of the shield that the dragon was running toward us around the lake, wings back and mouth opening for another blast.

"Hold it steady!" Zeb yelled as he and Carey raised their wands in tandem.

Their shots flew true and struck the beast on the

underside of her long neck, but she shook them off like mosquito bites and picked up speed. While the Joneses ducked back behind the shield, Hua took her turn, followed by Kip with the pistol, then Seamus, who flicked half a dozen blue fireballs toward the dragon's good eye. One of those managed to strike the target, and the dragon roared as she stumbled toward the lake.

We held our breath while the dragon plunged her head into the water, hoping she might not rise, but she did, blinded and angrier than ever. I could hear her pain and fear ringing over my thoughts, and from the looks on the others' faces, I wasn't alone. "Poor thing," I said over her cries. "Come on, all together, let's give the mercy shot—"

My sympathy was short-lived, as the dragon, unable to pinpoint her prey, took to the air. If her maimed wing troubled her, it worked well enough to let her hover a few meters above the ground. "*Shit*," Arnold hissed, "if she gets out of the canyon, I won't be able to make gates quickly enough to follow."

He had no need to worry, however—the dragon wasn't going anywhere. Though blind, she wasn't deaf, and we had been far too noisy in our attack. Taking aim as well as she could, she sprayed fire in our direction, turning her head to incinerate everything in our vicinity.

It took four of us—Arnold and me, then Hua, and finally Seamus, who threw a second shield on top of the one we'd built with spellcraft—to hold back the flames. The trees around us weren't so lucky, especially considering the fire our shields deflected onto them, and even the damp vegetation began to smolder. "We're about to have a forest fire on our hands!" Zeb shouted as he sneaked shots from around the shield. "Someone's got to put it out!"

"Jimmy, with me," said Carey, turning to the imminent inferno. "Stay behind the shield, try to cast around it…"

Jim followed his sister's lead, but their efforts were largely ineffective against the raging dragon's continual firestorm. I could see trees blackening and bursting into flame mere meters away from where we stood, and the acrid smoke from the new fires exacerbated the problem of the morning fog. We needed to concentrate on the dragon, but it was taking the four strongest fighters among us just to hold the shield together. Jim was a far weaker wizard than his sister, and though Zeb's talent for combat magic exceeded Carey's, it wasn't enough.

And then, through the haze and fire and fog, I saw Amy climb onto the boulder and take a knee. She shouldered her semi-automatic rifle while the dragon was incinerating another patch of forest, then took aim and let the bullets fly.

The dragon jerked as the projectiles ripped into her neck just below the jaw, momentarily too shocked to shoot flames, but Amy didn't let up. Weaving ever so slightly to match the dragon's frantic attempts to dodge the bullets, she fired off a rapid barrage until she emptied her magazine, and then, moving calmly, she pulled a fresh magazine from her bag and started to switch them out. But the dragon, though bleeding, had steadied herself enough to shoot a fresh blast. Down below, I stared in horror at Amy as she worked, seeing the spark at the back of the dragon's open mouth and knowing there was no way I could shield her in time from the flames to come.

But Kip also saw what I was seeing, and he was prepared. Sprinting out from behind the shield with nearly preternatural speed, he emptied his pistol into the dragon's neck, drawing her attention away from Amy. "Over here! Come get me!" he shouted as the gun clicked, then continued his mad dash through the burning woods.

The diversion was just long enough, and Amy sighted on the dragon while the lizard sought Kip. "Cover him, damn it!" she yelled down to us, then screamed as she delivered the killing blow, shooting through one of the dragon's wounded eyes until her second magazine emptied.

The ground shook as the dragon fell, landing half in the lake and half on the grass, and we turned our attention to the fire before it could spread. Seamus may have had the natural advantage at creating water, but with the thick fog, Arnold was almost as quick, and soon, the flames were nothing more than charred wood and curling smoke.

Coughing, Kip emerged from a partially burnt stand of pines, sooty but intact. "About time," he wheezed, then nearly fell as Amy plowed into him.

"What is the *matter* with you?" she demanded, holding him around the waist. "You don't run *into* the fire, idiot!"

"Me? You're the one who made yourself a target for an angry dragon!" he retorted, pulling her closer. "I thought she was going to crisp you!"

"You ran into a fucking *fire*…"

While the two of them chided each other, I turned my attention to the corpse. Casting as Arnold had taught me, I dissolved the body into dust—a spell nearly impossible to manage with a still-living being, unfortunately—and called upon a stiff wind to blow the evidence into the lake. As Carey, Jim, and Hua began covering up the worst of the fire damage, Zeb, Arnold, Seamus, and I headed for the five giant eggs, which had escaped their mother's wrath unscathed.

"You know," said Seamus as we contemplated them, "if Joey could raise a dragon, there's no reason that—"

"*No.* Unh-uh, no way," Zeb interrupted, fervently shaking his head. "No dragons on my ranch. Negative."

"Just a thought…"

"I don't even know how we'd incubate them," I said, folding my arms.

Arnold ran his hand over the nearest egg's smooth shell. "Localized warming spell…the construction wouldn't be complicated, and with regular reinforcement—"

"What part of 'no' was unclear?" Zeb snapped. "My insurance won't cover this."

I gave him a hard look. "We've got five dragon eggs on our hands, and you're worried about *insurance*?"

"I'm trying to find something that will get through your thick skulls. Wayward wizards, faeries, and even a centaur I can handle, but I draw the line at dragons."

"We can't just leave them," said Seamus. "Think Joey needs a herd?"

"Joey has enough on his mind," I replied. "Okay, what if we toss them back through the gate? Maybe someone over there can use them."

"Except they'll probably die if they're not incubated quickly enough," Arnold added. "And you saw how Kip reacted…"

In the end, there was no good solution. We smashed a hole into each of the eggs, then threw the lot back into the Gray Lands and cleaned up the dragon's fresh nest. As we finished the unsavory job, the others joined us, and I beckoned Kip toward me. "I wanted to give you the option before we close the gate," I told him, holding up my hand as he started to interrupt. "You've more than repaid whatever life debt you think you owe us, Kip. If you want to go home, the way is open."

Kip hesitated, then turned to look at Amy, who stood back with her hands shoved in her jacket pockets. "I'm sorry," he murmured.

Her face fell. "You're leaving—"

"I'm sorry about what I said. About you and Aiden, I mean. I…behaved poorly."

She nodded and gnawed her lip. "I'm…well, I'm sorry, too. For rubbing him in your face."

He began to speak, paused, then took a tentative step toward her. "Amy…do you want me to go?"

She shook her head, and her eyes began to well.

With a sigh of relief, he hurried to hug her, and I looked at Arnold and Zeb. "Let's close it and get out of here. I could do with a drink."

CHAPTER 8

The idea of walking out of Huangshan and seeing the natural beauty we'd missed on our overnight expedition appealed to no one, least of all Hua. With her adrenaline spent, she began to stumble over her own feet, and Carey ordered her to bed. "Come with me," Hua offered as she opened a gate into her tidy flat. "You are tired, too. At least let me make tea."

At that moment, I would have preferred a glass of wine, but the siren song of the promised tea was powerful. While we gathered our belongings and hurried to Hua's place, she arranged a line of small teapots on her kitchen counter, put out a selection of porcelain cups, then measured leaves and water with a weary smile. "With this, I leave you," she said, sweeping her arm to encompass the offering. "Stay as long as you like. The couch is comfortable."

Though most of our party went home soon after, Carey and I decided to stay and try to sleepwalk. "We seldom have sufficient overlap to seriously search," she explained to the others, "and it's not like Hua's going to mind. Plus, I don't know about Hannah, but I feel like I could sleep for a week."

"You're not alone," I muttered, and shooed the rest on their way.

Carey took the vouched-for couch, while I cast myself an inflatable mattress on the sitting room floor and snuggled down with a thin blanket. Another quick spell blackened the windows against the Beijing morning, and I relaxed into the familiar sensation of floating free of my body and out over the waking city.

Though I was weary, duty called—after all, it wasn't every day that I had the chance to sleepwalk from Asia. Granted, I could have chosen a better hour than midmorning to try to locate sleepers on the continent, but as I rose through Hua's ceiling and out over the shadow city, I told myself that if I didn't have any immediate hits, I could always turn my attention west.

Drifting in the constant twilight of the dream space, I gazed below as the sprawl of Beijing gave way to its suburbs and then, finally, the countryside. No unexpected flickers caught my immediate attention, a silent testament to Hua's scouting over the last year. China's lone sleepwalker stayed busy, and as far as I could see, she had located every last Fringer hiding in the capital—remarkable, considering how dimly some of our targets glowed. Looking south, I began to see the telltale bright gold lights of wizards, but before I headed that way to investigate, a flash below me caught my eye, and I waited as Hua rose to join me.

"How did I know I would find you at work?" she teased. "Go to sleep, Hannah. I'll resume the search when it's actually *night*."

"At least show me the terrain while I'm here," I replied, sweeping one hand over the shadows below. "I've yet to play tourist in your backyard."

"A pity, and I hope to host you again under better circumstances. Let's see…" Pointing to the lights to the south of our position, she said, "Shanghai. Most of the Minor Arcanum in China are based in that city, largely by chance. If you turn slightly and squint at the horizon…*there*"—she floated behind me and pointed over my shoulder—"you'll find another group in Taiwan. Due south is Hong Kong, and we have a small community there as well."

Hua spun around me as effortlessly as if she were lazing about a swimming pool, then pulled my shoulders into position as she indicated the strong golden haze to the northwest. "Arcanum," she said quietly, as if afraid to draw their attention. "Brighter in recent months as they've consolidated."

"Closing ranks," I murmured. "Any hint as to why?"

She shrugged. "You know as much as I do. And if you'll look east now, that's the Korean peninsula you're seeing. The bright splotch is Seoul—nearly every Korean wizard in our organization has moved to the city."

"Except him," I replied, pointing to a more northerly dot.

Hua's tone was guarded when she replied. "Her, actually. She's only ten."

"Has anyone made contact yet?"

"I have. I check on her every month or so, but I haven't yet convinced her to join us." Seeing my bemusement, she murmured, "You have heard of Kaechon?"

Unfortunately, I had. "The prison camp?"

Hua nodded. "Her grandfather was a dissident, I believe, but getting a clear answer from her is difficult. I've offered to break her out, but she worries about her friends and her family—if she escapes, she fears they will be punished. She's been padding their rations and patching them up for most of her life, too. Her mother had talent, she says, but she's been dead for several years." Looking back at me, Hua smiled grimly. "You seem surprised, Hannah."

"I…well, ehm," I stammered, "I know Beijing and Pyongyang—"

"I don't speak for the Party," she interrupted. "And having seen what I've seen, I don't *care* what the Party's official position is." She shook her head and sighed. "Anyway, those are the high points of what you can see from here. Come back and rest—we could all use a few hours of true sleep."

With a promise from me that I'd be along soon, Hua vanished as she returned to her sleeping body, and I surveyed the landscape in silence. As tempting as it was to pursue the North Korean child, I knew that Hua was better equipped to handle that delicate task and let the urge pass to head east. Instead, as if pulled mothlike toward the glow of the Arcanum installation to the north, I let myself drift toward Mongolia.

Though I kept my eyes peeled for the pale flashes of Fringers below, I didn't have high hopes of success as I crossed the shadow world of the dream space. Mongolia was sparsely populated outside of Ulaanbaatar, and to make matters worse, the brilliant glow of Arcanum 4—a repurposed cluster of Soviet-era concrete buildings, brought together and camouflaged with spells—washed out nearly everything around it like the full moon in a nighttime city sky. But during the last year, I'd cultivated an eye for detail, and it was that skill, plus a fair heap of luck, that showed me the lone golden flicker in the wilderness.

Given the location, I'd expected to see a ger when I descended, but to my surprise, I found myself standing outside a modern backpacker's tent, a construction of waterproof fabric stretched over bungee poles. That tent had probably come from the better end of a camping store, the kind that sells gear with detailed specifications and a suitably impressive price tag. But time and wear had been cruel—even in the shadows, I could see how ragged the cloth had become, and the structure's pronounced listing did little to inspire confidence in its stability. Puzzled, I passed through the zipped door on my hands and knees, as insubstantial as a ghost, and tried to make sense of the scene inside.

The long lump occupying most of the tent was a filthy sleeping bag, that much was clear. A backpack lay next to the opposite wall of the little tent, but not a hiker's kit—this was smaller, the sort of bag a child at a demanding school might use to carry his books. Scattered in the space between the bed and pack were a metal canteen, a plastic water bottle, and what appeared to be a waxy, empty cracker sleeve.

Before I could crawl closer to investigate, the sleeper stirred and sat up—a blond boy of perhaps twelve, I estimated, but no older. He blinked at me, squinting at my glowing form, then scooted away toward the back of the tent. "Am I dead?" he whispered.

Though speech was unaccented in the dream space, I guessed the boy was Russian—he certainly wasn't Mongolian—and I could only imagine what he was doing alone on the steppe. "No, you're very much alive," I reassured him, holding up my empty hands. "You're dreaming. I'm called Badger, and I'm with the Fringe."

His eyes narrowed in suspicion. "There is no more Fringe."

"Not many, not here. I've come to find the survivors and take you to safety." When he didn't continue his retreat, I sat back on my heels and smiled at him. "What's your name, love?"

"Sergei," he mumbled.

"Are your mum and dad around?" I asked, fearing I already knew the answer.

Sergei shook his head. "Dead. The women in black came in the night and killed them. I hid under the bed until they left, and then I ran." He considered his surroundings for a moment—I assumed he was seeing nothing but formless blackness—then looked back at me. "Are you *sure* I'm not dead?"

"Positive," I said, trying to smile.

The boy mulled over this information. "I thought I might be because I was sick when I went to sleep, and I don't feel bad anymore."

"Sick? How so?"

"My stomach hurt, and my eyes hurt, and everything was hot and cold together…" His voice drifted off, and he cocked his head as he considered me. "You're glowing."

"So are you," I pointed out.

"But you're brighter than me."

"Well, I'm a bit of a wizard, actually," I explained, and then, seeing his immediate panic, I rushed, "I only just found out. Fringe coordinator. It's all right, Sergei, I'm not going to hurt you."

I kept my hands where he could see them, and after an uncertain moment, he slowly began to relax. "You're a coordinator?" he asked.

"Last one running about over here. Listen, dear, I'm down in Beijing right now. Can you get to Ulaanbaatar? It's due east of here. I'll come up and meet you."

"How far?"

That stumped me—I was horrible at gauging distances from the air. "It's a fair distance," I admitted. "But I think I saw a road to the south. If you can get to that, then walk east…"

Sergei's face was drawn. "What if I'm still sick when I wake up? And my food and water are gone." Suddenly, he brightened as an idea occurred. "Could you make me some food, then? Or give me a healing spell? Or…I don't know, what about another blanket? My bag isn't warm enough, and the tent leaks."

He seemed so hopeful, and I hated to disappoint him. "I'm afraid I can't cast here," I began. "Magic doesn't work when you're sleepwal—"

Before I could finish the word, a woolen tartan blanket appeared in my hands, much like a throw I'd kept at my desk against drafts. I goggled in stunned silence, then slowly passed the blanket to Sergei, who beamed as he wrapped it around his shoulders. Pushing my luck, I picked up the cracker packet, which quickly filled with saltines and sealed itself shut. A glance at his canteen and a minute's concentration refilled that, too, and I smiled at the boy to disguise my unease. "Stay here. I'll find you as quickly as I can," I promised, then retreated through the tent and let my body pull me back until I could feel the firm air mattress beneath me.

I sat up and pushed myself to my feet, then tiptoed to the bath and stared in the mirror at my dark circles and mussed hair.

I'd cast in the dream space.

Dear God, I'd *cast* in there.

At that moment, I knew two things with certainty: I had to get to Mongolia, and Carey couldn't know what I had done.

We needed to hurry, that much my bleary companions agreed, but exactly how we were going to get to Sergei was a matter of debate. Tea in hand, Hua opened her laptop and tried to map a route, but the best she could suggest was a flight into Ulaanbaatar—a brief trip, assuming we could get the necessary documentation. Neither Carey nor I had brought a passport along, however, and while magically forging them would have been possible, we hesitated when we considered the possibility of having to spend quality time with the Chinese border agents. Driving was out of the question. Carey had begun to research rail routes when Hua, with a defeated sigh, picked up her mobile.

After a ten-minute conversation in rapid Mandarin, she hung up and looked at us sheepishly. "That was my mother. I had hoped not to call her, but under the circumstances..." She shrugged. "We do what we must sometimes."

Carey nodded, then glanced at me. "Mingyu is talented, but she's never been an active member of the Minor Arcanum. Every time Hua does something the slightest bit risky, the rest of us hear about it."

"*You* hear about it?" she muttered. "Her interrogation

tactics are unmatched. But anyway, she has a friend in Mosike…" Catching our blank expressions, her brow furrowed as she thought of the translation. "Uh…Moskva?"

"Moscow, yes," said Carey. "Go on."

"A wizard. She has traveled a long time—saw the world before the borders were relaxed. My mother thinks she can help us find the boy."

"That's lovely, but I don't know exactly where I left him," I cautioned. "He was in the mountains west of the capital, but I can't give her exact directions—"

Before I could finish, a gate opened in the middle of Hua's living room, and a middle-aged blonde with clattering gold bangles and a frosted updo, looking rather like she'd just come from the set of a fashion magazine photo shoot, swept into the room. Spotting Hua, she greeted our host with a smile and kisses, then held her at arm's length and clucked. Hua stood in silence while the newcomer lectured her, taking the unintelligible chiding until the blonde paused and Hua could direct her attention toward us. "Ayi, these are my friends…" was all she managed in English before the woman turned the force of her attention on us.

"Hello, how do you do?" she said, extending her hand as she strode toward us. "Zoya Fedkin."

I met her hand in a jangle of bracelets. "Hannah Parsons, pleased to meet you."

Her eyebrow quirked. "English? Hua, Mingyu said you were with Americans."

"Half right," Carey interjected, pumping Zoya's hand. "Carey Jones."

At that, Zoya's other eyebrow rose to join its mate. "Dr. Jones? I did not think you left the States."

"Well, yeah, my schedule's pretty tight, but we had business here," she said smoothly.

Hua's tension loosened a degree, and I supposed she'd realized that Carey wasn't about to rat her out.

"Nice to finally meet you, Zoya," Carey continued. "Though last I'd heard, you weren't on call for Minor Arcanum matters."

Zoya pushed up her pink silk sleeves. "I am not. But for a friend—or for my little one," she added, cutting her eyes to Hua, "who should not worry her poor mother so badly—I can make exceptions. Now, Mingyu mentioned Ulaanbaatar?"

She listened, nodding along as I filled her in on my findings, then seemed to take a decision. Reaching behind her back to extract the wand almost hidden in the folds her diaphanous blouse, Zoya pointed it at herself and whispered a word in Russian, and her finery reformed into a cotton shirt, khaki jacket, and sturdy trousers. "I have spent time in Mongolia," she explained, rolling her wand between her palms. "This is no great trouble."

I thanked her profusely as she, with a fluidity that could have been born only of long practice, cast open a gate into a cluttered cellar with a few precise flicks of her wand. "I'm afraid I can't give you his precise coordinates," I said as the rip widened, "but if we could find a guide—"

She laughed, favoring me with a sly smile. "My dear, you have one. Quickly, now. The morning is being wasted, and I have dinner plans."

Leaving Hua behind to return to her interrupted sleep, Carey and I followed Zoya into the storeroom of a café, which apparently belonged to an old chum of hers. "If he offers, do not drink the tea," she quietly cautioned as we headed up the concrete stairs toward the surface. "You will not like it."

"Strong?" Carey guessed.

"Milky and salty. And whatever you do, avoid the airag."

Zoya waved to the gap-toothed old man behind the counter, who smiled back at her in recognition, and then she hurried us out of the restaurant before there could be any suggestion of refreshments.

Half an hour later, she had negotiated the hire of a Jeep-like vehicle, large enough for the three of us but badly in need of new shocks. She took the wheel, but as I started to climb in beside her, she shook her head and pointed to the back. "You know where to find him. Sleep, see what you can see, and guide us. Carey, ride with me." We switched seats, and Zoya sighed. "The best way to see this country is on horseback. A pity you have no time."

"Maybe another day," said Carey, who clung to the door as the vehicle bounced onto the road. "Hannah, you okay back there?"

"Fine." I stretched out as well as I could across the back bench, curled my face toward the seat to block the worst of the sunlight, and tried to ignore the jostling while I made a practiced descent to the edge of sleep. For a moment, I feared that the shaking wouldn't allow me to concentrate, but then, with a silent *pop*, the world turned to shadow around me as I began to sleepwalk.

Sitting up, I saw Zoya and Carey's glowing forms in the seats in front of me, then floated out of the Jeep and spun around until I oriented myself. Rising higher, I scoured the landscape until I spotted the faint luminescence of the little witch, then flew toward his distant tent. From what I could tell, he hadn't moved in the time I'd been away, and I hoped he was sleeping off his illness. I looked about, trying to pinpoint a landmark, but the mountains blurred together, and the tent was alone on the grassy plain. Frustrated, I followed a narrow trail south until it ran into asphalt, and I made as careful a note of my surroundings as I could, given the limitations of the dream space.

Suddenly, with a jolt, I returned to my body and groaned at the sharp pain in my head. "Sorry," said Zoya, "pothole. Any success?"

I sat up, rubbing my bruised scalp, and pointed out the windscreen. "Head west until I say otherwise. I'll sleepwalk again in a bit and keep an eye on him."

The third time I dropped into the dream space, I found Carey waiting for me.

"I'll keep this brief," she said, leaning over the back of her seat as I abandoned the shadowy husk of my body. "No sense in making Zoya think we're conspiring. Whatever she does, roll with it."

"Who is she?" I asked, hanging on as the car hit yet another rough patch.

"Damn powerful."

I pointed to our driver's brilliant golden form. "Noticed."

"She's never been much of a team player. Good looking, married well, does her own thing. Best not to ask where she gets the money, know what I'm saying?"

I frowned. "You have that on good authority, or is this just speculation?"

"Little of both. Beyond that, the fact that she's here should tell you how far knowledge of the Fringe project has spread."

"Fair enough," I replied, puzzled by the strain in her voice. "We haven't exactly kept it a secret—"

"From the usual operators, no. But for *Zoya* to not only know about it, but drop everything and chauffeur us around the middle of God-knows-where…" She shrugged. "I mean, I appreciate her help, but this means our little secret isn't much of a secret anymore."

I paused, studying her drawn face. "You're worried about a leak."

"I trust my people," Carey replied. "But Zoya's barely one of them. Know what I'm saying?"

"I get the picture." When Carey made no move to wake, I asked, "What do you want to do about it?"

"Don't know," she muttered. "I don't seriously think anyone would turn you over to the Arcanum, but…"

"But shit happens," I finished. "Do you want us to move out?"

"We can talk about it later. For now…well, I suppose

the best thing to do would be to keep Zoya happy, yeah?"

"Yeah," I mumbled as she faded, then rose through the roof and flew off in search of Sergei once again.

Four hours and eight sleepwalks later, I finally guided Zoya off the road and up the barely marked path in the grass. "I don't know if this is legal," Carey began, but our driver cut her off.

"What no one knows, no one repeats," she said. "And we are not hurting anything."

Except my joints, I thought, gritting my teeth against the bumpy ride, but I held my tongue.

After another forty-five minutes of slow going, I spotted the tent—in the real world, a faded red—and called a halt. Letting myself out, I jogged toward it, grateful to feel blood in my feet and legs again, and Carey ran after me. I reached the tent first, signaled for Carey to wait, then unzipped the door and peered inside. "Sergei?" I whispered. "Hello, Sergei?"

Before I could stop her, Carey joined me at the flap. "Oh, that's not good," she said, pointing to the sleeping bag, from which a soft moaning emanated. Falling to her hands and knees, Carey crawled into the tent, then pulled back a corner of the bag to reveal the boy inside.

Sergei looked awful, pale and damp with sweat. He shivered in his sleep and muttered words I couldn't understand, and Carey dove into professional mode. "Move," she said brusquely as she lifted the child, bag and all, into her arms and knee-walked backwards out of the tent.

By then, Zoya had joined us, and she watched with concern as Carey lay Sergei in the grass and began patting his cheeks. After a few moments, his eyelids fluttered, and Zoya spoke to him in soft Russian before he could panic. Sergei's glassy eyes managed to focus on her, and he croaked out a response before slipping back into his feverish sleep.

"What did he say?" asked Carey.

Zoya turned her gaze on me. "He is glad you found him. The nice lady who gave him the blanket." She turned over the top of the sleeping back with the tip of one boot, revealing the tartan throw wrapped around Sergei's thin shoulders. "What magic is this?"

Carey's eyes widened in realization as she stared up at me, and I felt my face begin to flush. "I can explain—"

"Later," Carey almost growled, lifting the sleeping boy once again. "He needs medical help first. Open a gate home, Hannah."

"Carey, I—"

"*Open the goddamn gate!*"

Shocked into silence by her outburst, I cast the spell as quickly as I could, and the air split to reveal a welcoming sliver of the bunkhouse. "Ride with Zoya back to Ulaanbaatar," Carey ordered, then slipped through without waiting for my response.

I looked at Zoya, waved the gate closed, and awkwardly gestured to Sergei's tent. "Should we, ehm…pack this?"

She wrinkled her upturned nose, and with a flick of her wand, the campsite vanished into atoms. "Filthy. Come with me," she said, turning toward the Jeep. "This will not take long. If Carey thinks I am driving all the way back, she is a fool."

My mobile told me it was barely four in the morning once I dragged myself home to New Mexico. Zoya, who was far more experienced than I with gates, had opened one on a lonely stretch of road close to Ulaanbaatar and simply driven the Jeep through, cutting off all but the last few minutes of our return trip. Still, it took time to return the vehicle, and once Zoya led us back to the café, the friendly proprietor—a short, skinny fellow with the unlikely name of Chingis—insisted that we sit and take tea. Her mission accomplished, Zoya acceded to his request, and soon we found ourselves at a four-top with cups of the strangest brew I'd ever smelled. While Chingis drank with relish and Zoya with polite reservation, I struggled to finish my cup and wondered if I'd been too uncharitable to the iced nonsense Americans passed off as tea.

As I spoke neither Russian nor Mongolian, I could only smile and nod during the long periods in which Zoya and Chingis conversed, sipping my tea and trying to decide what on earth I was going to tell Carey when I got back. The blanket had been an accident, pure and simple—it wasn't as if I'd *tried* to cast in the dream space. Well, yes, there was the matter of the crackers and water, but she hadn't noticed those, and maybe Sergei wouldn't remember…

For crying out loud, all I'd done was give a sick child some food and a blanket! I had no reason to apologize…did I? Surely not, I'd done no harm, I told myself, then forced another sip of tea down and tried to look as if I was enjoying the experience. Carey wasn't *angry*. She was tired and stressed, and that was why she'd blown up at me. Simple. We would talk it out when I returned, and that would be that.

Ignoring my knotted stomach, which refused to go along with my forced optimism, I slipped off to Chingis's storeroom and opened a fresh gate, intending to find Carey and set things to rights. But when I arrived to the predawn darkness of the bunkhouse, I found no trace of her. Little Sergei lay unconscious in one of the private rooms, fitfully sleeping off whatever Carey had given him, but of the vet, there was no sign. Deciding that I should wait for daylight, I sloughed off my shoes and trousers, then crashed beside Seamus, grateful to be in a proper bed.

I could very well have slept until the next afternoon, and I might have done so, were it not for Carey's wake-up nudge around seven. Opening one crusty eye, I found her standing beside my bed, dressed but somewhat haggard from lack of sleep. "Morning," I mumbled, searching deep within myself for the motivation to sit up. "How is he?"

"Drugged. Penny's calling in prescriptions in my name."

Carey's voice lacked its usual warmth, and I forced myself to begin the unpleasant process of rising. "He's stable, though? And could you pass me my trousers, please?" She picked them off the chair and tossed them to me, and, modesty aside, I stood and slid them on. "What's wrong, then? You seem out of sorts."

"You're leaving today," she said calmly. "Get dressed and pack your things. You can stay for breakfast, but I want you gone this morning."

I froze, then recovered my wits enough to say, "Can I ask what I've done wrong?"

"You know damn well what you did," she replied, then marched out of my room and slammed the door on my sputtered protestations.

Two minutes later, once I was sure I was decent, I threw open the door and saw Kip and Amy sitting in the middle of the bunkhouse, wide-eyed and quiet. "Where did she go?" I demanded. They pointed toward the house, and I hurried after her.

I found Carey in the kitchen, leaning against the wall and glowering over her coffee as Zeb fried bacon and Seamus tried to change her mind. "Whatever she did, this is *Badger*," my partner pleaded. "She wouldn't do anything to hurt you, Carey! You know that!" I let the kitchen door swing closed, and Seamus wheeled about to find me. "What happened out there?" he asked, pulling me into the room and closer to our furious hostess. "Tell me what's going on. How have you two quarreled?"

"It's not a quarrel," said Carey, implacable as a glacier. "I will *not* have that monster in my house."

"*Monster?*" he echoed, looking back and forth between us. "What the devil did you—"

"It just happened!" I shouted over him, shaking as I

stared at Carey. "I didn't mean to! We talked, he asked for a blanket, I was telling him that I couldn't help him like that, and it just *appeared*. What was I supposed to do, take it with me? You saw him!"

My explanation had as much effect as a pebble tossed against the side of a mountain. "You're dangerous," she murmured. "We've risked everything sheltering you. The entire Minor Arcanum knows we're harboring Fringers— all it would take is one call to the Arcanum. *One*."

"And you told me you trusted your people!"

She placed her mug on the table and crossed her arms, ignoring my outburst. "I put a roof over your head, Hannah. Food on your plate. I don't even know how many trips to Arizona Zeb and I have made on your behalf. Hell, I taught you to sleepwalk in the first place. This is how you repay me?"

"I didn't mean—"

She cut me off with a raised hand. "You're finished here. The others can stay for now, but you're out. And if you'd repay our kindness at all, you'll go far, *far* away. Faerie would be a good start."

Seamus gripped my shoulder and steered me away from Carey. "We'll be gone by noon," he told her. "Come on, love, let's pack—"

Before we could retreat, the door banged open, and Arnold dashed inside in his damp sweats, red-faced and panting from his morning run. "Just heard," he gasped. "Kids told me. What happened?"

I looked at Carey, but when she made no move to explain, I sighed and mumbled, "I cast while sleepwalking. Didn't intend to, just happened."

Arnold leaned against the counter, catching his breath, then looked at Carey in confusion. "How is that bad? Sounds useful to me."

"The last person who could cast in the dream space was Simon Magus," said Zeb as he turned off the range. "He wiped out more than three-quarters of the wizards on this continent."

"Bloody *hell*," my cousin muttered, mopping his wet face with the dishcloth Zeb offered him. "During the Great War?"

"After the Asia conquest," I told him. "Apparently, the Americas weren't keen on joining up."

Arnold wiped off the back of his neck, then tossed the cloth over his shoulder and shrugged. "Well, if he was the last to do it, then I suppose it makes sense that you've got the knack."

"Come again?"

He looked at me strangely, then rolled his eyes as the realization dawned. "Your dad never talked much about the family, did he?"

A tendril of dread tightened around my stomach. "What about the family?"

"There's a reason the Parsons name carries so much clout, and it's not because we're a good-looking lot." Arnold leaned against the counter and met my worried stare. "We're descended from the Magus. One of the last families that can say that, actually. He had a few children before he broke his wand and went off to the monastery, you know."

"We're…" I groaned and sank into the closest chair. "Great. *Wonderful.* I could have gone my whole life without knowing that, Arnie."

"I mean, he *was* ridiculously talented. You've got a bit of that in you, yeah?" I could only shake my head, and, seeing that his attempt at comfort was an utter failure, Arnold resumed drying his face, the better to avoid our eyes.

Before Seamus could pull me out of the kitchen, Jim arrived from down the hall, his hair a squirrel's nest and his T-shirt inside out. "Are you crazy?" he snapped, pointing at his sister. "They're on our side! What are you doing kicking Hannah out?"

"Shut up, Jimmy," she barked.

Zeb reached for Jim's shoulder, but Jim brushed him off in his agitation. "Like hell I will! Hannah, if they're going to be weird, you can come stay with me. I've got a couch."

Seamus's hand tightened on mine, and I gave Jim a quick smile. "Appreciated, but I think we're going to move on. You've done more than enough, dear."

As Jim redoubled his efforts to yell sense into Carey, Zeb came around the counter with a plate of bacon. "Should be cool enough to eat," he said, holding the fragrant plate toward us like an offering. "I'll have the eggs and toast up in a few minutes."

But Seamus stepped away. "We'll find something on the road. Come on, Badge."

By the time Carey returned from the pharmacy with medicine for Sergei, Seamus and I had loaded our possessions into the back of the Suburban and were waiting as Amy, Kip, and Arnold finished their packing. Seeing Amy emerge from the bunkhouse with a cardboard box full of her unfinished wands, Carey frowned and cleared her throat. "I didn't say you had to go—"

"Package deal," Amy muttered, tossing her hair from her eyes as she carried the carton toward the vehicle. "Where they go, I go. Teamwork, you know?" Seamus took the box from her, and she headed back to the bunkhouse for her clothes. "Besides, I'm sure you'd like to have your privacy again."

Carey said nothing as Kip and Arnold brought their bags to join the luggage pile, but Zeb joined her and watched until we'd emptied the bunkhouse. Once the others had loaded into the SUV, Seamus cracked his knuckles and cocked his head toward the building. "I'll give the kid the language he needs, and we'll be on our way," he told the Joneses.

While Seamus enchanted the sleeping boy, I took a

final look around the building—our home for the last year—then swallowed the up-swelling lump and composed myself. Finding Jim standing forlornly by the door, I gave him a tight hug and murmured, "Call us if you need us. We'll be all right."

His eyes were wet when he released me, but he held himself together while he shook Seamus's hand and followed us to the Suburban. "I'll see that Sergei gets to Faerie, okay?" he called as Seamus started the engine.

"Give us a ring when you need to arrange pickup," I replied, then slammed my door and sneaked a last glance at the Joneses—Carey, ramrod-straight and as unyielding as steel, and Zeb, who had wrapped one arm around her taut shoulders as if she were the one in need of comfort. Seamus beeped the horn, and then we were off, accelerating down the long drive while the grazing mares watched us from the fenced pastures.

I lasted five miles before I broke down in ugly, angry, embarrassed sobs, and Seamus held my hand until I fell asleep against the window.

CHAPTER 9

When I woke again, the car had stopped at a McDonald's. Though my empty stomach complained, my face was gritty with yesterday's dirt and that morning's dried tears, and the thought of going inside to eat was nearly enough to put me off my breakfast.

As if he'd read my thoughts—which, to be fair, he might have done—Seamus handed a few bills to Arnold and asked, "Would you get us a couple of sandwiches or something, please?"

Arnold, who was clever enough to take a hint, escorted Kip and Amy into the restaurant, leaving me alone with my partner and the muted screams of a tantruming toddler on the playground. "All right, then?" Seamus murmured.

I shook my head.

"This isn't your fault, Badge—"

"Then whose is it?" I snapped. "I don't see the rest of you mucking everything up."

He leaned across the center console and hugged me, and I relaxed into the security of his arms. "It's going to be all right. Everything's going to be all right, love. You haven't hurt anything."

I clenched my jaw as my throat tightened in warning. "But I have. Carey's scared of me, and I—"

"You are *not* a monster," he whispered into my dirty hair. "So you had a distant ancestor who went on a conquering spree—so what? Would you like to discuss my grandmother? I'm *still* hearing stories." I laughed in spite of myself, and he tightened his hold on me. "We're just changing bases, that's all. Seeing the sights. You didn't want to live in New Mexico forever, did you?"

"Seamie…"

"Shh." He rubbed my back before he pulled back, then frowned, licked his thumb, and swiped at a streak of grime on my chin.

I swatted him away and finished the job myself with the visor mirror, then leaned back against the seat and closed my puffy eyes. "Where are we going? Where *can* we go? Do you know of another natural gate?"

"Well, I don't know if it's *natural*, but I do remember another gate," he replied, then waited until I looked at him. "Virginia. That little town where Coileán dumped us—Rigby, right? We went through a gate from his office into Stuart's old flat. He didn't close the gate all the way, remember? Just shrank it. What if we made camp there?"

"I mean, yeah, I remember it, but the whole reason we left Rigby in the first place is because the Arcanum was watching it," I pointed out.

"*Was.* It's been more than a year, and you know they've been circling their wagons—what makes you think they have anyone left in Rigby to watch for disturbances?" Before I could object, he rushed, "Think about it, Badge: we'd have our own building, plenty of space, and a gate right there! No more hikes in Sedona, no more being underfoot at the ranch…"

"If someone isn't already living there. And you realize this means we'll have to start cooking for ourselves."

"Hamburgers are easy. Come on, let's give it a try. What do we have to lose but petrol and a couple of days on the road? I've already routed it," he added, showing me his mobile. "We'll go by, scout out the building, see if anyone's moved in, and if not, we'll forge something showing that Stuart's sold us the place. Sound like a plan?"

"I suppose." The toddler's displeasure had advanced to the point of rolling on the artificial turf and howling. "And if we need a backup plan?"

Seamus hesitated. "There's always Faerie," he said, but seeing my expression, he put up his hands and added, "That's Plan C, at least. Maybe Plan D. It's just a plan."

"Right, because they're going to be thrilled to have a magus and a centaur running about over there."

"I didn't say it was a perfect plan," he replied, then pointed through the glass as the rest of our party emerged with cups and paper sacks. "Here's to Plan A," he said, taking my hand. "This is just a setback, love—we'll get through this together." As the others climbed back into the vehicle and Arnold passed us a grease-spotted bag of breakfast, Seamus looked at them over his shoulder and grinned. "Right, she's agreed. Rigby it is."

We made camp the first night just over the Arkansas border at a run-down motel outside of Fort Smith, the sort of establishment at which the staff sees and hears little as long as the television remains bolted to the furniture and the police have no cause to drop by. Seamus and I made the arrangements, paying for two rooms in cash, and Arnold chaperoned the kids while my partner and I huddled together on a questionable mattress, still feeling the road beneath us. I made no attempt to sleepwalk, but even with my emotional and mental exhaustion, I listened to Seamus's soft breathing for nearly an hour before I slipped into unquiet rest.

The next morning, after Arnold restored the other room to its former decrepitude—leery of the bedding, he had created a pair of pillow-top, vermin-free mattresses—we grabbed a quick bite at the Waffle House across the street and resumed our trek east on I-40. Having finally slept, I took the keys from Seamus and gave him a turn at handling the music, and we pressed on through Arkansas and Tennessee, calling a halt between Knoxville and the Interstate split. All of us were restless when we pulled into the motel—a Holiday Inn that time, questioning clerks be

damned, as Arnold's talk of bedbugs had made me itchy—
and after dinner, while Amy hit the hotel treadmill, Kip ran
around the spottily-lit streets until he was winded and
glistening with sweat.

The landscape improved the following day as we left I-
40 for I-81 and followed the rolling, verdant spine of the
Appalachians to the northeast, such a change from the arid
beauty of the Southwest that I'd come to know.
Eventually, we peeled southeast on I-64 to Richmond, and
then our map led us down a series of increasingly smaller
highways until we reached sleepy Rigby and the sea.

That night, we stood together beneath a wooden beach
pavilion and listened to the waves crash and retreat,
breathing the salt air in comfortable silence. I didn't know
if we were safe—I could never be certain, in any case—but
in that moment, leaning against Seamus and watching an
old beach walker's bobbing torch as he passed, I let myself
imagine that we could start over.

"Slow down, that's the place," said Seamus.

I tapped the brake, and the SUV crawled down the
town's quiet main street, past a row of mom-and-pop
stores and lampposts hung with civic beautification baskets
of flowers. Our target was obvious: a boarded-up,
padlocked, two-story brick storefront with a swinging
metal sign that proclaimed, in a vaguely Celtic script and a
flourish of blue-green swirls, *The Endless Knot.* The
plywood covering the plate-glass windows was winter-
weathered and graffitied, and a sad drift of dead leaves
from the previous autumn clung to the edge of the
building like stubborn mold. The narrow alley between the
building and its neighbor seemed maintained, but a
glimpse toward the rear of the structure revealed healthy
green tendrils of weeds growing out of the gravel on the
seaward side. Granted, the building across the street was
just as derelict, but only one of them was surrounded by a

deactivated ward system, a barely visible network of magic that crisscrossed the air like a massive fence.

There was little traffic at six that morning, and I whipped across the road to park in front of the abandoned store. "Well, obviously, Stuart didn't construct *that*," I said, pointing to the faint traces of the dormant wards.

"He'd have to be one hell of a wizard to have pulled that off," Arnold concurred behind me. "That's some tight spellcraft."

"I don't think it is," I replied, and let myself out for a better look. After a glance up and down the street, I placed my hand against the wards and pushed, trying to power up the magical fence, but despite my efforts, the attempt worked about as well as lighting a damp match. Stepping back, I beckoned my partner closer. "Go on, Seamie, give it a try."

He obliged after a moment's hesitation, but he'd barely touched the construction before it glowed to life under his fingertips. "*Whoa*," he whispered, leaning back to see how the wards ran over the top of the building. "That's...huh."

Arnold's mouth tightened as he studied the wards, a much easier task once they were fully visible to us. "Atypical for enchantment," he finally declared. "Almost *too* neat to be anything but spellcraft. You think Coileán made this?"

"It was his place before it was Stuart's," I replied.

My cousin nodded appreciatively. "All right, the old boy's good. Shut it down."

Seamus did so, albeit reluctantly. A ward system would have been a boon to us—the more protection we could cobble together in a strange town, the better—but any wizard who happened upon us couldn't have missed us with that fence glowing like a pulsing beacon. If the Arcanum's operatives were still keeping an eye on Rigby, we couldn't take the risk.

A quick inspection of the property was all we needed to ascertain that it was truly abandoned. The windows were boarded tight, every door was locked, and even the garage door appeared to have been left alone. As we rounded the corner from the alley toward our car, a couple in running clothes approached us on the sidewalk, pushing a double pram. "Pardon me," said Arnold, lifting his hand to get their attention, "but do you know if anyone's been in here for the last few months?"

The couple stopped and looked at each other, and the young mother shook her head. "No, neither one of them," she said, pointing from the warded building to its mate across the street. "There was a weirdo in here, sold New Age stuff for a while, and I think his grandma or something ran the old tea parlor over there until she died. But he skipped town a while back…" She looked at her husband again, then made a face and lowered her voice. "No one knows why. One day he was here, the next, it looked like someone had ransacked the store, and he was gone." She paused, sizing the three of us up, then asked, "Y'all visiting?"

"Not exactly," said Arnold, smooth as silk in the face of her questioning. "The fellow who used to own this place—Stuart Purcell, yes?"

"Sounds familiar," the husband chimed in.

Arnold stifled a laugh. "Stu is my brother's wife's brother. Free spirit if there ever was one." Dropping to a conspiratorial murmur, he said, "He was involved with some neo-pagan nonsense, people going into the woods and trying to cast spells and all that rubbish. Dick—that's my brother, Dick—still hasn't been able to get a straight answer out of him, but as far as he can tell, Stu got on the wrong side of the grand poohbah or whatnot, and so he skipped town. Packed up and moved to Oregon, of all places. I think he was afraid she'd cursed him," he added, and chuckled.

The couple laughed along with him and shook their heads. "Imagine," said the wife, "actually being afraid of *magic*. How gullible do you have to be to buy into that stuff?"

"Don't get Stu started—if you give him a chance, he'll tell you all about sasquatches and fairies and trolls," Arnold replied, grinning as the couple continued to laugh. "Anyway, long story short, Stu doesn't plan to come back, and his niece just graduated and is looking for a place to live, so he's sold her the building. Doesn't look like he's paid the property taxes, does it?" he added, thumbing his hand at the boarded-over windows. "Well, I'm based in D.C., and the little lamb's like family—I mean, she's Dick's wife's niece, so we're all practically kin—so I said I'd bring her down and see what crazy Uncle Stu has dropped in her lap. Arnold Parsons," he lied, extending his hand toward the pram.

The couple introduced themselves, Arnold explained me away as his visiting cousin and Seamus as my partner, and after final pleasantries, the locals wandered on. When we were safely back in the Suburban, Seamus asked, "Do you think it was wise to give them your real name?"

"What, Arnold? Why would that set off alarms? Not like I'm announcing myself as Magus Lowe, and besides, those two wouldn't know magic if their kitchen table started tap dancing," he scoffed. "I sincerely doubt they're Arcanum spies. Now," he said, buckling his seatbelt, "let's retrieve the kids and find the tax office. I do hope Amy doesn't mind being Stuart's niece for now. How strange was he, anyway?"

"*Is* he," I replied. "No word yet that he's come to harm, though I'd feel so much better about letting him go to Montana if he'd ever write. But yeah, the poor man is, ehm…special."

Arnold's eyebrows rose. "Special?"

"Thinks he's a wizard because he's *certified*."

"Oh." He looked pained. "Oh, no. Did you disabuse him of the notion?"

"We did our best, but…" I shrugged. "Special."

For all the trouble we can cause, there are certain perks to having a wizard around. For instance, let's suppose you're a seventeen-year-old girl who'd like to pass off a forged bill of sale on a piece of property, pay the back taxes, and set up housekeeping. Sure, you could find someone with computer skills to tweak your ID and cross your fingers at the county office, but it's ever so much easier to let a wizard alter your learner's permit into a proper driving license, pull together a convincing document, and cast a subtle spell on the clerk so that the handwriting on your forgery seems to match the exemplar on file. The ability to create large sums of cash through spellcraft doesn't hurt, either.

By mid-afternoon, Arnold and Amy had returned in triumph with the paperwork and receipts, and Amy had a new swagger in her step as she welcomed us all into her humble abode. "Cheeky," I said as I carried my bags past her. She laughed, then caught a lungful of the dust inside the shop and took a much-deserved coughing fit.

Aside from the boards on the windows, which we left in place for privacy, the three of us with talent spent the rest of the day cleaning and reconfiguring the building into habitability. Our first stop, however, was the upstairs flat's living room, which we found much as we'd left it the year before, but for a thicker layer of dust and cobwebs. Seamus and I pushed Stuart's cheap wooden entertainment center down the wall, then returned to the cleared space to inspect the plaster. There, we found a tiny hole, barely large enough for my thumb, through which a steady stream of magic flowed. I released the breath I'd been holding and grinned at Seamus, who mimed wiping his brow. "At least the gate's still here," he said to Arnold, who'd been watching from the dirty dinette. "One problem down, eh?"

For easier access, I created a large seascape in oils, nothing notable, and hung it over the gate. Even with the hole covered, magic seeped out from behind the faux-gilded frame, but there was nothing we could do about it. "Besides," said Arnold, inspecting my work, "if anyone's watching Rigby, they're probably using a detector to look for fluctuations in the background magic. This has been constantly leaking for a while, yeah? No change means no one develops an interest." He gave it another moment's consideration, then said, "Assuming there *is* background monitoring, we'll need to be judicious about using this gate. Widening it would show up as a surge of magic…"

"If you're paranoid," said Seamus, "you know the way to Sedona."

My cousin wasn't a great fan of canyon hikes, but he shrugged. "It's caution, not paranoia. But we'll cross that bridge when we must."

With the matter of the gate sorted, we turned our attention to the rest of the flat. Aside from the modest living room, the place had a decent kitchen—fortunately, we'd binned the spoilt food on our last visit—which flowed into a dining nook slightly set off from the living room. Down a short hallway were a full bathroom and two bedrooms, one of which had been serving as Stuart's office and storage unit. Having been given the tour, Arnold scowled at the setup and shook his head. "This will hardly do. One bath for five people—"

"Forget the bath," I interrupted. "Two bedrooms aren't enough."

"Well, if the kids share and I take the couch…all right, no," he muttered, seeing my dark look. "Honestly, I don't think they'd mind."

"Remember, we're supposed to be the responsible ones," said Seamus, running one hand over his glamoured stubble. "All right, what if we closed off part of the shop and made another bedroom and bath? Take the area around the stairs, wall it off…we could go wild and make two bedrooms down there so that no one need share."

"Except you two," Arnold pointed out.

"Naturally. Put you up here with us, the kids

downstairs, and no one cramps anyone's style."

His mouth twitched. "I thought the goal was to be responsible and keep them apart."

"We're not *actually* their parents," said Seamus. "Putting them in separate rooms is responsible. Should they fool around, that's on them, and I'd rather not know about it. Agreed?"

"Agreed," Arnold muttered with a grimace.

Begging Amy to be careful and keep to the speed limit—and feeling the teensiest bit hypocritical in so doing—I handed her the keys to the Suburban and sent her off with Kip to shop. True, the three of us could have stocked the kitchen with magic alone, especially with that convenient leak into Faerie hiding behind the painting, but I thought it best to keep the kids out of the way while we decided the arrangements. I watched from the door as Amy slowly backed out of the garage, sliding past cardboard crates of Stuart's odds and ends, and then they set off for the Kroger in the next town over, part of our plan to maintain a low profile in Rigby until we had the lay of the land. With them out of the house, Arnold and I made short work of the flat, banishing Stuart's furniture to the ether, repainting, and polishing the old wooden floors until they gleamed. By the time we'd spruced up the kitchen and renovated the bathroom—Arnold wanted a Jacuzzi tub, and I wasn't inclined to argue with him on that point—Seamus had reconfigured the store on the ground floor so that the staircase was completely walled off from the public space. A door from the shop now opened onto a tiny foyer, from which another door led into a bedroom, a shared bath, and a second bedroom nestled beneath the stairs. "I could cut another door through the wall here," he offered as he showed us his work, but we decided that we were better off with fewer unlockable routes.

Leaving the assignment of the bedrooms to the kids, we emptied the store, moving all of Stuart's wares into a bookcase-lined storeroom...well, all but a collection of gemstone-studded wind chimes that I fancied and a heavy set of geode bookends that Arnold lugged up to his room. With that accomplished, we stepped back and took stock of what was left: a generous shop space with a twelve-foot ceiling, one wall of exposed brick, and original wooden floors, dotted with an assortment of merchandise tables, a pair of repurposed china hutches, and a long wooden counter at the rear, complete with antique cash register and shelving beneath for special orders. Once the boards were down and the shades up, I imagined the place would be nice, well-lit and almost airy if we were careful with the furnishings.

"Now what?" said Seamus, mopping his sweaty brow with his T-shirt.

"Now we come up with a cover story," I replied. "Amy's got the building—what's she to do with it?"

The rumbling of the garage door cut short our musings, and shortly, Amy and Kip came in the back, arms laden with reusable totes. "The Cheetos are *mine*," she said by way of greeting, "but I'll share." She looked around the tidied shop, frowning. "Uh…someone want to tell us where the stairs went?"

Once the groceries were put away and the kids had used the time-honored rock–paper–scissors method of determining who got the bedroom with the outside door, Arnold and I fixed up their rooms, Seamus conjured a couple of pizzas, and we settled in around the living room for dinner by candlelight. "Better see about getting the power and water turned on in the morning," I told the others between bites. "And gas, I suppose. I didn't look at the water tank or the dryer…"

"They're gas," Seamus confirmed with his mouth full. "I mean, we don't *have* to—"

"But it'll look odd if we don't." I refilled my Sprite and leaned against the plush leather couch I'd made. "And how are we going to explain the rest of us loitering around here? Amy owns the place, Arnold's her sort-of uncle…"

"You're my cousin, Seamus is with you, and Kip's with Amy," said Arnold. "What if she's opening a shop, and we're here to help her get started? A little adult guidance can't be that objectionable, can it?"

"What sort of shop?" asked Kip. "She can't sell her wands in the open, can she?"

"Yeah, that would be a 'no,'" Amy replied. "If folks around here think Stuart was weird, then I'm not going to do anything to make the situation worse. The crafting's going to be a strictly back-room operation."

Arnold wiped tomato sauce from his cheek and grinned. "Pity. 'Levey's Fine Wands' has such a nice ring to it. A new sign, some velvet for the display windows…"

My guts clenched as he chuckled. "*Shit*. Amy, when you filled out the paperwork today—"

She shook her head and pulled her new license from her wallet for my inspection. "Amy Wilcox is five years older than Amelia Levey. If anyone in Charleston is still looking for me, I'm not going to ping on their radar."

"Let's hope," I replied, though my heart rate was already slowing. "So what would you like to do, Ms. Wilcox? A bit of light retail? Art studio? Palm reading and tarot?"

"Web design."

Arnold frowned. "You hardly need a storefront like this for web design…"

"Web design and minor tech assistance, then," she said, tearing off a fresh slice of pizza. "I did a handful of mockups when I was still in school—they're all in the cloud, so I can tidy them up and get one of you to make some glossy sample material. It'll take me a day or two to build my own page, and then I'll need to put out fliers…" She bit into the pizza and chewed as she contemplated.

Kip tapped her shoulder to get her attention. "What can I do, then?"

"You?" She chugged back half her Coke and stifled a belch. "Want to learn? It'll be fun," she hastened to assure him. "Whatever jobs I get, I walk you through them, and you'll have the basics in no time. Oh, and I'll get you a few books—shouldn't take you long to figure out HTML, but I want you to be comfortable with the hardware side of things, too…"

As Amy's excited chatter picked up its pace, I looked at Seamus, who shrugged bemusedly and stretched out his hand to offer me a little plastic tub. "Garlic sauce?"

Wilcox Webworks and PC Repair had its grand opening the following Monday, which was "grand" only in the sense that Amy ceremonially unlocked the front door and announced, "Ta-dah!" to our applause.

While she had spent much of the previous week ordering parts and tools—a process made much simpler with a credit card running on spellcraft—the less tech-savvy among us had done our bit to bring the store up to her specifications, adding comfortable chairs and display easels, moving the shelves into place along one wall, and hanging a flat-screen television that doubled as an impressive monitor. We had Internet service on Friday, and once the technician had departed, Amy pulled Kip aside for a long, intense discussion about how it all worked. She had then opened up a series of shipping cartons, extracted a large laptop, a book, and several slim boxes, and set Kip up on a stool at the back counter with instructions to install a series of programs and remove all conceivable bloatware. Kip was still no expert when Monday rolled around, but at least he had learned how to reset the router and work the Keurig, and Amy seemed pleased with his progress.

The neon green leaflets that we had tacked to community bulletin boards and tucked under windscreen wipers over the weekend seemed to have done the trick, as Amy had her first customer before noon, a pensioner with a misbehaving computer. She took notes as he relayed the problem, offered him a chair, a cup of coffee, and the remote to the television, then sat next to Kip for the next hour as she cleaned half a dozen viruses off of his machine. The man thanked her profusely and bought the antivirus software she suggested, and Amy waved him on his way, having made more than enough money for dinner. I pulled a dollar bill from the wad, smoothed it flat, then quickly framed it and hung it above the cash register in commemoration.

The first week was short—all of Rigby seemed to close for the Kiwanis Club's Independence Day barbeque and fireworks at the beach that Tuesday—but Amy considered it a success. Though she had yet to receive any enquiries about websites, she had done odd jobs for a steady stream of befuddled seniors and neighborhood shopkeepers in need of new chargers and printer paper. "I didn't think I'd get much interest in design work," she explained Friday night as we celebrated at Szechuan Garden, Rigby's lone Asian restaurant. "Not in this town, and not at first. No one knows me, yeah? But offer basic repairs and parts, and suddenly, people figure out where I am. For a lot of my customers, I'm just doing the stuff their grandkids would do," she added with a smile. "Easy money."

Dinner was on the house that night, as Amy had made the owner's ancient computer communicate with his wireless printer that afternoon.

But while Amy basked in the glow of modest entrepreneurial success and Kip read manuals late into the evening, I walked the midnight streets of Rigby in an effort to delay sleep, my nightly reminder that I was shirking my duties.

My sole purpose for being in the mortal realm was to find hiding Fringers and ferry them to safety. For a year, I'd put my life and my companions' lives on the line to do just that, and by almost any metric, we'd had a good run of it to that point. But since we'd left New Mexico, we hadn't made contact with a single target—not a soul in nearly a fortnight, the longest drought I'd had since learning to sleepwalk. Seamus and Arnold had been pulling shifts on a computer up in the flat, looking for activity on the old Fringe network, but the boards were silent, and of course, no one hiding out there could access the new network. The only way we were going to find anyone was for me to resume my nightly scouring of the dream space.

And I couldn't.

Oh, I remembered *how*—I could have sleepwalked at any time. What held me back was the fear of what I'd find there. Would Carey be waiting, furious and accusing me of crimes I'd never dream of committing? What about the others sleepwalkers I'd come to know, Hua and Jean-Claude and the rest? Surely Carey had warned them about me. What would they say when we met again?

Reluctant to find out, I walked the physical streets, telling myself that I was learning the town and looking out for trouble. I wandered through the square, past the competing churches and the squat mayor's office, and paused outside the glowing frosted window of the police station when a pang of homesickness made my eyes prick. I strolled past benches bearing donor plaques and wheelie bins put at the curb for predawn pickup, past scrounging feral cats and the occasional confused seagull, past closed shops and empty storefronts and a padlocked corner building whose window read *Slim's*, and I tried not to dwell on all the people and places and things and memories we Fringers had lost. On occasion, I ended up at the town's lone remaining bar, a beachfront establishment whose seaward wall could be rolled up like a garage door when the weather was fine—and it often was in Rigby on those nights, warm and breezy beneath a partly cloudy sky that disappeared into the starless sea. I'd buy a pint of whatever was local and on tap, take it onto the deck, and gaze into the distance as if I could stare all the way to home. By the time I dragged myself back to our building, the others were always asleep, and I'd tell myself that I could sleepwalk tomorrow, always tomorrow.

But that Friday night, as I watched the Atlantic throw itself against the sand, I nearly dropped my beer when Seamus came up behind me and called my name. "Want some company?" he asked, giving me a half-smile and raising his glass in greeting. "No need to drink alone, Badger."

I nodded, and he stood beside me in comfortable silence, both of us working on our pints while a girl and her Lab played on the beach with a glow-in-the-dark Frisbee. When our glasses were dry and the dog was finally winded, Seamus murmured, "I love you, Hannah Parsons. Don't do this to yourself."

Surprised to hear him call me by my name, I hesitated. "I'm not—"

"You think I don't know why you've been out late all these last nights? I'm not blind, love, and you're not hard to track."

"You *followed* me?"

He nodded, unapologetic. "Strange town, moderate risk of Arcanum, and you wandering the streets like you're out for a stroll in the park? Of course I followed you."

His explanation made sense, though it left me no less miffed. "I'm perfectly capable of taking care of myself, Malone."

"Sure, when you're actually paying attention. The fact that you didn't notice me kind of proves my point, eh?"

I snorted and looked back at the ocean. "It's cheating if you're invisible."

"I wasn't. And that's what worries me."

His fingers laced through mine as we stood together at the railing.

"We've all got our hang-ups," he said softly. "Carey just happens to think you're the antichrist right now, but something tells me she's a *wee* bit off-base. You help people, Badge. You protect them. Always have. That's something I admire about you, you know."

"Doing my job," I mumbled.

"Bollocks. You're a crusader, my dear, and you're doing the right thing. Don't let her tell you you're not." He squeezed my hand and leaned closer to my ear. "Come on, let's go home. Get out there and see what you can see. Or let me take you on a proper holiday, eh?"

I turned and smiled up at him. "Majorca?"

"Could do. I was also thinking, you know, there's this adorable little town in Faerie, lovely people, all-you-can-eat pasta night…no?"

"Not yet," I said, but kissed him. "I've got a crusade to win, haven't I?"

That night, with Seamus holding me, I closed my eyes and slipped into the dream space as effortlessly as if I were plunging into a warm pool. It felt good to be back, to float free of my body and the confines of physicality, and I let myself rise high above the eastern seaboard until I could barely make out the distinctions between the shadow earth and sea.

For a change, I directed myself northward and passed into Canada, orienting myself by the familiar constellations of known wizards scattered across the country. Suddenly, as I neared Québec, I saw a bight gold shape rising and sped toward it. "Hello!" I called, trying to hail the sleepwalker. "Jean-Claude, hello! Are you busy?"

The old man paused in his ascent, giving me a moment's glance at his fearful expression, then winked out of the dream space.

And there I hung, alone above the sleeping world, and understood that his departure had been no accident.

CHAPTER 10

I had known despair in the time since the Fringe unraveled, but I was also no stranger to stressful situations, and I was generally able to hold myself together.

Not now. Cast out not only by the Joneses, whom I'd considered friends and mentors, but also by the entire Minor Arcanum, I found the idea of climbing out of bed as ridiculous as if someone had suggested that I summit Everest in a bikini. What was the point of trying, anyway? I was at best useless, unable to control my own power; at worst, I was a danger to anyone in my path, a pariah for good reason. I'd failed as a coordinator—I never even knew the Arcanum was upon us until the assault was past and my parents had bled out. I'd lost my community, my *family*, because I wasn't strong enough to fight back. And now that I'd finally found a new community, I'd betrayed them all. Of course they'd rejected me. I brought nothing but death.

Seamus—my poor, darling Seamie—tried his best to rouse me in the days that followed my disastrous return to the dream space, but I rebuffed him. Telling him I needed to sleepwalk to make up for lost time, I instead allowed myself to sleep, ripping off the bedclothes as I thrashed in my nightmares. He knew me well enough to know I was lying to him, but Seamus continued to bring me mugs of instant soup and tried to tempt me with descriptions of the perfect summer beach that awaited beyond the walls of my self-made prison, all to no avail. I ate little, left my bed only when nature insisted, and kept the shades drawn.

I spent nearly a week lounging about in depressed quasi-hibernation, and then, one afternoon, my mobile rang.

Waking at the snippet of song, I pried my gummy eyes open, untangled myself from the sheets, and pawed at the nightstand until my fingers found my prize in the shaded bedroom. The limited light was on the wane, and I could hear no voices in the flat with me—either everyone was in the shop or they'd gone off to enjoy the day. Rubbing my eyes clear, I squinted at the screen while it came into focus, then frowned at the unidentified caller. The number wasn't from a US or UK line, that much I could tell, but all else was a mystery.

If only to stop the song, I tapped the line open and held the phone to my ear. "Yes?" I mumbled.

"Hannah, my dear, is that you?" asked a smooth female voice with an unmistakably Russian accent. Still, it took a moment before my rusty gears squealed together.

"*Zoya!*" I cried, sitting up in my messy bed. "Is this—"

"Ah, good, you remember me. I had worried you might have forgotten," she replied, her tone betraying a hint of a chuckle. "How are you, Hannah? Busy, I assume?"

I blinked at the wreckage of my nest—half-emptied mugs on the dresser, most of the duvet on the floor—and tried to sound more upbeat than I felt. "Oh, you know…little of this, little of that."

Clutching my mobile as if I could keep Zoya with me through touch alone, I desperately hoped that she hadn't yet heard of my banishment from the Minor Arcanum. Zoya had been so kind in my time of need, willing to run to my assistance and chauffeur me all over Mongolia on my mad quest. If she rejected me, too…

To my relief, she sounded pleasant, almost upbeat, as she spoke. "I apologize if this is a bad time for a call. I had to ask around until I found your number, and once I had it, I didn't want to wait."

"Oh, no trouble at all," I said, willing myself to project

an auditory aura of competence. "What can I do for you?"

She paused for the space of a long breath, just enough to make my inner senses prick up. "I need your help. Your particular...*skills*."

I closed my eyes and listened to what she wasn't telling me. "Zoya," I said slowly, choosing my words, "I don't know if you've heard, but I, ehm...I'm not on the best of terms with the Minor Arcanum at the mo—"

"That does not matter to me."

What should have been reassuring instead left me on alert. "Well, then, in that case, what do you need from me?"

Zoya sighed deeply. "It is my husband," she murmured. "He's having difficulty, and I need a friend to help us."

"Your husband?"

"Yes, my Mischa. He..." She hesitated again, a calculated breath in a prepared speech. "For six years, Mischa has been in business with a partner, Alexei. He made the agreement without truly knowing him. Alexei...he is a bad man, Hannah, the worst of men," she continued, speeding up as her agitation increased. "I've seen him beat his wife, hit his children...mistreat his employees..."

She fell silent, and, impatient, I followed my part in her script. "Yes?"

"And now, he is trying to cheat us out of everything. The company, our savings, our daughters' future...Mischa's reputation, Alexei will destroy him—"

"I'm very sorry to hear that you're having business difficulties," I said, cutting her short, "but I don't see how I can help you. Honestly, none of this sounds like it's at all in my wheelhouse."

Zoya paused again, and I knew in that pregnant silence what she had in mind.

"Mischa is a witch," she said softly. "So is Alexei."

I said nothing that time, letting her hang in the space

she'd created.

"I know what you can do," she pressed. "I saw it with the boy—Sergei, wasn't that his name? Poor little fellow. You made him a blanket, did you not?"

"By accident," I replied, resisting the urge to clench my teeth.

"But still, you made it," she purred. "In the dream space. You can cast in your sleep."

My fingers gripped the phone so tightly that they hurt. "A fluke, nothing more."

"You're too modest, Hannah. Your gift is remarkable." She waited for a response that didn't come, and when she spoke again, there was a hint of a smirk in her tone. "Power is a beautiful thing, dear. It should be celebrated, not shunned. I know what the others have been saying about you. I know what they've done to you. The things I hear these days…well, they certainly aren't kind."

I pushed the unspoken offer aside—hearing the rumors circulating about me wouldn't have helped the situation or my depression. "Appreciated, but as it stands—"

"Dr. Jones is a fool and a coward," she interrupted. "Why else would she drive away the greatest wizard of our age?"

"I hardly think *that's* accurate."

"Again, you are too modest. But I digress." Zoya's voice dropped to a seductive near-whisper. "I cannot sleepwalk, I'm not as talented as you. But other wizards have allowed me into the dream space on occasion. A sleepwalker can pull *any* wizard in, can't she?"

There was no point in lying to her. "I, ehm…I suppose…"

"What about a witch?"

"Probably," I allowed, liking our conversation less by the second. "Witch or wizard, it's all a question of degree."

"Then do this for me—a favor in turn, if you like, for my help in Mongolia. Find Alexei when he sleeps. I will tell you where to look. When you have him…"

She didn't need to finish that sentence to make her request plain, and she knew it.

Suddenly cold, I took a deep breath to keep myself from flinging my mobile across the room. "You're asking me to murder your husband's business partner?"

"He's a terrible man. It would be a kindness to us all."

"You in particular."

"Yes, Mischa and I would stand to benefit," said Zoya, sounding remarkably blasé about the affair, "but so would his family. His employees. His—"

"I don't know who or what you think I am," I interjected, unable to control my surging anger any longer, "but I am *not* a contract killer. How dare you! A 'favor,' indeed…"

"Yes, I suppose that was the wrong word." Though she still sounded unruffled, her voice hardened and sharpened, an unsheathed blade on the other end of the line. "This is repayment, Hannah. I am not a charity."

I stared at the wall, barely conscious that I was shaking my head in disbelief. "You helped me locate a sick child, and in return, you want me to *kill* a man? Are you mad?"

"Not at all. Do this for me, and our account is settled. If you won't…well."

"Well *what?*" I snapped. "If you're going to threaten me, go ahead and spit it out."

She chuckled. "Honestly, I'd hoped we would not reach this point. If you refuse to help me, then I will have no choice but to speak with certain…*friends*…of mine. They happen to be members of the Arcanum."

That smothered the fire in my veins, but even the embers were sufficient to propel me onward. "And say what? That you're a wizard living outside of the Arcanum's control and want to make amends?"

"Hardly. My associates are well aware of my feelings toward the organization. But since they have been considerate enough to overlook my non-allegiance, it would only be fair of me to repay their consideration with useful information. I should tell them that there's still an uncontrolled Fringe group active in this realm. Recruiting, even. And Faerie has been assisting them. This, my friends would find most interesting."

Her tone, which she carefully modulated to disguise the edge of the threat, only served to infuriate me. "This is nothing short of blackmail, Zoya."

"As I said, I had hoped we would not reach this point."

"You're talking about jeopardizing innocent people," I pressed, trying to appeal to her better sensibilities. "The Arcanum is holding Fringers hostage to keep Faerie at bay. What you're threatening to do could kill them all."

"And I would rather not," she replied.

"Zoya, they've taken *children*."

"A pity."

The silence stretched between us, marred only by the pounding in my head, as I tried to find a way to negotiate with her. Finally, I said, "Whatever this man has done to you and your husband, unless he has personally killed entire families, it pales beside the possibility of what the Arcanum could do if they found us. *All* of us, not just the ones they're holding captive. What do you want to do, lead them to the Joneses' doorstep? You think they'll 'overlook' Carey and Zeb?"

"No," she said simply, "I don't. Which is why I'm giving you three days to think about my proposition."

"Zoya, please—"

"Let me know, and I'll tell you where to find Alexei."

"I—"

"It's still Thursday on your side of the world, yes? Think about it over the weekend, if you like. I'll call on Monday if I don't have your response by then."

"For God's sake," I pleaded, "you can't—"

The phone clicked and buzzed in my hand, and I stared at it as if it were a living thing that had sprouted teeth while my back was turned.

Part of me—the rational part, the part that

remembered the benefits of teamwork—insisted that I find the others and break the news. At least Seamus needed to know, the little voice insisted. Surely Arnold could help, if in no other capacity than as a sounding board. Perhaps I could shelter the kids for a time, but they deserved to know if there was a heightened chance that the Arcanum could come in the night. And the Joneses—they would have to be warned, given time to run…

But another part, centered largely in the boulder in my stomach, told me to keep my mouth shut. I'd made this mess, and it was up to me to fix it, whatever that entailed. There was no sense in pouring more blood on my comrades' hands.

And so I put the mobile back on the nightstand, straightened the bedclothes, and returned to the semidarkness of my nest, my mind whirling as I tried to find a way out.

Friday came and went much as the previous days had passed: Amy in the shop, solving problems with a smile; Kip beside her, the devoted apprentice; Arnold at the kitchen table, holding vigil on the old Fringe network; and Seamus lifting the bedroom door to keep it from squealing as he cracked it open every few hours to check on me. With Rigby short on the customary comfort foods like sausage rolls, he brought me an overstuffed bagel sandwich from the bakery down the street, sat beside me on our rumpled bed, and ate with me, all the while suggesting that I at least step onto the landing outside the kitchen door and get a long breath of sea air. "It's not too hot," he assured me as he picked our crumbs off the duvet. "Lovely breeze. And if you're up for a walk, the bakery has these massive cheesecake slices that I'm *fairly* confident will trigger diabetes if consumed by only one person. For the sake of my continued health, I'm going to need assistance in this endeavor. Interested?"

I smiled but begged off, promising him I'd leave the room eventually. Unconvinced, he tidied up the rubbish and the leavings, kissed my forehead, and left me to my thoughts with a last worried glance.

The light faded toward evening. From behind my closed door, I could hear the rising voices as my companions talked and laughed over each other, the indistinct mumbling of the television, the clatter and banging from the kitchen as someone tried to cook, the blatting of the smoke alarm as the attempt hit a snag. Perhaps they weren't at peace yet—would we ever be truly at peace, knowing what was out there?—but they had found a comfortable rhythm.

Dinner ended, the voices slowly hushed, and I stared at the ceiling in the pitch blackness as Seamus slipped into the room to crawl into bed beside me. "Hungry?" he asked as he spooned against my back. "There's loads left to eat, and it's not all charred."

I murmured a demurral to the implied suggestion that I leave the room, and soon, Seamus's breathing slowed behind me, a steady pulse of air on the nape of my neck. Still, I lay awake in the darkness of the bedroom until I was certain that Arnold had retired and the kids had retreated to the ground floor, and then, ever so carefully, I slid out of Seamus's grasp, plucked my bathrobe from its hook and my wand from the dresser, and tiptoed into the quiet flat.

I felt my way down the corridor with one hand on the wall to guide me, then blinked in the den as my eyes adjusted to the faint yellow light from the streetlamp outside the curtained window. The flickering green indicators of Amy's cable box and router showed me approximately where the television was, and through the cutout window into the kitchen, I could see the red numbers of the microwave clock. Nearly midnight, and all was still.

Standing in the middle of the room, I closed my eyes

and listened for soft stirrings, but nothing reached my ear besides the faint hum of the air conditioner. When I was satisfied that I was alone and undetected, I padded to the far wall and lifted the hanging landscape just enough to show me the pinhole gate into Faerie, which shone with magic even in the darkness. Steeling my resolve, I aimed the wand at the hole and whispered an instruction. It began to grow after a moment's coaxing, but it did so with a clatter of falling books and knickknacks, a cacophony like the rumble of an avalanche in the silent flat. Panicking, I dropped the painting back into place and stepped away from the wall, hoping the others had slept through the racket.

A moment later, as I was convincing myself that no one had heard, there came a soft rapping on the back of the painting. Before I could investigate, it swung aside on its own, revealing Coileán's worried face on the other side of the gate. "*Detective*?" he asked, squinting into the darkness. "Is that you?"

Suddenly feeling foolish in my robe and bare feet—this plan, I realized, hadn't been my finest—I raised my empty hand and offered a little wave. "Ehm…hello," I whispered. "Sorry about that. The gate's in the back of your bookcase, isn't it? I forgot."

He shrugged it off. "What are you doing in Rigby?"

"Long story. Could I, ehm…"

"Sure." He stepped aside and gestured at the gate, which opened enough to give me passage. Once I'd come across and picked my way through the debris from the collapsed shelving, he returned the painting to its place and contracted the hole behind me, then straightened the mess with the flick of a finger.

There were, I mused, certain incontrovertible advantages to enchantment, particularly in seasoned hands.

Only starlight shown through the open windows of Coileán's spacious office, but a fire danced on the hearth, and a fat taper burned on the coffee table, which was spread with a stack of papers and an incongruous glowing laptop. "Sorry," I repeated, "you're working…"

"Nothing that can't wait." He headed for the bar, which, among its more mundane offerings, boasted enchantment-made bottles that hadn't been seen in the mortal realm in centuries. "Nightcap? Something stronger?"

"Actually, I'd love a cup of tea, if it's no trouble."

He shook his head and huffed his disappointment with me, but a fresh mug appeared on the coffee table, and I took the invitation to sit on one of the flanking leather couches. "Who drinks tea in the middle of the night?" he asked, settling onto the couch opposite mine.

"Someone who isn't planning to sleep. Cheers," I said, and blew the steam off the top.

An unadorned wine stem appeared in one of Coileán's hands, and he swept his other hand up and down himself, indicating his T-shirt and dark sweatpants, before closing the computer. "Tea and vino pajama party it is, then. Want to tell me what's going on?"

I sighed and leaned back into the couch, enjoying the warmth of the ceramic mug on my fingers. "Everything's gone pear-shaped with the Minor Arcanum, we've relocated to Rigby for lack of a better idea, and now…" I sipped my tea, then considered my host in the firelight. "Have you ever found yourself in a situation where you decide the best solution is to find someone better at being a responsible adult?"

"All the time," he replied—a bit too readily for my taste, considering his position—and drank. "Am I to take it, then, that I'm the responsible adult you've come to find?"

"More or less."

Coileán grimaced and put the glass aside. "You…*do* remember what I am, right? We're not known for making lauded choices."

"I'm desperate."

"Obviously." He pushed the papers and computer away, then propped his feet on the coffee table and tucked his hands behind his head, looking for all the world like a tousle-haired postgrad without a reasonable bedtime. "Okay, start at the beginning. What happened in New Mexico?"

Slowly, in between long, comforting sips—whatever else he might have done over the centuries, Coileán had learned to make a proper cuppa along the way—I told him about our China excursion, my sleepwalk, and Sergei's blanket. "I don't know how I did it," I murmured, and tucked my feet beneath me. "It's not like I had a wand in there. But once Carey learned what I'd done, she threw me out, and the others went with me."

The king refilled my mug with a glance. "Why was Carey so opposed?"

"It all goes back to Simon Magus," I explained, holding the tea close. "He conquered the New World by casting in the dream space, and…" I hesitated, suddenly unsure of the wisdom of my planned declaration. "And, ehm…apparently, we Parsons are his descendants. Arnie dropped that in front of Carey, and it didn't help matters."

If my ancestry gave Coileán pause, he didn't let on. "How'd she find out about this sleep casting, anyway?"

With the aid of my second cup of tea, I told him about Zoya, our relocation to Virginia, and the call I'd received the day before. "You see the problem, yes?" I concluded. "She's blackmailing me. But if I do what she wants—"

"She'll only keep asking for favors," he finished. Giving his wine a swirl, he downed the glass, then topped it up and held it toward the fire, considering the pale liquid in its glow. "Little sweet for my taste—I'm off my game tonight," he said, then shrugged and produced a coaster for the stem before turning his attention back to me.

To be perfectly clear, even if he means you no harm at the moment, it's disconcerting to find yourself the focal point of an aged high lord—rather like discovering that a large tiger has taken a particular interest in you. Mundanes can often pick up on the fact that there's something subtly wrong about them, even if they can't pinpoint the problem, but those of us on the magical spectrum, even the ones without the benefit of Arcanum training, can discern when we're in the presence of an experienced faerie. Coileán's face suggested he wasn't much older than Kip, but his eyes betrayed him, even in the firelight. The tell isn't easy to describe, but it's there—after all, the eyes of a man somewhere north of eight hundred are not the eyes of a twenty-something, and all the ratty sweats in the universe can't perfect the illusion.

Coileán's eyes were very green and fringed with dark lashes, and they seemed to flicker in the shifting light as he contemplated me. After an uncomfortably long moment, he leaned toward me, rested his elbows on his knees, and folded his hands. "What would you like me to say?"

"My lord?"

"You came here for counsel. What sort?"

"I…I'm not sure that I follow—"

"Not all advice is made equal. But I have an idea of what you're after." The corner of his mouth twitched. "I could tell you that you're doing your best and everything's going to be all right in time, but if you wanted a hug and a pat on the back, you'd have gone to your boyfriend. Which leads me to believe that you're here for honesty. Yeah?"

I nodded, tensing for the blow.

"In that case, you have two problems," he replied, holding up a crossed pair of fingers. "You're scared, and you're wallowing in self-pity. Your problems are exacerbating each other, I imagine."

Surprised and somewhat offended, I stiffened and frowned back at him. "Okay, perhaps I feel a *tiny* bit sorry for myself, but if you were in my place and had lost your family and—"

"This isn't about your family," he interrupted, placid against the assault of my indignation. "You've had one hell of a year, Hannah, and constant stress isn't good for anyone. Mourn your dead, there's no sin in that." He shifted deeper into the cushions and gave me a faint smirk. "But you can't sit there and tell me that's all you've been doing." My brows furrowed in bemusement, and Coileán slowly blinked. "I have it on good information that you've barely left your bed in a week."

"How—"

"It seems Seamus is panicking because he can't make you snap out of this funk, and he's been phoning for suggestions." Coileán waited, letting that sink in, then lifted his glass again and drank. "Never think for a moment that you're unloved, Detective. I say that in absolute sincerity. You've scared that boy half to death, you know."

He watched while I struggled for words, sipping his wine as the logs crackled beside us.

"It's been a difficult three weeks, all right?" I finally managed. "Carey kicked me out, we moved across the bloody country, no one in the Minor Arcanum will speak to me, and now Zoya—"

Coileán gave his head a firm shake to stop my explanation. "Self-pity."

"It's perfectly reasonable for me to be upset right now!"

As I fumed, he rolled his eyes and shook his head. "'Woe is me,'" he minced in a convincing impression of my accent, "'I'm a phenomenally powerful wizard, and now no one wants to be my friend.' Deal with it, kid."

"*Phenomenally?*" I scoffed.

He nodded and drank. "I never knew Simon Magus— he was gone before my time. But that doesn't mean I haven't heard stories. Hannah, if you're half the wizard he was, you're a force to be reckoned with. *Ah*," he interjected as I began to protest, "let me finish. You spent about forty years being, for lack of a better term, poisoned by your own wand. Not to be unkind, but the Fringe's magical instruction is fairly shitty, so you don't know most of what you should. But look how far you've come in just a year—the fact that you can already manipulate gates with *your* background should tell you how much potential you truly possess." He stared at me until I twitched. "You can sleepwalk, a form of magic so difficult and, frankly, arcane that the Arcanum itself has forgotten about it. And now you can cast in your *sleep*? Give yourself a few years—I wouldn't be surprised if your ability grew exponentially." He chuckled to himself and finished his second glass of wine. "If your family hadn't been so short-sighted, I'd say there's a decent chance you'd be grand magus now instead of Helen."

I goggled for a moment before I recovered my voice. "Grand magus—"

"Helen's powerful, but she's also highly trained. Look at what you've picked up piecemeal. Believe me, I've known my share of wizards, and I'm telling you that your cousin isn't the true magus of the family." With a flick of his wrist, the empty glass disappeared. "But instead of dealing with it, you're hiding away, feeling sorry for yourself."

Coileán waited, watching me try to stitch together a rebuttal. "I'm going to let you in on a little secret," he said after a long moment of silence. "Having considerable power means you will have precious few friends. Acquaintances, now, you'll have those in spades, and you'll probably find yourself with a number of hangers-on once you really come into your own, but friends? Nah." He reached for a glass that was no longer there, paused in momentary confusion, then leaned back into the couch and folded his arms. "Friendship is built on mutual trust and mutual vulnerability. There comes a point when you have to be open. Expose yourself, warts and wrinkles and all. Let the other person know who you really are beneath the mask. Now, generally, I suppose that's no problem, but how do you think someone would feel upon learning that you can kill him in your sleep from ten thousand miles away?"

He bent toward me again and met my gaze. "What we do—what we *are*—is terrifying," he murmured. "To mundanes, we're miracles and nightmares all in one because honestly, they have no real conception of what we're capable of. But wizards, now, they know. You may be Death, Destroyer of Worlds, but they know damn well that you're human beneath it all, and humans are capable of terrible, *stupid* things. Power like yours is dreadful when the person wielding it is anything less than perfect." He smirked as he leaned back, releasing his nearly hypnotic hold on me. "Let's not even discuss mine. You may have noticed that I don't exactly surround myself with dozens of bosom friends."

"I didn't ask for this," I protested.

"Tough. So you can either ignore it and hope it goes away—and you saw how well that worked for Seamus—or you can face it, figure out how to control it, and accept the fact that while you may still get invitations to Christmas parties, it's because they're afraid *not* to invite you. But lying about, feeling sorry for yourself, isn't going to change anything."

"And what if I *can't* control it?" I snapped. "You said it yourself—I don't have the training I should. Hell, I still can't get close to anyone in the dream space without taking a serious risk that I'm going to wake them."

Coileán laughed in disbelief. "Moon and stars, girl, you're living with a magus, aren't you? Use him!"

"Arnie can't sleepwalk."

"Maybe not, but I'd bet he knows a thing or two about spellcraft in general. Make him work with you. Private tutelage is nothing to scoff at. I'd ask Toula to give you the longer version of the intense course, but I assume you'd rather be back on the other side of the gate."

"Not going to find any missing Fringers from here," I mumbled.

"There you go. Now, let's talk about your Zoya for a minute. What would you like to do with her?"

I hesitated, pushing down the dark thought that had been rising into my consciousness for the last day. "Well, I suppose I—"

"Stop," said Coileán, raising both hands. "Put aside your scruples for a minute and try to think fae." I arched an eyebrow, and he shrugged. "It's seldom the prettiest approach, but in times like these, it's usually effective."

I felt a quick tingle in my mind, something altogether unexpected and alien, and began to cry out until I recognized the intrusion for what it was.

Coileán smiled, though his expression was far from reassuring. "Say it, kid. Accept it. If you're going to safely deal with your power, you'll have to recognize your less polite impulses instead of shoving them under the mental rug." When I remained silent, he added, "Everyone has them, but the vast majority of people can't effectively act on them. You and I can, and that's a critical difference." He waited until my eyes met his again, then said, "There's a certain safety in being a witch, isn't there? You can't do much, but you're not a threat, either. Largely unobjectionable. But Hannah, I've seen your aura—Toula showed me what you're working with. Yours is a magus-level gift, *at least*. Once you've mastered it, you'll have incredible power, but on the flip side, if you lose your temper and do something stupid, it can be fatal. Believe me, I know what I'm talking about."

I smiled weakly in spite of myself. "We're not nearly in the same league, my lord."

"No, but the principle's the same. And since I can't pull off that sleepwalking thing you do, I'm going to be a little wary now every time I sleep in the same realm as you. You can't walk between them in your sleep, can you?"

His tone was casual…but was that, I wondered, the slightest hint of fear I was hearing? From *Coileán*?

"I don't believe it's possible," I replied. "Part of the

reason why we're still based over there. I can't access the dream space here, so I can't track Fringers from this side."

"Mm." It could have been a trick of the firelight, but I thought I saw a slight relaxation in his face, a little hint of relief. "Anyway, you need to be honest with yourself—it's the best way to prevent nasty incidents you'll regret in the morning. So tell me, what do you want to do about Zoya?"

I forced myself to hold his gaze. "Kill her. I could find her in her sleep. She'd be defenseless, and I suppose it would look like a heart attack."

The king nodded. "*But.*"

"But that goes against just about every line of my moral code."

"And there's the rub—"

"No, the problem with that plan is more than my morality. Look at the moving pieces with me. Zoya's a wizard, Mischa's a witch. Even if he isn't involved with the Minor Arcanum, she is, and presumably, he knows who to contact in case of emergency."

Absently, Coileán rubbed his chin. "Go on."

"Zoya's asked me to kill for her—obviously, she thinks I can do it. But she also knows how precarious the Fringe's situation is, so she must have anticipated that I could turn on her. Hit me again, would you?" I added, holding out my mug. He obliged, and I drank my tea—slightly milky, sweetened just enough to bring out the flavor—while I assembled the jigsaw puzzle of my thoughts.

"Zoya probably knows I'm a cop," I said when the mug was again dry. "She's had time enough to ask questions, and I haven't kept my profession a secret."

"Cops are good and bad," he replied. "Like anyone else. She knows what you've been doing for the Fringe, though?"

"Assumedly."

"I'd think that's a better indicator of your character. Okay, go on."

"So Zoya knows, more or less, what I'm about, and

she's banking on the conclusion that I won't kill her to make the problem go away." Replaying our conversation in my head, I explained, "She said all the right triggers. She's a mother and a wife looking out for her family's well-being, her target's a bad, abusive man…all reasons for me to see things her way and not turn on her. Wouldn't want to orphan her daughters, would I?" I said bitterly.

"Assuming she has daughters at all," said Coileán. "She could very well be playing you."

"I know." I rolled my empty mug back and forth between my palms. "I also know she's not stupid. Zoya has a contingency plan."

He cocked an eyebrow. "Not much she can do if she's dead in her sleep."

"No, but hear me out. Let's go on the assumption that she's told her husband what she's asked me to do. If, for some reason, Zoya were to drop dead, who do you suppose Mischa would ring first?"

His eyes lit with understanding. "Two calls, I think. One to someone in the Minor Arcanum, giving some story about how his poor wife spoke with you and then didn't wake up…"

"And one to whomever Zoya knows in Arcanum 4. If she goes down, the Fringe and I go down with her, and we probably take the Joneses in our wake."

"What if you were to take out Zoya *and* Mischa?" he asked, steepling his fingers. "The problem and the backup?"

"Leaving the alleged children orphaned. No."

He smiled then in earnest. "Good girl. So you won't kill them both, you can't kill just one, and you can't ignore Zoya…I don't suppose you'd do the hit, would you?"

"*No*, and like you said, if I did, she'd come back the next time she wanted a 'favor.'"

"It'd be easier the next time. After all, you've killed for her before—why not do it again?"

My hands stilled, and I looked across the table at

Coileán. "Speaking from experience?" I murmured.

He was silent for the space of a long breath. "I'm no hired gun, but I do know *very* well that killing, like anything else, gets easier with practice."

That was one line of enquiry I had no desire to pursue. "So where does that leave me? I'm out of good options."

"From what I'm hearing, there never was a good option in this matter." Pushing himself to his feet, Coileán wandered to the fireplace and stared into the flames. "You look at the bad options, and you choose the one that best protects the people you care about. You do your duty."

I thought of Slim and Helen and all the missing Fringers whose lives would be forfeit if Faerie intervened in the Arcanum's madness. Coileán couldn't fix this for me.

"I…might have an idea," I said to his back. "Maybe not a permanent solution, but a temporary fix is still a fix."

"Few solutions are ever permanent, Hannah."

Hearing the weariness in his voice, I decided to take my leave. "Thank you. I should get back and try to put this to rights."

He turned as I unfolded from the couch and gave me a tired smile. "You've heard the chestnut about power and responsibility, yes?"

"Many times."

"Mm. You don't get one without the other, even if you wanted neither. But since you've been given the power to protect your people—"

"I have the responsibility to do so."

"Good luck to you, whatever you choose. And Hannah?" he said as I began to move away. "One suggestion."

"Please."

Coileán hesitated while he chose his words. "I realize you're somewhat spooked by Simon Magus. I can't give you any firsthand truth about him, but Grivam knew him."

"Grivam?" I echoed, frowning. "The merrow king?"

He nodded. "The one. When Simon divvied up his toys after the Great War, one went to Grivam. That can't be by chance. Once you've sorted your business with Zoya, take a week and drive down to the Keys. I'll send him word to expect you."

While I wasn't sure if a face-to-face meeting with a merrow would be the cure for what ailed me, prudence counseled against arguing with the king on that point. "Ehm...thank you," I managed. "Before I try to widen this gate again, do you want to move your breakables?"

Coileán started to follow me, then froze, closed his eyes, and put his fingertips to his forehead. "Now what?" he muttered.

"Are you all right?"

"Fine. Realm wants me to see something in Aiden's room...and she suggests you come, too," he said, opening his eyes again. "Shall we?"

I hurried after him toward the office door. "Did she say what we're going to find?"

"No," he replied, slowing until I caught up with him in the hallway, "but she's not happy. Come on, shortcut," he said, and opened a gate.

CHAPTER 11

The gate deposited us outside of Aiden's suite. Even with the door closed, I could hear shouting on the other side—muffled voices, but definitely more than one. Before I was able to identify the speakers, a second gate appeared in the dark corridor, and when the lightning-like afterimage faded, I found that Eleanor had joined us. The queen's coppery hair was bed-mussed into snarls, and she sported a purple silk dressing gown over sensible slippers. "Sorry for the intrusion," she told Coileán, "she said it was important…oh, hello, Hannah. Is everything okay?"

"I think we're about to find out," Coileán muttered, then pounded twice on the door to announce our arrival before flinging it open. "What the hell is going on?" he called across the room. "Do you have *any* idea what time it is, Aid?"

My eyes adjusted quickly to the dimly lit bedroom, revealing a long wooden desk against the window, a propped-up tablet open atop it, and a slouching shadow in a swivel chair, who spun about at the sound of our intrusion. The lamps around the room flared on, and I saw Aiden's flushed cheeks and blond ponytail. A voice continued to yell, however, and even with the distortion, I recognized it as Amy's.

"I can explain," said Aiden, holding his hands up as if to ward us away.

The looks on the king's and queen's faces suggested that whatever explanation he had in mind would need to be earth-shattering to get him off the hook.

Before he could begin, I crossed the room and snatched up the tablet. "All right, time out," I said, surprising Amy into silence. Her face was redder than Aiden's, and her hazel eyes glittered with angry tears on the verge of falling, but what surprised me more was seeing Kip standing behind her, gnawing on his lip. The monitor gave his bronze skin an odd cast, but the flyaway hairs that he quickly tried to smooth glowed almost orange in the computer's light. She was furious, he was worried, and Aiden…well, the kid looked like he wanted to crawl under the bed for safety.

Holding the computer so that the Virginia duo could see me, I beckoned Coileán and Eleanor closer, then pointed to the screen. "Amy, take a breather. Kip, you're being awfully quiet. Want to tell us what's going on?"

Reluctantly, Amy slid out of the way, and Kip cleared his throat. "Hannah? What are you doing over *there*?"

"Insomnia," I half-lied. "What's all this about?" Amy began to speak, and I lifted a finger to shush her. "Wait your turn, Amy. It sounds like you and Aiden have been doing plenty of talking already. Kip, fill us in?"

Ignoring her glare, he glanced to either side of my head as the rest of his audience moved into view behind me, then said, "Aiden wanted to talk. He sent me a message two days ago, asking to set up a time when we could discuss something in private."

"How?" I asked.

His dark eyes flickered toward Amy. "I have access to the new network now—Amy's been teaching me how it works. Aiden left word for me there, and I agreed to speak with him."

I looked down at Aiden, who nodded, then back at Kip. "What about?"

"The gates. I could give you the recap, but since he's there, let him tell you what he told me."

The three of us turned our attention to the swivel chair, and Aiden, who had calmed to a degree, spoke quickly while Eleanor drummed her fingers against her arm. "The new network is connected to Amy's dark magic detectors, right? I know there's been a rash of Gray Lands gates of late, so I pulled out the old Fringe records and started digging, just to see if there's a natural pattern in gate frequency or whatever, like sunspots. The Fringe tracked gates, you know? Arcanum took care of closing them, but the Fringe still kept tabs on what was going on."

Eleanor's peeved look began to shift closer to concern. "Your findings?"

"This uptick is unique. I looked at two hundred years of notes, and there's never been anything like this."

"Two hundred years isn't long," Coileán pointed out. "Not in the wider scheme—"

"I'm telling you, this is *wrong*," he insisted, shaking his head to silence his brother as he rose from his chair. "Look, bring the tablet in here. Let me show you the numbers."

We followed Aiden through a narrow wooden door into a stone-walled room dominated by a bank of darkened monitors. He slid into one of the chairs in front of the array and began typing to wake the system, then muttered to himself until the bottom-left monitor showed a simple line graph. "Gray Lands gate frequency over the last two centuries," he said, indicating the line with a red laser pointer. "You see the occasional blip, but it's been pretty constant, right?"

"Right…" said Coileán.

"Okay, same graph, but with the last twelve months tacked on." He tapped a key, and the jagged blue line shot toward the top of the screen. "That includes the latest ones—Tibet, the Everglades, and Huangshan," he explained. "Three natural gates in under a month is unprecedented."

"We had five in June," said Kip. "You forgot the one in Guatemala and the little one by Uluru."

"I didn't forget," Aiden replied, "and that's my point—

we've never seen anything like this."

"At least not since the Fringe began recording, you mean," Eleanor countered. "I see what you're saying, Aiden, but you have to admit that you don't have a large data set. Still…" She frowned at the monitor as her arms tightened. "That isn't reassuring by any means."

Aiden waited until we fell silent again, then said, "I can't tell you what's causing it. If these gates are all naturally occurring, then something may be very wrong— these could be like the warning tremors before a major earthquake. But if they're *not* natural—"

"Then something is testing the waters," Eleanor finished. "Some*one*."

"Nath?" Coileán murmured to her.

"I've never met her—you tell me."

He could only shrug. "I agree, the situation bears watching," he told Aiden, "but why the midnight shouting match?"

"And—no offense, dear," I told the tablet, "but why take this to *Kip*, of all people, in secret?"

As Aiden began to flush and stammer, Kip said, "Allow me." I turned the tablet back to face the three of us, and he leaned closer to the camera. "Given Aiden's concerns, he thinks it might be wisest if we evacuate and watch from there. But he also knows that you aren't about to abandon this realm, Seamus won't go without you, and Arnold and I are…problematic. He explained what he'd found to encourage me to make Amy evacuate."

"Which isn't your decision!" she shouted, still seething on the left side of the screen. "Neither of you! When are y'all going to get that through your heads? *Jesus*, if someone wants me to do something, have the decency to talk to me!"

Aiden, looking rather abashed by the mess, tried to interject. "You wouldn't have listened to me because you'd think I was trying to spirit you away. That's the only reason I got Kip involved."

"Oh, *sure*," she said, glaring into space because Aiden was out of view. "Play on Kip's emotions. That's not underhanded at all."

At that, Eleanor looked askance at Aiden, who sighed. "I just told him that Amy's defenseless against whatever comes across, and if he cares about her at all, he'll convince her to evacuate."

Kip nodded as Aiden spoke, and Amy huffed her anger. "That's what you want, isn't it?" she snapped, raising her voice to yell at Aiden. "Me stuck over there until whenever *you* think it's safe, Kip stuck back here…"

"Amy, it's not like—"

"We are *colleagues*," she continued over his protestations. "*Maybe* friends if you can get your act together. But even if you lock me away over there, I'm not going to change my mind!"

"I understand that," he replied through clenched teeth, "but Amy—"

"He wants you to be safe," Kip interrupted. "I also want you to be safe. And this—"

Ignoring her audience, Amy grabbed Kip by the chin and stared into his eyes. "You listen to me, Kippit, and you listen good. If you think for one minute that I'm going to run away from danger and leave you to face it without me, you're out of your damn mind." And with that, she darted across the space between them and pressed her mouth against his.

Kip's eyes widened in shock, but only for a second before he met her kiss and—at least from our vantage point—returned it with interest.

For Aiden's sake, I was glad that he could only see the back side of the tablet, though I suspect that our expressions might have told him what he was missing.

"You know," I said, lowering the tablet to get the others' attention, "Aiden has a point. If the situation were to deteriorate, could we send Arnold and Kip with Amy?"

The queen and king shared a grimace, and then Eleanor

turned to me. "Possibly. If the realm tolerates Toula and half of the Fringers living out there, then I don't see why Arnold would be a major problem. But Kip…"

Rubbing his head, Coileán quietly explained, "She's not happy about the idea. Bringing a Gray Lander across the border might be a bridge too far."

"I see." Glancing back at Aiden, who watched our conference with concern, I said, "Keep us posted—*all* of us. If the time comes…we'll play it by ear, yeah?"

I ended the video call before handing the tablet back to Aiden, and then, with Coileán on hand to stop me from ruining his bookshelf again, I took my leave. Before the gate constricted behind me, he said, "I'll work on her. Can't make any promises, but I'll do what I can."

"Thank you," I said, and swung the painting back into place. The flat was still dark, and I could hear no voices from downstairs. Deciding that the kids could deal with themselves for the rest of the night, I returned to my bedroom, slipped back under Seamus's arm, and stared at the shadows until my eyes finally closed.

When I woke, I was alone in bed, but the pale light through the crack in the curtains suggested that the hour was barely past dawn. I swung my legs over the side and stretched, feeling like I'd slept for an age, then pulled my robe from the floor where I'd dropped it and headed out in search of my partner.

I hadn't taken three steps from the bedroom before I heard his voice coming from the kitchen: "You're young, mate. A kiss isn't marriage, remember."

The voice that answered him was Kip's, and the boy sounded distraught. "But she…I didn't think she—"

"Liked you?" Seamus finished. "How'd you miss it? I mean, I'm no expert, but even I saw this one coming."

"But…you know…" He floundered for a few seconds, then blurted, "We're not of the same people!"

"No." I could almost hear his shrug. "Neither are Badger and I. And Rufus, have you met his partner? She shifts into a wolf when she's of a mind. Now, I don't know about you, but I think that Amy in her worst mood surely isn't scarier than the prospect of waking up next to *fangs*."

"Amy—"

"Has wizard blood and fae blood in equal measure. She's not strictly human, you know."

"And I'm not human at all," Kip muttered. "Take away…*this*…"

Seamus kept his silence for a moment, then said, "I wouldn't lose sleep over it. Obviously, she thinks you're close enough."

"But—"

"Let it *ride*, Kip. Maybe it works out and maybe it doesn't, but for now, enjoy it." After a brief pause, he added, "By which I mean get to know her, maybe fool around if you two get that far, but, ehm…remember that she's seventeen, okay? You're…nineteen?"

"Twenty, I think."

"Yeah. Just…do us a kindness and keep the brakes on the sex until she's legal. Right, then, go on," he said, and the chairs scraped against the floor. "If you want the bear claws, you need to be there before seven."

I lurked in the shadows until the kitchen door slammed and I heard Kip's rapid steps on the fire escape, then wandered in and found Seamus with his hands wrapped in oven gloves, filling the steel kettle. "Let me," I said, reaching for the handle.

He relinquished it with a grin. "Look who's up! Kip's gone round to the bakery for doughnuts, if you can stand the wait."

I cut off the tap and kissed his cheek. "Suppose I'll manage. Sleep well?"

"Like a rock."

As I put the kettle on and turned the dial, Seamus

peered at my sleep-puffy face as if trying to memorize the tracks of my crow's feet. "You *look* better," he finally declared. "How do you feel?"

"Better." I pulled a mismatched pair of mugs from the cabinet and slid past Seamus to rummage for the tea things in the pantry. "Had a word with Coileán."

"Did you?"

"Mm. English Breakfast or Earl Grey?"

He pointed to the box in my left hand. "Too early for bergamot. And what did he have to say?"

"Gave me some advice. Also, Aiden's worried about the frequency of Gray Lands gates—something to keep an eye on for now." I began unwrapping the tea bags, saving Seamus the trouble of avoiding the staples. "Kip told you about that bit, I take it."

"More or less." He pulled the milk out of the refrigerator. "And about Amy. I gather you heard us, then."

"The last of it. Sounded like you had it well in hand."

We waited in comfortable silence until the kettle whistled, and I poured for us both and began doctoring my cup. When the tea was the correct shade of brown, I drew closer to my partner and murmured, "Hey."

He looked up with a query on his face, teabag string in hand, then closed his eyes as I leaned in to kiss him properly. When we parted, he smiled in earnest. "Hello to you, too."

"Thank you, Seamie."

"For what? You made the tea."

"For everything that isn't the tea." Grinning back at him, I tidied the counter and binned my teabag. "And if you'd told me two years ago that we'd be here, *together*, and you'd be giving pointers to a lovelorn centaur—"

"Madness, isn't it?" He took a long sip and sighed with the pleasure of an addict getting his first fix of the day. "So, now that you've deigned to join the waking world, how about we tackle that cheesecake this afternoon?"

"I'll pencil it into my diary," I replied, "but there's something I need to do first."

"Oh? What?"

I hesitated, unsure of how much I wanted to tell him. "It's a sleepwalking thing. And since time is of the essence," I added, lifting my mug in salute, "I'm afraid I'm going back to bed."

Seamus stood aside while I exited the kitchen, but he called my name when I was halfway down the hall. "Anything I can do, love?" he asked when I turned.

There was hope on his face—cautious optimism, perhaps, but optimism nonetheless—and any thought I'd had of telling him what I was going to do died unspoken.

"I'll see you for cheesecake," I told him, and closed the door behind me.

My computer informed me that Moscow was only seven hours ahead of us in Virginia—not ideal for my purposes, but at least I would have time to scout around. Hoping that Zoya wasn't planning a long Saturday night out on the town, I finished my tea, made myself comfortable, and steadied my breathing until I slipped into the dream space.

After my time away, the sensation was akin to sliding into a warm bath. I took my time rising from my body, then from the building, until I saw Rigby spread beneath me and the vast Atlantic rolling in from the east. The only signs of wizard or faerie I could spot in the town were in our flat, and as I continued to rise, the landscape remained reassuringly dark—no Arcanum assassins creeping closer to ambush us, no rogue faeries lurking one town over. Soon, the eastern seaboard spread below me, dotted with the few and distant stars of Fringers we'd yet to coax from hiding, and I floated out over the empty ocean.

I drifted across Europe, making notes of potential targets, but I stayed high above the occasional glimmers below me. There was no sense in descending; Europe was well into its morning, and I couldn't drag people into the dream space for a word if they were still awake. Carey had impressed that upon me during our lessons, and I had no reason to doubt her. But another part of me counseled me to keep well above my targets in case Carey was wrong—with my control imperfect, I didn't want to be responsible for yanking someone into unconsciousness when he was, say, trying to drive.

It took me a fair amount of time to locate Moscow—the Minor Arcanum had few members in Russia, and most wizards in the area were clustered inside Arcanum 4 to the distant east. Eventually, however, I was able to pick out the shadow metropolis, and then my search led me to an impressive penthouse in a well-to-do section of the city. Passing through the glass windows, as insubstantial as a ghost, I studied my surroundings and the glowing yellow forms I found inside.

Zoya was easiest to spot, brilliant and gleaming in the darkness of the dream space. She sat at a desk, staring into a thin laptop. I couldn't make out the picture on the screen, but from the movement of her mouth, I supposed that Zoya was video-chatting. I couldn't hear her, not while she was awake, but then again, she couldn't hear me, either.

In the living room sat a middle-aged man in an old T-shirt and a girl of perhaps ten, both of whom glowed with a fainter light than Zoya's. Mischa and one of their daughters, I surmised, both focused on a chessboard. He sat with his stubby fingers interlaced, watching with a slight smile as the girl frowned at the board. Her forehead furrowed into deep grooves with the mental strain of deciding her next move. Across the room, forgoing the comfort of the sofa for a spot on the oriental rug, a younger daughter lay on her stomach in front of the television, her chin propped in her hands. From my vantage point, unable to see the program being broadcast, it appeared as though the girl were staring raptly at a blackened screen, but such were the limitations of the dream space.

I had no real concept of the hour—no later than eight in Rigby, I supposed, which would be no later than three in Moscow—and so I settled down to wait, anticipating that I would have to spy on the family until well past nightfall. But not half an hour after my arrival, Zoya rose from her desk, yawned, and kicked off her expensive flats. I watched her step into the main room and say something to Mischa, who nodded and waved her on, and then, my heart quickening, she headed for the master bedroom.

A Saturday afternoon nap. How fortuitous, indeed.

I waited by the wardrobe as Zoya made herself comfortable beneath an afghan and closed her eyes. Ten minutes later, her chest rose and fell like a metronome beating a dirge, and I seized the opportunity. Touching her blanket-covered shoulder, I jerked her into the dream space, then stepped back from the bed and smiled while she gathered her bearings. She could see nothing of the room about her—no one but a sleepwalker could see anything but formless blackness and the person who brought him into the shared dream—and part of me enjoyed witnessing her confusion.

Catching sight of me, she collected herself quickly enough, and her mouth moved into a little smirk. "Hannah. What a surprise."

"Enjoying your nap?"

"I was." She stood and smoothed her bed-rumpled blouse. "You decided quickly. That was wise."

"You haven't heard my decision yet," I replied, and her shoulders stiffened. "Here's my proposition for you, Zoya," I continued, leaning against the wardrobe. "I'm not going to kill your little inconvenience."

Her eyes narrowed. "That would be a mistake."

"No. What would be a mistake would be if I were to learn that the Arcanum had received any indication of my presence in this realm or of the workings of the Fringe.

You see, if that happened, I'd have no choice but to return here and kill you."

Before Zoya could speak, I summoned a weak bolt of energy—so much easier there, freed from the binds of my body—and threw her across the room. Her glowing form hit the heavy dresser, and she slumped to the carpet with a groan. "That was nothing," I told Zoya, watching her frantically try and fail to assemble a shield. "We both know you're powerless here, and unless you never plan to sleep again, I *will* have you at my mercy."

Her face registered shock, but her eyes blazed in defiance. "You would not kill me. You, the brave little detective, would not rip me from my children—"

"Plenty of children have been orphaned in the last year," I interrupted. "*Loads*. And if the Arcanum comes for us, there will only be more orphans and widows and grieving parents, so spare me. I'm not your attack dog, Zoya, and if I have reason to believe you've betrayed us or our allies, I will *not* hesitate to destroy you. Fair's fair."

"I helped you in Mongolia."

"And I'm not killing you today. We're even."

Though she pushed herself from the floor, Zoya seemed more guarded even as she threatened. "If you kill me, the Minor Arcanum will know, and they will hunt you down. You can't touch me."

"Can't I?" I shrugged. "You speak as though I'm bound by the Minor Arcanum."

"They will find you—"

"Not before I find them, and remember, they have to sleep, too." I permitted myself a predatory smile. "You think I'm scared of them? They're the ones fleeing from me, love. So tell them I paid you this visit. Tell them I threatened you—I don't care. Do your worst. Just remember that if I have the *slightest* feeling that you've endangered me or my people, I'll kill you here. Like shooting fish in a barrel, really."

As I stared at her, I realized with an unexpected thrill

that Zoya was nervous—no, not nervous. *Afraid*. She maintained her stiff upper lip, but the tight hunch of her shoulders betrayed her, the posture of a frightened animal preparing to spring for its life. And as the tip of her tongue darted out to moisten her lips, I realized a second truth: I was enjoying this. Zoya had threatened my people, had threatened *me*, and now, she was one sudden movement away from frightened tears, frozen under my gaze and powerless to fight me.

Make her pay, something in me whispered in a voice like silk. *Make her ache and bleed. Show her what you can do…or kill her.*

My plan had been to merely scare Zoya into silence—I thought I'd found a solution, or at least a first step before escalating to more drastic measures. But then I thought about how easy it would be to end her…how much simpler it was to cast in the dream space…

She would scream, and no one would ever hear her. No one but me. And she would know that I—

God, what was I *thinking*?

Snapping out of my reverie, I gave Zoya one last look that I hoped conveyed the precariousness of her situation, then flung myself back toward my body like a taut rubber band released.

I opened my eyes to full morning in Rigby. Slowly, I sat up, letting myself adjust, and blinked at the daylight. My sheets were wrinkled with use, and something smelled odd. Giving my shirt an experimental sniff, I realized it was me.

When the world had solidified under my feet once more, I stood, picked up my stained mug, and made my way toward the kitchen and the promise of more tea. From the quiet, it seemed I had the flat to myself. I selected a glazed doughnut from the half-empty box on the counter, and as I ate one-handed, I focused on the smoothness of the kettle's handle and the quiet rush of the tap to distract myself from my internal turmoil.

I'd just threatened to kill Zoya, and part of me had

enjoyed every second of it.

I was deep into my second doughnut and third cup of tea when Seamus opened the door from the shop, noticed me standing by the stove, and smiled. "All better, then?" he asked.

"Yes. Maybe," I amended, then put the mug down and folded my arms. "I have to get out of town."

Seamus stood at our bedroom door with his arms folded, glowering at my well-used duffel bag as if he could cow it into sliding back into the closet. "It's only for a few days," I told him again as I plucked an armful of T-shirts from their cheap wire hangers. "I'll hire a car—you lot keep the Suburban here—and I'll ring you when I get there."

"Absolutely not."

I draped my shirts over my arm and gritted my teeth, fighting the urge to snap at him. "This isn't up for discussion, Seamie," I said as calmly as I could. "I need a little time, and this trip—"

"Is madness," he interrupted. "First you tell me that bitch threatened you, and now you're running off to who-knows-where, *alone*, chasing after a mermaid?"

"'Merrow' is the preferred term. And this would be their king—"

"Whatever. We need to circle the wagons in case she gets any bright ideas, Badge—this is no time to be splitting up, and certainly no time for a solo holiday a thousand miles away."

"It's a straight shot down I-95," I said as I began to roll my shirts into tight tubes, tensing under the pressure of his glare. "I've already mapped it. Anyway, Coileán said I should speak with him, and—"

"Coileán can go fuck himself. We have no idea what's happening in the Minor Arcanum right now, Aiden's predicting Gray Lands Armageddon, and in case you've forgotten, there's a very real chance that one of our friends in black will pop by any day now."

I counted to ten as I packed, focusing on the soft cloth under my hands to keep myself from escalating the argument. "I took a look while I was out this morning, and there's no sign of a wizard within three hundred miles, at least."

"All it takes is one gate, and you know it," said Seamus. "Look at me, Badger."

"The situation is stable."

"*Look at me*, damn it!"

Collecting myself, I rolled up the last shirt and wedged it into my bag before I turned to him. "Yes?"

"You're not going."

"That isn't your decision," I replied, and headed back to the closet for my trousers.

With a frustrated huff, he stalked after me and cornered me between the closet's accordion door and the adjoining wall. "Are you hearing a word I'm telling you? This whole spree of yours is dangerous. You're asking for trouble. *Begging* for it. What if you run into another wizard down there, eh? Or two of them? Ten of them? What do you do then? You'll have no backup, no support—"

"You're catastrophizing," I countered, shouldering him out of my way as I returned to the bed to pack.

"Because I don't want anything to happen to you! Am I not making sense?" Seamus hurried to my side and caught my wrist as I reached for my jeans in the stack of unfolded clothing. "Badger, please," he said more softly, but with no less urgency. "At least wait a few days. Let's see if we hear any rumblings, yeah? We'll call Jim, find out if he's heard anything. Make sure you scared what's-her-face well enough."

"Zoya."

"Fine. Make sure you scared Zoya straight. There's no rush, love."

Gently, I freed my arm and resumed folding. "Something tells me that if Coileán is going to send word to someone old enough to have known Simon Magus, I don't want to keep him waiting."

Seamus sat on the bed beside my pile of trousers and watched me silently fit them into the bag. As I retreated next door for my toiletries, he followed me into the narrow bathroom and blocked my exit. "Why?"

"Why what?" I muttered, digging in the drawer for my travel-sized toothpaste.

"Why are you suddenly so obsessed with Simon Magus? He's got nothing to do with you."

Nearing my breaking point, I slammed the drawer closed and wheeled on him, using the half-flattened toothpaste tube as a pointer. "He's got *everything* to do with me. He's the last person who could do what I can do, and he turned into a genocidal maniac. I need…I don't even know," I snapped, "but whatever this Grivam can tell me, I *need* to hear it."

He caught me by my shaking shoulders and stooped to look into my eyes. "Whatever he did, that's no part of you. So you've got a rare talent. Fair enough. That doesn't mean you're destined to repeat whatever the hell it was he did."

His deep blue eyes had softened, and I knew that if I swam in them too long, I'd likely drown. "You've got no idea what it's like," I said, breaking away to hunt down my extra shampoo bottle in the cabinet beneath the sink.

"Oh? What, finding out I've got family with a less than perfect past?"

I glanced up from my crouch on the fluffy bathmat and saw him watching me. "I'm a walking bomb. I don't have perfect control in the dream space, and now I'm casting in my sleep. *Anything* could happen in there, and no one would be able to stop me. That's why Carey drove me away. That's why every other sleepwalker runs as soon as I appear. I am *death*, Seamie," I said, straightening, "and even if I get this under control, I'll still be death, just a little less likely to spontaneously go off. So yes, Simon Magus has got everything to do with me. I need to know, I…I've got to face this," I said, hating myself for the pricking in my eyes and raising my voice to cover. "So don't stand there and tell me what to do right now, because you've got no fucking *idea* what I'm going through."

I'd expected him to shout back at me, or at least to scowl. Instead, he spread his hands and shrugged. "You think I don't know what it's like? Hell, all you have to worry about is what happens when you *choose* to sleepwalk. Until last year, I lived with the fear that at any moment, I was going to kill someone by accident. Forty-seven years of that fear, Badger. I ran away from everyone I cared about, just to be on the safe side. And I'll be damned if I stand back and let you make the same mistake."

"I'm only going away for a few days…"

"You say that now. I know that look on your face all too well—I am *intimately* familiar with it because I used to see it in mirrors all the time." Before I could react, he wrapped his arms around me and rubbed my stiff back. "I don't want you to go because I don't think it's the safest plan you've ever made, and I don't know what I'd do if something happened to you," he murmured. "But if your mind is set on going, then by God, you are *not* going alone. If it kills me, you're not facing this alone. And whatever Aquaman tells you about some wizard wanker who's been dead a thousand years, I'll be there to remind you that you are Detective Inspector Badger Parsons, and you don't have to take shit from a fish."

Exhaustion made me laugh, though it felt almost like a sob as Seamus held me tightly against his chest. "Okay," I finally said. "All right, you impossible man, you can come on holiday with me."

"Brilliant plan. Our last trip to Florida left something to be desired."

His arms didn't loosen their grip, but I wasn't bothered.

"Want me to take care of the car?" he asked.

"Okay," I mumbled into his shirt.

"Something sporty? Something *not* the Suburban?"

"Sounds good."

I raised my head from his shoulder, and he wiped away the tear I hadn't felt escape. "Maybe a convertible. Let's live a little, why don't we?"

"I love you, too."

"Splendid. I'll hire a car and pack, and you…" He pulled back to hold me at arm's length, then gave me a critical examination. "Out to the beach with you, madam. You've been in your little cave here for far too long."

He released me and headed back to the bedroom, where he'd left his mobile, and I followed with my toiletry kit. "You're awfully bossy today, Malone."

"I'm only bossy when I'm right," he countered, and began to search for a car hire. "Now, on to important matters. Assuming I can find a Maserati in our price range, have you any preference as to color?"

CHAPTER 12

The best Seamus could do on short notice was a red Mustang convertible, but it suited our purpose and zipped along the highway without complaint. I'd been surprised that Arnold and the kids had let us leave without protest, but Seamus explained their willingness to see us off once we were half an hour south of Rigby, doing a steady eighty in the light Sunday morning traffic. "Did you think I was the only one worried over you?" he asked, twisting off the top of his Sprite. "I told them you needed a quick change of scenery, and they understood." He took a long swig and stifled a belch. "Amy says for us to bring her back a shot glass, if we find one sufficiently terrible. Maybe one with a mermaid—that would be appropriate, wouldn't it?"

When we stopped for lunch at a lonely Wendy's off the Interstate, Seamus went inside to place the order—he could have built my preferred burger in his sleep—while I sat in the car with the windows up and rang Coileán to let him know I was on my way south.

"Good, he's expecting you," he replied, sounding pleased but not surprised. "Basically, you're going to take 95 until it runs out, then pick up Highway 1 and head out to sea. Look for East Rock Key—it's not well marked, and Aiden says it's nothing but an empty island now, but there should be a turnoff all the same. Pull together a boat, then go around the back of the island. You'll find an inlet, and you should have decent tree coverage between you and the road."

"You couldn't just give me an address, could you?"

He snorted. "Hard to do that with the only landmark vanished into thin air, but I have faith in your navigational skills. I mean, it's an island chain—if you hit Key West, turn around. Now," he continued, "here's the tricky bit: to let him know you're there, put your hand on the surface and shoot a beam of light down. Think more like a headlamp than a laser. There's no telling how long he'll make you wait on the surface, but in my experience, he tends to regard flashes rather like a blinking red light on an answering machine, know what I'm saying?"

"And he knows why I'm coming?" I pressed.

"I told him. You should be in no danger…" He paused to clear his throat. "You…haven't had any dealings with the merrow before now, have you?"

"No…"

Coileán sighed. "Okay. Remember your manners, don't stare, and if his eyes roll in different directions, just focus on the spot between them. He has a smile only a piranha would love, but unless you really anger him, you won't need to worry. And he's fluent in Fae, so you shouldn't have trouble there. What else…" he muttered to himself, then snapped his fingers. "Ah, *yes*. Grivam doesn't do anything for free. Know your limits going in. If you can make him a gift, so much the better."

"Thanks," I replied, mulling over what one might give a merman. A box of cigars seemed right out.

"I take it your problem has been resolved?"

The interruption sent my thoughts down a path I'd been trying to avoid all day, but I kept my tone light. "Yes, it's sorted."

"Glad to hear it," he said, then hesitated. "Are you all right, Hannah?"

"Never better," I lied, then said my goodbyes and hurried inside before Seamus came searching for me.

My partner took the wheel after lunch, and I let myself

sleepwalk, flying far ahead of our borrowed car to look for wizards in our path. The land below me remained unbroken shadow, however, and I woke with faint relief, blinking through the mild sleepwalking hangover, the shock of once again being at the mercy of gravity and surrounded by the riotous colors of full daylight.

"And?" Seamus asked when I began to stir beside him.

"All clear." I stretched my legs and yawned as the mental fog thinned. "Should be smooth sailing down the coast."

He nodded, squinting back at me as the sun continued its slow dip outside my window. "Good news. Where were we thinking about stopping tonight? We should be in Florida by dinner—Jacksonville, I think," he said, giving his dash-mounted mobile a pat. "We'll have light still if you want to press on, or we could split the trip. That's the halfway point, more or less."

"I don't mind driving by dark."

"Your wish is my command, milady," he replied, touching the brim of an imaginary chauffeur's cap, and I laughed weakly as I looked away toward the endless green of the summer-bright woods that closed the road in like the living walls of a canal. After a few minutes, when I made no attempt at conversation, Seamus glanced my way and reached across the seat to take my hand. "All right, then, Badger?"

Though usually reassuring, the warm pressure of his fingers entwined with mine did little to pull me from the edge of the funk on which I'd been teetering all day. "Fine," I told him, smiling too brightly. "I'm fine."

"Try again."

"Really, I'm just knackered after yesterday."

His grip tightened, but he turned his attention back to the road. "I *know* that's not true, but if you don't want to talk about it, I won't push you."

My first reaction was relief—having someone force you to dredge through muck you'd rather leave undisturbed is never fun. But the longer I held Seamus's hand, the more I realized that I wanted to talk. The trouble lay in pinning down the words to express my jumble of thoughts. To his credit, Seamus halfway ignored me, keeping watch but saying nothing while I stewed, until finally, I found a loose thread in my mind and began to pick at the knot.

"Yesterday, when I went after Zoya…"

"Mm?" he replied when my voice faded, a study in careful nonchalance.

I forced myself to continue, letting his hand anchor me even as my eyes darted to the passing pines. "Yesterday, when I found her, I told her, ehm…I said I'd kill her if she betrayed us to the Arcanum."

"Right."

"Well, I…I thought about doing it, anyway," I said in a soft rush, squirming as my guilt resurfaced. "Then and there. I had her at my mercy—"

"I wouldn't have blamed you."

"*I* would've. But it's not just that." I hesitated, briefly paralyzed as I tried to predict what his reaction would be to what came next. "When I thought about it…about killing her, I mean…"

He waited, giving me time, then gently prompted, "Yes?"

"I liked it," I whispered. "It felt good."

Seamus nodded pensively, but he didn't retract his hand. "Okay."

"I wanted to kill her, Seamie," I said, wishing for a confessional's protective screen between us. "Right then, with her husband and children in the next room. He and one of the girls were playing chess, and the little one—"

"It happens," he interrupted as I ramped up. "We've all felt it. Someone throws a punch or gets mouthy with you, or you separate the same idiots at the pub three nights in a row…maybe things got better in Durham after my departure, but I know *I* wasn't always pure of thought on the job," he joked.

"No, of course not. Nor I. But…"

He passed a trailer loaded down with wrecked cars, an insurance nightmare on eighteen wheels. "But what?"

"Now that I can, you know, cast in there…what if I lose my temper? What if I lash out before I know I'm doing it and hurt someone, or worse?"

"Your temper's fine, Badger."

"My *control* isn't," I countered. "I still wake people into the dream space without intending to. Maybe I'm clumsy, maybe I'm doing it subconsciously, I don't know. But if I can accidentally wake someone, I can accidentally kill someone just as easily." I softly sighed and leaned against the headrest. "Perhaps the best thing to do right now is stay out of the dream space. Until I'm positive that I have this sorted, I can't trust myself in there."

"Trust me, you're not going to snap," Seamus insisted. "I know you better than that. You've never been unnecessarily stabby."

"You're not listening to me," I said, my voice rising toward a shout in the too-small car. "I *liked* the thought of killing her! I was standing there, imagining how her face would look when I struck! My God, if I'm capable of that…"

As I fought the clenching in my chest, Seamus pulled off onto the shoulder and parked the car. "I'm fine, really," I lied, glaring at the door. "We can keep going. I'll take a turn if you're getting bored—"

"Badger." He waited, then tried again. "Badger, look at me, please."

Reluctantly, frustrated with myself for throwing the matter into his lap, I turned to find his expression a careful neutral instead of the pitying I'd expected. "I'm okay, Seamie."

"Be that as it may"—his tone told me that we both knew I wasn't okay in any sense of the word—"I need to show you something."

"What's that?"

He unbuckled his seatbelt, then peeled off his thin gloves. A flicker of hesitation crossed his face before his fingers stretched across the car to find my temples. "You might want to close your eyes. This will probably feel weird."

Experience had taught me that seldom does anything immediately pleasant result when a young faerie gets anywhere near someone else's head, and I stiffened under his touch. "What are you—"

"I don't know how else to make you understand," he muttered, and my world went black.

Speaking as a wizard, the problem with fraternizing with the half fae is that we become complacent. Get to know one who's a decent person, not too flashy with the fireworks, and still well within a mortal lifespan, and soon, you tend to forget all the precautions you should be taking. *Sure, technically, he's fae*, you tell yourself, *but he's just like us.* Enchantment's kind of like spellcraft without the wand, and besides, he's your friend—can someone who laughs at your jokes and argues with you about which Christmas number one was most overplayed really be that different?

We are, as a species, particularly adept at lying to ourselves when it's convenient.

To the mundane, spellcraft and enchantment must seem like one and the same—whether you're producing a cup of tea from thin air or raining lightning down upon your enemies, you're manipulate the magic around you to generate an effect. Those of us on the other side know better, of course. Most of the time, you can use an enchantment or a spell to achieve the desired result, but the *process* is vastly different, as is the amount of magic expended. Pretend you're trying to get into a bank vault. Spellcraft is all about precision and economy, rather like picking the lock. Enchantment is quicker and easier, and it has the potential for a messier result—here, blowing a hole through the vault door with ten kilos of PE-4.

But we're limited to the skills we have, and so we teach ourselves ways around our weaknesses. Wizards learn to make bigger explosions and to focus their casting to lessen the interval between thought and outcome, while faeries who work at it can tame their wilder sort of magic into something almost approaching spellcraft in its technicality. Still, there are areas in which each side naturally surpasses the other. No faerie could ever produce an equivalent to the most complex spells, such as the intricacies of aural examination, and no wizard will ever equal a faerie at mental manipulation.

Faeries can throw flames when they're of a mood, but they can also get inside your head as easily as blinking. That's all glamour is, really—making everyone around you (and sometimes yourself) see what isn't there. If a wizard wants to alter his face for more than a few minutes, he'll go to the trouble of transformation, but since a faerie can make you see what he wants you to see, why bother with the extra work? And as they're adepts in this area, a moderately skilled faerie has the unsettling ability to jump inside your head and poke around, with or without your permission. If you ever see two faeries suddenly making eye contact for no apparent reason, odds are there's a bit of telepathy at play.

Finding yourself with an older, well-practiced faerie inside your head isn't a painful experience. Certainly, it feels odd—depending on the faerie, the contact can seem like anything from an unscratchable itch in the middle of your brain to a fluttering sensation like an insect bumping into a lightbulb—but it doesn't *hurt*. Seamus was neither old nor particularly experienced, however, and his touch hit me like a pair of jackhammers attacking my temples.

I know I screamed when everything went dark, but before I could focus on the pain, a picture resolved around me, as if I'd put on a pair of virtual reality goggles. There was our old primary school playground, the wooden towers and creaking drawbridge and mildewed cargo net and yellow fireman's pole, long-gone victims of modernization and safety standards. I blinked, but the image remained, large as life, dappled with shade as the clouds flew overhead in the stiff wind. The air smelled crisp—October, perhaps—and all around me, I heard the sounds of children at play, feet running over the pea gravel that never cushioned a fall, voices raised in the shrieks of young people with energy to burn.

I knew those voices. Friends, acquaintances, annoyances—I knew them all, knew where they sat in our classroom, knew who was likely to have done the homework and who would spend most of the next period quietly making spitballs in the back of the room. These were my people—Jack and Richie, Pauline and Sandra, Will and Jill, the twins—but I was seeking one in particular.

I paused on the pavement surrounding the playground and surveyed the scene while a few errant leaves fell from the tree above me, flashing red when they hit the sunlight in their erratic descent. My sock had wrinkled under the arch of my left foot, as usual, and I balanced while I reached under the frayed cuff of my trouser leg to yank the sock taut—

Trousers?

I'd never had trousers in primary school—the girls' uniform required a pleated skirt and jumper. From the corner of my eye (which, I noticed with growing alarm, I wasn't controlling), I caught a glimpse of my hands—a child's hands, still stubby, the fingers tipped with short, slightly dirty nails. Having favored pink polish or at least a clear coat at that age, surely a holdover from my mother's Texas upbringing, I knew those hands weren't mine.

This was *Seamus's* head, and I was caught in the middle of his memory.

With a moment's concentration, I could separate my consciousness from his, but still, his thoughts flowed through mine, strange sensory impressions of a body I'd never worn. Judging by the faces I recognized on the playground equipment, he couldn't have been more than eight or nine. He was still searching for someone—me, no doubt, we'd been thick as thieves at that age—so where *was* I?

And then, from past the swings and the flat place where the younger girls had chalked out a hopscotch grid, came a voice that stirred up unpleasant memories in my own head and made Seamus's fists clench. Doug Stewart, the new boy, the tosser who—

No. Focus.

Seamus started across the playground, growing tenser and faster with every step, sliding socks be damned. He gave the swings a wide berth—no sense in risking a run-in with a metal chain. I felt welling up from his mind the memory of his last iron burn, which had blistered his finger like a glowing poker, before he suppressed it and ran around the hopscotchers. And then, as he neared the far wall of the playground, he rounded an overgrown bush and found Doug—and, I realized with a jolt, me.

That was *me*. The skinny girl in the skirt and dirty shoes, all elbows and knees, with the red face and trembling jaw—I knew her, if only by the white streak running from her forehead back through her black ponytail. She'd hunched her shoulders and turned away from the stocky blond boy behind her as if bracing against a winter wind, but his words cut through her defenses all the same: "You're a *freak*, Parsons. Did you run away from a freak show, eh? Why are you crying, crybaby? Because I'm right? Because you're a weird freak?"

My own thoughts at seeing that moment replayed were almost immediately subsumed by the rising tide of Seamus's anger...but no, this wasn't anger. Anger was unpleasant but manageable, a beast on a leash. This was white-hot rage, swelling to fill every inch of him, a searing brilliance that negated all else.

The girl I'd been covered her face to hide the worst of her weakness, and as her sob escaped, Doug turned to look at Seamus. "What do *you* want?" he said with a smirk, and pounded his fist against his palm, a threat against interference.

His rage was still growing, but there was nowhere else for it to go but *out…*

Seamus jerked with the uncontrolled release of power, and then Doug flew into the brick wall with a wet splat and the sharp crack of breaking bone. Doug wailed his shock and pain, I watched with my mouth open as his broken arm dangled in his torn jumper, and Seamus, free of the sanity-stealing grip of his anger, shook with the fear of punishment to come as he saw what he had done.

The blackness fell again, a welcome curtain, but lingered only an instant before clearing to reveal a small interview room. I didn't recognize the place—it wasn't in Durham, I knew—but the setup was familiar: cinderblock walls covered in cheap white paint, a table the length of a loveseat, four chairs of gray plastic over steel tubes, two of them occupied. The fluorescents glowed overhead, and I—no, Seamus—opened the manila folder on the table in front of me. The middle-aged man across the table was a stranger: mousy brown hair trimmed short, a white tracksuit jacket over jeans, the scraggly beginnings of a moustache. Whoever he was, Seamus was losing patience with him.

I watched Seamus's hands riffle through the folder until they found a set of snapshots. A small, pale throat, bruised. The same throat from the side. A little hand, scratched in places. Its mate. He slid the next few photos to the back of the stack, uncomfortable with the images of the trauma to the girl's privates, then lingered on a headshot of the victim. Susannah Duncan, ten, goalie for her youth football team. One brown eye was blackened from the fist that she said had struck her to stop her screams. Her hair was as dark as the bruise…all but the white streak that framed the left side of her swollen face.

Seamus slid that picture and the one of Susannah's throat across the table to the suspect, her assistant coach, who watched with affected disinterest. "She told us everything," he said. I could feel my borrowed throat buzz, my lips and tongue produce the words. His voice sounded strange until I remembered that I was hearing it as he did, from within his own head. "Named you. We'll have the lab work soon enough, and you know *that* won't lie. This"—he tapped his finger against one of the photos—"will go before a jury. These pictures here in front of you. What do you suppose they'll think about a man who'd do that to a little girl?" He paused, letting that sink in, then said, "Tell me the truth. Explain this to me."

The man considered the photos for a long moment, then picked up Susannah's headshot and held it closer. "You want the truth? Going to give me these and hope I feel guilty?" he finally said. I could pinpoint his accent to Belfast, and I knew, to my horror, what was coming next. "Yeah, right, I was too rough," he said as he put the photo back on the table by its mate. "She panicked. But if you could see the way she's been asking for it—"

The rage rose, faster than before, until the world was nothing but his anger and his burning need for a target. I felt it snap from him like a cracking whip, a flaming line that wrapped itself around the man and squeezed.

Seamus sat in shock for only a second before pushing back from the table and scrambling to his feet. The man screamed as he burned alive, and Seamus, his breath coming in terrified, hitching gasps, moved away until his shoulders hit the wall. The smoke detector in the ceiling began to blatt, and then the sprinkler engaged in the room, turning all of his papers translucent. Still, the man burned, flailing in the ineffective rain as he tried to save himself. Seamus watched, frozen, until the door flew open and a young man ran inside with a fire extinguisher.

The darkness returned, but not before I heard the

rescuer yell, "Medic! Someone help, my God, he's turned black…"

And then, I recognized the Joneses' kitchen, the morning sunlight, the back of my rumpled T-shirt. Carey was staring at me with her arms folded, and my shoulders shook under her gaze. "We've risked everything sheltering you," she said, implacable. "I put a roof over your head, Hannah. Food on your plate. I don't even know how many trips to Arizona Zeb and I have made on your behalf. Hell, I taught you to sleepwalk in the first place. This is how you repay me?"

I heard myself try to protest—if Seamus's voice sounded odd from the inside, my own sounded almost foreign from within his head—and then Carey raised her hand, silencing me. "You're finished here. The others can stay for now, but you're out. And if you'd repay our kindness at all, you'll go far, *far* away. Faerie would be a good start."

The memory was fresh enough in my mind, and I certainly didn't need to see it replayed in Seamus's to recall that morning and how much her dismissal had smarted. But before I could analyze the situation, I felt his rage flare like a deadfall struck by lightning. He stared at Carey for an instant, an ocean of rage heading for the shore, straining against its bounds…

He exhaled, wrestling it back into the depths from which it had arisen, and squeezed my shoulder. "We'll be gone by noon. Come on, love, let's pack…"

When the blackness lifted that time, it did so with a silent *pop*, and I found myself back in the Mustang, staring across the hand brake at Seamus. "Badger?" he said, waving his hand in front of my eyes as they tried to focus. "Badger? Come on, wake up. Hey—"

He reached for my shoulder, and I reflexively pulled back until I felt the glass behind my head, putting as much of the car between us as I could. Seamus froze, then withdrew his hand and retreated. "Say something," he murmured. "Please, love."

It took me another moment to collect myself—yes, I checked, I was back in control of the body I was inhabiting—but my mind continued to whirl. What I had felt in him, even in memory, was horrifically violent, and I tingled with the phantom sensation of the power that had exploded from his deepest core. By turns, I wanted to scream and be sick.

And he was watching me with a look that bordered on terror—the grownup's counterpoint to the expression I remembered him wearing when he attacked Doug on the playground. But what was *Seamus* afraid of? I was the one who'd been dragged through the darkest corners of his soul, who'd felt his twinge of satisfaction at incinerating his suspect. If either of us had something to fear, it was me, and that something was a monster wearing my Seamie's face...

Then it hit me: of course Seamus was afraid. He stood before me, as naked as he could possibly be, and waited to see whether I'd run from him. I'd seen his worst, and maybe his best wasn't enough balance the scales.

Though my tongue tried to stick to the roof of my mouth, I managed to meet his eyes and croak, "How do you *live* like that?"

Seamus seemed almost relieved at the question, but then again, I hadn't ordered him out of the car. "I didn't realize it wasn't normal until Val started working with me. You...don't get that feeling, do you?"

I shook my head.

"Apparently, it's a faerie thing. I've always had it," he quietly explained. "But I realized that if I didn't rein it in, bad things happened. You see what I mean."

Trying not to think of the man in the track jacket as he flailed and burned was taking most of my discipline. "Carey..."

"Exactly. It's harder to control when someone I care about is hurt, but with practice..." His shoulders rose and fell. "I'm sorry to have done that to you, but I didn't know how else to make my point. That's my reality, Badger. It doesn't happen every day, but it's often enough that I know it well. And if I can keep *that* in check, then I'm not at all concerned about your ability to control yourself in the dream space." He paused, studying my expression, then mumbled, "Are you okay? Did I hurt you?"

I saw his anxiety, rubbed my face, and pulled myself together. "Please don't *ever* do that again," I muttered. "At least not without warning me."

"Intense?"

"You don't know the half of it."

He bit his lip. "Sorry, love. I should have—"

"I'm all right. Let's go, we're wasting daylight."

Though Seamus still regarded me with unease, he guided us back onto the road and reset the cruise control. After a long few minutes of no sound but the hum of tires on asphalt, he asked, "Are you cross with me?"

"No."

He hesitated, then said in a rush, "I have it under control, I swear. I've only really lost it three times, and that was before Val. I promise you, I can control it…"

Seamus's voice petered out as I reached toward the wheel and took his hand. His grip on me was that of a drowning man.

We stopped for the night at a Holiday Inn near Daytona Beach and curled together on the unyielding mattress while the overly excited children in the next room screeched at each other and the television. The air conditioner hummed too loudly to be in perfect working order, and the thin sheets were perhaps somewhere in the neighborhood of one-hundred-count, but I was grateful to be horizontal once more. While I lay on my side and my body tried to accept the fact that it was no longer moving, Seamus fit himself into my curves and held me in the darkness, his breath warm and slow on the back of my neck.

I thought he'd fallen asleep when he mumbled, "Badger?"

"Mm?"

He swallowed audibly. "If it's too much…I understand."

At that, I rolled over to face him, another shadow in the void, and scooted closer until our foreheads touched on the flat pillows. "It's not too much," I murmured. "It's never been too much. You know that."

"Yeah, but today, the look on your face—"

"That was because of your little magical mystery tour. 'Disorienting' doesn't begin to cover it, love."

His hand found the valley of my waist—which, to be frank, had risen closer to the peak of my hip in recent years than I preferred. "I just wanted you to understand that you're not alone. It's scary as hell when you aren't in control of it, right? I *get* that. And I…" He paused, choosing his words. "Platitudes and reassurance are nice, but I wanted to get through to you."

"And how."

"Sorry."

I snuggled closer to Seamus. "Points for effort, minor deduction for execution."

"So you're not going to kill me in my sleep, then?"

"Not tonight."

We lay there in silence, listening as an advert for an erectile dysfunction pill blared through the wall.

"Are you going to hex that, or shall I?" he muttered.

With a grunt, I pulled one hand free of the bedclothes, pointed at the headboard, and whispered until the television shut off and the children began to whine. "Better?"

"Much," he yawned, and waited while I readjusted myself before kissing me. "Sorry about the onion, too."

"If I'm not tossing you out of bed over your anger management issue, then I'm not going to be bothered by a little onion."

He was quiet for a minute, then whispered again, "Badger?"

"Yes?"

"Were you planning on sleepwalking tonight?"

"Nope. Even if I wanted to, I can't concentrate with the screaming kids."

"We could hex—"

"*Good night,* Seamie."

My partner chuckled and shifted on the mattress. "You're driving first tomorrow, yeah?"

"Seeing as I'd like to make it to the Keys before I'm fifty…"

"I was going perfectly fast," he mumbled in protest.

"For a granny."

"You wound me, Badge."

I kissed him again, tasting the ghost of his onion rings once more, then let myself drift to sleep as the restless neighbors began jumping on the bed.

With traffic on our side and my lead foot unleashed, we sped down I-95. Shortly after two Monday afternoon, having made only a couple of false turns as we navigated, I pulled off onto East Rock Key, a little island of no consequence in the chain of inhabited patches. A two-lane road spread over with white sand led across the length of the island and dead-ended in an irregular cul-de-sac of cracked asphalt. To the south of the road stretched an empty beach, unbroken but for the occasional palm standing sentinel above the tide line. The northern half was partly covered by a scrubby undergrowth of sea oats and palmettoes beneath more of the towering palms. If there was a path through the trees, I couldn't find it. A weathered wooden sign at the turnoff named the island, but there was no other hint of recent occupation, not even a sunbather in search of a quiet beach.

Despite its beauty, the place was shunned by locals, as I'd learned when I stopped to top up the thirsty Mustang and asked the elderly clerk inside the convenience shop for directions. He'd startled at the name, then quickly crossed himself and gave me a hard look. "What do you want with East Rock?" he'd asked, staring at me as if I might be primed to leap across the counter and attack.

"Friend of a friend said it was lovely," I'd lied, smiling to sell my story. "He was down here a few years ago—"

"*Ah*," he'd interrupted, as if that explained everything, but his demeanor softened by a degree. "Must have been here *before*."

"Before what?"

The clerk, bald as a bowling ball and tanned the color of milkless tea, had looked left and right for potential eavesdroppers before leaning toward me and muttering in a conspiratorial tone, "There was a bar on East Rock. Houses. People lived there. Other folks'd go out there, have a couple drinks, nice time, you know. Weird stuff happened every now and then, but no one really gave it a second thought. And then, one day, it was gone."

"What was gone?"

"*Everything*," he'd said, giving careful emphasis to each pulled-taffy syllable. "Buildings, cars, people—poof. Like nothing'd ever been there at all." He'd shaken his head and retreated to the safety of his stool. "Y'all don't want nothing to do with that place, trust me. Ain't natural."

To be fair, though, neither were we, and so I parked the car and stepped out to have a look round the empty island. Seamus climbed out after me in his T-shirt and jeans, then slipped on a pair of sunglasses to survey the placid ocean. "Right, then," he said, unkinking his back. "If you were a mermaid, where would you hide?"

"Merrow," I reminded him.

"Yes, yes," he said absently. "I don't think any of them are listening in right now unless they can make themselves invisible." He paused, frowning. "They can't, can they?"

"Not that I know of." Considering the sandy expanse, I peeled off my trainers and socks, rolled up my trousers, and padded to the hard-packed shore. The water felt nearly like a bath in the July heat, rather different to the Atlantic we'd left behind in Virginia, and I resisted the urge to toss aside the rest of my clothing and plunge in. Seamus joined me at the water's edge, similarly freed of the constraints of footwear, and we soaked our feet in comfortable silence as a pair of gulls swooped and dove overhead, chasing a school of baitfish.

After a time, when my toes were beginning to prune, I told him, "Coileán said we're to take a boat to the back of the island and signal him from there."

He nodded. "Want me to do the honors?"

"Be my guest."

Seamus turned inland, squinting behind his sunglasses as he contemplated the task, then twisted his hand as if he were trying to scoop water from a stream. As I watched, the sand rose and coalesced into the shape of a skiff, then hardened as it transformed into white fiberglass. An outboard motor—or at least a facsimile of the shell of one, as I doubted that Seamus knew what went into a motor, let alone had the power to enchant steel into being—appeared at the back of the boat. He traced one finger through the air, and a trim blue stripe appeared along the hull. "How's that?" he asked.

I stepped closer to inspect his work—a pair of benches inside, a couple of life preservers, and even a stone anchor—and smiled back at him. "That'll do. Shall we?"

With the path clear, I levitated the boat over the sand and plopped it into the shallows, then climbed aboard. Seamus jumped in after me, and with another magical push, we were free of the island and puttering over the waves, being propelled by something that was decidedly not mechanical. I sat at the rear and steered while Seamus kept an eye out for underwater obstacles, and in short order, we'd reached the sheltered side of the island, a wooded bay hidden from passing drivers. We dropped anchor, and then, hoping I'd heard Coileán correctly, I put my palm just over the surface of the sea and sent a white beam shooting into the depths. There was no immediate reaction, and I could see nothing disturbed below us, so I dried my hand on my trousers and shrugged. "I think this is the part where we wait."

Seamus made a face. "Any idea how long?"

"No. Coileán was rather vague, all things consid—"

With a splash, a pair of gray, webbed hands rose from the water and grabbed the side of our boat, followed almost instantly by a quasi-cetacean head, like that of a dolphin gone horribly wrong. Seamus yelped and slid toward the other end of the boat, but I held my ground and tried to suppress my unease as the creature's side-set eyes rolled to focus on the two of us. "Ehm…Lord Grivam?" I asked.

The merrow opened its mouth, displaying enough razor-sharp teeth to give a shark pause, then threw back its hairless head and laughed. I waited uneasily until it composed itself, and then it said in Fae, still chuckling, "My father will be amused to hear of this."

Judging by its voice, I surmised that the merrow was female. "My apologies, I—"

"Cannot distinguish us, I know," she interrupted. "You're no easier, you realize. I'm Ilunna."

"Hannah," I replied, automatically extending my hand.

She hesitated, then hooked one elbow over the side of the boat to steady herself and met my grip. "You're expected, but he's busy," she explained as she released me.

I fought the urge to again wipe my palm dry of sea water. "Is there a better time? Should we return later?"

"No, he'll speak with you tonight. He said to tell you to wait on the island." Her head tilted toward the trees, and her mouth moved into an expression that nearly approximated a smile. "There is a beach on the other side, not so cluttered. Perhaps you could wait there. Leave a signal to show him the way."

"Will do," I said, and glanced at Seamus, who continued to watch us from a distance. "Excuse my partner, he's…surprised."

Ilunna's off-putting smile widened. "Understood. And should you see Joey, tell him hello from me," she replied, then pushed off from the boat and back-flipped beneath the water with a splash of tail fin.

Once the ripples had stilled, I sighed and began to raise the anchor. "Would you like to go back to dry land, where it's safe?" I asked Seamus.

"God, *yes*," he muttered, then snapped the anchor rope and sped us to shore.

CHAPTER 13

With hours to spare before sunset and no indication of when we should expect Grivam after that, Seamus and I took a hard look at the empty beach and waving palms, then decided to make the best of the situation.

To avoid giving any passing locals heart attacks, Seamus cobbled together a massive glamour around the island, which gave it the appearance of being undisturbed. While he toiled, scowling at the sky as he built his largest enchantment yet, I took the additional step of erecting a magical barrier at the turn-off. Anyone who tried to drive onto the island that night would find himself the proud owner of four flat tires—an unfortunate deterrent, to be sure, but I felt better with the spell activated. Blocking off water access was another matter, however. While I could work out a spell to blockade us, I wasn't entirely certain that I knew how to build in an exception to give Grivam access, and so I crossed my fingers and hoped that the boaters out that Monday afternoon weren't the curious sort.

When Seamus had completed his task, we turned our attention to the question of shelter, particularly as both of us had begun to burn in the subtropical sun. Remembering what it had taken to put together the bunkhouse, I opted to keep my project to a smaller scale. Waving my wand like a marker on a whiteboard, I sketched and doodled in the air, using fine tracers of sand to draw the shell of my design, then cleared my mind, focused on the desired building, and muttered mantras until the structure popped into being. I waited for a moment, blinking sweat from my eyes, but when the cabana didn't waver or dissolve into dust, I climbed up the beach to see what I had wrought.

The cabana was gorgeous, if I do say so myself, an airy construction of dark wooden beams and gauzy white curtains. I'd covered the roof with oversized palm fronds to block the worst of the sunlight and lined three of the low walls with plush white couches. A woven ceiling fan rotated lazily overhead, stirring the waters of the deep hot tub in the middle of the floor, which I'd accented with a pyramid of rolled towels in easy reach. I climbed the three wooden stairs from the beach, threw together another small spell to remove the sand from my feet as I entered the cabana, and nodded with satisfaction. "Think that'll do?" I asked Seamus.

"I don't know," he replied, climbing up after me. "It's not exactly in keeping with the unspoilt aesthetic of the island…"

His grin told me the truth, and I dismissed him with a snort as I peeled off my shirt. "Well, you can go sit outside and bake if you don't like it. I'll be in here if you need me," I said, testing the hot tub with my toe.

While I changed, he quickly tossed his clothes onto one of the couches. "Aesthetics are overrated. Were you planning on—*ah*."

My eyebrow arched as he turned to face me, and I planted one hand on the hip of my new red bathing suit as he gave me a once-over. "A little decorum, Malone, if you please."

He smiled sheepishly as a pair of shorts materialized in place. "I didn't know—"

"This is Florida, not the Med."

"We *are* invisible behind the glamour right now," he pointed out. "I mean, if you wanted to…"

He left the invitation unspoken, and I stepped down into the perfectly steamy pool. "I'll stick to the suit, thanks. Excellent camouflage for the jiggly bits."

Seamus rolled his eyes and followed me into the water. "You know how I feel about the jiggly bits," he said, catching me around the waist.

"You're blind and incorrigible."

"Yes, and in case you haven't noticed, we're *very* much alone."

I started to push him away, but to my surprise, what I saw in his eyes wasn't mischief or pity—it was hunger, pure and simple, which gave me pause. I was forty-eight, hardly a model or a beauty queen, yet Seamus was staring at me as if I'd just sashayed off a runway in my knickers. True, glamour aside, we *were* in public, and prudence warned that we should be making preparations to receive company, but still…

"Oh, look at that," he said, running his dripping hands over my shoulders. "You're soaked, love. We should get you out of those wet things, shouldn't we?"

"Smooth." I grinned and motioned the curtains closed around us.

As the sun sank, I curled up on the end of the couches, facing the turquoise sea and enjoying the warmth of my new bathrobe while Seamus tended the bonfire on the beach below. The smell of baked fish wafted toward me on the breeze—Seamus's attempt at recreational fishing had ended in defeat, but the enchanted version was good enough—and he had thrown together a fireside table for two with a lovely view of the sunset. Personally, I was in no hurry to leave my perch. The afternoon's recreation and a long soak had done wonders for my mood, and even though the knot in my stomach periodically reminded me of what was to come that night, I felt better than I had in weeks. A spa robe, fresh salt air, and a partner handling all the dinner preparations—what wasn't to like?

Seamus pulled a pair of foil packets from the fire, gave them a quick inspection, and nodded. "Dinner's up," he called. "What are we drinking?"

I unfolded myself from my seat and padded down the stairs and across the warm sand. "I'd be happy with manager's choice, though might I suggest something white?"

He motioned a ceramic platter into being and decanted the fish from their baking packets. "Chardonnay?"

"Could do." I settled into my place, a generous wooden folding chair with a white cushion, and watched as plates, utensils, and wine stems appeared. "You're getting good at this, Seamie."

"Just practice," he said with a grunt, but I caught his satisfied smile.

In a matter of minutes, the table was laden with side dishes, jasmine rice and steamed vegetables and a salad tossed with a balsamic vinaigrette barely on the cusp on too sweet, and he lifted his half-filled glass toward me. "To doing this holiday thing more often."

"Cheers," I replied, clinking my glass against his. "This is lovely, dear."

"Good." He took a sip and set his stem aside. "I have a couple decades' worth of missed holidays to make up for, so…"

"You're off to a fair start." I cut into my fish with the side of my fork and inspected the meat. "Bones, be careful. And how were we going to show Grivam where we are? With the glamour in place—"

"Ahead of you. See that?" he asked, gesturing toward the waves with his knife.

I squinted at the surf. "Is it glowing, or is that just me?"

"I anchored a few lights down there. Should give him an idea of where we're hiding, yeah?"

"Clever boy."

With my mind at ease—or as close as it was going to come that evening—we lingered over dinner until the fire burnt low and the stars came out in the moonless sky. Seamus cleared away the evidence while I threw together a shower behind the cabana and freshened up, and by the time I'd reluctantly dressed, he'd traded our dining set for a pair of cushioned wooden chairs by the fireside. "They're loungers," he said, grinning as he demonstrated the improbable movement. "Go on, give it a try."

I settled in, kicked the sand from my bare feet, and leaned back to stare at the sky. "We could use these in Rigby."

His chair creaked as he mirrored my pose. "I was thinking about that. Our roof is flat, right? Couldn't we extend the outside stair and do something like this?"

"Maybe not the bonfire."

"*Maybe* not," he conceded. "But some loungers, a summer breeze, a few adult beverages…potential?"

I began to respond, but I fell silent and sat up as I saw motion at the tide line. Whatever was rising from the sea appeared to be nothing more than a blot against the sky at first, but as my eyes adjusted, the shape resolved into that of a thin old man, hobbling precariously up the sand with the aid of a cane. The decorative gold handle atop it glinted in the firelight, but to me, it seemed woefully unsuitable for the terrain.

By the time Seamus had flipped back his chair and risen, I had intercepted the newcomer, who was white-haired, wizened with age, and dripping. His skin seemed to hang from his limbs like the wrinkled, borrowed suit of a much larger man, but his dark, deep-set eyes regarded me with interest. "Young Hannah, I presume," he murmured in Fae.

I hesitated, hoping I wasn't about to step in it a second time. "Lord Grivam?"

To my relief, he nodded. "Perhaps I could trouble you for a towel."

"Sure, sure, of course," I said, rushing to create something sufficiently fluffy. "Evaporation's only pleasant when the sun is out, isn't it?"

He accepted my offering and carefully wrapped it about

his waist. "The wind does not bother me. If memory serves, your people have a custom involving clothing, do you not?"

"Oh…ehm, well, yes," I stammered. "But there's no need to put yourself to any—"

The merrow patted my shoulder and shook his head. "This is not my first time ashore. Shall we?"

I offered him my arm, and we began our slow trek up the beach, giving Seamus time to add a chair beside mine and put another few logs on the fire. Grivam's balance was shaky at best, and his towel repeatedly attempted to fall off as he walked, to both of our frustration. Finally, with a whispered incantation, I converted the towel into a firmly tied bathrobe, and after a moment's inspection, he nodded his approval.

Seamus was waiting by the new chair when we tottered up. "Here, allow me," he offered, taking my place at Grivam's side, and guided him off his wobbly feet. "Something to drink? Eat?"

Grivam gave him a quick look and faintly smiled. "You must be young Seamus."

His brow furrowed. "How did you—"

"Young Coileán warned me that the lady would likely not be traveling alone. And yes, a drink would be acceptable. Whatever you're having."

Seamus poured him a glass from our second bottle of chardonnay and brought it over as I took my seat. "You needn't have come here, my lord," I said while he sampled the wine. "We have a boat…"

He smacked his thin lips and held the glass toward the fire, the better to see its contents. "Dry, but acceptable. And this was easier—I have much to say, and…well," he added with a chuckle, glancing my way, "my daughter informed me that your friend is ill at ease on the water."

I couldn't tell in the firelight, but I was fairly confident that Seamus was blushing.

We waited, listening to the logs crackle and the waves

roll while Grivam drank, and then he wedged the glass into the sand with a satisfied sigh and turned to me. "You have his look."

"I…do?"

"This," he said flicking his thin hair with one gnarled finger. "Dark with a white patch, I remember it well. He was always sensitive about it—thought it made him seem older than his years. There were those who used to tease him, but not once he came into his power. Simon was a mighty man in his season, and by mortal reckoning, his season was long." He paused, watching as I digested that. "Coileán told you that I knew Simon, correct?"

"Yes."

"*That* is an understatement, but he was unaware. What would you know of him?"

I struggled to pull my thoughts into coherence, anxious that I was wasting Grivam's time. "I…you see, well, it's…ehm…well." Clearing my throat, I tried again. "It seems I've inherited certain of his abilities, and I…I'd like to avoid making his, ehm…more *impressive* mistakes. Does that—"

"I understand." Grivam leaned back against his chair, then yelped as it reclined and the footrest shot out. Catching his breath, he laughed with surprised pleasure and tucked one arm behind his head as a cradle while he regarded the heavens. "You have strange ways of marking time. Give me a reference point in Simon's life, a year."

Seamus shrugged helplessly, but I racked my brain for what I knew of the Magus's career and came up with a starting date. "The Great War began in 1014. Does that help?"

"Mm. Roughly thirteen moons to the year…yes, I suppose." He shifted against the cushion and crossed his bony ankles. "Before your war, my people were at war with ourselves—eight petty kings and queens, all of us vying for supremacy. I sparred with one of the younger upstarts and was run through. See?" He opened his robe above the belt just enough to reveal a faint, oblong scar on his chest. "Nearly killed me. I fled, and trying to escape my pursuers, I let myself wash ashore. This would have been"—he pursed his lips and thought for a moment— "perhaps 1009 or so. A few years before your war."

Even having dealt with faeries, it still unnerved me to hear stories from a man who had distinct memories of the turn of the previous millennium. "You must have been rather young then," I ventured.

He tidied his robe and smiled. "Youth is entirely relative. It was half my span ago, but was I *young*? Now, I would say so, but then, I thought myself rather wise and mature. As we all do in our folly."

Grivam shifted again, apparently uncomfortable, and Seamus took the hint and thickened the cushion. I couldn't fault the old merrow for his sensitivity; at his age and in his condition, losing the buoying weightlessness of the sea surely hurt. Still, he voiced no complaint, and he acknowledged the adjustment with a nod to my partner before resuming.

"When I came to land, I was half dead already, and I made the cardinal error of not shifting," he said, tracking the flight of an airplane high above us. "I can't say how long I lay there before Simon found me. I know I lost consciousness at least twice, and the tide had receded when he walked up, but much of that day is a blur. Anyway, I remember waking to see his boots beside my head. Scuffed, they were, and black, and covered with sand. I realized then what I had forgotten to do, and I shifted before fainting again."

His lips twitched as he turned his head to look at me. "I had no conception at the time of how fortunate I was to have landed on that stretch of beach. When I next woke, I was on a bed in a small house, and he was standing over me with a wand, trying to close my wounds. It was dark in the room—he'd laid a fire, but he'd covered the windows and barred the door."

"Underground wizard?" I asked.

Grivam briefly pondered the term—too late, I saw that the word in Fae didn't carry with it all of the nuances of the English use—but then his face relaxed. "Metaphor, yes? He lived above the ground, but he did not want the others in the town to know of his abilities."

"Sorry, yes, that's what I was asking…"

"No need to apologize." His mouth quirked with a hint of mirth. "I feel fairly confident that I've spoken this tongue longer than you have. But Simon…he was a priest, you understand. A young man—somewhere between twenty and thirty, I believe. Fortunately for me, he was learned enough to recognize my kind, he had pity, and he lived alone."

He paused as he slowly sat up to retrieve his wine. "Telling tales often brings thirst, does it not?"

In an instant, Seamus had the bottle at the ready. "Do you need—"

"Not yet, boy, not yet," he interrupted, waving Seamus away. Seamus hesitated, then twisted the bottle into the sand beside Grivam's chair and took his seat.

I had no idea of what the merrow tolerance for alcohol was like, but I wasn't about to question Grivam as he drained his glass, poured himself another, and quickly chased the first.

"You have a term for wizards like Simon, young Hannah, which now escapes my memory," he continued once his thirst was momentarily slaked. "He was the first of his kind—his parents lacked the talent."

"New-blooded," I replied.

"Ah, *yes*." Tapping the side of his head, Grivam sighed. "Age is not always helpful. Anyway, yes, Simon was new-blooded. Lucky for him, *his* childhood priest was also a wizard—there were many such in those days, wizards hiding in the clergy—and that man steered Simon into their ranks. The boy was taught to read and write, and for his years, he had an extensive understanding of spellcraft when I met him. Even then, his diary was an impressive work of magical scholarship. And he taught himself this tongue from books, did you know that?"

"No," I admitted, feeling momentarily inadequate. "I…I grew up Fringe, I was never taught Arcanum history in great detail…"

"Coileán mentioned that your education was lacking in places," he replied, which did nothing to help my ego. "But your grasp of the language is better than Simon's was then—we partly communicated by signs until he better understood it in its spoken form, and I was slow to learn his tongue."

Whether Grivam had intended or not to throw me a bone, I smiled my gratitude.

"In any case," he continued, "his linguistic skills weren't his greatest gift. Simon was immensely talented—more than he realized. I'd had dealings with wizards before him, and none compared to this boy with a homemade wand and threadbare tunics."

He coughed as the breeze shifted the bonfire's smoke toward us but motioned us down when we were halfway out of our chairs. "I'm not as feeble as you think," he wheezed, and paused for more wine while I threw together a spell to divert the smoke toward the water.

"So," said Grivam, sand-crusted glass in hand, "by the time I woke in Simon's house, he had dragged me to shelter and set his healing spells to work. I told him who I was—as well as I could, that is, with the linguistic problem—and he filled in the gaps in my memory of that day. I would have left him that evening, but even with his spells at work, I was weak. I lost a great deal of blood, you understand, and magic can only do so much. Simon offered me his bed, and in the morning, when I told him of my people's war, he offered me sanctuary while I planned my next move."

"Bet the Arcanum loved that," said Seamus on my other side. "Or did they know?"

Grivam craned his neck to see around me. "And which arcanum would that be? There were ten on that island alone at the time." Catching my surprise, he added, "I know far more of wizard politics in those days than you would imagine, but then again, I was there."

"For the Great War?" I pressed. "*You?*"

"Yes, but that came later. First, let me find…ah, there you are." He finished the wine bottle, and Seamus surreptitiously refilled it, this time with a red. "So, the arcana situation. It wasn't then as it is today, you understand," he said, keeping his eyes on me. "There was no single arcanum. Simon's order primarily studied and taught, and they hid themselves in the priesthood to avoid the attention of the mundane world. They saw magic as a gift, and they considered it their duty to assist those who were less gifted. Truly, I could not have chosen a better rescuer."

He lifted his glass and the wine bottle again, then paused and considered the liquid level. "Wasn't this—"

"Just topping it up," Seamus offered.

"Ah. Very well." He poured again, examined the change in color, then looked past me at Seamus and smirked. "You needn't be so concerned, boy. This has very little intoxicating effect."

Seamus mumbled something that might have been a denial, and Grivam gave me a brief look of long suffering.

"But as for the arcana," he continued between sips, "no two were alike in their governance or policies, and they squabbled—not only with each other, but with the arcana on the mainland, some of which were substantially larger than the English arcana. Simon's arcanum was one of the few that didn't engage in the petty wizard wars. His fellows had no great designs on power. They wanted their books and the occasional hearty debate, and they were content, or so Simon told me. I met several of them over my many moons with Simon, and nothing I saw in them made me doubt his assessment."

Grivam sighed and watched the fire's breeze-tossed sparks for a moment before he spoke again. "They were fools. Clever fools, but fools all the same."

"What do you mean?" I asked.

"A wise man may wish peace and prosperity to others, young Hannah, but only a fool expects the same wish in return. Six days after Simon found me, one of the other arcana descended on his village. They had declared themselves supreme some time ago, and Simon's order had ignored them. The massacre of his village was a message of what would befall the rest of his people should they retaliate."

"Massac—"

"They left no one alive. Male, female, the young, the livestock—no one. And they burned every structure to ashes."

"My God," I whispered. "How did you two escape?"

There was no levity in his smile. "By your standards, I barely sleep, and Simon was ever quick to stir at unexpected sounds in the night. I saw the glow of their torches and roused him, and when we realized how many of them had come—and how defenseless the village was— I dragged Simon down the beach and into the sea. Oh, he fought me," Grivam added, "and he tried several times to swim back, but it would have been suicide, and he soon saw reason. By then, there was nothing we could have done to save the others."

He fell silent again, and from the way he contemplated the bonfire warming us, I could only imagine what he must have been seeing in his mind's eye.

"The boy who walked out of the sea with me the next morning, choking on smoke and the stench of burned flesh, wasn't the boy who went in. He barely spoke while he sifted through the rubble of his home—his diary, spell-protected, was the only thing that survived. Then we walked together through the ashes and the smoldering ruins, and when Simon had seen the extent, he wept. And then, when he had control of himself again, he asked me why I was so unbothered by the carnage." Grivam drank, slowly blinking. "I told him I had seen worse. That all of my people's factions were at war with each other, and this was nothing compared to the worst I had seen."

Seamus coughed beside me. "What, ehm…"

"Humans fight with fire and sword. Too clean. My people prefer teeth."

I decided not to pursue that line of enquiry, and to my relief, Seamus seemed to concur.

"In any case," said Grivam, returning to his tale, "Simon was horrified, but more importantly, he was *angry*. Not so angry that he ran after the attackers in a blind rage, you understand, but angry enough to plan. He built himself a shelter on the beach, then wrote a message in the sand. I can't speak to the spell he used, naturally," he continued, "but when he finished, the writing flashed purple and disappeared. He told me he was alerting the rest of his arcanum and calling them to war."

"But I thought you'd just told him about how bad the situation was with the merrow," I replied. "Why would he—"

"The problem with the merrow was that we had eight leaders with eight armies. There is peace under the rule of one, but under *eight?* Chaos. Simon realized this, and he said that he would unite the arcana to stop the fighting, for the good of wizards and the mundane alike. I almost laughed in his face," he added, and smiled at the memory. "But I saw something there that I could respect. Something hard within the soft priest. And since I had nothing to gain but scars by throwing myself back into our war, I offered him my friendship and my assistance."

"In other words, you sat out your own war," said Seamus.

"A strategic withdrawal," he countered. "A chance to, as you say, lick my wounds. Truly, I didn't plan to be away as long as I was—I thought Simon would meet his end quickly. But he surprised me. The boy was a *peerless* wizard." He sat up, the better to look around me at Seamus. "What he lacked was a leader's skills. Strategy, diplomacy, the best way to make a threat…these, I could teach him. And by the time I returned to the sea, I was stronger and wiser, and my opponents were much weakened from fighting each other. It was little trouble for me to conquer them all. Now, shall I continue, or do you have other criticism for me, young Seamus?"

"No, sir," he mumbled.

"Very well." Mollified, Grivam leaned back again and glanced at me. "All that season, I worked with Simon, toughening his softness in body and mind. By day, he ran the beach until he bled and swam until his lips turned blue. By night, he pored over whatever books of magic and history he could find, committing battles and tactics to memory. All of this was merely in preparation, of course—he had no army to command yet, but I knew his time would come, and soon.

"At the turn of the year, by his reckoning—when the days began to lengthen into spring again—Simon summoned his fellows and announced that he would challenge the dominant arcanum, the one that had burned his village. Only four wizards joined us, but Simon was undaunted. They were merely there to bear witness, you see," he explained, lowering his voice as if he were delivering a great secret. "No one told *them* that, but Simon had no intention of taking his fellows into battle."

I frowned as I listened. "Then how—"

"Single combat. For three days, we marched to the fortress of the other arcanum, deep inland. While we watched, Simon presented himself to their leaders and challenged them for power. They laughed at him—I can hear them now," he added with a smirk, "but how were they to know? Simon was young and slight, and these were men of arms and power, graying and battle-scarred. But they agreed to fight him, I suppose for their amusement.

He slew twelve of them before the rest of the arcanum yielded."

"Quite a magus," said Seamus.

"I have not seen his like," Grivam agreed, and refreshed his glass. "But with those wizards behind him and his four fellows spreading the news to all corners of the island, Simon brought the other arcana under his leadership within the year. Not all came willingly—conquered peoples are seldom eager to cast off their crowns—but from the most powerful of those who knelt, Simon chose his circle of advisors, and he sent the loyal and deserving away to keep peace in his name."

"The first council?" I asked.

"Precisely. And it worked. I dwelt with him while he consolidated his arcanum, offering my assistance when he asked it of me, but to my pleasant surprise, Simon proved capable, worthy of headship. He sent magi to the mainland to broker formal alliances, and he even offered his aid in my war, though I declined his help."

"Why not take him up on it?"

Grivam smiled at my question. "A wizard is a fine thing on land, but in the deeps, he drowns as well as any human. As a people, you are remarkably poor swimmers."

I shrugged at that and helped myself to the wine. "Nothing to be done for it, I'm afraid."

"You are what you are. But back to Simon…as I was saying, he maintained peace in his territory for several years, but news came more and more frequently of fighting on the mainland. Arcana were allying themselves with each other, forming new factions and rebuilding old ones. We knew war was imminent—it was a question of where it would begin, not when. So Simon recalled his messengers, gathered his most skilled wizards, and crossed the sea to conquer the foreign arcana before they could tear each other apart."

I nodded. "The Great War. 1014, Simon lands in Calais and begins the long march across France."

"It is as you say, young Hannah. The march was very, *very* long. Bloody, despite his best intentions. For season after season, Simon waged war and brokered peace, drawing arcana into his arcanum—*your* Arcanum, I should say."

"Not mine. They don't care for my kind," I muttered, and swigged.

The old merrow cocked his head. "No? And you of Simon's blood?"

The wine was almost astringent enough to dry my mouth, and I forced it down. "My father was a witch, my mother mundane. I'm a genuine freak of nature."

He considered that, then offered a half-smile. "Remember, then, that Simon's parents were both mundane, and he conquered the world. Perhaps the Arcanum should be reminded of its past…someday, when it's not busy killing its weakest."

"You've heard about all that, have you?" Seamus interjected.

Grivam nodded. "The young king and queen and I speak in Faerie. But to the topic," he said, adjusting his robe as he crossed and uncrossed his bony legs. "Simon tolerated no holdouts, no neutral parties. Those who refused to join him were battered until they bent, and Simon guarded his peace jealously. He was content to allow local wizards to rule for him as long as they swore absolute fealty. It hardened him, the war," he explained, sounding pensive. "The boy grew into a man, made mistakes, lost soldiers he should have protected. Somewhere along the way, he finally abandoned the vows he had made to his church and took a mate, Béatrix. She was a good woman, strong, fertile. He seemed to find her attractive enough."

"My many-times great-grandmother?" I asked.

To my surprise, Grivam made a face. "Probably. Simon took other lovers, but I never knew of him to sire children on anyone but Béatrix."

"Girlfriends, eh?" Seamus added.

"Not only girls. There was a young man…" He paused and chuckled at my expression. "This was not discussed in your history, was it, young Hannah?"

"Not, ehm…not exactly," I stuttered. "Simon, ehm…"

"The boy's name was Cuthbert," he said once I fell silent. "Some years younger than Simon. He joined the main camp before Simon took the war to the lands of the caliphs and the deep deserts." Grivam looked uncomfortable at the thought of the arid wastes. "He was, to Simon, beautiful, pale of hair and eye, slim like a girl and quick on his feet. A servant to one of the magi. Witch-blooded, you see. He had no talent for spellcraft."

The thought of Simon Magus, venerated father of the Arcanum, slipping off for a rendezvous with a witch-blood made me nearly giddy. "Did Béatrix know?"

At that, Grivam's smile took on an almost wolfish quality. "I should think so. Simon did not always limit himself to a single partner in bed. After so many years of denial, I imagine he was only making up for lost time."

Part of me knew I shouldn't ask, but my curiosity took the reins. "You and Simon, ehm…"

He seemed nonplussed at the question. "I taught him a few things, as the mature should instruct the young. Pairing in this form is not unpleasant, though I don't prefer it. Still, after moons away from another of my people…" He shrugged. "Simon was an excellent pupil."

That, at least, was never going to make the Arcanum's textbooks. "But he really had an affair with a *witch-blood*?" I pressed.

Grivam nodded emphatically. "He took Cuthbert as his manservant, and they were seldom apart. The boy was as clever as he was appealing, and in time, Simon realized that Cuthbert could craft. His wands far surpassed anything any wizard was making, and Simon entrusted him with equipping his best magi. And when he'd finished *that*, Simon put him to work on the larger problem."

"What was that?" asked Seamus, who had produced a bowl of crisps while Grivam was talking.

"Magic is a fixed thing, yes? It isn't limitless. In Simon's larger battles, he and his army would fight with other massive armies, and eventually, both sides would be forced to retire because they had exhausted all of the available magic. It could take a day or two until there was sufficient magic to recommence, and by then, the armies might have had a chance to rest and find supplies. Simon wanted a way to carry magic with him so he could strike when his enemies were weakest. It was Cuthbert who perfected the design. Golden spheres, crafted by Simon's magic, filled by Cuthbert's hands. Those changed the course of the Great War."

Grivam refilled his wine yet again, and I took the opportunity. "The war didn't end until 1062, yeah? He fought across Europe and the Near East, then split the Arcanum forces until Africa and Asia fell. Were you there all along?"

"No." With a swirl of his glass, Grivam took a long sip and licked his lips. "Once the spheres were created, I knew Simon's future was secure, and I took my leave to win my own war. Once a year, I would return and seek word of him, and one day, I was able to greet him in his hall, the greatest wizard of his age, home and at peace. He bade me stay with him for a season, and I agreed."

Grivam's face clouded as he reminisced. "He had changed. For nearly fifty years, he had waged war across the known lands. Though he was grown gray and had passed most humans' span, he was still a warrior, all scars and sinews beneath his robes. But he was very much alone in those days," he explained. "Béatrix and several of her children had died, as had Cuthbert and his other lovers. Simon was surrounded by his magi, most of whom had once been his enemies. And every day would come at least a message or two about a disturbance to soothe or a rebellion to crush. He was...*paranoid*, I suppose, would be the best term. Not without cause."

I hesitated, then asked, "Were you there when he learned to sleepwalk?"

"I was. He came into my chamber like a madman at dawn, raving about the things he had seen, of peoples beyond the water. When I confirmed for him that there were other lands out there, I thought he would strike me—he was furious that I'd never mentioned the far side of the sea. I told him there was no need to concern himself with those lands unless he planned to build a boat strong enough to cross, but he wouldn't leave the matter alone."

The king finished his wine, then twirled the stem in his hands while he stared into the bonfire. "One morning, he told me he had conquered the far west in his sleep, and he relayed how he did so as we broke our fast. He ate with the vigor of a man half his age. That was when I took my leave again. I was deeply fond of Simon, you must know that," he added, looking me in the eye, "but the man I left was not the Simon I had known. The Simon who set off to bring peace would not have recognized him." Grivam paused. "I take it you know of what he did in these lands. Else, you would not have asked for me."

"I've been told, my lord. About three-quarters of the wizard population murdered as they slept because they refused to submit to him."

"That's my understanding. I know he meant well," he continued, and reached across the space between our chairs to grasp my hand. "He wanted only safety and peace. But when he insisted on peace at all costs…as I said, fifty years of war changed him." He gave me a squeeze before releasing me. "What do you know of the end of his days?"

I searched my memory, trying to come up with a halfway intelligent answer. "Not much," I finally admitted. "I know he had a religious conversion late in life, swore off magic, and left the Arcanum, but that's all."

Grivam sat in silence, and I listened to the crackling of

the fire and the low rush of the waves on warm sand until he cleared his throat and spoke again. "Simon's mistake that you fear repeating is his sleepwalking massacre, I assume?"

"More or less."

"And that is because you don't know what happened after." He took a moment to pour, then handed me the wine bottle and nodded to my glass. "Go on, you'll want it."

I did as I was told and sipped, wishing Seamus had come up with a sweeter blend.

"When I left Simon, I stayed away for nearly a year," said Grivam as I wedged the empty bottle back in the sand. "I returned to pay him a visit, hoping his paranoia had abated. It had not."

"He'd conquered the world by then," I said. "What other enemies did he have?"

In response, Grivam glanced past me at Seamus. "He told me that all he had done was for naught as long as there was an unchecked threat from Faerie, and he meant to destroy them."

My jaw dropped, and I caught myself before I could spill my wine. "He tried to take on the *Three*?"

"Two, then. Mab was expelled before the Great War, as I recall. But yes, he had a plan to wipe out the fae."

I turned to look at Seamus, who seemed as flabbergasted as I was. "How the hell was he going to do that? He couldn't have been *that* strong."

"Oh, he wasn't," he agreed. "Simon was mighty, but he was still mortal. His plan, as he told me in our conversation, was to cross the border, wait until nightfall, then sleepwalk and kill the king and queen while he had them at his mercy. With them out of the way, he was going to pick off the courts much as he had the wizards in the far west."

I thought then of Coileán and his unease with the knowledge that I was casting in my sleep. Sure, he was safe from me as long as I remained in the mortal realm, but if I could somehow find a way to sleepwalk in Faerie…

"Did you tell him that was a bad idea?" Seamus asked, interrupting my train of thought.

"Emphatically," said Grivam. "I told him that provoking the courts would do nothing but draw their attention to the Arcanum and make enemies of the fae, and I warned him that the plan was folly. He refused to be dissuaded, and so I took my leave." He drank deeply, then looked out toward the rolling waves. "I left Simon, and once I was back at sea, I found the nearest gate into Faerie and sent word that I needed an audience with all haste."

"You gave him up," I murmured.

His dark eyes swiveled back toward mine. "I was very fond of Simon, but what he was planning was madness. I told Titania and Oberon that he was old and sick in the head, bent under the load he'd taken up, and that he would be acting alone. You see, young Hannah, I tried to save him, to keep them from waging war on the Arcanum for his madness."

"And you put them in your debt," said Seamus. "Telling them about an assassination attempt—that couldn't have been bad for you."

He acknowledged this with a slight nod. "Neither of them was particularly pleased with that knowledge, but yes, each granted me a boon. But such is the way of my relationship with the courts, you understand. Knowledge is precious and valuable."

"Did you tell Simon what you'd done, then?" he asked.

Grivam softly sighed. "I was on my way back to warn him when he made the attempt. What I know of that time came from Titania much later—"

"What happened?" I pressed.

He collected his thoughts, then said, "You are aware that the realm has a consciousness, yes? She speaks to whomever she wills."

"Yes, we've had…ehm…"

"She wasn't fond of me for a while," Seamus interrupted.

"I see. Well, Simon made the crossing, and the realm alerted the king and queen. They caught him in minutes and brought him to Titania's palace. He fought, but they overpowered him and threw him into a cell. For nearly a moon, every time he tried to sleep, someone would wake him. Titania said his howls were most entertaining, but they eventually tired of the game and allowed him to sleep, just to see what he would do."

Grivam shook his head. "Simon was a scholar, but he didn't know everything. He told me that when he sleepwalked, he entered a sort of land of shadows...you know this place," he said, seeing me nod. "What he learned the hard way was that this place doesn't exist in Faerie."

"I can't find it there," I muttered.

"Then it wasn't simply his failing. Simon saw nothing but formless blackness in all directions." He looked away, his thin lips tight, then glanced back at me. "They kept him as their prisoner for five years. One would play with him, then the other, back and forth until they wearied of him. Before she cast him out into this realm, the queen castrated him. I believe she wanted a souvenir."

I looked Seamus's way in time to catch his grimace. "And that's when Simon swore off magic?"

"Soon thereafter. The Arcanum welcomed him home, but he'd had a long time in Faerie to ponder the things he'd done, and he wanted nothing more to do with the organization he built. Simon repented of it all, changed his name, and rejoined his church under his new identity. But before he did, he scattered the golden spheres Cuthbert had made so that the Arcanum would never again use them to wage war. He gave me one as a parting gift—I don't believe the queen and king ever told him that I'd warned them of his coming," he added, sounding almost guilty. "He kept the last sphere for himself, bound his diary in spells so that his secrets would remain protected, and moved to Ireland. I visited him once at his monastery, but when I returned the next year, he was freshly dead. I took his few possessions, including the final sphere, and buried them in a field. All but his diary—I never saw it again."

With a grunt, Grivam swung his legs over the side of his chair, and I hurriedly sat up to face him. "I tell you this so that you learn, young Hannah," he murmured, clasping my hands. "Simon was unparalleled as a wizard, and he tried to use his gift for good. Deep within himself, he thought he was doing the right thing, and in many ways, he was. He made the Arcanum strong. But peace seldom comes without violence, and Simon…he was so afraid of anything that could disturb his peace. He spent his life trying to achieve it, and in the end, his pursuit of absolute security destroyed him." Grivam paused and studied my face. "Did I answer your questions?"

"I…think so."

"Good. Then my tale is done." Using me to steady himself, he slowly stood and reached for his ineffective cane. "There was goodness in him," he added, finding his footing on the loose sand. "Goodness and darkness alike. But so there is in most of us, is there not? It's a question of balance."

I offered him my arm, and Grivam hooked his elbow around mine as we made our slow way down the shore. "Thank you for coming," I told him. "I, ehm…I don't know how to repay you for your time and this information…"

The old merrow chuckled. "Young Coileán warned you, did he? I never give gifts without asking for payment in kind."

"And I suppose I'm in your debt now."

We paused at the water's edge, and Grivam gently turned my chin toward him as the warm water rushed over our bare feet. "If you would repay me," he murmured, "learn from Simon's mistakes. Coileán told me you can work magic in your sleep. That is a dangerous gift, little one. Control it. And someday, should it whisper to you of all the worlds you might conquer, all the peace you might forge through your own might…" He squeezed my arm and looked me in the eye. "Just remember what I told you."

"I will," I promised.

With that, Grivam released me and took a deep breath of the spray-damp air. "This garment," he began.

"A bathrobe, my lord."

"Mm. Will you be wanting it back?"

"If you'd like it, please take it with my compliments."

"Thank you. I think I will," he replied, then tottered into the surf, leaning on his cane. When he was chest-deep, he slipped beneath the water without so much as a splash to mark his departure.

Seamus joined me at the tide line as I scanned the sea. "What use do you suppose he has for a *robe?*" he asked, wrapping his arm around my shoulders.

"Buggered if I know," I said, and to my surprise, I found myself laughing.

CHAPTER 14

We laid a floor over the hot tub in our cabana, converted the benches into a bed, and stretched out beneath the roof of rustling palm fronds while the curtains billowed around us. Dawn found me back on the beach, however, and I was only mildly surprised to hear Seamus's feet shuffling through the sand shortly after I returned to the water's edge. "You're up early," he said as he stretched, his bare chest pink in the pale light of sunrise.

"Just thinking." I rubbed my elbow and watched a pair of gulls dive for their breakfast.

"About Simon?" he asked. I nodded, and Seamus began to rub my tense shoulders through my T-shirt. "Want to tell me?"

I let him continue his massage in silence for a few minutes, enjoying the warming morning and the pressure of his hands as he kneaded my muscles. "Arcanum thinks he's a saint," I said at last, "or at least worthy of veneration. Minor Arcanum thinks he's evil incarnate."

"And the truth's somewhere in between?"

"It usually is, isn't it? *Ooh*." Though I winced as he bore down on a tender spot, Seamus was merciless in his assault on my trapezius. "I suppose he tried. Fucked it up royally, but he tried to do the right thing."

Seamus's fingers stilled, and he came around to face me. "You're not going to do what he did, Badger."

"I *could*," I protested, rubbing my friction-warmed neck. "I told you what I felt with Zoya—"

"And you know what I felt with Carey. You can

control this, love." He ran his hands over my shoulders and arms, up and down, as if he could reassure me through touch alone. "You can do it. And should the day come when you're unsure if you can, or should you ever feel particularly genocidal, I'll be there to talk you off the ledge."

I rested my hands on his waist, keeping him close to me. "If I ever get to the point of genocide, I expect you to do the clever thing and run."

"Why would I do that? I'm not afraid of you."

"Oh? Remember that part about how I could kill you in your sleep?"

"And I could throw fireballs at you right now, but that's not going to happen."

Seamus pulled me against his chest, and I wrapped my arms around him, smelling the hints of salt and bonfire smoke that lingered on his skin. "You're like my second soul, Badge," he mumbled into my wind-tangled hair. "I know you at least as well as I know myself."

"Likewise."

"Exactly. I respect the hell out of you, and not just because you've got that fancy stick of yours in the back of your trousers." I chuckled at that, and Seamus tightened his hold. "But I don't fear you. I don't care what you can do—I know you well enough to know what you *won't* do, and that makes all the difference." After a moment's hesitation, he pulled back slightly to see my face. "You're not afraid of *me*, are you?"

"No, Seamie."

"Thank you," he said with a sigh, unable to fully disguise his relief.

I closed my eyes and held on to him while the waves washed our feet and a lone gull cried overhead. "Maybe I should go to Faerie after all," I mumbled. "Just to be safe."

"What do you mean?"

"I mean I appreciate the vote of confidence, love, but I can't sleepwalk over there. In case we're both wrong about me…"

I left that thought unfinished, and Seamus waited for the space of a long breath before he spoke again. "You know I'd do anything to keep you safe, yeah?"

"I've been getting that impression."

"Right. *Good.* Well, this is me telling you that going over would be a mistake."

I disentangled myself enough to step back and frown at him. "You think Coileán would kick me out?"

"No, not at all. But if you give in to your self-doubt and give up now, before you've found the rest of the Fringe, you'll hate yourself forever. Don't make my mistake," he said softly, cupping my cheek in his palm. "I ran because I was afraid. You're braver than I am, Badger, always have been. If you need someone in your corner now, count on me. But honestly, you've helped loads of people already, and I think you're where you're meant to be. Am I wrong?"

I tried to read the emotion in his deep blue eyes— concern, yes, *so* much concern, but there was love in his gaze, and if I wasn't mistaken, more than a touch of pride.

Smiling, I nodded and rested my head against him once again.

Seamus grunted as he hugged me. "Was that a 'Yes, you're wrong' nod, or was that 'Yes, you're right about everything'?"

"I wouldn't say *everything.*"

And so we stood there together on the beach, holding on to each other as the morning brightened and the wet sand shifted under our feet, until I finally sighed and brushed my hair out of my face. "We've got to go back to Virginia, you know."

"Says who? We've got this lovely place all to ourselves…that hot tub…a little wine, a little sea air, very little clothing…"

"*Seamie.*" Pulling my wand free, I waved the cabana out of existence, then pointed to our convertible. "Hop in. I'm driving."

To our relief, we found Rigby and our apartment much as we'd left it when we rolled into town with the rain on Wednesday night. While Amy hid away in her back room to work on her wand stock, Arnold and Kip had plopped on the couch with a five-hundred-piece jigsaw puzzle of the Eiffel Tower and a six-pack of beer. "We're making progress," my cousin assured me, but what I saw spread across the coffee table was largely a litter of lonely pieces, accented with a few bottle caps from the evening's libations. Still, the boys seemed to be enjoying themselves, so I left them to their labor and retreated to my room to unpack while Seamus asked for an update.

The last four days had been quiet for them—light traffic in the store, long evenings on the beach with takeaway from the sandwich shop and a Frisbee, and nary a blip on either Fringe network. Unless the Minor Arcanum had managed to destroy all of Amy's dark magic detectors, that meant that no one we knew was anywhere close to a fresh Gray Lands gate, which came as a welcome discovery. Carey might have thrown me into the street, but I still didn't like the thought of her, Zeb, and Jimmy attempting to close a gate on their own, particularly not having seen what could come through them. When I logged on to the new network late that night to check with Vivi and see whether Sergei had made it across the border yet, I briefly entertained the thought of shooting Carey an e-mail to ask about the gate situation, but prudence stayed my fingers. If Carey were ever desperate enough that she needed me, I decided, she'd be in touch. In the meantime, it was wiser not to pick at that particular scab.

Seamus might have thought I was brave, but I still had to convince myself. This meant that although I could put off my return for a time, I couldn't avoid the dream space forever.

The trick, I told myself, was building up my confidence, which would come with familiarity and control. Trust your training, your weapon, and your people, and you can walk onto a scene like you've just stepped into the garden. As for me, I could sleepwalk reliably in those days—I just needed to practice until I figured out how to draw my subconscious desires back under my impulse control.

Arnold and Seamus might not have appreciated being my guinea pigs, but then again, I didn't give them a say in the matter. I had two potential targets on hand who didn't need to sleep well enough to operate delicate electronics on a daily basis, and so I focused my energy on them when I sleepwalked night after night. Besides, I knew where both of the guys slept, and I couldn't say the same for Amy— nor did I especially wish to find out whether she and Kip were getting cozy in their downstairs bedrooms.

The fortnight that followed our return from Florida was grueling for me and little better for my targets. Every evening, I waited until Seamus and Arnold fell asleep—an event that came earlier and earlier with the passing days— then sleepwalked and chose a person on whom to focus my attention. In my first attempts, I inevitably woke the target into the dream space, once a spectacular eight times in a single night. My men bore the interruptions stoically enough, but the circles under their eyes in the morning were testament to my failures of the night before.

Not until the fifth night of solid practice was I able to avoid waking Arnold, and then only on one occasion. By the seventh night, I managed to keep both of them under on three-fourths of my attempts—a personal best, even if the sleep-deprived men were less than enthusiastic about the speed of my progress. To give them a break, I turned my attention toward casting for a few nights, spending hours exploring the limits of my power while sleepwalking. I didn't need a wand in the dream space, and if I wasn't careful, I was likely to cast without intending to do so. To control my talent, I tried meditating within the dream, making myself acutely aware of my mind and ethereal body to prevent myself from acting unintentionally. The process took work, and in the end, I had to bring Arnold along one night and force him to grapple with me until I felt closer to confident that even distracted, I had my impulses in check.

I allowed myself to truly sleep only in the mornings, once Arnold and Seamus were up and had put at least a few walls between us. Though I was often exhausted enough to drop off again as soon as my head hit the pillow, sometimes sleep evaded me, and my thoughts circled through my nagging problems: Carey and the Minor Arcanum, surprise gates into the Gray Lands, the many names still on my list of missing Fringers. But more and more frequently, my mind drifted toward Helen and Joey.

I knew neither of them well—I'd met the kidnapped grand magus, and I'd seen enough of Joey in Faerie to decide he was a decent sort—but I wanted to help them. Joey's dejection had been heartbreaking the last time I saw him, and his words stuck with me: *You're my only hope.* No one in Faerie could storm the silo, nor did they have any solid information about what might be going on down there. But if I could keep myself under control, then I could sleepwalk right through the door, find Helen…

Or maybe, I allowed myself to think, I could end this. Part of me felt ill at the notion, but another part—the part that had thrilled at finding Zoya at my mercy—shouted that my time had come.

It was all so simple, really. What but my own trepidation was stopping me from killing Grand Magus Mulligan in his sleep?

For three days, I napped, stared at the television, and tried and failed to concentrate on a book while I debated with myself the wisdom and merit of going after Mulligan.

This wasn't murder—this was an act of war. Killing an enemy combatant, not a civilian. It was Mulligan who had declared war on the Fringe, after all—*we* certainly hadn't started the conflict. And this would be a highly targeted mission with little chance of collateral damage. All I'd need to do would be to sleepwalk into the silo, locate Mulligan, drag him into the dream space, and throw lightning at him until he was crispy. His people would find him dead of a heart attack or a seizure or something in the morning, none the wiser that I'd been there, and with Mulligan gone, surely someone less genocidal would come to power.

Unless Mulligan's replacement was just as bad as he was. Or unless the Arcanum blamed Faerie for Mulligan's untimely death and killed the hostages in retribution.

All right, then, what if I didn't stop with the grand magus? It might take me a night or two to pinpoint them all, but what if I eliminated the entire Inner Council? Lopped all the hydra's heads off at one go? They'd have to bring one of the installation magi in as a replacement, wouldn't they? And hadn't the installation magi been more favorable toward Helen? We'd get someone sensible in power in the silo, and then Coileán and Eleanor could make overtures toward ending the standoff...

No, that was still too risky. Perhaps the installation magi had changed their minds about Helen in her absence. So I'd need to kill—no, *execute*—the entire Council in one night, thereby leaving the Arcanum leaderless and in chaos.

But who was to say that any of the rank-and-file knew where the hostages were being kept?

Well, I could find them, couldn't I? They couldn't hide from me in the dream space—even in a silo full of wizards, a cluster of witches would be visible to me.

Unless they weren't. Unless some spell I'd never imagined was blocking them from all possible detection.

If I killed all of their jailers and no one could find them, they'd die in captivity.

Fine. So I needed to scout out the silo, see if I could locate the Fringers and Helen, *then* take out Mulligan and the rest of his magi, thereby plunging the Arcanum into turmoil and giving the faeries a chance to storm the barricades.

But how many magi were there, anyway?

And what if some of them didn't support Mulligan? What if there was a quiet Arcanum resistance I knew nothing about, working on the inside to free the captives? What if I executed our allies by mistake? How much collateral damage was I prepared to accept as the cost of liberating my people?

They were just wizards, though, yes? They'd never given a damn about us—hell, Arnold hadn't even known of my existence before we joined forces. Why should I care if a few wizards died who perhaps didn't entirely need to, if it meant recovering the kidnapped Fringers and Helen...

...who was herself a wizard. The biggest wizard of them all, wasn't she?

Well, now, she *had* married Joey, and she was half sister to Aiden. Sure, she was a wizard, but she wasn't a *wizard* wizard, right? She wasn't one of the bad ones.

Maybe some of the other magi weren't, either.

Arnie was a magus, after all...

Finally, once I had considered and reconsidered my plan until all I had in mind was a tangle of competing voices and salient facts, I cornered Seamus in the kitchen, where he was stirring a pot of macaroni cheese, and tapped his shoulder. "I need my partner's opinion," I told him once he looked up from his work.

Seamus nodded. Gripping the steel stockpot with one towel-shielded hand, he continued to melt the cheese into the noodles and said, "Talk to me, Parsons."

"What would you say if I offed Mulligan in his sleep?"

To his credit, Seamus didn't pause in his cooking. "Just Mulligan?"

"Probably not. I might need to take out the entire Council as well, to be on the safe side."

"Hmm. This would be in hopes of getting new leadership amenable to ending the hostage situation, yeah?"

"Or giving the powers that be a chance to rescue the hostages while the Arcanum straightens itself out."

He checked the noodles' color, and then, satisfied with the cheese distribution, moved the pot from the range and covered it. "Could work."

"It's possible. I've thought through the variables."

"I'd assumed as much," he replied, leaning against the counter with his arms folded. "Logistically…I wouldn't say it's *perfect*, but it's close enough for me. If you wipe out all of the Arcanum's leadership…yeah, that might do the trick."

Silence hung between us, and I knew he had more on his mind. "But."

"But as your partner, I think it's a bloody awful idea."

"Would that be speaking as my partner, or as my *partner*?"

"Speaking as someone who knows what you're capable of and how you're likely to react." He arched an eyebrow. "You're telling me you're willing to knock out, what, a dozen wizards?"

"More than that, I think. I'd have to ask Arnie."

Seamus sighed and frowned at the floor. "You have good cause," he finally told me. "I can't say it wouldn't be justified, especially considering the losses the Fringe has sustained."

"You still don't like it."

"I think it would eat at you for the rest of your life," he murmured. "You may be a fine detective, Badger, but you're not Rambo. Killing that many people, all in one go…honestly, I think you'd regret it."

He was only confirming what my gut knew to be true, but I still fought back. "What if I freed the hostages by doing so? I don't think I'd lose any sleep over *that*, Seamie."

"Granted, but that's the best-case scenario. What if something goes wrong?" he countered. "You're getting better at this, but what if you panic and wake the wrong people? Or you wake the right people, then have second thoughts and back out? Or someone manages to escape somehow? Now the Arcanum knows what you can do, and what if they hold that against the courts for letting you run about unchecked?"

"It wouldn't be the courts' fault."

"You think Mulligan cares about the technicalities?" He crossed the distance between us and rubbed my shoulders. "I'd love to get the bastard, but I'm more concerned about you. Wait and see. Let yourself get stronger, more secure. There's no need to rush this."

I felt my muscles tense and go limp under his practiced hands. "It's already August," I muttered. "How much longer is it going to be before I'm useful?"

"You're already useful, and you know it," he said, and kissed my forehead. "Fishing for compliments, eh?"

"I'm serious," I protested. "How long is it going to be before I'm a competent wizard? I don't have forever to get this right, and while I muck around, my people are stuck in the silo or God-knows-where..."

Seamus squeezed my shoulders one last time before releasing them to take my hands. "You're one person," he said softly, looking me in the eye. "One brave, talented, and considerably *sexy* person"—I snorted in disbelief at that—"but you can't do it all. You can't always win wars on your schedule. If it takes another year or another ten years before you've got yourself sorted, then so be it. You're doing your best, love. No one can fault you for that."

"*I* can."

"Which is why you have your partner here to be objective. Give it time. Keep practicing on us until you're sure, if you have to. And hey," he added, brightening, "maybe Mulligan will do us all a favor and drop dead of his own accord. Wouldn't that be nice?"

"I wouldn't count on it," I said, then slipped free of his grasp and lifted the lid of the cooling pasta. "Was this all for you, or may I graze?"

"Help yourself." He pulled a pair of plates from the cabinet and spread them on the counter. "If you wouldn't mind doing the honors—"

Before I could fish the ladle from its drawer, I heard footsteps pounding up the staircase, and then Amy burst through the door with her laptop in her hands. "Problem!" she puffed, and spun the screen around.

She'd logged on to the new Fringe network—I recognized the world map and its overlay of white diamonds showing the location of dark magic detectors. The map had gained a flashing red border, however, and the diamond over New Mexico was blinking along with the alarm.

"Gate?" I asked.

She nodded. "That's Jim's detector going off. Gate's somewhere in a thousand miles of him."

"Show me."

She put the computer on the kitchen counter, then tapped at it until a circle appeared around the flashing diamond. "Anything in there. Missouri, Arkansas, Texas, Oklahoma, Louisiana…"

I counted out the rest of the states that fell under the detector's shadow, noting that the gate could just as easily be in Mexico. "We need to narrow the field," I said, and headed toward my bedroom.

"Wait!" Seamus called after me. "What about your lunch?"

"All yours. I need to get out there, *now*."

"It's the middle of the day," he protested, following me down the hallway. "You're not likely to find anyone asleep in the affected area."

I paused at the door and shook my head. "Maybe not, but I might see people massing. Worth a try," I added, and gently closed the door behind me.

I could literally find New Mexico in my sleep. Hovering over Jim's flat in San Angelo, I saw no trace of him, but a glow from several miles away showed me that he was still at the radio station, and ostensibly awake. Rising higher to see my surroundings, I pinpointed the Joneses' ranch to the northeast—Carey and Zeb had yet to leave in search of the new gate, I surmised—and then I started the slow process of scanning hundreds of thousands of square miles for abnormalities.

In the end, I stumbled onto the gate by sheer luck. The higher I floated, the more of the terrain I could see at once, mountains and valleys spread out below me in shades of black and gray. By the time I was high enough to take in most of the detector's wide radius, I had a new problem: the glow of the Arcanum silo, a brilliant, golden haze like a distant city on a dark night. The concentration of wizards in one spot hid anyone living too close to the installation, subsuming them within the light of the small city. More annoyingly, if I looked to the north, the glow left an afterimage in my vision, making it harder for me to search the shadows for the new gate. Taking my chances, I flew as close to the silo as I safely could, then turned my back on it, the better to keep my eyes attuned to the nuances of the shades below me.

Even then, with my vision mostly unimpaired, I almost missed it. Gates emit no special light in the dream space, and my hope was that one of the Minor Arcanum's members had stumbled onto it before me or that several were congregating on it with their own detectors, letting me triangulate the location of the gate by the angles of their progress. I had no such luck on that front, but what I spotted instead was much better—and much more ominous.

The gate was southwest of the Arcanum silo, tucked against a mountain range I couldn't name, on the border of what appeared to be a tiny town. Fences crisscrossed the little flat land nearby, traces of habitation in the wilderness, but no buildings I could see below me were larger than two stories. But the size of the local population made little difference—there was a gate within shouting distance, and someone would have to move quickly to neutralize the threat.

As I floated closer to the hole in space, I realized the extent of our problem. The gate was perhaps thirty meters across, not the largest I'd seen, but certainly not something to be overlooked. What made my stomach knot was the wave of shadowy forms erupting through the gate, what appeared to be several dozen cloaked forms riding horse-like creatures. Though the details were obscured in the dream space, I assumed I was seeing another pack of the raiders that had massacred Kip's family. That was bad enough, but flanking the gate were ten figures on foot, all of them wearing swords at their hips and glowing with a strong bluish light. The guards weren't human—most had far too many eyes for that—but all were bipedal and armored.

I backed away, irrationally fearing that they might see me, and glanced up in time to spot Carey as she flew toward the target. "Over here!" I called, and she stopped short, looking about wildly until she noticed me below her. "This is bad!" I added, cupping my hands around my mouth as a megaphone. "Let us help you."

She hesitated, hanging in midair as she considered her options, and I slowly rose to her level, albeit at a distance. "Are you seeing what I'm seeing?" I asked her. "They're glowing, Carey—if gold means wizard and white means fae, what are the odds that blue means someone skilled with dark magic?"

Carey folded her arms and regarded me warily. "We

don't know that."

"It's a safe assumption. And do you see the rest of the horde?" I said, sweeping my hand over the riders below. "We've dealt with them before, and they're not fun. Come on, you know you can use the help."

Before Carey could reply, I felt someone give my shoulder a violent shake, flinging me back into my body like a released spring. Shocked, I gasped as my eyes flew open, only to find Seamus standing over me with my mobile in his hand. "Badger? Hey, Badger, are you in there?" he asked, patting my cheeks. "Come back, love, you need to take this."

"Wha—" I mumbled, struggling to sit up. The transition from sleepwalking had been far too rapid for comfort, the mental equivalent of rising from a deep dive without bothering to decompress, and my head pounded.

"It's Jim," he explained, putting the phone in my hand. "I said you were out scouting. He wants us."

Though impatient, Jim waited on the line for a few minutes while I regained my bearings. When I could stand without listing, I took the mobile from Seamus and leaned against the window, watching the distant sea from the corner of my eye. "This is a disaster," I muttered.

"How bad? And hi, nice to hear your voice again," said Jim. "Carey was going to look into it, but she hasn't called me back yet."

"I just left her," I replied, relieved to hear that Jim, at least, hadn't begun crossing himself and spitting at the sound of my name. "The gate's big, up in the mountains, and it's too close to a town."

"Where?"

I sighed, feeling the glass warm against my forehead. "Damned if I know. Southwest of the silo, but that's the best I can do for you. Out there, without real landmarks…"

"It's okay. Hang on…"

The rapid clicking sound on the other end could only be Jim's fingers on a keyboard. "Can you describe the mountains?"

I frowned into space for a moment, trying to pick out pertinent details. "Ehm…not the biggest I've seen. Not the heart of the Rockies, but probably something in that range. The gate's on the eastern edge, where the mountains rise. The town's tiny," I continued, wringing whatever I could from the memory. "One main road, a two-lane highway. Nothing sticks out. A handful of houses. Ranch or two, perhaps."

Jim was quiet for a moment but for the occasional click and tap at his computer, and then he grunted in frustration. "Assuming the radius for Amy's detector is right at a thousand miles, I'm guessing this is somewhere up in Wyoming, maybe near Yellowstone. The park's probably too far, but there's tribal lands to the south, along the eastern part of the range."

"Diné?"

"No, not ours. Some of the settlements through there aren't more than wide patches in the road with names. Going to be a pain to get everyone in until we lay eyes on the place and can get gates going, but I guess there's nothing to be done but start driving. Did you see any activity around it?"

"Loads," I told him. "Raiders, maybe fifty or sixty."

"Those things that—"

"Were going to eat Kip, yeah. Plus some sort of guard force at the gate."

"What kind of guards?"

"Beats me, but I think they're dark magic users. Looks like someone on the other side wised up and sent border patrol."

Jim muttered to himself—of the limited Navajo he spoke, much was profane—then switched back to English. "Carey and Zeb can't fight that alone, and I'm not going to make much of a difference. We need you guys out here."

"I offered, but Carey didn't seem thrilled with the idea."

"Carey can get over herself," he retorted. "Just one question."

"Shoot."

"Did you try to kill that Russian woman in her sleep? Zoya Fedkin?"

I hesitated, looking for the best answer. "If I'd tried to kill her," I finally said, "she would be dead right now. All I did was explain to her what would happen if she decided to tell her Arcanum friends about us."

"She was going to do *that*?"

"She tried to blackmail me into killing someone who inconvenienced her," I said, balling my fist. "Said she'd tell the Arcanum about the Fringe still active here if I didn't do the job for her. She also said she'd lead them to your sister's doorstep."

"*Shit*," he whispered. "Hannah, I'm sorry, she's been telling everyone that you—"

"I can imagine."

"Look, I'd tell you to come here and caravan toward Wyoming with me, but I'm stuck right now," he said in a rush. "Work thing. A bunch of stations are heading up this dance telethon to raise money for cancer research, and I'm supposed to be emceeing all night tonight. But I have a backup plan. Hang tight and stay by the phone, okay?"

"Roger that," I said, and ended the call.

Ten minutes later, once I'd straightened the mussed bed and Seamus had shepherded me into the kitchen to reheat my abandoned lunch, the phone rang again. "I don't know the number," I told my wary partner, but I perched on the counter and tapped the line open. "Yes?"

"Badger? Lou Martinez."

"*Lou*?" I echoed. "I didn't know you had—"

"Jim gave me your number."

He sounded tense—guarded—and I continued with

caution. "There's a gate open somewhere between you and the silo, Jim thinks maybe in Wyoming. Carey's seen it sleepwalking, but I have no idea who's on the scene and who may be en route."

"He said you'd seen civilians."

"I saw signs of habitation far too close to the gate to make me happy," I replied. "And I saw bogies on our side."

"How many?"

"Several dozen mounted—they fight with knives—and maybe ten with actual talent. Listen to me, Lou, I've got Seamus and my cousin here, plus two marksmen. Carey's going to need help."

"Yeah, that's my thought, too," he said. "You in?"

"Unless you people were planning to shoot me on sight."

The trooper grunted. "Been hearing stories third-hand about you having a little run-in with a woman in Moscow. Jim said there's more to it than she's letting on."

"I take issue with attempts to blackmail me into assassinations."

"That so?" He hissed a long breath through his teeth. "Okay, how were you planning to get up there?"

"You believe me?"

"You know, there's something to be said for the brotherhood, Detective."

I smiled, then nodded my thanks as Seamus put a plate of pasta beside me. "Didn't know if I still qualified. Unofficially retired and all."

"True. But be that as it may, I like to keep my mind open until I get statements from both parties, know what I mean?"

"Too well." I slid off the counter, fished a fork from the cutlery drawer, and tucked in. "And to answer your question, I've got no idea how we're getting to the gate, let alone where it actually might be. Thoughts?"

"Up for a drive?"

"If that's what it takes," I said around a mouthful of pasta.

"All right. You know that spot on the border where I pulled you over? I-40, couple months ago?"

"Sure…"

"Give me about half an hour, and I'll meet you there. You can make a gate, right?"

"We'll see you," I replied, then hung up, wolfed down the rest, and looked up to find Seamus waiting for an explanation. "Lou Martinez is going to convoy with us. Grab Arnie and the kids—we need to pack."

CHAPTER 15

Driving through a gate in the middle of the day is hardly anyone's idea of stealth or safe practice, but desperate times call for questionable actions.

Fortunately for us, traffic was light at the Arizona border that Saturday afternoon, little more than the occasional passing car and speeding lorry, and if anyone noticed us appear on the side of the Interstate, they didn't slow. Part of that could have been due to the patrol car parked a hundred meters ahead, nose pointed toward traffic in a pose that promised imminent ticketing. So caught up were the other drivers with braking toward the speed limit that they never saw us drive onto the gravel.

"Sure about this?" Arnold asked behind me.

I nodded. Still, in case of ambush, he and I had our wands close at hand, and I didn't need to look in the mirror to know that Amy and Kip had armed themselves. She'd stuffed enough ammunition behind the third row to overthrow a small country, and Kip had added his boot knife to the arsenal. I hadn't been downstairs when Seamus told them of the plan, but my partner had said that Kip's expression was at best murderous as he hurried to pack.

Just as I cut the engine off, the patrol car turned away from the road and slowly drove down to join us. It parked facing us, and as a precaution, I raised our bonnet, conjured up a pair of cables, and stepped out. "Give us a jump, officer?" I called, lifting my prop to show him the plan.

The patrol car's door opened, and Lou grinned as he climbed out—to my surprise, wearing jeans and a loose-fitting T-shirt instead of his uniform, and carrying a black shopping bag over one shoulder. "Not a problem, ma'am," he replied, ambling toward us. "Battery, huh?"

"Sadly."

When he'd closed the distance, Lou hurried to my open door, peeked inside, and dropped the act. "Hey, folks. Hope everyone brought snacks—this is going to be a long haul."

Amy lifted an open bag of barbeque crisps and a two-liter bottle of Coke. "Armed and ready."

"Awesome." With that, Lou deposited his bag on my seat and extracted the contents. "Dash array," he said, affixing a red and blue LED set to our windscreen with suction cups. "And here's your CB," he added, passing Seamus a handset. "No time to install this in your vehicle, and I don't have an extra external antenna, so keep it plugged into the lighter and hope the walkie-talkie antenna works. This is mostly for you to listen, anyway—let me handle any LEO chatter." He glanced toward the back again and pointed to Amy. "Got a detector on you? Something more helpful than Jim's?"

"Uh...*yeah*." She held a black box aloft. "Thought it might be easier than guessing. Head north."

Lou chuckled and slid out of the SUV. "Okay. It's up to you to keep me straight on directions. Either call me or use the CB. I don't have a handle—just go with 'Smokey' if you need me."

With that, Lou pulled his wand from the back of his trousers and beckoned me closer. "Little spell I worked out when I was younger and dumber and liked to drive at NASCAR speeds. It won't hide your ride, but it'll make it seem unremarkable to anyone we pass. You shouldn't get stopped for speeding, and if you have to throw your lights on, you're not going to get questions from local police. I mean," he added, thumbing toward his car, "I'm taking my baby *way* out of jurisdiction. No need to deal with nosy cops."

"Be my guest," I replied, and while I blocked him from traffic, Lou quickly cast the spell on our Suburban.

As he finished, paying careful attention to our registration plate, he asked, "You driving, Badger?"

"That was the plan."

"Got much experience at high speed?"

Lou seemed slightly unnerved by my smile, but he climbed back into his car as I lowered our bonnet, then turned around, put on his indicator, and sped off.

Almost immediately, we left I-40 and veered north on a two-lane road through the Navajo Nation, weaving back and forth across the New Mexico border as we raced through the red rocks and scrublands at nearly one hundred miles per hour. We made the Utah line in an hour and a half, having only had to turn our lights and Lou's siren on twice, then continued on the oft-patched road as it passed out of the tribal lands. I'd expected to pick up an Interstate, but not until another two hours had passed did we catch I-70, and Lou called a stop for petrol.

"Thoughts?" he asked Amy upon her return from the shop with another giant bottle of Coke.

She deposited her prize in her seat, then turned on her mobile's mapping app and pinpointed our location. "The signal's getting stronger, and the detector is still pointing north," she explained, then showed him the map. "We're not going to keep 70 long, no matter which way we go. There isn't a north-south Interstate to pick up unless we go through Salt Lake or Denver."

"Which will only slow us down." He motioned me into their huddle, and Amy showed me the map. "I propose we head east for a bit, if only to keep the sun out of our eyes, then veer north on 139 once we're in Colorado. We'll be up in the mountains for a while, and then we'll head northwest back through Utah and into Wyoming. See?" he asked, maneuvering through Amy's map until I followed the route. "It's not great, but there are only so many roads out here."

"It makes sense, and don't apologize—you didn't lay the bloody things," I replied, popping a handful of M&Ms. "How long until we lose the light?"

Lou squinted at the blue sky, then glanced at his watch. "Not until eight or later. At least another two and a half hours. If we're quick about it, we should be out of the mountains by then."

"*If* we're quick," I said, then spotted the others loitering by the ice cooler on the shop's front porch. "Come on, boys, we're going!" I called, waving them over, and the three, looking rather weary already, climbed back into the Suburban.

"Road trip amateurs," Amy muttered, holding out her palm until I shared my sweets.

Amy's detector began to beep more insistently as the sun set and we crossed into Wyoming. Lou kept us on his planned course until we found I-80, then suggested a dinner break. To my relief, my passengers were enthusiastically on board with his plan, and we regrouped over burgers.

The problem was that Amy's navigator still insisted that the largest dark magic source in the area was due north of us, but our options were limited. "There's a national forest in the way," Lou explained. "No direct route. We're going to have to head northeast, then drive most of the way through the Wind River Reservation. I'd say it's a scenic drive, but given the current conditions…"

I glanced at the night beyond the glass. "You're confident that it's there?"

Lou, tackling his packet of ketchup-soaked chips, nodded. "I've been getting chatter all day, mostly by text message. There's about ten of us in the area already. Carey knew her way to Casper, and everyone trekked west from there."

"So they've found the gate?" Seamus asked, dropping his cheeseburger.

"From what I can tell. Haven't had an update since seven, but I think it's safe to say they're on site."

"Well, then," said Arnold, "couldn't you just call Carey and ask her to open a gate for us?"

Lou pushed his chips aside and wiped his mouth clean. "I could, except Carey doesn't know I'm heading up with you. Less chance of anyone saying no if we waltz in unannounced, right?"

"Good point," my cousin muttered into his drink.

"I'll let you know if I get any news," he continued, "but until then, everyone who isn't driving or navigating should try to get a nap. This may be a long night, even without Carey chewing me out."

Easy for Lou to say. I knew he was tossing back energy drinks to stay awake, but as for us, we had the steady, nagging chirp of the detector to yank us from the brink of sleep. As the night wore on, Seamus looked over his shoulder and finally asked Amy, "Is it possible to remove the batteries in that thing? Lou knows where we're going."

"I take no chances," she replied, but as a concession, she wrapped a sweatshirt around it to muffle the noise.

In the end, only Arnold was able to catch a few minutes of sleep. Even having ridden with me as long as he had, Seamus was too tense to doze off as we zipped through the dark night. Amy was preoccupied with her detector and map, and as for Kip, he stared silently out the window, occasionally passing his knife from hand to hand. I could guess what was on his mind, but I had no desire to plumb those depths.

Lou and I slowed slightly due to the darkness, but even

still, we stumbled onto the Minor Arcanum's perimeter shortly after ten that evening. Throwing on his emergency lights, he pulled off on the side of the road behind a pickup truck hauling a camper—the nearest in a long double line of abandoned vehicles—and I followed suit.

"Badger?" came his voice over the CB. "All right there?"

"Affirmative," I replied, taking the handset from Seamus as I killed the engine. Lou's lights continued to bathe our car in alternating bursts of red and blue. "Detector's beeping like mad back here."

"I hear it. See the shield?"

The pulsing, multicolored construction of spellcraft rose in front of us like the lights of the Vegas Strip blasting forth from the desert. "Can't miss it."

"I recognize some of these cars. Going on foot from here. You coming?"

"Copy that," I said, and put the handset aside. Turning to see the back of our SUV, I took a deep breath and nodded. "Ready?"

It took Amy only two minutes to disembark, put her sweatshirt back on against the night, unpack her favorite rifle, strap a pair of pistols across her hips, and fill her pockets with extra ammunition. Kip moved nearly silently beside her, snapping on his own gun belts and checking his boot knife, and Arnold waggled his wand like a drumstick, expending nervous energy through his twitching fingers. When we were prepared, we followed Lou toward the shield, which stood at least ten stories tall and extended across the road in both directions before curving off toward the north—a bubble perhaps three or four miles in diameter, I estimated.

We'd walked only a few minutes before we reached the back of the Minor Arcanum's line. "How's it going?" asked Lou, and the supposed guard, a teenage boy, yelped and nearly dropped his torch. "Whoa, easy, kid," said the trooper. "What's with the shield?"

The boy looked from Lou to the rest of our pack, and his eyes grew wide.

"They're with me," said Lou in a practiced no-nonsense tone. "Go get Dr. Jones, if you can. We'll stay here."

The guard sprinted away, and we stood quietly to await his return, all of us examining the shield except Kip, who couldn't see it, and Amy, who tried to point out to him its contours. Soon enough, however, the bobbing torch gave away the guard's return, and with him was Carey, looking haggard and tight-lipped.

"I brought them," said Lou before she could speak. "They just want to help."

She glared at him, then cut her eyes to me and squared her shoulders. "Hannah."

"Hi, Carey," I replied, and showed her my empty hands. "How bad is it?"

Carey hesitated, seemingly wavering, then sighed and slumped again. "It's a fucking bloodbath," she muttered. "We were too slow in getting here. Got the shield up before the bastards could spread out, but I don't think there's a human alive inside the bubble. They may have gone after the pets and livestock by now, for all I can tell."

"Shield's holding, though?"

"For the time being. There's an illusion built in, which should be more useful once we hit dawn, and we're getting roadblocks set up to the north and south, but there's not much we can do until it gets light out and we can see just how many we're up against. Lou," she added, turning back to him, "if you'd like to supervise the traffic situation, I'd be grateful."

He nodded, and Seamus offered, "What about some flashbangs? I'll step inside and light it up for you, and maybe we can take out a few while they're distracted."

"Might work but for the second shield."

"Second?" I asked.

She nodded wearily. "You were right—blue glow

means proficient with dark magic. The guards at the gate built a second shield inside of ours, I suppose to protect their buddies."

"Can we punch through it?" Arnold asked her.

"Conceivably, but we'd need more juice than we have right now. It's taking most of what we can muster to keep our shield up, especially with the outflow from the Gray Lands."

"So the gate's still open, I take it," said Lou. Carey gave him a pointed look, and he held up his hands in pacification. "Sorry, sorry, dumb question."

"Right. Okay," I said, looking behind Carey as a few of the exhausted wizards on break wandered closer. "You need help. Aside from Lou, who's driven since lunch to get here, we're offering you two wizards, a faerie, and two kids with guns. No strings. We're here at your service."

She hesitated, looking at me long and hard with her arms folded, and I sighed. "You don't honestly think I tried to kill Zoya, do you?"

"Don't know," she said, and shrugged. "I *do* know you're capable of it."

"And I'd be lying if I told you the thought hadn't crossed my mind, but as God is my witness, all I did was threaten her. And throw her against a wall," I admitted, "but we were sleepwalking, so I don't know if that actually counts."

Carey's mouth tightened to a white line. "Zoya told me you attacked her as revenge for me throwing you out, and the only way she saved herself was by forcing herself to wake."

"Yeah, that's *entirely* bullshit. Zoya threatened to go to the Arcanum if I didn't do a sleepwalking hit for her, and she said she'd send them your way, too. I tried to impress upon her the stupidity of that idea."

Her dark eyes narrowed. "Zoya did *what?*"

"Said she'd tell her Arcanum friends about me, and about you as well. Little extra incentive for me to play along." When Carey didn't respond, I said, "Look, you're worried that I'm going to turn out like Simon Magus, I get it. I've already had a long conversation with someone who knew him well, and I'm deeply aware of what he did. What I did in Mongolia—and where's Sergei, by the way? Did he ever make it across?"

"Still back at the ranch," she murmured. "He and Zeb hit it off."

"Fine. But what I did there, I did accidentally. I've been working to control it, and I've made good progress."

"She has," Arnold offered, and Seamus nodded along. "Speaking as her practice partners, we should know."

"Carey," I said, taking her hands before she could pull away, "I know it scares you. It scares the shit out of me, too. And I know we haven't always seen eye to eye on things like binds and transformation. But if you think for one second that I'd do something on purpose to hurt you or Zeb, then you're absolutely mad. You took us in, dear. Why would I do anything to bring you harm?"

She looked down at our hands, then turned her eyes back to mine and nodded. "Okay," she mumbled, "you can stick around. We need whatever help we can get. But I…"

Carey left the thought unspoken, and I released her and stepped back a pace. "You're still uncomfortable. It's all right, I understand. Just put us to use."

"No problem there," she replied, and turned to go. "Follow me. Hope you got some rest on the drive."

The wizards taking their turns at the shield gave us a wide berth once they realized who we were, but I ignored them and listened while Carey resignedly gave us the details of the situation.

"Shield's stable for now," she concluded, waving at the massive construction. "I've got a couple of folks walking the perimeter tonight, patching as needed. The outflow of dark magic was problematic at first, but once they built their own shield inside, the pressure on ours hasn't been so great."

"Have you tried to get through the inner shield?" Seamus asked.

"A handful of times, but no dice. We need something focused and strong, but with the manpower it's taking to keep the shield up, we don't have the resources to spare."

I pressed my hand against the brilliant magical wall, feeling it flex against me like a sheet of rubber. "Can you let me through? Or drop the illusion, either way. I just want to see what's inside."

She nodded, took out her wand, and whispered a few words, and a door appeared in the bubble. "Light it up once you're in there."

I waited until Carey had sealed the door behind me, then closed my eyes for a few seconds to remove the after-image of the glowing web of spellcraft, which was nearly as blinding as the Arcanum had been in the dream space. When I opened them again, the night was dark but for the distant edge of the Minor Arcanum's shield, still bright not intolerably so. I took five steps forward before I hit the inner shield, which was similarly unyielding to me but nearly invisible in the night. The only indication of the shield's presence was a faint bending of starlight around the edges of the bubble.

With my eyes adjusted, I picked out at least twenty campfires on the other side, decent conflagrations that sent smoke skyward and out the top of the inner shield—a selectively permeable membrane, apparently closed to anything more substantial than air. But smoke wasn't the only thing I could smell from within the encampment. Someone was roasting meat in there, and the aroma was enough to make me salivate until, to my horror, I remembered that dinner was probably the ranchers who'd lived nearby.

"Fuck that," I muttered, then raised my hand and shot

a streak of lightning up the skin of the inner shield. When it reached the top, it held its position and sent a volley of glowing leaders down the sides of the barrier, giving me enough light to count the creatures inside. I saw a couple of lumps that might have been dead raiders or their mounts, but most of the ones I'd seen while sleepwalking were alive and well, and they shouted an alarm at the disturbance.

Before I knew what was happening, Carey opened the shield again and pulled me back through. "Seen enough?" she asked.

"Too much," I muttered, hoping to get the smell of meat out of my nostrils. "But I think I've got a plan."

Kip grabbed my arm and stopped me before I could walk away from the shield. "Raiders?"

"Dozens of them."

"Then this plan of yours had better have a place for me in it."

"We can talk about it in the morning," Carey began, but I shook my head.

"No time to wait. We do this tonight," I said, and squeezed Kip's shoulder. "That is, assuming those bastards in there don't have supernatural vision. What says the expert?"

He smiled grimly at the acknowledgement. "Not as far as I know. What did you have in mind?"

"Flashbangs," I replied, grinning as I glanced at our bright shield—a shield that the non-talented raiders, presumably blind to magic and dark magic alike, couldn't see. "Emphasis on *flash*."

All right," said Carey, "listen up. We have a game plan. I'm not wild about it, but right now, it just might work."

The wizards on break clustered closer to her, while the ones sustaining the shield cocked their heads toward the sound of her voice.

"We can't do anything until we break through their shield," she continued, then muttered her quick thanks as Zeb wrapped a woolen shawl around her shoulders. "Hannah and Arnold should be able to do that if they work in tandem. It won't necessarily be a *big* hole, but we're not trying to drive a tank through. Once they gain entry, Seamus will send up a signal—something bright and loud. When that happens, drop our shield."

"*Drop* it?" one of the other wizards echoed incredulously. "But if we—"

"As long as their shield is up, everyone inside is still contained," Carey interrupted. "What I want all of us to do is cast spotlights—fire, flares, whatever you can do. The bigger and brighter, the better. I want a ring of light where our shield is now, bright enough to show us what the bogies are doing. Make the light stronger than the shield's glow, if you can. If we do this right, they won't be able to tell what we're about because the glare will blind them."

"And then what?" the wizard asked. "Sit back and hope they run home?"

"No," I said, raising my voice to be heard about the rumbling of the crowd. "Then *we* bring the heat while *you* hold the line. Got it?"

The Minor Arcanum wasn't thrilled—whether with the plan or my presence, I couldn't say for sure—but after a little more nudging from Carey, they took their positions at intervals around the shield just past midnight and waited with their wands drawn. In the meantime, the five of us stood with Carey and Zeb at the edge, checking our gear one last time before entry. As I flipped my wand between my fingers, Zeb stepped closer and cleared his throat. "Uh, Hannah?"

"Mm?" I replied.

"Lou told me what you said about Zoya, and Jimmy confirmed it the last time he called in."

Hearing his discomfort, I downplayed the situation. "Well, she's not getting a Christmas card from me this year, that's for sure."

I looked up to find him watching me, his face working as if he were struggling to put a thought into words, but after a moment, he stuck out his hand and said, "Be safe in there."

I shook it and nodded. "You, too."

"Assuming we make it out of this, how about I throw together huevos rancheros in the morning?"

"Looking forward to it," I said with a smile, then released him and took my place at Arnold's side. "Ready?" I asked Carey, who had decided to handle the door herself.

"Ready as I'm going to be," she said, then muttered into existence a hole in the glowing shield and stepped back. "I'll leave it open, just in case. And the shield should be down in a few minutes, anyway, if all goes according to plan…"

"Be careful," I told her, then stepped through with Arnold on my heels. I heard Seamus and the kids follow us, but my attention was fixed on the inner shield, and Arnold readied his wand.

"Hey," said Amy, sniffing the air, "does anyone else smell barbeque?"

"Just go," Arnold muttered, and produced a laser-style beam of energy from the tip of his wand. I did likewise, and cautiously, we maneuvered the two together, joining the streams to double their effect. The shield flexed with the strain and tried to absorb the concentrated energy we were throwing into it, but after a minute's work, as the nearest of the raiders began to sound the alarm, we broke through. Slashing at the shield, we widened a gap large enough to admit us, and the five of us ducked inside before the breach could heal.

"Ready when you are," Arnold told Seamus, who nodded and pointed at the sky. High above us, a brilliant yellow explosion went off like a firework in a submarine, nearly loud enough to deafen me, and the raiders ran for their mounts.

Before the ringing in my ears had ceased, our shield fell, and a circle of blinding light burst into view around us. I groped in my pocket for my sunglasses, then slipped them on with a sigh of relief and watched as the confused raiders spun around, looking for order in the chaos. Even with protective lenses, I couldn't make out much detail, but the raiders' silhouettes against the distant light gave their positions away.

"Are you—" was as far as I made it before Kip had raised his gun and started firing. He emptied it in short order, then pulled Amy's rifle from her shoulder, took a knee, and began spraying the night with bullets. Apparently unfazed by the loss of her gun, Amy simply readied another and joined Kip, passing him ammunition from her sweatshirt pouch as needed.

"No quarter," Seamus muttered.

The lightning I shot into the screaming crowd flew beside a stream of fireballs from his fingertips, and Arnold joined the fray with a barrage of boulders he'd plucked from the ether. "Nice!" Seamus yelled to him over the cacophony. "If we don't burn, electrocute, or shoot them, squashing them should do the trick."

"Keep the fire going," I cut in, and pushed up my jacket sleeves. "I'll do Arnie one better."

I admit that a rain of knives wasn't the cleanest way to kill the raiders, but it had such a *satisfying* result.

By the time dawn broke, the fight was over for everyone but Kip, who made a point of driving his knife into every raider's throat. Gore-spattered and snarling, he shouted incomprehensibly with every strike, and Arnold held Amy back while he did his work. "Trust me, you don't want any part of that," he murmured as she sullenly reloaded her magazines.

As for the guards, there was no sign of them. Surmising that they'd escaped through the gate in the chaos, we turned our attention toward patching the hole and covering up as much of the gristly evidence as we could. While Arnold and another ten wizards started working on the gate, the rest of us walked around the encampment, smothering fires and zapping corpses into atoms, hoping to finish before local law enforcement could drive past and wonder about the parked cars with out-of-state plates. Finally, when we were down to the last handful of bodies, Amy walked over to Kip, who stood with his dripping knife over his last victim, and reached up to rub his shoulder. "Okay?" she murmured.

"No."

"I know."

He looked at the knife, then crouched to wipe it clean against the raider's black cloak and sheathed it. The emaciated creature's mummified face was half gone and singed around the edges, its fangs bared in a death grimace, and Kip spat on it before he turned away and found Amy's arms. "Come on," she said, guiding him toward the perimeter. "Zeb's making breakfast."

"I don't think I'm hungry," he replied.

"Try for me, then."

With a bit of gentle prodding, he allowed her to lead him away toward the mess tent. I couldn't blame him for his lack of appetite—even with the fires out, hints of roasted flesh wafted on the morning breeze, and Kip knew better than anyone what we were smelling. He'd been forced to lie by another raider band's fire, after all, bound and gagged, while his family were killed and eaten one by one. I didn't know how to help him through that trauma, but if hacking the dead raiders around us into pieces soothed his soul, I wasn't going to stand in his way.

Seamus, looking as haggard as I'd ever seen him, joined me at an empty bench and wrapped his arm around my shoulders while we watched the exhausted wizards eat. After a time, Zeb emerged from the camp kitchen with two steaming mugs and pressed them into our free hands.

"Get *something* down you before you drop," he chided. "If you're not feeling the spice this morning, Joyce is making cheese grits." He cocked his head toward the far end of the kitchen workbench, where Joyce and Boone Killian were taking turns stirring the contents of an enormous stockpot. "They got here just before you did," Zeb added as we sipped our tea. "After the gate in the 'Glades, I think they felt obligated."

I glanced over the rim of my mug at a nearby table, where Hua was shoveling rice into her mouth as quickly as her chopsticks would fly. "Nice of her to make the trip."

Zeb followed my line of sight and nodded. "Most of the sleepwalkers came. Them and the gate makers. If this one had opened anywhere but the middle of nowhere—"

"Then there'd be more dead, and maybe rioting in the streets," Seamus interrupted. "You did the best you could, Zeb. Stop punishing yourself."

"Those people never had a chance," he muttered.

"That may be, but you stopped it from getting worse. And look," he said, gesturing with his mug toward the knot working on the gate, "it's almost closed. Arnie knows what he's doing."

"Yeah." Zeb watched the other wizards for a moment, then mumbled, "Missed you guys."

"Missed you, too," I told him.

"Hasn't been the same around the ranch. Sergei's a good kid, but...you know."

Seamus chuckled. "You can't take him to the bar, you mean."

"It *is* frowned upon to go drinking with minors. But no, in all seriousness...I'm sorry things ended up the way they did. I'm not quite as worried as Carey about the threat of you killing us all in our sleep," he said to me, "but if she's that concerned, I'm not going to fight her."

"Nor should you," I replied. "It's her house, too."

"Still..." He shrugged and turned back to us. "Sucks that it went down that way. Hope you understand."

Before we could respond, a cheer went up from the gate team, followed by a round of hugging and hearty back slaps. "Looks like that's the hole patched," said Seamus. "You're bound to have hungry customers soon, Zeb."

"I left rations enough for them in the kitchen," he said, and waved the group toward the tent. "Come on, folks, food's getting cold!" he called. "Hurry up and eat so we can go home, huh?"

The first of the pack hadn't reached the mess tent door when a dark streak ripped across the sky with a sound like thunder. Those of us nearest the edge of the tent made it outside in time to see the carefully sealed gate reopen, then vomit forth twenty blue-skinned guards in black uniforms. Lightning played across one's fingers, while another drew a blade of flame from midair and moved its mouth into an expression that might have been a smirk. As we gawked, the apparent leader, another man with no hair and far too many eyes, stepped in front of his companions and began to bellow across the burn-pocked pasture.

Zeb listened for a moment, then scowled and wheeled on us. "Are you getting any of this? What's he speaking?"

Seamus tightened his grip on my shoulders. "It's Fae," he murmured. "The accent's weird, but that's definitely Fae. He's saying that the queen demands a parley."

"Queen?" Zeb echoed. "What does Eleanor have to do with—"

"Not Eleanor," I interrupted, then reached up and covered Seamus's hand with my own, squeezing so hard that he winced. "He's talking about Nath."

CHAPTER 16

Seeing as there were precisely three people on the ground that morning who knew more of spoken Fae than the basic curses, the Minor Arcanum was willing to step aside and let Seamus, Amy, and me take the lead. Kip, all pretense of eating forgotten, protested that there was no reason to put Amy in the line of fire, but she quickly talked him down. "The more of us who know what's going on, the better, just in case someone starts shooting. Besides, I'm not going empty-handed," she added, checking her rifle. If she noticed the blood spatter on the stock from where Kip had used it as a club on a half-dozen raiders, it didn't break her rhythm.

Once Amy was prepared, the three of us made our way across the pasture, flanked by a crowd of anxious wizards, who parted and fell back as we neared the waiting invaders—all, that is, but Carey, who continued with us as if she were oblivious to the understood tactical configuration. "What are you doing?" I muttered, trying to keep my face neutral and my stride confident.

"In case our girl's trigger finger slips, you're going to want backup," she replied.

"Carey—"

"Don't push me."

There was no time to argue with her, so I let the matter drop and turned my attention to the guards' leader, whose six black eyes squinted slightly in the rising sun. On closer inspection, I began to make out his details: dark bluish-green skin stretched taut over the planes of his face; a pair of slits where a nose should be; lips full and almost navy, parted slightly to reveal the points of his upper teeth; a steel breastplate contoured to his apparently well-muscled form. What I had originally taken for black cloth down his arms and legs was actually finely-woven chain maille in a dark metal, which clinked and rustled as he shifted his weight. His hands were empty, but as a wizard, I knew too well how quickly that could change.

When we were within a few meters of the guards, I stopped and extended my arms, blocking the others from closing the distance. Seamus arched a brow in query, and I nodded, then turned to address their leader. "Your presence here is unwarranted and unwise," I began, dropping my voice into the no-nonsense tone I'd once employed with uncooperative witnesses and green officers. "Your friends slaughtered innocent civilians last night. That's unacceptable."

He shook his head. "Those were no friends of ours."

"Really? You were with them, were you not? Some of you, at least," I amended, scanning the crowd.

"We were. But those are lesser creatures...entertainment, you could say." He flashed more of his teeth in a gesture that almost certainly wasn't a smile. "For us. For you, a test from my lady."

"And why would Lady Nath be testing us?" I countered. "She has no business in this realm."

"Perhaps, perhaps not." He folded his arms across his breastplate and gave our line a cursory inspection. "My lady wishes to speak with your leader. It would be exceedingly unwise to refuse her invitation."

My guts began to clench. "She wishes to speak here?"

"No. Her palace is far more comfortable than...*this*," he added, glancing at our tent with a flicker of distaste.

Before I could reply, Carey caught my arm and murmured, "What's he saying?"

"A moment," I told the guard, then turned from him and raised my voice to address the waiting Minor

Arcanum. "Lady Nath wants to speak to our leader in the Gray Lands. I get the impression that this isn't so much a request as an order."

"Second that," Seamus muttered beside me.

"Of course," Amy began, "there's the little problem of the Minor Arcanum not *having* a leader, per se—"

"Dr. Jones."

The voice was young, male, and American, but I couldn't pick the speaker out of the crowd. "I'm sorry," I said, "what was that?"

"Dr. Jones," he repeated, still hiding in the throng. "She's our leader. She should go."

The rest of the crowd held its breath, and I cut my eyes to Carey, who seemed rooted in place. "Look," I replied, scanning the closest wizards for a clue as to the speaker's identity, "whoever goes needs to appreciate the risks."

"There's no guarantee that anyone who goes over there is coming back alive," said Seamus. Glancing at him, I could tell that he was making the same examination of the crowd. "Lady Nath may want to have a chat, but that doesn't change the fact that whoever goes will be unarmed. Let's be reasonable about this. Carey's an excellent healer, but would you want her in a brawl?"

"Hey, now," Carey snapped, poking him in the chest with two fingers, "I'm perfectly capable of taking care of myself."

True, Carey could doctor a bull without breaking a sweat, but she was still on the short side. Without saying a word, Seamus pressed his palm against her forehead and stepped back, holding her at bay while she tried to either dislodge or hit him.

"So if we put our heads together," I resumed, keeping an eye on the combatants, "then maybe we'll have a shot at bringing everyone home intact. Now, I don't know all of you—"

"Dr. Jones," a girl called from the crowd. "Send her."

"She's our leader," said the boy.

"Yes, Carey can do it," added an older man—Jean-Claude, to my surprise. It was difficult to tell with his accent, but I thought he sounded unsure of himself. "Send her. She is our leader."

As the nominations rang out from the assembled, Carey stopped trying to fight Seamus and stared out at the wizards around us, baffled and slightly panicked. Searching the crowd, I picked out familiar faces in the first rows, some tight-lipped, others calling for Carey to do the job. A few even had the grace to look guilty as they shouted her name, but still, they were willing to sacrifice her.

Carey's mouth opened and closed as she fumbled for words, and then she clutched my arm. "I don't speak the language," she said in a frightened rush. "How can I talk to her if I can't understand her? Seamus, can he do that thing—"

"No worries," I murmured, smiling to myself as Zeb forced his way through the crowd to defend his wife. "It's under control."

With that, I turned back to the waiting guard and nodded. "My people have given their assent. I will gladly speak with your lady." Seeing Seamus's jaw drop, I held out one hand to still him and focused on the guard. "As you can see, the situation here is somewhat chaotic. Your 'entertainment' has caused us great trouble. I ask that you return for me at sundown in order that I might oversee the work that is still to be done here."

He considered that for a moment, then flashed his teeth again. "Sundown. I will return to escort you," he replied, then barked a sharp command to the others, who rapidly retreated through the gate. The leader was last out, and he left the rift open behind him.

I counted to ten, giving them time to walk away from us, then faced the waiting wizards and raised my hands for silence. "I'm going, all right?" I said once the noise had subsided to an agitated rumble. "Honestly, I cannot *believe* you people."

My plan was to stomp away in a righteous huff, but Seamus grabbed me before I could take more than a few steps. "Are you mad?" he exclaimed, pulling me around to face him. "Or suicidal? It's one or the other."

"It's neither, Seamie," I murmured. "I'm better suited for this than Carey is."

"And I'm not? You're not going anywhere. I'll see what Nath wants, and you—"

I laughed once and shook my head. "Right, because *that* would go over so well. The only way you're going into the Gray Lands is over my dead body."

"I'm just as qualified as you are—"

"You're Mab's grandson."

His brow furrowed in bewilderment. "*And?* What's that got to do with anything?"

I sighed and consulted the sky for patience. "Mab ruled the Gray Lands for a thousand years. Remember that little wrinkle about how her court was expelled when Nath came to power? Now, how well do you suppose you'd be received?"

Seamus's eyes narrowed in discomfort. "They don't know who I am."

"Maybe not, but Toula told you me you look rather like her. And without magic, how would you block them from your thoughts?"

That gave him pause, but before I could make my exit, Carey called my name. "Get out of here," she said once I met her eyes. "Go on. I'll handle it. When they come back, I'll tell them you were trying to protect me."

Extricating myself from my partner's grip, I took Carey's hands and tried to smile. "I'm *fairly* sure that I still owe you for room and board. This is on me."

"Hannah—"

I squeezed until she stopped protesting. "I'm a cop, a coordinator, and if it matters, the freaky descendant of the greatest wizard in history. This is my job." As Zeb finally wrapped his arm over Carey's shoulders, I released her and smiled in earnest. "You've got people counting on you. Might want to have a word with the rest of the group about choosing representatives for cases like this, but that's up to you."

I could read the conflict on her face—guilt at the fact that I was taking the bullet for her, mixed with relief—and I tried to nudge her in the wiser direction. "They called your name because they know you're usually right. If the Minor Arcanum lost you, what would they do? A healer *and* a sleepwalker? It's okay," I added, mentally bracing myself as Arnold and Amy neared.

But before the others could confront me, Seamus caught my wrist, and I saw the mobile pressed to his ear when I turned around. "Yes, I have her here," he said in rapid Fae. "Will you... thank you."

Without further preamble, he pressed the phone to the side of my head until I reached up to take it. "Hello?" I said.

"What are you *thinking*?" came the agitated reply. "You're not ready for this!"

"Hi, Val," I sighed, and pushed through the knot growing around me for privacy. "Seeing as I haven't got a better idea—"

"*I* have one: run. Come across, you'll be safe here."

"And then what happens to the people I leave behind?"

"You mean the ones who threw you out of their little club and have been shunning you for the last few weeks? Those people?"

"I have a better chance of making it back than any of them do."

He laughed in disbelief. "Moon and stars, girl, you'll have *no* protection. None. There's no magic in the Gray Lands, you will not be able to cast—"

"Yes, I'm aware," I replied, hearing the testiness in my tone.

"You aren't. I've been there, Hannah. It's unlike

anything you have ever felt." Grunting his frustration, Val asked, "How long do you have?"

"Until I go? Sundown…at least twelve hours. Probably a bit more. Why?"

"Stall as long as you can. I will try to convince the king and queen to assist you."

"What?" I pressed the mobile more firmly to my ear and waved my followers back. "They're already on the Arcanum's bad side. I can't ask them to intervene against Nath."

"No, but I can," he said quietly. "They listen to—oh, Aiden, hello. What is…"

Val's voice grew muffled for a long moment, and I assumed he'd pressed his phone against his shoulder to block out his conversation. When he returned to the line, he sounded somewhat peeved. "It seems Amy and Seamus had similar thoughts. Aiden is aware of the situation."

"Is that a problem?"

"He wants to speak with you. Amy should be entering the network…"

I glanced back at the crowd and saw Amy waiting, tablet in hand and tapping her foot. "She's in," I told Val, then took the computer from Amy and gave Seamus back his phone. "Got any brilliant ideas, then?" I asked Aiden, who watched me from his computer's camera.

"Not this time." Looking up at a sound, he slid his chair to the right and waited as Val pulled a seat into the frame. "Heard what Val said about getting Coileán and Eleanor involved. Even if they were willing to jump in, it wouldn't do you any good."

"Why not?" asked Amy, pushing me to one side as she joined the conference.

"For the same reason that no one wants to hang out in the Gray Lands—no magic. Take that away, and my brother's just another grunt." He hesitated, gnawing on his lip, then said, "Amy, before the realm messed with me, I could do something weird. Can you move magic around?"

Her face scrunched in bemusement. "Come again?"

"Like, you know, push it without activating it."

"I *can't* activate it, that's the problem—"

"Not for what I'm talking about. I used to be able to move raw magic—I pumped it into the Gray Lands the last time any of us had to go over there. Can you do it? What happens when you touch magic?"

"Nothing," she replied, growing more puzzled by the second. "My hands go through it. I don't know what you're talking about."

"I do," I cut in, and both of their heads swiveled toward mine. "Aiden, you're in the old Fringe files. I've read accounts of your talents, before and after. What you could do before...there hasn't been a witch-blood in centuries who could do that. The last known was the one who helped Simon Magus with his canned magic—his name was Cuthbert," I added, hearing Grivam in my thoughts. "Unfortunately, you're an anomaly."

"Shit," he muttered, and rubbed his forehead.

"Sorry," Amy mumbled.

"Not your fault." He looked at Val, who shrugged helplessly, then back at me. "So yeah, without magic, you're not going to get much help from anyone here. No offense, Hannah, but I don't think my brother or Eleanor are crazy enough to go on that field trip with you. If you go, you're probably on your own."

A chill like cold water ran down my spine, but I forced myself to nod and project serenity. "Understood. I'll be careful."

"I'll ask," said Val.

"Don't. They've done enough for us already—no sense trying to guilt them into this fool's errand." With that, I handed the tablet back to Amy, then turned to find the rest still watching me, listening to our incomprehensible conversation. "Ehm, hello," I muttered. "If you'll excuse me, I need a nap."

Throughout the long day, Seamus did his best to dissuade me from my plan. "If not me, then why not Arnold?" he tried at lunch. "Let the certified magus handle this. I can set him up with the language, and he'll be fine to go."

I gave him a look of weary reproach over my sandwich. "He can't read people like you and I can. I don't trust him alone with Nath."

"Nath's inhuman, her body language is probably different—"

"And I still have a better shot at this than he does. We're not sacrificing Arnie."

Frustrated, Seamus swept our dishes aside and gripped my hands. "Then why are we sacrificing you, Badge? You have no business doing this."

"Someone has to."

"Like hell. If we run, she won't be able to find us. Go to Faerie until this blows over," he pleaded. "Let the Minor Arcanum tidy its own mess."

"Last time I checked, this was everyone's mess," I countered, matching his squeeze with my own. "I'll be fine, Seamie. I'll come back in one piece."

"You can't make that promise," he murmured, shaking his head. "And what am I to do if you don't make it out of there?"

I held on so tightly that he flinched. "If that happens, then I expect you to look after Amy and Kip. Keep them safe. If you can figure out a way to sneak Kip into Faerie, so much the better. But in any case, I expect you to carry on, Malone."

Seamus stared at our entwined fingers, then met my eyes. "I don't want to do this without you. Forever is a *very* long time to spend coming up with ways everything could have gone better."

I tried to smile and managed a twitch at one corner of my mouth. "Don't count me dead before I'm actually stiff, love."

He raised our hands and kissed my fingers, telling me

everything in silence that he couldn't bring himself to say.

As the sun set behind the mountains, I stood before the gate and waited for my escort, counseling myself to keep breathing and to focus only on the now. Try as I did, however, my thoughts raced onto a score of tangents if I let them drift for even a moment, and I wrestled them back before I could panic. After all, it wouldn't do to show weakness, either in front of the other wizards or in front of Nath's envoys.

This was for the best. Really.

No one among the assembled, save Seamus, had my background. Lou was a solid trooper but young, and his work had kept him largely on the roads. I could talk to people, even the unpleasant ones, and generally keep my temper in check. As for talent, there was no point in sending a better-trained wizard in my place—what could he do without magic to draw upon?

And besides, the little voice in the back of my mind whispered, I'd come *awfully* close to killing Zoya, hadn't I? Maybe it would be for the best if I didn't make it back. Safer for everyone, at least. Carey wasn't stupid.

I silenced that thought and looked to my left, where my foursome waited a few meters away. All had offered to go, either with me or in my place, and none looked happy. Kip, in particular, had volunteered to be my second. "The spell on me will break once I'm home, yes?" he'd insisted that afternoon. "I'll be faster then. If there's trouble, I'll be able to carry you away."

"You're not faster than magic, dark or otherwise," I'd reminded him.

He stood in the growing twilight with his arm around Amy, who wore a pair of pistols and glowered at the rift between the realms. Beside them waited my cousin, ostensibly for the kids' benefit but really to keep Seamus from bolting after me. My partner's expression would have been inscrutable but for the valley between his brows, a look he'd always worn during training while concentrating before a dangerous scenario.

Lou, who came bearing a gun and a wand, stood to my right with Zeb and Carey, neither of whom spoke while the crowd muttered around us. Somewhere in the throng were all of the wizards who'd volunteered Carey for this task, and I wondered what they were thinking that evening. Were they disappointed that I was going in her stead? Ashamed for having chosen a scapegoat? Embarrassed by their own cowardice? Happy to see the back of me?

I didn't have long to ponder the answer. As the last rays pinked the western clouds, a trio of the guards from that morning stepped through the gate. The leader, who'd taken point, stopped and nodded to me. "You are here," he said in his odd Fae.

"I am."

"This surprises me. I had expected you to flee."

I shrugged, taking care to show him and his fellows my empty hands. "Your queen wants to talk. Let's talk."

He stepped aside and swept his arm toward the gate. "After you."

With a deep breath, I headed for the hole, but I paused just before I crossed and found Seamus in the shadows. *Love you*, I mouthed, then held my head high and crossed into the Gray Lands.

The first thing I noticed was the light. It seemed to be quite a bit earlier in the day on the other side of the border, and my eyes smarted while they adjusted to the glare. Still, the thick clouds overhead dampened the worst of the sunlight, and the grove of silver-leafed, black-barked trees through which my escort led me cast the forest floor into thick shade. I could see the path we followed, but anything more than twenty meters away faded into nondescript shadow.

The light, though, wasn't truly bothersome. For me, finding myself in a realm suffused with dark magic, the greatest annoyance was the feeling almost like a tingle along my skin, a warning field that made the hair on my arms stand on end. I'd been conscious of the dwindling magic supply during that disquieting week in March a few years prior, of course, but at least the background dark magic in the mortal realm had been relatively low. Here, at its source, it pressed around me like a fine, electrified net, always *this* close to administering a nasty shock. The fact that we were passing through a forest of shadow alder did nothing to make the situation any more welcoming.

The guards walked in silence, one ahead and two behind me, though where they thought I might run, I had no idea. Without magic, without any weapon, I was at their mercy—there was no way I'd reach the gate before they could catch me.

Our forced march was mercifully brief. As we topped a little hill, the thick trees gave way, and I looked into the valley to see an enormous palace rising from the midst of the grove, as tall as one of the showier cathedrals. But unlike Coileán's stone-and-glass confection of a palace, this one was alive, its walls formed by the knit-together branches of oversized trees. The structure was an awesome, yet deeply disturbing, twist on a fairytale treehouse, both fascinating and foreboding, and I stopped in my tracks and craned my neck to examine its living spires.

"My lady's home," said the leader of the guards. "She awaits you within."

Forcing myself to look away, I straightened my shirt and gestured toward the palace. "Lead on, then. Don't suppose she'd rather take this outdoors."

"Her chamber is close enough."

Quickly, we crossed the brown lawn to the palace. While I searched in vain for a door, the first guard in our line touched two of the twisted branches in the palace wall.

With a creak, the branches bowed away from each other, forming an opening perfectly sized for the four of us. I swallowed hard and stepped through, wondering how severely Nath punished anyone foolish enough to light a match in her house.

Given the outside of the building, I hadn't known what to expect indoors, but I'd hoped for at least solid flooring. Here, however, the trees continued to bend to Nath's will, sending thousands of thin runners back and forth across the wide foyer in a living floor. These branches grew flat on top, making a smooth path between the now-sealed door and the arched entrance to the structure's inner maze. Glancing about me in hopes of noting a landmark, I followed my escort into the heart of the palace.

We must have walked for half an hour through the semidarkness, always climbing with each new turn, and soon, I admitted to myself that I was lost. Beyond the problem of the many branching pathways was the general lack of signposts in the palace. One hallway looked much like the next, the only differences being the presence or absence of irregularly spaced windows. The twisting interior corridors were instead lit by glowing yellow orbs set into the walls—the queen's construction, I had no doubt. She had no need for tapestries, as the inner branches curled into decorative designs, some floral, some reliefs of scenes I had no time to study as we hurried on. Finally, the guards directed me through a cavernous space at the heart of the palace that could only have been Nath's throne room—the tree at the center growing in the shape of a massive chair was a bit of a giveaway—and then we passed out a side door and up another series of winding halls before, at last, we paused beside a seemingly unmarked stretch of wall. The lead guard placed his hand upon the nearest orb, which flickered, then turned green beneath his palm. He smiled at me as the wall's branches parted and led the way inside.

The chamber beyond the wall—Nath's office, I

understood—was large without losing the intimacy of a personal space. The omnipresent black branches stretched across the floor and up the walls to form a shallow dome in the ceiling. We'd gained a fair bit of altitude in our walk, and the arched windows, which cleared the treetops around the palace, offered a sweeping view of the countryside. The brown pelt of a massive beast, beheaded but still in possession of six sets of clawed paws, covered much of the floor...and there, beside the far windows, stood two plush red chairs, angled to give the occupants views both of each other and of the vista. The one on the left was as yet empty, but the queen sat in the chair to the right, staring out the window. Only once the door sealed behind us did she deign to look our way. Rising, she smoothed her diaphanous purple robe over her simple black shirt and trousers, then cocked her hairless blue head and spoke to the guards.

While they conversed, I studied my hostess. Like the guards, she had six eyes, all deep black and difficult to read, and nostril slits that flared with her breathing. Her ears were slightly too small for her head, at least in my estimation, and they came to points below her temples. The queen's lips were slimmer than the guards' but similarly dark, and when she opened her mouth, I saw that her teeth, like theirs, were closer to fangs.

With an impatient snort, Nath finally looked at me and folded her arms over her flat chest. "You came alone," she said, switching to Fae.

"I did, my lady," I replied. "Your envoy suggested that you didn't wish to entertain a crowd."

She couldn't disguise the surprise in her tone. "Unarmed?"

"As I told your men, I'm here to talk. I came in good faith."

Nath considered my response for a moment, then returned to her chair and extended her hand toward its mate. "Join me," she said, then dismissed her guards, who retreated through the wall while I made myself comfortable—or as comfortable as I could be with a blue creature out of a nightmare sizing me up with at least four of her eyes.

Unsure of where to begin, I decided that protocol dictated that I should let the queen make the first move. After a long moment of silence, a technique I knew all too well, she cleared her throat and crossed her legs. "What are you called?"

"Hannah, my lady. Hannah Parsons, if you prefer."

She grunted in affirmation. "And you are the…what do you call yourself, the grand magus?"

I paused, trying to gauge from her expression and tone how much she knew. "No. I don't represent the Arcanum."

"Indeed? My sources tell me the Arcanum has withdrawn into its holes. Is that the truth?"

"More or less, my lady."

"Why?" she asked curtly.

She knew more than she was letting on, I was sure of it, but without any sort of recent intelligence on the Gray Lands, I was at a disadvantage and proceeded with caution. "Ehm…well, honestly, I'm not sure. Not quite a year and a half ago, the Arcanum's magi kidnapped the grand magus and put another in her place. They turned on my people, and then they called their own into their installations. Aside from a few known operatives, we see little and less of them these days."

She steepled her fingers beneath her chin. "Security? The new grand magus is afraid?"

"Perhaps, my lady. I haven't spoken with him."

"He fears Faerie?"

I tread as carefully as I could. "He may, but the courts have no current plan to attack him. The Arcanum is holding many of my people hostage."

All of her eyes narrowed as I spoke. "And your people are…"

"The Fringe, my lady. And now, the Minor Arcanum. I'm here on behalf of both."

Nath turned away and stared out at the leafy canopy for a long moment in silence. "Why would Faerie be concerned with your people?" she finally asked.

"Because the king and queen would rather not see innocents die," I replied. "They've held their fire against the Arcanum this long for our benefit."

"Truly?" She didn't look at me. "Then they are insane, are they not?"

That took me aback. "My lady?"

"Coileán and Eleanor. My sources tell me their blood is impure."

"Oh. Ehm...they're half fae, yes," I said, shifting uneasily in my seat as I tried to predict the direction in which she was taking the conversation.

She seemed almost bored as she surveyed her realm. "I suppose it is to be expected, then, that they would suffer the insanity common to mortals. Concerning themselves with you is against their interest."

"Yes, my lady. It's...altruistic, I suppose."

"Insanity," she repeated. "But no matter." With that, she swiveled back to face me, resting her elbow on the carved arm of her chair and her head on two fingertips, as if the conversation wearied her. "I have made a study of the recent gates out of this realm, natural and induced. All were closed, but not by anyone recognizably Arcanum."

"They *have* been somewhat derelict in their duty," I admitted.

"They have abandoned it entirely," Nath countered. "It seems to me that the Arcanum has relinquished its claim to that realm."

I hesitated, looking for the best non-committal answer. "The Arcanum's motives are unknown to me, my lady. As I said, we've not been in contact."

"The Arcanum has long defended its claim," she continued, blinking each pair of eyes in a slow sequence.

"If they have abandoned it, then why should I not stake mine?"

Though Nath was affecting boredom, I could see through the mask. "Because *this* is your realm, my lady, and—"

"My people want new hunting grounds. How can I deny them the opportunity when it arises?"

"They're hunting *my* people," I said, struggling to maintain control over my surge of anger as I thought of the morning's cleanup. "Your raiding party took out an entire town last night before we could contain them. Prior to that, we killed a pair of snakes and a dragon before they could go on a proper rampage. Your people's incursions only put my people at risk."

If my description of the night's events disturbed her, I couldn't tell. "That may be, but your leaders have forfeited their claim. What right do you have, child, to impede my progress?"

Without reconsidering my options, I blurted out, "Because I am the true heir to the Arcanum, and I say you have no right to my realm."

She straightened in her seat, surprised. "Is that so? And the basis for your claim?"

"I sit here before you, the scion of Simon Magus, he who was first and greatest of magi," I heard myself say. "The Arcanum is held by a false magus. Until he is overthrown, I take up the claim as my right and responsibility. And you, my lady, have no right to allow your people to attack mine. Every gate you make is a declaration of war."

It was a bluff—a complete, utter, ridiculous bluff—but I put enough conviction in my voice to give it a bit of weight and prayed that I was a better actress than I believed.

To my relief, Nath didn't laugh me out of her office. "My people have a right to eat," she replied. "I am bound to protect them. You must understand this."

"And you must understand that I protect the ones among us who can't protect themselves," I told her. "Need I remind you, my lady, that when your people cause damage and kill mundanes, they risk exposing themselves—and you—to the mundane world?"

She shrugged. "You tell me this as a threat?"

"No, as a fact. If mundanes knew about this realm and its inhabitants, they'd do everything in their power to destroy you."

"They have no talent," she said, waving her hand dismissively.

"They don't need it. Mundane technology is deadly in its own right. Even Faerie respects it." I paused, giving that not-quite-fib time to sink in, then leaned toward the queen. "I'm not about destruction. I just want you to recognize our borders. Keep your people on your side, and you'll have no quarrel with me."

Nath mulled that over, once more contemplating the view, then cut some of her eyes to me. "If you are so opposed to the inhabitants of my realm, then why do you tolerate one among you?"

My muscles tensed at the enquiry. "You've got quite a spy network, haven't you?"

"It suffices. Will you answer the question?"

"Kip's a good kid, and he lost everything to raiders," I said, trying to sound unconcerned. "Are you demanding his return?"

At that, the queen chuckled and shook her head. "No, I have no need of your little pet." She gave my poker face a moment's study, then asked, "What do you know of the kadalin?"

"The which, my lady?"

"The kadalin. Kip, was it?"

"I, ehm…sorry, I didn't recognize the word."

Nath smiled coolly. "It is their name for themselves. We have other terms, but I had assumed your Kip would have told you of this. No?"

"He seldom speaks of this place, my lady. Too many bad memories."

Unperturbed, she rose and strolled to a curtained opening in the line of windows, then onto a balcony. I followed her outside, though I kept a fair distance from the wooden railing. "In my tongue," said Nath, closing her eyes in the wind, "*kadal* means 'monster.'"

"I confess, my lady, I'm unfamiliar with your language—"

"It is no matter. I tell you only to explain the term." She turned to lean her back against the railing, letting the wind ruffle her robe while she watched me. "In the long-ago, before my time, my father discovered that a band of your mundanes had crossed through a gate that closed shortly after their arrival. You are aware of my father?"

If the Fringe's records were accurate, Nath had been born of the Gray Lands' consciousness itself—or, I supposed, *him*self. "Yes, my lady."

"Very good. My father watched as the mundanes tried to find a way back, and he saw them picked off one by one—the old, the young, the weak. They were too slow," she explained. "Their sticks and slings were ineffective, and they could not fight off the hunters who pursued them with claws and teeth. He decided to improve their odds."

I frowned. "Why not just send them home?"

"Why would he do that?" she replied, equally bemused. "He had a solution. The mundanes traveled with mounts—creatures similar to chinols." When I frowned at the word, I said, "Pack animals. My people use them, and the 'raiders' of which your Kip speaks have a bad habit of stealing them."

I recalled the raiders' nightmarish companions, creatures like black-scaled horses with wicked teeth, and nodded.

"As I was saying," Nath continued, "when those long-ago mundanes rode, they could often escape, but their survival was contingent upon them having mounts ready and at hand. So my father combined the mundanes and their mounts, giving them a better chance at running from danger. It was more sporting."

My jaw tried to sag, but I gritted my teeth to hide my shock. No wonder Kip's anatomy was so bizarre—his race had been cobbled together, victims of the realm's whimsy. "He, ehm…transformed them?"

Nath thought about the term, then shook her head. "No, more permanent than that. The children born to them were augmented as well. Oh, they complained," she said with a smirk. "Father said that they were horrified with his gift, but he knew best. Besides, they were more entertaining when they could put up a fight."

"And you named them monsters," I murmured.

"Not us. Once they learned a bit of our tongue, they used that term for themselves. They have their own tongue, you know, the kadalin. Perhaps by now the word has lost some of its meaning among them."

She seemed relaxed, a stark contrast to the rigidity with which I held myself to prevent my true feelings from showing. "You keep using 'us' and 'them,' my lady," I said. "Do you not consider the kadalin your people?"

Nath laughed, deep in her belly, and smiled in earnest. "They are prey, nothing more. I make no claim upon them." Sobering, she gripped the railing and gave me another once-over. "And now, speaking of claims, I challenge you for yours, Hannah."

The vise around my gut tightened, but I forced myself to breathe. "Do you think that's wise?"

She smiled again. "You are confident. I will enjoy this."

"Oh, yes," I said, thinking quickly, "I'm rather confident about my chances. But if you insist, let's make it…*sporting*, wouldn't you say? My realm, my terms."

"I am listening."

"If you want to stake a claim to my realm, then you should be able to defend yourself there. We fight on my side of the border. Let's say…tomorrow morning, give us both a few hours to prepare. Agreed?"

Nath smiled again, and I had a feeling that she showed me more of her teeth than was strictly necessary. "I accept your terms. The morning, then. My guards will escort you back to the gate," she added, and turned away, giving me as much regard as she might a fly throwing itself against a window pane.

"Until morning," I replied, and shuffled back into her office to wait for my entourage, wondering what the hell I had just done.

CHAPTER 17

Nath's guards left me at the edge of the gate, and I walked through alone, willing my legs not to shake until I was out of their sight. Night had fallen in earnest while I'd been away, and beneath the star-sprinkled sky, I saw a small campfire and the shape of a lone watchman. Before my eyes had fully adjusted, he was on his feet and running toward me.

"*Badger!*" he cried, and then I was in Seamus's arms, gasping for breath as he squeezed my ribs almost to the point of cracking. When he loosened his hold and the black spots cleared, I looked up to find him beaming with joy and relief. "That was quick," he said, smoothing my hair back from my face. "What did she want? Are we to have an apology, or what?"

The dim light of the nearby fire might have hidden the worst of my expression, but I couldn't mask the tremor in my voice—certainly not from Seamus. "Not exactly."

"Then what?"

I took a deep breath, though it did little to calm me. "Long story short, she'd like to rule this realm, too, and now I've got to fight her in the morning. Where's Carey?"

Seamus shepherded me directly to the mess tent, plopped a fresh mug of tea on the table at which he'd dropped me, then waited until I took a few sips before running out to gather the others, who'd made tents for themselves over the course of the afternoon and were settling in for the night. While I drank, I gazed out at the shield around our camp. We'd moved all of our vehicles off the road and behind the illusion of an empty field, giving passing motorists no reason to suspect anything was out of the ordinary. A cleanup crew had done its best with the ravaged town, removing the bodies and scrubbing the blood and ash, and a few lights in the houses beyond the shield suggested that someone was still home. It was barely ten, or so said my watch, though my body insisted it was much later and that sleep was in order. My overly wired brain, on the other hand, was circling ever closer to the edge of full-on panic.

Fight Nath? What was I *thinking*? Might as well go toe to toe with Coileán, for all my skill would do. The Fringe's knowledge of the Gray Lands was woefully scant, but I had to assume that Nath was as powerful as her counterparts in Faerie, and I knew she wasn't young. And me—what was I, then? A half-trained wizard with a good stick and access to decent firearms, blathering about a long-dead ancestor who'd probably have laughed me out of the Arcanum. I doubted that Simon could have beaten the lady of the Gray Lands, so why did I ever imagine that I stood a chance?

Unless…

The sound of tramping boots pulled me from my dispiriting reverie, and I looked toward the gate to find a double line of guards walking through, lighting their way with hovering orbs. I jumped to my feet, but rather than run to engage us, the newcomers spread out behind the gate, waving tents and campfires into existence along neat rows. While I watched, their numbers swelled, first to a few dozen, then to a hundred and more. Their features were obscured with the darkness and distance, but I could see variety among them—more of the blue guards, a shorter people who seemed to be purplish in complexion, multi-armed and -legged beings of all shapes and sizes, a cadre of raiders, and even a pair of towering things that had to be trolls, so large that they barely fit through the gate. Voices rose from their new encampment, the sounds of men and beasts making themselves comfortable, and then a shout erupted from the throng as a curtained litter appeared from the gate and the queen climbed out to survey the field.

When I turned back to the table, my tea had gone cold, and I found my crew and the Joneses staring at the horde across the way. "I have one idea, and it's a long shot," I murmured as their shocked faces swiveled in my direction. "I can't win this alone. How many sleepwalkers are still here tonight?"

"Five," said Carey, who looked quite green. "You, me, Jean-Claude, Hua, and Rosaria."

"The Chilean girl? She's all of twelve, yes?" She nodded, and I forced a sip of cold tea down. "Right. How many more can you bring me?"

With a few frantic phone calls, Carey managed to coax another five sleepwalkers to Wyoming, even with the threat of an army parked nearby. Though scared— probably of me as well as the Gray Landers, to be honest—they and a few translators followed me into a tent on the edge of our encampment and listened as I spelled out my plan. "I'm not saying this is going to work," I concluded, looking around the semicircle gathered about me. "There are too many 'ifs' for my taste, but I don't have a better plan, and this realm needs us to pull this off. Are you in?"

When the last of the translations had been muttered, all nine gave their assent. "Thank you," I said with a sigh, enjoying the reprieve of momentary relief. "Get some rest. Stay close. I'll tell you when it's time."

The others filed out of the tent and toward the camp beds waiting for them, but Carey lingered at the door while I stepped outside and surveyed our forces. "If this doesn't work?" she murmured, folding her arms against the night chill.

"Run like hell."

"Seriously."

"That was serious. If they catch you, you're probably dead." I glanced down the line of tents, where Zeb was coaxing a couple of agitated teens back to bed. "If this fails, I'll stay and handle the fallout. You and Zeb will need to open gates and evacuate as many as you can. If you're able to get to Faerie, do it. Tell them we sent you." I looked back at Carey and waited until she turned my way. "Make sure Amy and Kip go with you. Arnie can look after himself, and Seamus…"

"You know damn well he won't go anywhere without you."

"If it comes to it, if you could knock him out and drag him away, I'd be grateful."

Carey smirked and looked out at the distant tents. "You want me to piss off a faerie? That's low on my bucket list, not going to lie."

"Granted, but if everything goes pear-shaped, I'd prefer it if we could keep the heroic sacrifices to a minimum."

We stood in silence for a moment, listening to the sounds of the camp trying to settle down, before Carey coughed and quietly said, "Thanks for coming."

"Sure."

"You didn't have to."

"No point in sulking at home, is there?"

She hesitated, then gave my arm an awkward pat. "Maybe I should have listened to Jimmy."

"You've got a lot of people looking to you, Carey," I replied, zipping my jacket. "And you're trying to keep them safe. Can't blame you."

"Maybe…" She cleared her throat, then tried again. "Maybe, assuming we don't all die in the next twelve hours, you and I could get coffee or something. Clear the air."

"I'd like that very much. Assuming we're still alive, of course."

"Naturally. So," she sighed, "what do you want to do with the rest of this sorry bunch?"

I checked my watch, considered the distant fires of the Gray Landers' camp, then shrugged. "Give them until midnight, then bring them to the mess tent, if you would. I think we can use them, but you'll have to be the one who gives the order."

"I don't know," she said, nudging me in the ribs, "you seemed to do all right with the sleepwalkers. Coming back from the Gray Lands intact does give you a bit of street cred."

"Yeah, but half of them probably still think I tried to kill Zoya, and the rest *know* I could have done it. They trust you. This is your circus, Carey—I'm just butting in and setting the tents on fire."

"Not *my* circus," she muttered. "Got a couple of elephants, some drunk clowns, and a cage full of rabid monkeys, and two or three of us trying to keep the show together."

"But they look to you, all the same."

Giving her shoulder a squeeze, I took my leave and found the tent Seamus had thrown together, where he was playing solitaire by the light of a glowing orb. "Couldn't sleep," he said, shuffling the pack together as I lowered the flap. "Going to try?"

"Best if I did," I replied, setting the clock on my mobile, then slid beneath the blankets of our double-sized camp bed. He climbed in beside me, and soon, we were spooned together in the darkness, Seamus holding on to me as if he feared I'd float away.

No one was thrilled to be crammed into the mess tent on the wrong side of midnight, but at least there was body heat in the middle of the pack. When the last of the stragglers had been forced from bed and onto a bench, Carey stood on a table, blinked her torch for attention, then turned the floor over to me.

"I'm sure you've been hearing rumors," I began, taking Carey's spot on the tabletop. "There is a plan. You have a part to play in it."

To my right, Kip nodded and cracked his knuckles, and Amy flashed her thumbs.

"This will be a long night for you," I continued, letting my eyes roam over the crowd. "When we disperse, I'd like for you to pull together whatever light you can and form a line in front of our tents. Fire, lightning, whatever. We're not trying to blind them this time, just show them we're here. Can you do that?"

"You're making us targets."

I recognized the voice—the boy who had championed Carey's nomination as envoy to Nath—and spotted him slouching to my left. The speaker was young, probably no more than eighteen, and had shaved the sides of his head into a blond fauxhawk. He sounded confident enough, but there was fear in his eyes.

"Have you got a better plan?" I asked him. "I mean, you were so keen on sending Carey earlier today—what's your great idea, hmm?"

"Not using us as bait. How about *that*?"

"Kid," I said, aiming my torch into his eyes, "I'm the only bait here. If this falls apart, you're to run away. How does that suit you?"

His skinny chest began to puff. "You calling me a coward, bitch?"

On the floor in front of me, Seamus balled his fists, but I held out a hand to stay him. "Coward?" I told the boy. "No."

Before he could be clever again, I called upon the little force I needed to yank him off the floor and toss him over the heads of the crowd into the grass. He cried out and bounced on landing, but he managed to pick himself up once he'd skidded to a stop. "I'm calling you a little punk whose mouth is bigger than his brain," I yelled after him. "Now's your chance to prove me wrong."

A few of the wizards around me clapped, and the boy skulked back into the tent, head down and slightly limping.

"Right," I told the others. "Take your positions, and if Carey tells you to run, then you run like the devil himself is after you. Agreed?"

In a matter of minutes, the tent was nearly empty, and I jumped off the table to give Seamus one last hug. "Be careful out there, no heroics, and try not to punch that wanker, eh?" I told him. "I know he's a little beast, but we have bigger problems."

"I'll be waiting," he mumbled into my hair, then released me and gripped Amy's shoulder. "Ready, kid?"

"Locked and loaded," she replied, passing her rifle to Kip, and gave Carey and me a salute as she led the stragglers into the night.

Everything—our safety, our future, our chance of walking away with our lives—depended upon two variables: would Nath catch a few minutes of sleep, and if so, could she be pulled into the dream space?

"There she is," Carey told us as we floated above the Gray Landers' camp. Nath and her kind glowed with the bluish light of the dark-magically adept, but only a few were asleep. I stayed well above the tents so as not to accidentally draw anyone into our huddle, though I itched for the chance to experiment. No one among us had ever attempted to sleepwalk with a Gray Lander, and the uncertainty drove me mad as we waited.

But there was nothing for it—we couldn't do anything until Nath slept. To my dismay, she seemed to be in no hurry to lie down, instead walking the avenues of her modest tent city and having the occasional word with her captains. She inspected armor, watched weapons be forged and sharpened, and smiled as her soldiers tested their power in the gate's shadow. True, there was far less dark magic on this side of the border, but that didn't seem to stop them.

I had kept my watch on so that we would have some idea of the hour, in case Nath decided to pull an all-nighter and the Minor Arcanum needed to be evacuated. Minutes turned to hours, and the seconds ticked painfully slowly as we huddled above the camp, biding our time.

Finally, Nath slipped into an empty tent, and I held my breath—well, metaphorically speaking—while I watched her through the cloth. She surveyed her modest quarters, created a few more pillows for her bed, then threw off her shoes and robe and plopped into her cushioned nest. It was hardly a graceful landing, but then again, Nath couldn't know that she had an audience.

The others gathered around me as Nath rolled onto her side and tucked her knees to her chin, and then, a few minutes later, her chest rose and fell with the slow rhythm of sleep.

"Come on," I told my companions, and one by one, we drifted into the queen's tent and surrounded her bed. With a moment's concentration, I created a white orb for each of us and suspended them above the others' heads. Though we all glowed golden in the dream space, I thought it couldn't hurt to add a little extra decoration. A few of my companions stiffened—even though they'd surely heard of my talent, seeing it for themselves must have been unsettling—but no one ran. "Spell seems to be holding," I told them, then glanced at Rosaria, the youngest of our pack. "Ready?"

"Ready," she said, and put her hand over Nath's body. The others did likewise, and with a last, rushed prayer to any kind deity, I joined them.

The plan would only work, I'd explained, if we used subterfuge. Nath needed to know that I had an army behind me—a suitably *powerful* army—and the only way she'd believe that would be for her to see us all in the dream space. Ordinarily, a non-sleepwalker would only see the person who pulled him in. We didn't know if having ten people attempt to simultaneously yank someone into the dream space would work, but we tried.

"Three…two…one…" Carey murmured.

In unison, we made the effort, working as hard as we could to rip Nath from her sleep. I was beginning to fear that we couldn't wake her when suddenly, she opened two of her eyes and gasped.

"Hello, there," I said as the other wizards fell into place behind me, their lights blazing and their faces stern. "Nath, my dear, we need to have a little chat."

She sat up, confused—but then again, since all she was seeing of her surroundings was blackness, a little confusion was to be expected. "Who are they?" she asked, pointing to the others. "And how did you come to speak this tongue?"

"A few of my associates, and magic, of course," I replied, grateful for the dream space's translation effect. "I know we'd agreed to start in the morning, but technically"—I tapped my watch's face—"it *is* morning, so why wait for daylight?"

"Why, indeed?" Nath murmured, straightening her clothes as she climbed out of her bed. "Where am I?"

"Where you were. This place is slightly outside the physical," I explained. "Though what happens here can have physical repercussions."

I didn't flinch as Nath flung her hand toward my face, but when I wasn't immediately incinerated or blasted into pieces—whatever she'd had in mind—she jerked and stared at her fingers as if they had turned traitor.

"I happen to like this place, myself," I said as Nath tried again to kill me. "Puts me at a certain, oh…advantage."

With a flick of my wrist, Nath was flung twenty meters into the air. "You won't be able to break your fall," I told her as she clawed for purchase. "If I drop you, you'll almost certainly feel it. I doubt that it would kill you, so if I have to do it again, I'll take you higher on the second round. Or maybe I'll just throw you into one of those mountains over there," I mused, pointing into the distance. "You can't see them, but *I* can. Stone, I find, is unforgiving."

After a moment, Nath seemed to realize that her efforts were futile, and she ceased her struggling. "Why are you doing this?" she called down to me.

I floated up to join her, and the rest of the wizards followed suit. "Why? To spare you the humiliation of seeming weak before your people," I explained. "None of them can see what happens here. You're going to yield, but if we do this in private, then you'll be able to save face when you pack up your tents and go home."

"*Yield?*"

"Unless you'd like me to kill you right now," I murmured. "That can also be arranged."

"I don't believe—"

The rest of her response was cut short by the vise I threw around her neck, which tightened until her eyes bulged. With a wave, I loosened the bind, and Nath gasped and choked as she recovered. "As I said, what happens here has physical consequences," I said over her coughing. "You'll have a lovely bruise in short order. Might want to cover that up, spare yourself the questions."

"I'll…kill you…for this," she managed between heaving breaths.

I allowed myself to smile. "Go ahead. If you do, any one of my associates here will be happy to pick up where I left off. Or you're welcome to test the ones waiting back at camp—you'll see them if I release you. Trust me, they can be creative. If you don't like the thought of falling, would you rather die by drowning, or by being burnt alive? Really, I'm open to suggestions."

Nath rubbed her purpling neck, looked at the formless

ground below her, stared at us for a long, silent moment, then bowed her head. "I yield to you, Hannah."

"Very well," I replied, and gently lowered her as I drifted back to earth. "And as for us, we'll say nothing to your people of how this arrangement was made. Now, what assurance do I have that you won't come after me in my sleep?"

She bounced on her toes, feeling the ground below them once more, and sighed. "I swear by my realm, my throne, and myself that I will not challenge your claim while you live to defend it. My oath is binding, and my word is good."

"I believe you," I said, having seen the faint flash of silver around the edge of her glowing form as she spoke. The oath of a magical adept—one who is aware of the potential consequences for breaking it—is never given lightly. "But your terms aren't my terms. You'll leave this realm and never make a claim on it again."

She cocked her head. "That I will not swear. A claim endures only as long as the one who makes it. Each successive claimant must defend it in turn. While you live in this realm, I will respect your claim, but I will not bind myself for eternity." She regarded me calmly, using her bit of height over me to its full advantage. "Kill me if you must, but I reject those terms."

It wasn't perfect, and I thought furiously, looking for holes to patch in our negotiations. "You'll keep your people out of this realm?"

"That I cannot promise," said Nath. "Gates form on their own—you know this. But should any of my people cross the border and come to harm, I swear that I will neither defend them nor retaliate against you." She paused and considered me as I wrestled with the implications of the deal, then asked, "Do we have an pact?"

My mind raced. She was agreeing to stay away as long as I lived. That was a start, wasn't it? All I had to do was remain in the mortal realm and keep myself alive, and we'd be safe from Gray Lands incursions…well, at least for the next thirty years or so, right? Longer, if I went to Faerie…

No.

I *couldn't* go to Faerie.

Nath's terms meant that I had to be in the mortal realm to defend my claim. If I went to Faerie, I'd be abandoning it, leaving the realm wide open to invasion.

That wasn't fair. I was supposed to go to with Seamus someday, maybe before I grew too old, and now…

I could renegotiate. Tell her the terms were unacceptable. She didn't have much to bargain with in the dream space…but then again, if someone shook her awake, all bets were off. I had lives down there, so many lives, counting on me to make the monsters go away…

I stuck out my hand. "Agreed."

Nath clasped it briefly, and our forms glowed in tandem, binding us to the terms. Once I'd released her, I cast her from the dream space, then threw myself back into my body before the other sleepwalkers could congratulate me.

I just couldn't take that.

Sleep—true sleep—was the only thing I wanted, and I allowed myself to drift until the alarm I'd set in case of watch failure went off just before dawn. Feeling sick at my stomach, I dragged myself from bed, ran a brush through my snarled hair, then stepped out into the pale light in time to join the wizards still holding the line.

As I neared, Carey caught my arm and pulled me closer. "I told them to be quiet until the gate is sealed," she whispered. "No sense in jeopardizing this now."

"I don't think we need to fear that," I replied, but I let her lead me to Seamus, who held me as the end of Nath's forces retreated through the rift. The queen herself was the last to depart, carried away in her litter. I couldn't imagine what she might have told her soldiers, but that was Nath's problem, not mine. One of her guards stepped aside as the litter passed, then waved his hands at the gate until the skin between the realms knit itself back together.

When the gate was well and truly shut, the people around me burst into cheers and a few tears. I accepted the thanks of the nearest dozen wizards, then gratefully allowed Zeb to usher my crew into Seamus's and my tent. "Let us worry about crowd control," he said, and winked as he dropped the flap.

While the others happily chatted and compared notes, I sank onto our bed and buried my face in my hands. I must have sighed too loudly, as the voices fell silent, and Amy asked, "You okay, Hannah? Tired?"

"Very tired," I replied, and looked up at the ring of concerned faces. "I'll be fine. Ehm…I hate to ask, but would it be possible to have a moment with Seamus?"

"Of course," she said, exchanging a knowing look with Kip, and the two of them and Arnold slipped out past Zeb and the excited throng.

Once we were alone, Seamus sat beside me and pulled me against his shoulder. "Well, now," he murmured, stroking my hair, "how does it feel to save the day?"

"I didn't."

"Oh, I don't know about that. Carey said you were marvelous."

I looked up to see him smiling, and my heart clenched. "Carey didn't tell you everything."

Seamus's brow creased. "No? I think she hit the high points, and as Nath's no longer around, I doubt that she embellished too badly."

"Seamie," I said with a sigh, sitting up again, "there's something I need to tell you."

He took my hand even as I began reaching for his. "What's the matter, love? You're not moving to the Gray Lands, are you?" he weakly teased.

"No, but…the negotiations didn't go as well as I'd hoped."

"What do you mean? Nath took her army with her—"

"Only as long as I'm here to defend my claim to this realm. Once I'm gone, she'll be back."

His expression shifted toward shock as the implications hit. "Badger," he whispered, "you—"

"I can't go to Faerie," I said in a rush. "Not now, not…well, not unless someone comes along who's able to fight her off. Until then, I can't leave this realm undefended, Seamie, I *can't*." I paused, trying to read him, then murmured, "Go on without me. Be safe. I'll come if I can…*when* I can…and I'm so sorry, but—"

He pulled me into his arms and held on, rubbing my back as I cried. "I'm not going anywhere. Not without you. I promised you that, and I intend to keep that promise."

After a moment, I sniffed and rubbed my eyes dry. "It's not fair. I could have pushed her, but if she'd woken before the ink was dry—"

"You did what you had to do." He produced a tissue from thin air and dabbed at my smeared mascara. "Sacrifice was always a possibility with the job, you know—more so with this one, I guess."

"Seamie…"

"And what's this gunk made of, tar?" he muttered, dampening the tissue with a glare. "How the devil do you take it off?"

"There's a special remover for it. Seamie, I'm sorry—"

"Stop." He cupped my chin in his palm and put the dirtied tissue aside. "When we were kids, we signed on with the Constabulary because it was the right thing to do, and because we knew we could do it. Once the Arcanum got stabby, you could have stayed safe in Faerie and let the stragglers fend for themselves, but you didn't. You came back to find them because you could, and because it was the right thing to do. I get it, Badger. You've been trying to do the most good, and I love you for it. I *admire* you for it. So stop apologizing for saving this realm from a hostile takeover."

"It's not fair to make you stay here—"

"Who's making me? I'm *staying*. And this isn't forever, love—you're going to have to retire someday, one way or another. You'll have to pass the baton at some point."

"Any when will that be?" I replied. "When I'm eighty? Ninety? If the Arcanum situation doesn't straighten out, I may bloody well still be at this when I'm a hundred—*if* I live that long."

"They'll come round," he murmured, resuming his makeup removal. "And until they do, I'll be here. You waited twenty-three years for me to come to my senses. The least I can do is return the favor."

I watched his eyes as he tried to clean me up, then waved my hand over my face and whispered a word to wipe it clean. "It really is impossible to remove with just water."

"Mm. I like your method better," he said, then kissed my forehead and tossed the tissue into the ether. "So that's settled, then. We're here until you decide otherwise." He looked at me closely, then frowned again. "What is it? Something else on your mind?"

Seamus looked so earnest, but the concern that had risen to the top of my thoughts seemed horribly petty, and I shook my head. "No, I'm, ehm…I'm fine."

"Liar," he countered with a knowing smile. "Go on, then. If I've said something wrong, tell me."

"You haven't," I hurriedly replied, "but…well…" I paused as my cheeks flamed, then forced myself to spit it out. "Seamie…let's say it's another thirty years before I can go. I'll be seventy-eight."

"So will I. Thanks for the reminder."

"But I'll look it and feel it, and you…" I struggled for the words and settled for waving one hand awkwardly at his face while I stared down at our linked hands. "Under the glamour, you'll still be young. And…I mean, I wouldn't *blame* you if you didn't want me then, but…"

He said nothing until I looked him in the eye once

more, and then he rested his free hand against my cheek and shook his head. "Please hear me, Badger," he said softly. "If you believe nothing else I've ever told you, I need you to believe me now. All right?"

"All right," I mumbled.

"You are the only woman I want. No one in the universe knows me like you do, and there is no one I'd rather grow old with, whatever that may entail."

"But—"

"I love you," said Seamus. "For the rest of my life, I'll love you. The stars will go out, and I'm sure it'll be bloody freezing, but I'll still love you."

I couldn't help but crack a smile.

"And so what if we get older?" he continued, smiling back at me. "I won't exactly be young, right? Maybe on the surface, but I plan to enjoy being a cranky pensioner. Someday, you and me, maybe three hundred or so, sitting in rocking chairs and yelling at the neighborhood kids to stop being so noisy. What do you say?"

"You're impossible," I told him, feeling my smile widen. "And you can't pull off the pensioner shtick if you still look twenty-five."

"Which is what glamour is for, love." He took my other hand and squeezed. "Sure, Faerie will always be full of pretty, fit people. So what? The only partner I want is you."

I leaned forward, and he met my kiss with fire in his touch. When we parted, I looked at him and chuckled. "What's so funny?" he asked.

"Well, typically, when someone makes a pronouncement like that, it's followed by a ring."

With a snort, Seamus raised my hand, and my own tiny diamond flashed back at me in the light of the orb he'd left burning. "You're already wearing mine, Badger. As far as I'm concerned, you're stuck with me."

I pretended to mull that over for a moment, then kissed him again. "Suppose I can live with that."

CHAPTER 18

By the time Seamus and I emerged from our tent, half of our company had departed, and the rest were on their way home. Still, the smell of bacon wafted from the mess tent, where Zeb and Boone were manning a grill half-covered in scrambled eggs and browning toast. "Vittles?" Boone offered when we peered at the industrial setup. "If it's chicken or pork you're after, we've got y'all covered."

We each took a heaping plate with thanks and settled down at an empty table, only to be joined a few minutes later by Amy and Kip. "Oh, my God, *bacon*," Amy mumbled through a mouth full of food, rolling her eyes in pleasure. She'd stuffed her breakfast into a sandwich and was making remarkable progress, considering her size.

Across from her, Kip shook his head and grinned as he tucked in. "You would think she'd never tasted it before, hearing her go on about it."

"You love it, you know it," she managed, then washed the oversized bite down with a swig of coffee. "I forget how good this is. Seamus, you can make bacon, right?"

"Passably," he replied, "but *that* hardly qualifies as bacon. Far too thin…"

Amy pulled a piece from her sandwich and crunched it in half. "'Murica, bub. No worries, I'll figure it out. Can't be that hard."

"Need an assistant?" Kip asked.

"Oh, definitely. Maybe someone to taste-test for poison."

He raised his hand. "You have a volunteer, then.

Though you're asking much of me, I will do my best. *Hey*," he snapped as Amy's fingers shot across the table and grabbed an unguarded slice.

She smiled coquettishly before eating it in two bites.

Watching them flirt, I thought about what Nath had told me and realized I couldn't keep it to myself. "Kip, dear, could I speak with you for a moment? Maybe in private?"

Blushing, Kip dropped his fork, then glanced between Seamus and me. "We haven't done what you think we've done," he mumbled.

"What are you…oh. Oh, gosh, *no*," said Amy as she realized what he was talking about. "No, that's…I mean, I don't want to be rude, but that's not really any of y'all's business, and—"

"This isn't about *that*," I cut in, and lowered my voice. "Though I suppose this might be of interest to both of you, come to think of it. Ehm…" I hesitated long enough to put my thoughts in order, then turned on the bench until I was directly facing Kip. "You're kadalin, are you not?"

He started at the term. "Yes, but where did you learn that name?"

"From Nath. She knows you're with us, and she told me a bit about your people. Where you came from."

Kip cocked his head in confusion. "The Kint Porda? My family lived near those lakes for generations."

"No, not you specifically—*you*. Your people. Why you don't claim Nath as your queen."

"Because we're a free people," he replied, returning to his abandoned eggs. "We've never accepted a monarch. Not Nath, not Geheret, not Mab before them. No offense," he added, glancing at Seamus, who shrugged it off.

"That may be, but Nath barely considers you people at all," I continued, watching him tense. "You, ehm…your people aren't native to the Gray Lands, Kip. They came from this realm in the beginning."

At that, Amy put down her sandwich and leaned across the table toward me. "Wait, we had centaurs in *this* realm?"

"No," I told her, and turned my attention back to Kip, who had once again pushed his food aside. "Nath told me your ancestors were mundanes who happened to wander through a gate. They brought their horses with them. Nath's father—the consciousness of the Gray Lands, best not to ask, but I assume he's much like Faerie—she says he…well…fused them."

My companions stared at me, flabbergasted, but Kip was first to recover his voice. "Wait…Hannah, are you telling me I'm—"

"*Human*," Amy whispered, staring at him.

"Your ancestors were," I said. "You, not so much, but deep in there…*well*." I pointedly glanced at Amy, and Kip nodded in comprehension. "It explains a lot about you. Your race is basically the Gray Lands' arts-and-crafts project."

Absently, Kip massaged his forehead and stared at the table as he processed that information. "If my people were once human…" he muttered, then sat up straight and looked at Amy. "Perhaps…*this*"—he waved his finger back and forth between the two of them—"isn't so unnatural after all."

"Could be," she teased. "I still think you're pretty cute."

"Amy…" He rubbed the back of his reddening neck as he chose his words. "Not today, but, uh, someday…knowing this…would you ever, um…I mean, would you ever consider—"

"*Kippit.*"

He froze. "I'm sorry, I shouldn't—"

"No, no, wait," said Amy, grabbing his hand across the table. "Go on."

"Really, it was nothing," he mumbled. "Forget—"

"Dude," she sighed, "if you're trying to propose to me,

that's not *nothing*."

Looking about wildly for a hint of how to proceed, Kip finally found Amy's smiling eyes and steadied himself. "Would you…*someday*…have me as your mate?" he asked, looking slightly nauseated. "I would do anything for you, Amy, and if you'd have me—"

"Not *if*," she interrupted, and started to grin. "When."

He seemed shocked at her answer. "Truly? Even with the—"

"The spell?" she finished. "Kip, I really don't care how many legs you have, okay? I love you," she said, and shrugged. "I mean, I don't want to get *too* freaky, but as long as the spell holds…"

"Oh, let's not go there," Seamus muttered, looking pained at the notion.

Unperturbed by my partner's discomfort, Amy kept her attention on Kip. "And not right away. I'm not sure I want to be a teenage bride, but, uh…two, three years? Time to get the shop running well, get you proficient…"

"Whenever you're ready," said Kip, beaming back at her.

She held out her palm for his other hand, then laced their fingers together. "We'll start over, you and me," she murmured. "Maybe forget some of what came before."

"Once you've shot the grand magus in the balls," he replied.

"Yeah, after that."

The two of them stood, leaned across the table, and kissed, and Seamus and I shared a look. "Ehm…congratulations, kids," he said, sliding off the bench. "And while I have no idea whether it's possible for you two to procreate, should you have questions about the getting or prevention of children, you know where to find us."

"*Seamus!*" Amy yelped, mortified. "Okay, *wow*, that's—"

"We're going," I said, and dragged him away as Amy flushed crimson.

Before we could go far, however, we ran into Carey, who was seated with several of the Minor Arcanum's senior members. They flagged us down as we passed, and we paused beside their table. "Everything all right?" I asked.

"We have a question for you," said Carey. "Need a truthful answer."

I folded my arms. "Shoot."

"Are you planning on taking over the Minor Arcanum and turning us into your personal army under threat of nighttime execution?"

"Of course not," I said with a frustrated sigh. "I'm not a conqueror—I may look a bit like Simon Magus, but believe me, I have no interest in fighting the Arcanum head-on."

"Uh-huh," she murmured, glancing at her fellows. "And all of this talk about you defending your claim to this realm? That's a second question, I realize."

I looked around the table, meeting everyone's eyes in turn, before I spoke again. "I did what I had to do to make Nath go away. That's all. And I'll be here to make sure she honors our bargain. But beyond that, what you do with yourselves is none of my concern."

Carey considered my response, then gave me a curt nod. "Works for me," she said, and extended her hand. "We'd like to offer you our cooperation in the continued effort to not be eaten by monsters. How does that sound?"

I shook her hand and chuckled. "Sounds fair enough. You know where to find us?"

"Jimmy said you'd gone to Virginia. If you need a place to stay...I mean, we've got that bunkhouse..."

"Generous of you," I replied, and glanced at Seamus. "But I think we'll stay on the coast for now. We've got a place."

"You should come visit sometime," Seamus offered. "You two and Jim, what about dinner one night? Summer by the sea can't be worse than summer in New Mexico."

Carey released me with a smile. "Might just have to take you up on that."

Never had I been so happy to see the flat above Amy's shop as I was that afternoon when we finally climbed the back staircase and piled through the kitchen door. "Bed," Kip grunted, rummaging in the refrigerator for a drink.

"*Shower*, then bed," Amy countered. "You smell."

He pulled out a root beer and took a swig. "You're no better."

"Exactly, which is why I'm going to do the civilized thing," she said, half-dragging him toward the interior staircase. "If you don't give me grief, I'll save you some hot water."

Arnold shook his head as the door closed behind them. "Kids. What are we to do with them?"

"Stay out of their way, I'd think," said Seamus, filling the kettle. "Considering the arsenal downstairs…"

"*Right*. I'll get mugs. Have we bought anything better than store brand of late?"

"Doubtful."

With a mutter and a flick of Arnold's wrist, three mugs floated down from the cabinet, and a trio of proper teabags materialized inside them. "You're on your own for sugar, but I'll get it out," he said, heading for the pantry closet, then stopped in his tracks. "Ehm…guys?"

A silhouette had appeared on the other side of the frosted panes of the kitchen door, a form human in dimension but otherwise undiscernible through the clouded glass. On first glance, I thought it might be male, but I couldn't be certain. "Wands," I murmured, pulling mine out of my waistband, and Seamus preemptively bounced a fireball in his palm.

The visitor rapped at the door—a polite shave-and-a-haircut knock—and Arnold, who was closest, turned to us and frowned. "The assassins' style is more along the lines of kicking down the door," he whispered. "Might not be Arcanum."

"Might be what he wants you to think," I replied.

He nodded, lips pursed, then motioned us back. "Around the corner, watch through the cut-out window. I'll handle this," he told us. When we were in position, Arnold readied his wand in his right hand, then flung the door open and aimed at the stranger.

One thing was certain: the stranger on the landing wasn't a member of the assassin corps. They typically didn't go for white linen suits. He wore a black dress shirt underneath, but no tie, plus a coordinating pair of bucks. Somehow, he'd managed to keep his clothing unwrinkled in the humidity, a feat often managed only with magic. I estimated his age as early forties—closer to my cousin's age than mine—but that estimate could have been skewed by his head of blond curls, which gave him the air of a cherub masquerading as a country lawyer. He was taller than Arnold—perhaps Seamus's size—but otherwise similar in build, healthy without being skinny. But the thing that caught my eye more than any other was his half-eaten ice cream, a melting vanilla double scoop in a rainbow-sprinkled waffle cone from the shop down the street, which he licked even as Arnold leveled his wand to strike.

"Good afternoon," he said in a surprisingly deep voice—American, I could tell, but nothing more particular than that. "My card."

With his free hand, he reached into his pocket and extracted a piece of black cardboard, which he passed to Arnold before taking another bite of his snack. If the man was at all concerned at being on the business end of a magus's wand, he hid it masterfully.

From my vantage point, the card was entirely black, but Arnold rubbed his thumb across the surface, then held it to the overhead light. "Black on black embossing? Classy," he muttered.

"Tradition," the man replied, catching a runaway drip with his tongue. "But if it's too difficult to read, my name is Tanner Adler."

"Yes, that unique color scheme gave you away," said Arnold, handing his card back to him. "Your business, Mr. Adler?"

"Best discussed with all parties on the same side of the door. May I come in? I mean you no harm," he added, raising his voice. "You can put the wand away, Detective. I see you."

Arnold glanced back at us, then stepped aside to let the stranger in. "Anything funny, and you're dead."

"I'd assume nothing less," he said, pulling out a chair at the kitchen table. "And before we get down to business, could I trouble you for a napkin? My ice cream seems to be leaking."

Once he'd wrapped a paper towel around the cone, he smiled as the rest of us joined him at the table. "Really, I'm not here to hurt anyone," he said, cutting his dark eyes to Seamus. "You can put out the fireball now."

"I'll be the judge of that, thank you," Seamus muttered.

"Suit yourself." Tanner shrugged and bit a chunk out of the cone. "This is good stuff, by the way. Fresh. That's a nice little ice cream parlor you have."

Arnold sighed impatiently. "Mr. Adler," he explained, looking at Seamus and me, "is the head of the Dark Company."

Seamus looked at him blankly, but I was back on my guard. The Fringe's practice had been to avoid the Company, an espionage organization composed entirely of shifters. While the Fringe couldn't be bought, the Company was more than willing to negotiate, and they didn't seem to consider 'mercenary' to be a dirty word. The fact that the Company knew I was back in the mortal realm was troubling, but to have their leader sitting in my kitchen was enough to make my wand hand twitchy.

"What do you want, Mr. Adler?" I forced myself to ask

instead.

"Tanner, please," he said, still smiling. "First, I'd like to congratulate you on your performance last night. That was quite a stunt you pulled off with Nath. I'll admit, we were concerned by what we heard during the day, but you came through. Well done, you," he added, saluting me with his cone.

"Thank you," I murmured. "And second?"

"*Second*, and partially in light of recent events in Wyoming, I came to offer you a little intel."

"Your price?" asked Arnold.

At that, Tanner sobered. "Gratis. We don't make a habit of this, but under the circumstances, it seemed right."

"Since when has the Company been concerned with *right*?"

"Since the Arcanum decided that the Gray Lands wasn't their problem anymore." Tanner considered his cone, then spread out the paper towel and rested it on his placemat. "Two months ago, I got a call from James Mulligan. He seemed to think you were active in this realm, Detective Parsons, and he wanted to know your whereabouts. He also wanted to know whether you were still alive, Magus Lowe. And he was quite generous with the compensation. *Wait*, let me finish, please," he said, holding up his hand as the three of us started to speak. "We took the job because we're not stupid, but we have yet to deliver a final report."

"So you're here to blackmail us, then," said Arnold. "Have you any idea what my cousin here does when people try to do that?"

His eyebrow quirked. "I've heard stories. Zoya Fedkin, wasn't it?"

"They're remarkably good at espionage," I told Seamus.

"Please," Tanner replied, "it's easier than you think when you have operatives who can shift into, oh, standard houseflies. Like that one," he added, rising from the table, then crossed the den and raised the window. "Go on, Rudy, I have it from here."

We hurried across the room, and I reached the window in time to see the fly spiral down to the quiet alley between our building and the scrapbooking shop next door. In seconds, a middle-aged man with a prominent bald spot was standing in the building's shadow, naked as a newborn. He began rummaging behind our neighbors' bin and produced a plastic bag, from which he quickly extracted a shirt and trousers. By the time Seamus had picked his jaw off the floor, Rudy had vanished down the street.

Tanner grinned and closed the window. "He's quite good. It took a bit of doing to find you, I'll admit, but once we had you, it was simple to monitor the situation."

"Not if we buy more bug spray," Seamus growled.

"There's no need to resort to chemical warfare. The monitoring stops as of now. Well," Tanner amended, "I mean, we'll keep a general eye on you, but nothing quite so intense."

"Why bother?" said Arnold, still gripping his wand. "Once the Arcanum has confirmation, they'll hunt us down."

Tanner smiled at him, still unruffled. "You're assuming that the Arcanum is going to receive confirmation, Magus. What's that line about assumptions making asses of people, again?"

"Just spit it out," he snapped. "What do you want?"

"Only to tell you that as far as the Dark Company is concerned, revealing your whereabouts to the Arcanum would be against our best interest. Believe me, we don't like the idea of living under Nath's rule any more than you do."

"So...what?" I asked. "Are you going to return the money? They'll kill you if they know you're hiding us."

"But they won't know," Tanner replied, and tapped his temple. "Can't read a shifter's mind, remember. Or is that in the Fringe files? Been so long since I've had a look, I really can't recall. And no," he said, giving his ice cream a lick, "the fee stays with us. My people have to eat, too."

Tanner was halfway to the door when I said, "Why bother telling us about any of this?"

He turned back to me, but this time, there was no trace of mirth on his face. "Because you need to be aware that you're not as far off their radar as you think. If you're the one thing standing between us and the Gray Lands, Detective, then you need to take care of yourself, for all our sakes. And you should know that they've been investigating your old haunts. We've seen them in Durham in recent weeks."

"No one there knows where I am," I told him. "I cut ties when I went on the run."

"Maybe, maybe not. Folks like to say they've cut ties, but in the end, no man is ever really an island. There's always some thread to follow. Anyway, be careful, will you?"

"Wait," I said as he reached for the doorknob. "Do you know where they're keeping Helen and the rest of the Fringe?"

At that, Tanner sighed. "No. Somewhere in the silo, that much we can tell, but I'm not putting my people at risk to learn more. I'm sorry," he added, glancing at me over his shoulder. "But you couldn't pay me enough to go in there. Not with the wards on that place."

He closed the door behind him, and we stood in the kitchen until the metal staircase ceased to ring with his footsteps.

"What, ehm…what does he shift into?" Seamus asked. "Out of curiosity."

"Cougar," Arnold muttered. "Or so we've been led to believe."

"Mm. Whatever," he replied, and headed for the interior staircase. "I'm going to the store for DEET. Anyone want to come along?"

As it so happened, Tanner was either prescient or knew more than he let on, and given his line of work, I tend to believe the latter.

Seamus and I retired early that night, just after eight. There was still light in the sky, but blackout curtains solve a multitude of problems, and our exhaustion took care of the rest. I was no happier about my situation post-Nath, but that evening, I was simply too tired to care, and Seamus's slow breathing behind me soon lulled me to sleep.

Barely an hour later, my phone began to chime on the nightstand, and I forced my eyes open enough to see whether it was anyone of importance. The name on the readout surprised me into full wakefulness, however, and Seamus grunted as I sat on the edge of the bed and answered the call. "Hello, Mary? Everything all right?"

"Hannah?" came her whispered reply, her familiar brogue distorted by decades in Durham. "Hello, love, so sorry to bother you, but…ehm…"

Your mum, I mouthed as Seamus switched on the lamp and frowned at me. "Are you okay?" I asked her. "Is Tom? What…what time—"

"Half-two, I think. Hannah, I'm sorry, but…but there's prowlers in the garden."

"Prowlers," I repeated, conscious of Seamus's eyes on me. "Have you rung the Constabulary?"

"They're not that kind of prowlers, I think. They've got wands."

"*Wands?*"

"Yes. Tom was in the loo, and he looked out the window, and he saw two of them skulking around the back. I think they're poking about in your parents' house. What should we do?"

"Stay away from the windows," I said, pressing the phone close to me. "Both of you. No lights, no sounds, no movement. Don't let them know you're awake. They're probably Arcanum, and—"

Before I could finish, Seamus snatched my mobile away. "*Mam*? Mam, it's me. We're coming," he said, and ended the call.

"Wake Arnie?" I asked, stuffing my feet into my trainers.

"No time." Quickly, he belted his bathrobe on, then looked about the room. "Where did you leave your—"

"Forget the robe. Take us in," I said, snatching my wand from beneath my pillow.

A second's concentration was all it took for Seamus to rip open a gate into his old bedroom, which his parents had partially converted into a guest suite once he moved out. I followed him through, and he sealed the gate behind us. "Think they're looking for background fluctuation?" he muttered, groping for the door. "We were quick, weren't we?"

Footsteps thundered down the wooden floor of the upstairs hallway, and as the door swung open, someone pointed a torch in our faces. "Oi, you!" shouted Tom Malone, sounding far too aggressive for a man with wizards in his garden. "What do you think you—*Seamus!*"

The light dropped, and Seamus squinted as his eyes adjusted. "Dad?"

Moving with the speed of a much younger man, Tom ran into the room and threw his arms around his son. Seamus hugged him in turn, ineffectively thumping his back in an indication that it was acceptable to stop crushing his ribcage, but Tom held on for a solid ten seconds, until Mary found us and took her turn. I couldn't blame them—they hadn't seen their boy in decades—but in light of the circumstances, I stepped in to pry Mary and Seamus apart before she was entirely ready. "Sorry," I said, hearing Mary sniffle, "but let's have a look at your prowlers first, eh?"

Muttering reassurance to his mother that he wasn't about to do anything foolish, Seamus followed me downstairs to the back door, and we peered out into the night. "See anything?" he whispered. "The gate's unlatched, but other than that—"

He fell silent as my parents' back door opened, and two men wearing familiar black suits and face-concealing helmets stepped out into the grass. Both openly carried wands, and my hand clenched around my own.

"Think they're going to leave?" Seamus asked. "Surely they wouldn't come over here, not with the neighborhood asleep…"

His assessment made sense—if the Arcanum was just looking for me without any real sense of where I might be hiding, then it would have been stupid for their operatives to invade an inhabited home in the middle of the night on less than a hunch—but seeing those two casually walk out of my parents' house made my blood boil. My parents had died in there, shot through by assassins like those, because my father had been a coordinator. My mother wasn't even a witch. She'd been murdered by association.

"Badger?"

Before Seamus could talk me down, I opened the door and stormed into the shared garden. "Hey!" I hissed as the wizards turned my way. "Looking for something?"

In the second they hesitated, I fired off two blasts of lightning, striking one of the assassins. The other managed to shield, and while his companion lay smoking on the lawn, he began to fire at me in turn. My shield took the worst of the impact—I was too infuriated to feel the strain in my arm—and I was preparing to go on the offensive again when Seamus flashed past me, reappeared an instant later at my assailant's side, and slapped his hand against the man's helmet. The wizard dropped, dead of a bolt to the brain, and Seamus panted as I jogged through the dew-damp grass to join him. "Bloody *hell*," he muttered as I tucked my wand into the back of my pajamas. "Slightly uncalled for?"

"Justifiable," I replied, nudging my victim with my toe. "Got a problem with it?"

"No, but...*shit*," he groaned as his worried parents appeared at the door, clutching their torch and mobile. "When these two don't turn up, what do you suppose HQ will do?"

"Send more," I mumbled. "Your parents..."

"They can't stay here." He waved one hand until the bodies disappeared, then returned to the house, tightening his belt as he went. "Wizards," he said once I'd nudged the Malones inside and locked the door. "You were right. They're after Badger."

"Well," said Mary, "if you keep *killing* them like that—"

"So they won't kill you," he interrupted. "Anyone ever associated with Badger is a potential target. We've got to get you out of here before the Arcanum notices those two are missing."

Tom glanced out the window again, but we'd left no trace of the bodies. "How...what did you..."

Seamus sighed and rubbed his arm. "Do you remember what Brian told you about me?" When his father turned back to him, Seamus held out his hand and produced a little blue flame in his palm. "Half fae. I...I've had some help with it in the last year, I can control it better now, but, ehm...yeah." He made a fist, and the flame snuffed out without a hint of smoke. "It's magic, Dad. Different to what Brian could do, but same principle. And Badger...she's so much stronger than her dad was. Proper wizard, she is. All she needed was a good wand," he added, and I pulled it free for their inspection. "We've been in the States, more or less, trying to keep those bastards from doing what they did to Brian and Kathy to anyone else. Evacuating people."

"There's a place you can go where they won't be able to find you," I explained. "People like Dad have been over there for months. They've got a lovely little town and everything, and you'd be safe there."

Mary and Tom shared a look, and then she asked, "Where, exactly? The States?"

"Ehm…no," said Seamus. "Faerie. But it's safe enough," he hastened to add, "and you wouldn't be the only ones there without any sort of talent."

"Yeah, Joey's parents are there, too, aren't they?" I added. "Bit older than us, you'd like them. And there are certainly mundane Fringe spouses—people like Mama."

Seamus took his mother's hand. "Please let us get you out of here before they come back. *Please*, Mam."

Mary hesitated, then dropped her phone into her robe pocket and reached up to pat Seamus's scruffy cheek. "My sweet boy," she said with a note of wonder in her voice. "You turned into such a handsome man, didn't you?"

"*Mam…*" he mumbled.

"I agree," I said, cutting in to spare him further embarrassment. "But the longer we stay here…"

Tom seemed to get the hint, even if his wife was too thrilled to see their son again to focus on the larger problem. "Tell us what we need to do, Hannah."

"Take only what you can carry," I replied. "Anything you can't live without. Mementoes, pictures, things like that. Maybe some clothes. They'll help you resettle once you get there."

"And this place is…safe?"

"More or less," I admitted. "We'll explain on the way. Hurry, now."

Tom managed to drag his wife out of the kitchen, and we met them upstairs in Seamus's old room a few minutes later, now wheeling overstuffed suitcases. "We bought these last year for our Paris holiday," Mary explained, "but you should have *seen* the tiny lifts—*oh*!" she cried as Seamus opened a gate back to Virginia. "How did you—"

"Magic, Mam. Explain later," he said, and ushered them through.

While we waited for nightfall in Sedona—I didn't think it'd be prudent for us to barge in on Coileán every time we needed to send someone across the border—we parked the Malones at the kitchen table and tried to give them the condensed update as Arnold made tea. After a time, confused by the voices above them, Amy and Kip wandered upstairs to see what was going on. Upon realizing who the elder couple were, Amy proceeded to the liquor cabinet beneath the sink, found our bottles of gin and rum, and brought them to the table with her best hostess smile and a cheery, "Who needs a shot?"

Tom took her up on the offer, but Mary was content to sit beside her boy and pat his hand, as if reassuring herself that he wasn't about to vanish—a possibility, yes, but not an idea that I was about to put in her head. Once we'd explained what we'd been up to in the last year, Seamus excused himself for a moment and retreated to our room with his mobile. He left the door open, though, and I heard half of a rapid conversation in Fae. "His uncle," I explained to his perplexed parents. "Making sure we have clearance to take you over and that there'll be someone there to help you."

Mary frowned. "You're not going with us?"

"I can't," I said slowly, "and Seamie…he may for a bit, but—"

"But nothing," he said, returning to the kitchen. "Sorry, Mam, but Badger needs me more than you do right now. I'll visit," he promised before she could protest, "but with the Arcanum looking for her again…"

"And he'll call," I said, giving him a look until he nodded.

Tom cleared his throat. "Your…uncle, was it? You, ehm…you found—"

"My birth parents? No," said Seamus. "But there are ways of testing, and I found my aunt and uncle. They're expecting you. I told them that if anything happened to you, I'd be *exceedingly* cross, and they assured me that you'll be fine." He glanced at the microwave clock. "It's probably dark in the canyon by now. Val said to give them a few minutes, and they'll be at the gate. Shall we?"

"Sure," I replied, "but would you like to put on real trousers first?"

Mary looked at us in confusion. "Canyon? What canyon?"

"Bit of a hike, nothing to worry about," said Seamus, helping her from her chair. "And then there's the *tiny* matter of getting you through the gate, but we'll cross that bridge once we come to it, eh?"

I had to admit that the Malones were excellent sports, all things considered. Toula was waiting at the gate when we arrived—throwing caution to the wind, Seamus opened a gate straight onto the canyon trail—and she hoisted herself over the rim and floated down to the ledge to introduce herself to his overwhelmed parents. With a little reassurance, she levitated both of them and their luggage through the hole in space, then hugged Seamus and me and promised they would be taken care of. "And *you*," she added, jabbing her finger into my chest, "are crazy, and I like it. Nice job."

Shortly thereafter, though still slightly wired on caffeine, Seamus and I tumbled back into bed and curled up together. "You didn't tell them about the glamour," I said through a yawn, spooning against him.

"They *did* just watch us kill two people. Didn't think it would help if I changed my face, too."

"Later, then," I mumbled, and closed my eyes.

Soon enough, Seamus was asleep, but I found that I couldn't shut my mind off. It wasn't the chemical surge—I was still too angry.

They'd come looking for me. Those fucking bastards had come looking again, in the middle of the night, in *my parents'* house. And what would they have done if they'd known the Malones had spotted them? Probably would have killed them—Tom and Mary, as mundane as they came, people who by rights should have been my in-laws years ago. They'd done nothing wrong. Hell, this wasn't their war, and now we'd shipped them off to a new life in order to save them from assassins.

It wasn't fair. *Nothing* was fair. The bloody stupid Arcanum...

I didn't realize I was letting myself sleepwalk until I looked down and saw Seamus's body glowing next to mine, our limbs entwined beneath the duvet.

What was I doing? I could look for more Fringers, hope that someone I'd missed would have landed in my vicinity, but another idea pushed its way to the fore.

I'd taken on Nath in my sleep and made the Gray Lands stand down. What was stopping me from going after Mulligan?

I could do that, couldn't I? Sure, the Dark Company couldn't get past the Arcanum's ward network, and no wizard could do it awake, but how could wards stop me like *this*? And so what if I woke the wrong person? They suspected I was still in this realm, anyway, and they couldn't track me out of the dream space. But I wouldn't wake the wrong wizard—I'd been practicing, hadn't I? No, I'd take myself to the silo, find the grand magus's bedroom, and kill him in his sleep. He wanted me so badly? Fine. I'd pay him a visit he'd never forget...well, if he were going to wake up. That was looking less likely by the minute.

Fueled by my anger, seeing flashes of my parents' bodies in my mind's eye, I flew across the sleeping continent toward the bright hub of the Arcanum silo, buried deep beneath the Montana soil. It blazed like the sun across the shadowy world of the dream space, a golden light that drew me like a moth.

I landed outside the silo's perimeter and walked toward the entrance, a seemingly normal static caravan in a circle of other caravans, all of them dilapidated or at least grungy. Whatever wards existed in the waking world did nothing to stop me as I passed into the entrance caravan, then descended through the floor to the proper silo entrance. There were plenty of wizards still awake—it was barely ten in that time zone, after all—and I drifted above them, insubstantial as a thought, as I searched for my quarry.

Having never been invited into the silo, I was unaware of its floorplan, and so I was forced to conduct my search room by room. Ordinarily, I could look through structures and find my targets, but here, the collective glow of the wizards packed into the silo was obfuscating, to say the least. I couldn't see the bottom of the silo, let alone pick an individual out of the crowd, and my heart sank as I realized that whatever glow the captured Fringers gave off would be lost in the brightness of the wizards around them. Still, I knew that I could find Mulligan if I had patience, and so I continued my slow descent.

And then, perhaps an hour into my search, I located his office.

There he was, the son of a bitch, sitting on his couch, watching the television on the wall with a glass of wine in hand. He was pudgier than I'd imagined, grown soft around the waist with middle age, and his gray hair had thinned so much that his pink scalp showed through. He wore a plain red sweatshirt and jeans, plus a pair of navy bedroom slippers, which he propped on the coffee table beside a half-eaten plate of nachos. Beside him, leaning against his chest, was a woman of approximately the same age and physical condition—his wife, I assumed. She, at least, was sleeping, and he'd wrapped a steadying arm around her, holding her close while she dozed. Perhaps they were watching the end of a movie, and she'd simply drifted off.

I stood beside the couch, studying him. All I had to do was wait until he fell asleep, and that would surely come in the near future. I'd follow him back to his quarters, watch as his breathing slowed, then stop his heart—presumably after I confronted him with a list of his crimes and gave him a chance to beg for mercy. I could do it. I *would* do it. Mulligan's tenure as grand magus would end that night.

But.

Mulligan knew where the Fringers were being held, didn't he? What if he'd kept that a secret from all of his magi? Arnold certainly couldn't give me a precise location in the silo, so what if, in killing Mulligan, I inadvertently doomed his prisoners?

Or what if the magi blamed Mulligan's death on the courts and killed everyone in revenge?

No—I was catastrophizing, that was all. Less ruminating, more destroying the man who had killed my family, ripped apart the organization I held dear, and sent me running for my life. I could do this. If I could stare down Nath as the scion of Simon Magus…

Oh, *God.*

I stepped away from the Mulligans and rested my head against the insubstantial wall. This was exactly what Simon would have done, wasn't it? Well, no, he wouldn't have stopped with the grand magus, but still, it was the *principle* of the thing.

I could do it…

But no.

With a groan, I flung myself out of the silo and back into my bed, where I opened my eyes and stared at the darkness around me. As I stirred, Seamus woke and pulled me closer. "All right?" he mumbled. "Phone?"

"Nothing, love," I whispered. "Go back to sleep."

When he was once again unconscious, I lay still and told myself I'd made the right choice. I could go back there—every night, if I so chose. If I had a think and decided I'd been right the first time, I could pop back into the silo and kill Mulligan before he knew what had hit him.

But I wouldn't. Not like that. Yes, I wanted to beat the life out of him, but not as an assassin in the night. If I did it that way, I'd be no better than the black-suited wizards who'd shot my parents.

I'd keep fighting, but I'd do it as one of the good guys. And we could bide our time.

Still, I told myself as I tried to sleep again, I'd done well, hadn't I? I'd breezed around the silo, and no one was the wiser. Maybe I finally had this sleepwalking thing under control.

And with that thought, I had another idea.

It took me hours to find her. They'd buried her under levels upon levels of flats and libraries and common spaces, deep in one of the silo's subbasements, but there she was—Helen Carver, the once and perhaps future grand magus, asleep on a padded table. She glowed with the powerful radiance of the truly talented, and I knew I'd hit my target.

I couldn't see the details of the room in which she was being held—the shadowy contours of the dream space were vague enough without Helen's light making me squint—and I knew that the wards on the silo would prevent us from reaching her by gate, in any case, but still, there she was. Grinning like a fool, I put my hand on her shoulder and shook her to wake her into the dream. "Hello, there," I said as I jostled her. "It's Badger Parsons. I'm here to talk to you. Helen?"

But she couldn't be wakened, no matter how hard I tried, and finally, perplexed, I stepped back to take stock of the situation. Then it hit me: of course I couldn't wake her. Mulligan would have had to put her to sleep with magic—else, she'd surely have broken free by then, wouldn't she? Perhaps she couldn't dream at all in that state. She might simply be in suspended animation, distantly conscious of the voices around her but unable to free herself.

I didn't know if she could hear me, but it was worth a try. "Helen, it's Badger," I said, taking her limp hand. "If you can hear me, this is a dream, but it's not a normal one. I'm so sorry that I can't free you, but…you haven't been forgotten. The Arcanum is using you as a hostage, along with many of the Fringe, and no one's quite figured a way to get you out of here yet, but they're trying."

I bent closer to her, looking for any sign of movement, even a flicker beneath her eyelids. "Joey loves you, dear. He's beside himself, but he's safe. So is Aiden. Joey's mum and dad are with them. I know Joey's desperate to find you, and I'll tell him you're alive and…ehm…" Glancing down her institutional pajamas, I realized what I had missed when I first laid eyes on Helen: I couldn't see any hint of the child she had been carrying when she was captured. "You're not pregnant any more, are you? Did you have the baby? Did you lose it?"

Helen gave me no sign, and I sighed as I straightened. "No matter. I don't know when, and I don't quite know how, but we're going to rescue you, dear. And until then…we'll be out there. Maybe it seems like it now, but you're not alone."

A few minutes later, once I'd surfaced from the dream and reoriented myself, I slid from Seamus's grasp and took my mobile onto the back steps to watch the sun rise pink over the sea. I selected a number and waited, then smiled as I heard a greeting. "Hello, Aiden. Tell Joey she's alive."

ACKNOWLEDGEMENTS

If you're reading this, then it's a safe bet that you and I have been together for six books now. That's…well, from my end, that's staggering. I sit in my den and type—usually with my dog sprawled nearby, waiting around in case of sudden snacks—and you, at some distant point in the future, make yourself comfortable and read these words. It's almost like we've been sharing a peculiar sort of dream, isn't it? Thank you for letting me be your guide.

My continued thanks go to the Novel Chicks for their advice and friendship, and for our many working dinners. My sincere gratitude goes to Adam Domby, beta reader extraordinaire, whose suggestions are always great.

And yes, here's to you, Mom and Dad.

ABOUT THE AUTHOR

When not writing fiction, Ash Fitzsimmons is an appellate attorney and an unrepentant car singer.

Find her online:
www.ashfitzsimmons.com